THE
STARS DOWN
UNDER

Tor Books by Sandra McDonald

The Outback Stars
The Stars Down Under

SANDRA
McDONALD

THE
STARS DOWN
UNDER

A TOM DOHERTY
ASSOCIATES BOOK

NEW YORK

TOR®

THE STARS DOWN UNDER

Copyright © 2008 by Sandra McDonald

Edited by James D. Macdonald

A Tor Book
Published by Tom Doherty Associates, LLC
175 Fifth Avenue
New York, NY 10010

www.tor.com

Tor® is a registered trademark of Tom Doherty Associates, LLC.

Library of Congress Cataloging-in-Publication Data

McDonald, Sandra, 1966–
    The stars down under / Sandra McDonald. —1st ed.
        p.   cm.
    "A Tom Doherty Associates book."
    ISBN-13: 978-0-7653-1644-8
    ISBN-10: 0-7653-1644-7
    I. Title.
    PS3613.C3874S73   2008
    813'.6—dc22   2007042146

First Edition: March 2008

Printed in the United States of America

0   9   8   7   6   5   4   3   2   1

To Sue Factor, Janine Shahinian, and Angela Gabriel
for a decade of friendship and encouragement

ACKNOWLEDGMENTS

Writing the continuing adventures of Jodenny Scott and Terry Myell would have been much more difficult if not for the gang on Kelleys Island, Ohio. Their kindness and goodwill will not be forgotten. Special thanks go to the very talented Sarah Prineas and Paul Melko, who read the entire manuscript in its raw form and offered invaluable advice.

Thank you also to Jeff Kellogg, James Macdonald, Patrick Nielsen Hayden, Stephanie Wojtowicz, Terry Berube, and my family.

THE
STARS DOWN
UNDER

The boy fled for his life.

Across the sun-baked plain, his bare feet kicking up dust, he ran from his father and brothers and uncles. He was a good child, known throughout the tribe for his kindness and laughter. He was helpful to his aunties and respectful to the old men. But fear had stained and ruined him.

His brothers shouted, "Coward!"

His uncles shouted, "Become a man!"

The boy carried no water, and soon his parched throat was closing up. Sharp rocks and dried brush scratched at his legs and tried to trip him. The ocher painted on him for the initiation rites streamed off in the wind. He fell once, scrambled upright. Fell again, pulled himself up with a strangled moan. Managed several more steps and then felt the hot jarring thud of a spear as it pierced his right leg and shattered the bone.

He fell for the last time, sobbing. His father and brothers and uncles gathered around him.

"You shame us," they said. His father spat on him.

The circle of men parted for the arrival of the aunties, his kind and loving aunties, who came at the boy with their sticks and landed a dozen blows.

No one spoke in the moments afterward. The boy's family stood back from their grisly work. The boy's eyes stared at them sightlessly. The descending sun had left red streaks across the sky and the bitter air smelled like blood. At last one of the aunties glanced up and saw the great Rainbow Serpent coiling down from the clouds with fire in its eyes.

The boy's family screamed and fled.

The next day, when they came for whatever parts of the corpse had been spared by the gods and wild animals, they found only a smooth black sphere. By noon the sphere was taller and wider than any man of the tribe. By nightfall it was larger than five men. The wind pushed dust against its side. The ground beneath it cracked, then heaved upward. For the next thousand years the sphere grew and grew until it was the largest rock in all the world. In the shifting light of day it turned pink and green, yellow and red, much like a rainbow.

The locals named the rock Burringurrah, in memory of the murdered boy.

The white men who came later called it Mount Augustus, in the land down under.

Terry Myell, when it was his turn to be murdered atop Burringurrah, was also visited by the Rainbow Serpent. They say the Serpent saved him and his wife and his wife's lover. They say the three of them rode the Serpent's back into the sky, where even now, on those rare clear nights, they can be seen riding the tails of comets and dancing on the face of the moon.

Those stories are wrong. This story is true.

CHAPTER
ONE

Terry Myell drizzled oil on the vegetables in the wok, reached past his comm-bee for seasoning, and jumped back in surprise as a crocodile scurried through his kitchen.

"Christ!" he yelled, bumping up against the hard countertop. It was just after seventeen-hundred hours, a sunny afternoon in the military suburb of Adeline Oaks on the planet Fortune. His wife, Jodenny, would be working until midnight and he was cooking dinner just for himself. The last thing he had expected to see was a three-meter-long reptile with sharp teeth, gray scales, and black, hook-shaped claws that screeched against the floor tile.

The creature whipped around the refrigerator and was gone so quickly that surely he had imagined it.

"Betsy!" he said to the house computer. "Report."

A soothing woman's voice flowed out of the microspeakers in the ceiling. "Inside temperature is twenty degrees Celsius. A front stove-top element is operating at a setting of two point seven. There's a slight leak in the guest shower—"

Myell fumbled for the longest knife in the silverware drawer. "Any mammals, reptiles, supernatural creatures?"

"There's a spider in the living room closet, and several termites burrowing through the rear foundation. A gecko is hanging off lanai screen number four. That's all I have to report, sir."

Myell crept forward. The floor showed no gouge marks or smeared dirt. The dark beige carpet in the living room was similarly unmarked, and the front door was closed. With cold sweat on his neck, he headed for the master bedroom. He edged past half-empty packing boxes in the hall to the ajar door. From outside came the sounds of a neighbor's kids kicking around a soccer ball and the hum of flits as parents returned from work. Everything else was quiet.

"Come out, come out," Myell murmured. "Show yourself."

The master bedroom was awash with afternoon sunlight. His dress white uniform hung neatly on a hook outside the closet doors, the ribbons and insignia carefully aligned. The bed was a messy rumple of blue linens and pillows. Beneath them, a hump moved back and forth slowly, obscenely.

He steeled himself and yanked the sheets away.

Karl the Koala blinked up at him with golden eyes and rolled over.

"Rub me, rub my tummy," he sang.

Myell let the knife drop. "Go to sleep, Karl."

The bot rolled to his haunches and scratched himself. Though he understood basic commands, the programming defaulted to mild disobedience. A real koala would never follow orders like a dog, anyway. Nor would it talk. Myell still wasn't convinced they needed any mechanical pets underfoot, but Karl made Jodenny happy.

"He's so cute," she'd said when they saw him at the mall.

Myell could think of something much more adorable and cuddly, but Jodenny had said she wasn't ready for kids.

Betsy spoke up. "You have new imail in your account, sir. Four challengers have questioned your score in the latest Izim tournament. And I believe your dinner is burning."

Cursing, Myell hurried back to the kitchen and pulled the wok off the stove. Betsy's vents began sucking up smoke that reeked of burnt oil and blackened string beans. He dumped the mess into the disposal and accidentally knocked the knife off the counter. When he tried to catch it, the blade cut into his finger.

"I detect blood, sir. Do you have a medical emergency?" Betsy asked.

"I'm fine," he said through gritted teeth. The slice was long but shallow. "And I've told you, stop calling me *sir*. It's Chief Myell, or Terry. Got it?"

"Yes, sir."

A little self-sealant took care of the cut. The stir-fry was ruined, so he threw together a salad instead. Afterward he checked the imails and saw three more media inquiries. Reporters, always damn reporters. He deleted them, as he had all the other requests that had come in during the last four weeks.

He took a beer to the sofa and kicked his feet up. "Betsy, are there references to crocodiles in Australian Aboriginal mythology?"

"I find several instances in which people are reputed to have been eaten or transformed into crocodiles. One tribe revered the crocodile as a totemic god. Would you like me to send the information to your bee?"

"No. Forget I asked." On the *Aral Sea* he had experienced visions of an Aboriginal shaman, and on a long, strange top-secret trip across the galaxy he had seen a Rainbow Serpent. He'd hoped he was done with all of it.

Karl climbed up onto the cushions beside him.

"Koala, my ass," Myell said. "You're probably a god in disguise."

The robot rolled backward and repeated his plea for a tummy rub.

"Talk to Mommy," Myell said.

Betsy was the oldest house in the neighborhood, and her nighttime temperature controls were erratic. Though he meant to stay up for

Jodenny, Myell fell asleep on the sofa and woke every hour or so because he was too cold, or too hot, or too cold again. When he did sleep, he dreamed of crocodiles in a deep cave, hissing and snapping their razor-sharp teeth. At oh-four-hundred he woke shaking with dread, and stumbled to the bathroom to splash cold water on his flushed face.

He went to the bedroom and burrowed into the sheets. He was just dozing off again when the wallgib beeped and Jodenny's image rolled into view.

"Betsy told me you were up," she said. "Everything okay?"

"Fine." Myell turned his head into a pillow, then turned to eye her. "Why aren't you home?"

"There was an accident with some academy students, a big mess." She was as beautiful as ever, but dark circles hung under her eyes. Her lieutenant commander bars glinted on the screen. "They borrowed a birdie for fun and crashed into the ocean. I've been fending off the media for hours. I don't think I'll be home before you leave."

He shrugged one shoulder.

"I wanted to send you off to your new job in style," she said. "I'm sorry."

Myell was sorry, too. Their last ship, the *Aral Sea,* had barely entered orbit before new duty assignments arrived in their queues. Fledgling plans for a honeymoon had been abruptly discarded. Jodenny's new position at Fleet was prestigious but demanding. Lately he'd seen more of his reflection than he'd seen of her.

Jodenny touched the gib screen, as if trying to pat his cheek. "Be kind to your students, won't you? I remember how hard it was for me to memorize everything."

"I don't think they're going to throw me in front of a classroom today."

"They should. You'll be great." A gib pinged, and Jodenny glanced offscreen. "Got to go. Call me later."

"Love you," he said, but the connection was already dead.

Further sleep eluded him. He played Izim for a while but got killed multiple times. Just before dawn he pulled on some gym clothes. He opened the top drawer of his dresser and palmed a small dilly bag. Inside were two carved totems of geckos. One had been a gift, and the other had been his mother's.

For the first time in months he tied the bag around his waist and felt its comforting weight.

Outside, the air was hot and dawn was just lightening the sky. The faux-brick homes were a bit affluent for his tastes, but Jodenny's rank had its privileges and he supposed he'd have to get used to them. At the end of the street was a steep wooded hill dotted with senior-officer homes. He jogged up it, the dilly bag bouncing against his skin. The exertion left him winded but the view at the top was worth it.

"Good morning, Kimberley," he said.

The rising sun sent yellow light streaking over Fortune's capital city. Myell could see the Parliament buildings, the graceful expanse of the Harbor Bridge, and a wide, disorienting expanse of silver-blue ocean. He hated the ocean. In the center of the city stood the Team Space pyramid, blue and clean and beautiful, the hub of its interplanetary operations.

The birds had woken up, kookaburras and doves mostly, and over their song he heard the unmistakable sound of an approaching security flit. Myell kept his gaze on the city and his hands in plain sight on the railing.

"Good morning, sir," a woman's voice said behind him. "Routine security check. Everything all right up here?"

Slowly he turned. "Good morning, officers. Everything's fine."

The woman was a brunette with the insignia of a regular tech. Her nametag read M. CHIN. Her partner, Apprentice Mate H. Saro, was smaller and slimmer, and had the coiled tenseness of a dog with something to prove.

"Do you live here, sir?" RT Chin asked.

"Chief Myell. I just moved in. Twenty-four hundred Eucalyptus Street," he said.

"Chiefs don't live in officer housing," Saro said.

Myell pushed down a flare of annoyance. He reached carefully into his pocket and handed over his identification card. Chin retreated with it to the flit. Saro rested one hand on the mazer in his belt and tried to look fierce.

"Are there regulations against people taking a morning walk?" Myell asked him.

"Most people don't walk around when it's still dark out."

"Sun's up," Myell pointed out.

Saro glared at him. "And they have the common sense to exercise in the gym."

"Fresh air's better for you."

Chin returned. "Sorry, Chief. You're all clear. People get nervous when they look out their windows and see a strange face, that's all. Welcome to the neighborhood."

"But he's not—" Saro started.

"Shut up, Hal." Chin nodded briskly at Myell. "Can we give you a lift home, Chief?"

"No. I'll walk."

Saro gave him one last suspicious look before the security flit drove off. Myell started downhill. He imagined eyes watching him from every window. An hour later, after forcing down breakfast and checking his uniform for the tiniest flaws, he joined the morning crowd at the monorail station. He hung back against the railing so he wouldn't sprain his elbow offering salutes. A few curious glances came his way, but no one spoke to him or challenged his right to be there.

He didn't flaunt his Silver Star, but a lieutenant with bloodshot eyes said, "Earn that the hard way?"

"Is there any other way, sir?" Myell asked.

The lieutenant squinted at Myell's deployment patches. "That's the *Aral Sea*'s emblem. You help beat off those terrorists at Baiame?"

"Something like that."

The lieutenant raised his coffee cup in salute, then turned away as a train pulled in.

Kimberley's public transportation system was a hub-and-spoke design. At Green Point Myell transferred to another train and rode several stops with civilians, students, and other military personnel until they reached Water Street. Supply School was easy to find. It occupied a pierside base wedged between shipping companies and freighter lines. The flags of Fortune, the Seven Sisters, and Team Space flapped overhead, bright in the sunshine. The air smelled like fuel and vile salt water.

"Second building to the right, Chief," a gate guard told Myell. "They'll help you over there."

Once Myell was inside the steel and glass building, a receptionist took him past cubicles where RTs and civilian staff were busy socializing. The enlisted men saw Myell and got to work. The civilians were slower about it. Large vids on the walls displayed student status, lists of instructor assignments, and announcements for Saturday's graduation ceremony. The name of the Supply School commander, Captain Kuvik, was prominently displayed everywhere.

The cubicle maze ended in a small office where Moroccan rugs hung on the walls and hand-woven baskets decorated the shelves. A bald sergeant with brown skin rose from his desk, offering a smile and a handshake.

"Bob Etedgy, Chief," he said. "Welcome back to Supply School."

"Thanks. In truth, I never came through in the first place."

"Got all your training in the fleet? Me, too." Etedgy cleared off a chair for Myell. "Don't let them hear you say it around here, but direct experience is always better than sitting on your ass in a classroom."

Etedgy had already arranged for Myell's security pass, had requisitioned a parking slot in case he ever wanted to drive in, and had put together a bright red orientation folder emblazoned with the Supply School emblem.

"You'll be meeting with Captain Kuvik at oh-nine-hundred. He meets with every new instructor, nothing to worry about there. Until then I'll take you on the guided tour. Officer training is down the street, in their own building with their own faculty and staff, so we'll skip that. I'll also get you set up with a locker down in the training room. Most of us commute in civilian clothes and change into uniform here—saves on the wear and tear, you know, and it's okay as long as it's before the students arrive. Captain's not keen on us being seen as regular human beings."

He said it with a smile, but Myell didn't think he was joking.

The classrooms were on the second and third decks of the building. Khaki-clad chiefs were already lecturing, administering tests, or conducting multimedia presentations. The upper decks contained computer labs, a library, and a chapel. The mess hall was in an adjacent building, and beyond it was the gymnasium.

"So where did they stash you and your wife for quarters?" Etedgy asked. "Widen? Sally Bay? My wife and I have been on the waiting list for Lake Lu for a year."

"Nice, is it?"

"Best you can do for enlisted housing around here."

"Is that how long you've been here? A year?" Myell asked, and successfully diverted the topic.

Just before oh-nine-hundred they returned to the main building and rode the lift to the fifth deck, which offered marvelous views of the sea traffic heading in and out of port. Myell kept his gaze averted. Captain Kuvik's suite was impeccably furnished and much larger than a shipboard captain's. The walls were vidded with photos of square-shouldered graduating students, all of them ready to march off into the fleet and inflict invoices for every last roll of toilet paper.

Not that Myell thought poorly of his career track. Supply sailors didn't earn the same glory as flight crews and didn't save lives like the medical corps, but someone had to keep food, equipment, uniforms, materials, and weapons moving down the Alcheringa and throughout the Seven Sisters.

"Chief Myell to see the captain," Etedgy announced.

Captain Kuvik's secretary, a thin man with antique glasses perched on his nose, gave Myell an unfriendly look. He pinged the inner office and repeated Etedgy's words.

"Send him in," a man replied.

Myell stepped into Kuvik's office. Windows screened out the sunlight. Classical music from pre-Debasement Earth played softly on a hidden radio. Kuvik, an older man with rugged features and white hair, nodded Myell toward a chair. Five rows of ribbons were pinned above his left pocket. Some of them were for enlisted sailors only, meaning he'd worked his way up through the ranks. The office smelled like peppermint.

"Sergeant Etedgy show you around?" Kuvik asked.

"Yes, sir." The chair was hard under Myell, and a little low to the floor. "It's an impressive complex."

"The enlisted school graduates three hundred ATs a month, and we teach advanced courses to twice as many RTs and sergeants. Do the job right or don't do it at all, I tell them. I disenroll anyone who doesn't take the job seriously, and I won't have any instructors who think this is a three-year vacation after years of running down the Alcheringa."

"I don't think of this is a vacation, Captain."

Kuvik gave no indication of having heard him. "Just because Fleet assigns someone here doesn't mean you get to be in front of one of my classrooms. My instructors are role models for young ATs who need direction and guidance. You don't pass muster, I'll stick you in a basement office and make you count requisitions eight hours a day."

Myell knew all about being shoved into dead-end, tedious jobs. "I hope I pass muster, sir."

Kuvik's gaze hardened. The music on the radio rose in crescendo. Something by Beethoven, Myell thought. Or maybe not.

"I know you were instrumental in saving your ship after the insurgent attack off Baiame," Kuvik said. "That Silver Star they gave you proves that. Commander Wildstein on the *Aral Sea* speaks highly of you, and she's damned hard to please. But you also married your supervisor, Lieutenant Scott, which indicates an appalling lack of decorum and brings up serious issues of fraternization."

"No fraternization charges were filed against Lieutenant *Commander* Scott or myself," Myell said, making sure Kuvik knew her current rank.

"I'm not interested in whether your former captain had the balls to court-martial you for violating regulations." Kuvik leaned forward, a muscle pulling in his cheek. "Worse than your playing house with

Lieutenant *Commander* Scott is the fact that you've never undergone chief's training."

Ah, Myell thought. *The true crux of the problem.* He and Jodenny had discussed the ramifications of his refusal, rehearsed possible scenarios, but he'd sincerely hoped the issue wouldn't arise.

"I was promoted in the field while recovering from my injuries," Myell said. "Authorized by my captain on behalf of Team Space to wear the insignia and uniform, and receive all the ranks and privileges of a Chief Petty Officer. When we arrived here, seven other sergeants on the *Aral Sea* were also approved for promotion."

"And those seven sergeants immediately volunteered for chief's training over at Fleet. You refused."

"Because the training is voluntary, and has been ever since the death of that sergeant on Kookaburra."

Kuvik wagged a finger. "One mistake shouldn't override hundreds of years of tradition. Initiation marks the transition from sergeant to chief. You don't just put on the uniform. You're expected to be a leader, and being a leader means being accepted as an equal by your peers."

Myell could already picture that basement office with his name posted by the door.

"That's where we disagree, sir. A leader rises above his peers instead of hovering in the pack with them. Team Space promotes us because of who we are and what we've done, not so we can reinvent ourselves. You can do whatever you like with me, but you're not going to convince me that a month of being humiliated and bullied will make me more fit to wear this uniform."

Myell realized his voice had risen. He clamped his mouth shut. He'd given the captain enough to hang him with already.

Kuvik leaned back in his chair. The radio fell silent, and a cormorant cried out behind the windows as it swooped down toward the water.

"There are some people from Fleet in my conference room," Kuvik finally said. "They want to talk to you. Something hush-hush and very important. Any idea what?"

Myell thought instantly of the Rainbow Serpent, and of the jobs he and Jodenny had turned down in a secret underground complex back on Warramala a few months ago.

"No, sir," he said.

Kuvik rose from his chair. "Go talk to them, Chief. And if they offer you a transfer, you'd better take it. It'll be a better deal than anything you're going to get here."

The outside world was too bright, even with sunglasses shading her eyes. Jodenny Scott resisted the urge to lie down on the sidewalk for twelve hours of sleep and kept walking down Sydney Boulevard. Train, home, bed. Those were her only goals.

She thought about pinging Myell, but he would already be at Supply School meeting his co-workers and getting settled in. The last few weeks hadn't been easy for him. Her part, going off to work every morning, had been simple. He'd had to lease a flit, get them moved into housing, buy furniture they'd never needed before, and organize their personal lives. He had done it all without complaint, and had even arranged for a dozen long-stemmed red roses to be on her desk her first day at Fleet.

She hadn't been able to send him off in style, but maybe she could make his first night home special.

"Jo?" a woman asked from nearby. "Jo Scott?"

Jodenny stopped. Sydney Boulevard was a wide avenue of shops, cafés, and office buildings, an eclectic mixture of old and new architecture. Foot and street traffic were both heavy. A redhead with a baby in a back carrier was standing nearby, her smile wide.

Jodenny asked, "Noreen? Is that you?"

"Yes!" Noreen Cross threw her arms around Jodenny in an exuberant hug. "It's great to see you! You look fabulous!"

"And you look like you've got a baby on your back," Jodenny replied.

Noreen juggled the carrier a little. A chubby-faced baby in pink clothes gave Jodenny a wide-eyed look and waved a clenched fist.

"My daughter Emma," Noreen said. "My second. She's my best sweetheart."

Jodenny waggled her fingers at Emma, who responding by drooling. "Two? Already?"

"Tom and I want four. Tommy Allcot. You remember him, don't you? He was in the class ahead of ours at the Academy. Big guy, soccer player?"

"I remember." Jostling pedestrians forced Jodenny to step closer. "How do you do it? Kids and husband and work?"

"Oh, I resigned my commission." Noreen wiped Emma's drool from her shoulder with practiced ease. "They let you, you know, if you get pregnant. I figure one member of Team Space was enough for this family, and I still get all the benefits of being a dependent."

The military word *dependent* was old-fashioned and politically incorrect. Jodenny was glad she didn't "depend" on Myell, or he on her.

"But look at you, Miss Lieutenant Commander!" Noreen eyed Jodenny's uniform with admiration. If she'd heard about Jodenny's heroism on the *Aral Sea* and the *Yangtze*, she didn't say anything. "Look at that ring on your finger. The girl who never dated. Who'd you marry?"

Jodenny pulled her hand free. Her wedding ring was a single diamond, purchased in haste on Baiame. Myell had promised to upgrade it. "He's in Team Space, too. Supply."

Baby Emma's fists began to wave in earnest, and tears spilled down her cheeks. Noreen said, "You'll have to come to dinner. Your husband and my husband, you and me—we'll do a barbecue. We live in Adeline Oaks."

"Sounds wonderful," Jodenny lied.

Emma's wails grew in volume, and her face turned red.

"We're off to her pediatrician," Noreen explained. "Call me! I'm in the base directory!"

With a wave and another hug, Noreen hurried off. Jodenny blew out a relieved breath and went up a flight of stairs to the monorail station. That Noreen and her husband lived in Adeline Oaks was an unfortunate stroke of luck. Myell was already uncomfortable enough living surrounded by officers. He'd never enjoy a barbecue with Academy graduates.

A train was already on the platform. Jodenny found a cushioned seat, wedged her briefcase between her ankles, and scanned the news on her gib. The upcoming election for Fortune's Parliament had turned vicious and cutthroat. Other candidates were vying for positions open in the Parliament of the Seven Sisters. The Prime Minister of Fortune was secure in his job for another year or two, but increasingly strident action by the Colonial Freedom Project terrorists was affecting his agenda. Though they hadn't discussed it, Jodenny had registered with the Prime Minister's Liberal party and assumed Myell had done so as well.

A woman in a smart blue suit brushed by Jodenny's knees, took the seat facing her, and murmured a question.

"Sorry?" Jodenny asked.

"Are we going outbound?" the woman asked brightly. She had a broad accent, from somewhere in the north.

"Yes. Last stop is Killarney," Jodenny replied.

"Excellent. Thank you."

She carried no briefcase, only a small purse. Her shoes were expensive but practical. She wore her red hair in a sleek ponytail. Although Jodenny ran for exercise, the other woman had the lean, disciplined look of an athlete. Someone used to hardship and success.

"I'm Dr. Anna Gayle," the woman said. "It's a pleasure to meet you, Commander Scott."

Jodenny eyed her warily. "Is it?"

"Yes. To be frank, I need your help."

Another crackpot, Jodenny thought. She attracted them like flies to shit. She reached for her briefcase and checked the overvid for the train's progress. "I can't help you."

Gayle leaned forward. "It's not about the *Yangtze*."

Even now, Jodenny had difficulty hearing the doomed ship's name. Her leg had healed up fine, as had the injuries she'd received later. Her nightmares had mostly faded. If at times she saw the faces of the dead in the crowd, or heard their whispered voices, then she was certainly allowed.

Jodenny asked, "Then what's it about?"

"My husband. He's an archaeologist. He's been missing for four months."

"What do I have to do with it?"

"You may have crossed paths with him in some remote, uncharted lands."

Jodenny's fuzzy brain took a minute to process that. "No," she said firmly, and headed for the double doors.

Gayle followed her, still earnest, but with a hint of desperation in her voice. "It's not only him. There are eight other people as well. People who have families that love them and desperately want them to return. Just as you returned."

The monorail slid to a stop. Disembarking passengers jostled Jodenny, but she didn't move. Gayle's careful words were clear enough. Her husband and she were somehow affiliated with the secret project known as the Wondjina Transportation System. Traversing the system by accident had nearly killed Jodenny and Myell. They had turned down a subsequent offer of employment with the project, and vowed to put it all behind them.

Working at Team Space headquarters was an excellent career step. No one made an issue of Jodenny being married to an enlisted man, though they had yet to present themselves together at any social or formal events. Jodenny's co-workers all seemed nice, and more importantly, competent. All in all, she anticipated a challenging but satisfying tour of duty.

And if her new job wasn't quite as exciting as working with alien technology that could fling people across the galaxy, that was the price she would pay for a few years of stability with Myell in a home they built together.

Gayle asked, "Can we talk? One married woman to another?"

The doors gave a warning beep.

"He's my heart," Gayle said. Her face turned pink. "He's all I want."

The doors closed. Jodenny took a seat again, her briefcase clutched tightly against her chest. Myell was all she wanted, as well. But sometimes, without fully admitting it, she wondered if she might *need* a little more.

A gray, unmarked flit was parked outside Jodenny's house.

"They're just to make sure we're not interrupted," Gayle assured her, easily keeping pace with Jodenny's quick strides down the street.

Adeline Oaks was quiet and drowsy in the morning heat, the children in school and the spouses off to their jobs or whatever kept them busy on a Monday morning. Jodenny thumbed open her front door and let Gayle follow her inside. Myell had left the house only slightly messy. They had yet to decide on a formal decorating scheme, though he'd bought a green sofa for the living room and put floor plants in all the corners. The plants were okay, but the sofa was ugly.

"Coffee?" Jodenny asked.

Gayle sat at the kitchen island. "Black and hot. Thank you."

"Start talking, Doctor. I'm eight hours overdue for my bedtime."

Gayle showed her gib to Jodenny. On the screen, a good-looking man with a thick beard and bright blue eyes smiled for the camera. "Robert. We met as graduate students. About two years ago Team Space recruited us both for help deciphering the Wondjina Transportation System. Robert was far more eager to conduct field work than I was. He went with teams on two trips through the Spheres at Swedenville. He was very ill, afterward. As everyone is. You and your husband found that out on Warramala, right?"

Jodenny handed over a cup of black coffee. "Keep talking."

"I told him it was unsafe to keep going. And unfair to our children. Then the medical branch, which had been experimenting with pro- phylactic treatments to ward off the travel sickness, announced a breakthrough. He volunteered for one more mission, as much to test the new treatment as to satisfy his insatiable curiosity. They left just before you and your husband stumbled through the Spheres on War- ramala. They've never returned."

Jodenny poured herself a glass of soy milk but didn't drink it. Trav- eling through the Wondjina Spheres had made her worst, most vile hangovers seem like minor headaches. She remembered the sickness working all the way through her skin and bones, and the way Myell had gone lax and unseeing in her arms.

"No one was sent after them?" she asked.

Gayle abruptly shut off the gib. "We tried. The system wouldn't activate. None of the Spheres on Fortune would send a token ring— what you call an ouroboros. When you and Chief Myell arrived on the *Aral Sea,* we read the classified file about your exploits. Obviously the problem was local. But then the *Alaska* docked yesterday."

The *Alaska* was a month behind the *Aral Sea.* News on the Big Alcheringa traveled only as fast as the ships riding it along the route of the Seven Sisters.

"Our branch office on Baiame sent word that their Spheres also aren't functioning. It's believed they stopped working after you and Chief Myell returned to Warramala."

"No one said anything to us there," Jodenny protested.

Gayle replied, "I understand there were more pressing problems to be dealt with."

Well, yes, if one counted the attempted overthrow of the local government. Jodenny said, "Whatever the case, you can't blame us. We didn't do anything that would make the system stop working."

Gayle ran her fingers around the rim of her coffee cup. "We're hoping that if you step into a Mother Sphere here, the system will respond—"

Something moved in the corner of Jodenny's eye. Gayle saw it as well and bolted from her chair. Karl, the mechanical koala, had lumbered out of the bedroom and was rubbing himself against a potted plant. He turned his eyes on them and said, "Hungry, hungry."

"He's harmless," Jodenny said.

Gayle turned her back on Karl. "Commander, all you have to do is give up an hour of your time. The nearest Spheres are at Bainbridge. If a token appears, we'll take over. If the system ignores you, then you go home. No harm done."

Jodenny didn't answer. Karl scratched himself and lumbered toward the floor plants. He wasn't programmed to eat, but sometimes he chewed on leaves.

"I'll have to talk to my husband," Jodenny finally said.

Gayle looked almost pathetically grateful. "Thank you, Commander. You don't know how much I appreciate it."

When she was alone, Jodenny made sure the doors were locked. She slid into the softest T-shirt she could find, which happened to be Myell's. She collected Karl. The bot agreeably snuggled up against her in the wide, warm bed. The mattress molded to her shape, Betsy screened down all the windows, and Karl snored softly. Quiet and stillness enveloped her.

The Wondjina Transportation System, dead. The most important discovery since the Little Alcheringa, the wormhole that connected Earth to Fortune. Or even since the Big Alcheringa, which linked Fortune to the six other planets of the Seven Sisters. Gayle's husband and eight other missing scientists, lost and stranded somewhere. Jodenny's former lover Sam Osherman was out there too, maybe injured, maybe dead.

She didn't fall asleep for a long, long time.

No," Myell said.

He was sitting in a windowless conference room with the two representatives from Fleet. One was a woman named Leorah Farber. She had dark black hair cut very short and a heart-shaped face currently expressing a frown. The other, Teddy Toledo, had wide shoulders, a thick neck, and curly brown hair. Both wore business suits. Farber was standing by the door, and Toledo sat across from Myell at a long table made of faux wood. The smooth brown walls were vidded with the same Supply School pictures that hung in Captain Kuvik's suite.

Farber had done very little talking, but she watched Myell with an intensity that was perhaps meant to be intimidating. Toledo had done nothing *but* talk, at about two thousand words a minute. The fast pace made him sound like a teenager talking about Izim or Snipe.

"—I don't think you're understanding what's at stake, here, Chief, we're talking about the lives of people who were stuck in a system that stopped working because of something you or your wife did while you were in it, otherwise how can anyone explain why nothing works now, nothing at all? I'm not saying sabotage, no one's saying that, but you have to admit the timing is bad, and maybe you found some equipment you didn't want to tell anyone about, maybe you pressed a button or two—"

Myell wondered if Toledo had played football in school. He had the hulking, menacing build for it. But he was more earnest than menacing. Not the captain of the team, then. Maybe the co-captain. American football had fallen out of favor over the years, but on Myell's first ship, the *Kashmir,* some of the sergeants and chiefs had enjoyed scrimmaging on the flight deck using Australian rules.

"—Don't you understand, Chief? All you have to do is stand in the Sphere. We'll be there if the token ring activates."

Myell could almost hear the mournful horn already, the warning that an ouroboros—"token ring" seemed such a dull phrase—was about to arrive in one of the ancient structures left by the creators of the Alcheringa and Seven Sisters.

He repeated, "No."

Toledo threw up his hands. "Don't you feel any responsibility at all?"

Myell had his doubts about Toledo's claim that he and Jodenny had somehow broken the system. The fault, if any, rested with the Rainbow

Serpent. The Creator God that Myell had spoken with and turned away from.

"If it's so important to you that we try, why hasn't someone given me a direct order?" Myell asked.

"You've refused orders before," said Farber. "In such a delicate situation as this, we agreed to try to enlist your help rather than demand it."

"Because you're a man of principle, and you don't like seeing innocent people get hurt," Toledo added.

Myell almost asked which innocent people Toledo was referring to. Anyone who tried to use the system had to know the risks involved. Not only the physical side effects, but also the possibility of getting lost in the vast, unmapped maze of stations and spheres.

Then again, perhaps the missing team of "scientists" was something else entirely.

Toledo said, "All you have to do is step inside a Mother Sphere. We can be there in twenty minutes. If it doesn't work, it doesn't work. If it works, then we're golden."

He made it sound so easy. So reasonable. But Myell had made his choice in front of the Rainbow Serpent, and he would abide by it.

"Teddy," Farber said suddenly, "I'd like to talk to Chief Myell alone."

Toledo flicked a gaze her way, then back to Myell.

"Go," Farber insisted.

When they were alone, she sat down and laid her hands flat on the table. "He's not telling you everything, Chief. We want you to do more than just activate the transport ring."

Myell waited. The room was soundproof, but he imagined Toledo standing at the door trying to listen.

"I know that when you were debriefed on Warramala, the agents didn't believe your story about a serpent telling you how to get home. The official conclusion is that you were hallucinating, and that you were enormously lucky navigating the network back to Warramala."

He stayed quiet.

Farber leaned forward. "I think you did encounter some kind of intelligence. It communicated with you. The first alien sentience that mankind has ever made contact with, and you were chosen for the honor. That makes you our liaison. Our best chance to establish a dialogue with the beings who created or control the Wondjina Spheres."

Myell phrased his answer carefully. "Miss Farber, whatever's out there, it doesn't want us using the system. It's not my place to go against that. If it's meant to be, those scientists will find their way back."

If the *Rainbow Serpent* meant it to be.

"You're condemning them to death," she told him.

Not true. They had done that themselves, the minute they stepped into a transportation system they knew nothing about.

"I'm sorry you feel that way," he said.

Myell walked back to Captain Kuvik's suite alone. The secretary gave him a sideways look, made a discreet call, and then said, "Your office is on the equipment deck."

"Is that the basement?" Myell asked.

The secretary smiled coldly.

Myell took the lift down. The equipment deck was dim and airless, with machinery sounds muffled behind thick locked doors. One door bore a sign with his name printed neatly on it. He'd seen closets that were bigger, but inside was a desk and a chair. No deskgib. He used his bee to ping Betsy.

"Where's Jodenny?" he asked.

"She's sleeping, sir. Shall I wake her?"

"No. Let her rest."

He sat there, alone with nothing to do, pondering snakes and lost travelers. Fleet would ask Jodenny, of course. They would appeal to her sense of honor. But she would say no. Together they had made their decision, and there was no going back on it now.

CHAPTER
THREE

After a while the view of four blank walls grew claustrophobic. Myell searched through the desk drawers but found nothing to write on. He ventured down the passageway and tried other doors. Most were locked, but close to the lift he found a closet filled with unwanted office supplies. Old deskgibs sat piled in boxes, their screens cracked or coated with dust. Printers and copiers with missing power units filled shelves. After sneezing a few times Myell dug up boxes of envelopes bearing the name of Captain Kuvik's predecessor, and at the bottom of a filing cabinet he found some pens and thumbtacks.

He brought the discovered treasures back to his office. On the backs of envelopes he began to sketch out the most common shipboard duties of a supply tech. The envelopes went up on the wall in decreasing order of importance. He sorted through the old course-ware. He was even coaxing one deskgib into clicking, flickering existence when footsteps hurried past his door and farther down the passage.

Myell hadn't heard anyone else since coming down. He suspected students weren't allowed in the area. Curious, he followed the sound down to one of the mechanical rooms. The hatch was open, revealing a dim and noisy interior full of water pipes and hot-water heaters.

"Hello?" he asked. "Who's down here?"

Something clattered to the floor. Myell turned to a corner.

"I could just leave you alone," he said casually, "or I could turn on the fire-suppression equipment for this room. It'll be hard to remain inconspicuous later when you're soaking wet."

After a moment a young sailor emerged from the shadows behind a boiler. He was a scrawny kid, barely old enough to shave, tall and gawky in a flagpole sort of way.

"Sorry, sir," he said.

Myell sighed.

The sailor noticed Myell's insignia. "I mean Chief, not sir."

"What are you doing down here, sailor?"

A frown, a shrug. "Just being derelict, Chief."

Myell scratched his chin. "Dereliction's a pretty serious charge. You might as well come down to my office and be useful instead."

"Chief?"

"It's over here. It's the luxury suite."

Myell led the way. Out of the corner of his eye he saw the sailor wipe at his eyes quickly. No worries there. Myell had done his own fair share of retreating to dark corners over the years. By the time they reached his office, the sailor's face was splotchy but dry.

"Romero, is it?" Myell asked, eyeing the sailor's nametag.

"Yes, Chief. AT Putty Romero."

"Well, AT Putty Romero, what do you think of my palace? Too gaudy? Maybe I should tone it down."

Romero blinked uncertainly.

"Don't be afraid of hurting my feelings." Myell turned to the deskgib and slapped the side of it, hoping to cease the clicking noise. If anything, the sound grew worse. "I'm told interior design isn't my forte. What's yours?"

"My what, Chief?"

"Your special area of expertise."

Romero's face scrunched up. "I'm not so bad with gibs."

"Can you fix this one?"

Romero examined the deskgib, pried open the back panel, and began fiddling with the insides. "Power unit's okay but the brain's fried up. You'll need a transplant."

"Let's go shopping," Myell said, and showed him to the supply room.

It took thirty minutes with improvised tools for Romero to have the unit working properly. Myell would have taken twice the amount of time on his own. Once powered up, the gib didn't get him to Core, but Myell could sync his bee to it if he wanted connectivity, and Romero jury-rigged a printer that was excruciatingly slow but serviceable.

Romero was mostly silent as he worked, but Myell did worm out of him that he was part of the class graduating on Friday. He had orders to the *Kamchatka,* which was deploying soon for Earth. He'd never been off world before.

"You're from around here?" Myell asked.

"Pennefather. The boondocks."

Myell's grasp of Fortune's geography was still tenuous. "Where I grew up, the nearest town was called Pink Skunk. You don't know the definition of 'desolate' until you've been that way."

Romero brushed dust off the top of the printer. "I guess I'd better get back to study hall. I only have one exam to take before graduation Saturday."

"Which exam is that?"

"Fifth-generation X-relation databases." Romero was still gazing at the printer, as if it contained secrets of the universe. "I hate them."

"They're not so hard, once you understand them."

"Oh, I understand them. They're kinda easy. But clunky, you know? No beauty at all."

Myell asked, "Do you find the courses here too easy?"

Romero shrugged. "They're not so bad."

"But not what you're interested in."

That was it. Romero's eyes gave him away before anything else did.

Myell had heard many recruiting horror stories. "Recruiter lie to you? Promise you some other rating, and then switch you at the last minute?"

"Aeronautics tech. They said I could crew on birdies and foxes, though only officers get to pilot them. But then they said there weren't enough openings, and I could be in supply aviation. That I could still be in a crew."

"It's possible."

"You've been on freighters, Chief. Any chance?"

Myell didn't want to lie. "Small one."

Romero looked down at his boots. "That's what I thought."

The bells for eleven-hundred began to chime. Romero said, "First lunch period. That's mine. You want me to show you where the mess is?"

"I think I'll wait. Thanks for your help."

Romero rubbed the side of his head and went off. At high noon Myell ventured over to the mess, which was teeming with students and staff. The high, airy room was separated into a large space for students, a smaller room for enlisted staff, and a mess for officers and chiefs decorated with banners, ship models, and plaques.

He was sorely tempted to grab a tray and bring it back to his sub-terranean office. The chief's mess on the *Aral Sea* had welcomed him well enough, though it had been with the tacit understanding that he'd undergo initiation at Fortune, as they had. He forced himself through the chow line, picked out a plate of spaghetti and soy meat-balls, and headed for the staff dining room.

Six male chiefs sat at a table in the center of the room, with no chairs free. They had the jocular air of old friends, of drinking bud-dies. Two female lieutenants were dining in the corner, their heads bent close in conversation. A lieutenant commander, two ensigns, a senior chief, and Captain Kuvik's secretary sat at a long table near an aquarium. One chair was free there, but cowardice overtook him and he aimed for an empty table along the bulkhead instead.

He supposed it was meant to be humiliating, their ignoring him, but he'd had plenty of experience eating on his own. He used his bee to skim the day's news. He ate with deliberate leisure, and sipped at his coffee long after it had grown cold. He was aware of sideways glances and whispers. One of the senior chiefs at the head table, a thickly built man with muscled arms, glared Myell's way more than once, as if personally affronted by his presence.

Well, then. If his tenure at Supply School was going to be shot down before it even got started, Myell might as well make it a spectacular flame-out. When the lunch period ended he followed the senior chief to a large auditorium classroom on the third deck. Two hundred or so sailors were already crowding into the tiered rows of blue chairs. Myell took an aisle seat halfway down and settled in.

"What class is this?" he asked the sailor beside him.

"COSAL reporting," the sailor said, surprised. Apparently chiefs didn't sit in on each other's classes here.

"What's the instructor's name?"

"Senior Chief Talic. Like *italic,* you know? But not like parentheses."

Myell nodded gravely. "I'll remember that."

Senior Chief Talic didn't notice Myell in the audience, or chose to ignore him. Myell believed the latter, considering he was the only one in dress whites in a sea of gray jumpsuits. Talic began his lecture by saying, "All right, settle down, thumb your way to chapter seven. Your homework assignments show an appalling lack of understanding of basic regulations. Let's review the priority sequencing for all class-two general requisitions."

Ten minutes in, the sailors had glazed expressions and Myell was starting to yawn. Sequencing was a silly thing to spend time on. Young ATs would face much more interesting problems in the fleet. But mastering regulations and procedures meant doing well on tests, and high test scores led to promotion. Didn't mean a person could handle an issue room, or deal with unhappy customers, or fix DNGOs that decided to shut down on their own.

The second half of the class picked up a bit when Talic sprang a pop quiz on the students. As they bent to the task, furiously keying in answers on their gibs, Talic came up the stairs. He motioned for Myell to follow him out to the passageway.

"Who said you could sit in?" he demanded when they were alone. His cheeks were ruddy with anger.

"I took some initiative," Myell said.

"Smart-ass. Everyone says that about you. You're not welcome in my classroom and you're not welcome at this command. My students have a hard enough job as it, memorizing all this bureaucratic bullshit. They don't need a bad influence. Stay the fuck away from them and from me."

Talic stalked back into the auditorium. If he could have slammed the doors behind him, he probably would have.

"That went well," Myell said to the empty air around him.

When he got home that afternoon he found Jodenny in the kitchen, frying tofu in a pan and nursing a burn on her finger.

"Our kitchenware is cursed." She kissed him soundly. "How was your first day at school?"

"I think I made a big impression."

"In a good way?"

"In the only way I could." Myell eyed the tofu warily. Cooking wasn't Jodenny's strong point. She was dressed for the summer weather in a white blouse and blue shorts that set off her long, slim legs. He was tempted to carry her over to the sofa for some overdue affection.

Instead he pulled a beer from the refrigerator and took a long, satisfying swallow.

Jodenny said, "I vowed I would cook you dinner on your first day back to work, just as you've been cooking for me these past few weeks."

He nuzzled her sweet-smelling neck. "I have a secret to confess. I've been ordering takeout and making it look like I cooked."

"You lie like a rug," she said, and kissed him until Betsy began to chime a warning.

"Forget dinner," Myell said, turning off the stove. He lifted Jodenny up onto the countertop and nudged her knees apart. She looped her arms around his neck, her hot kisses spicy against his lips, her hair brushing his face. He unbuttoned her blouse as her hands ran down his shoulders to his waist.

"Missed you," she murmured.

"Quit your job," he said.

She smiled. "When you quit yours, sailor."

Then there were no words, just some urgent needy noises and giggling. He carried her not to the sofa but to the bedroom, where Karl was unceremoniously rousted from his pillow. Myell slid Jodenny's shorts off. His own uniform was too hot, too tight. He shucked the pants off, but Jodenny's hands stopped him when he reached for his shirt and tie.

Her eyes wide and dark, her cheeks flushed, she said, "Leave them on."

"Anything else?"

"Socks are optional."

He peeled off the socks, twirled them over his head, and cast them into the corner. Jodenny used the tie to pull him down and he mouthed a trail from her breasts to her navel. She shifted, her breath fast, her hands tight on his hips. Her gaze was locked on his face.

"Love you," she whispered.

"Love you more," he said.

Her fingers touched his waist and found the dilly bag. "You're wearing this again?"

Myell untied it and tossed it onto the pillows.

Afterward, when they finally got around to dinner, they settled for cold sandwiches, sweet pickles, and vegetable chips. They played a little footsie under the table as she tried to worm more information out of him about Supply School. Myell described Captain Kuvik's office, the well-equipped gymnasium, Sergeant Etedgy and AT Romero. He briefly related Senior Chief Talic's lecture.

"I don't know how people keep from keeling over in boredom," Myell said.

"Did anyone give you a hard time about not going through chief initiation?"

"The subject came up," Myell allowed.

She waited him out.

He reached for another pickle. "There's some hard feelings. But we expected that."

"I don't like it."

"Also expected," he said.

Neither of them mentioned anything about the Wondjina Transportation System.

After dinner they took glasses of wine to the new sofa. He was proud of that sofa. It had taken him three days of computer research and visits to four stores before he found one that fit perfectly. Jodenny wriggled her bare feet hopefully, and he took them into his lap. She searched through the drawer in the coffee table, pushing aside honeymoon brochures, and tossed him a small bottle of massage oil.

"So," he said, rubbing her arches with strong, steady pressure. "Anything else happen to you today?"

"Is this an interrogation?"

The windows were open to the fine summer evening, with the occasional whoosh of a flit and the hum of lawn-bots cutting grass.

"I have my fiendish ways." Myell concentrated on the shape and feel of her feet, the delicate toes, the well-shaped ankles. She had painted her nails a cheery shade of red. She knew he loved red on her toes.

Jodenny's breath hitched a little as he pressed more strongly. She said, "A woman came to see me from Fleet. She said her husband and eight other people are lost in the network. That the whole thing's closed down."

He kept his head down, his hands moving.

"You're not surprised," she said.

"I had my own visitors."

"She's desperate to find him. As I would be to find you, if you disappeared."

"I'm right here." He gently tugged at each toe, rotating and soothing them. "Not going anywhere."

Jodenny cocked her head. "If you disappeared, I'd scream and scream until someone helped. Someone who knew about where you'd gone, who had experience traveling that path."

Myell squeezed more oil onto his palms. "They've been gone for months."

"Every minute would be like the first minute."

"And if there were other considerations?"

Jodenny's voice was very serious. "What's more important than finding the love of your life?"

The western sky was gold with sunset. Karl the Koala wandered out of the bedroom and climbed onto the coffee table. Very carefully Myell said, "Keeping to what we decided before. It's not our business."

Her legs tensed against his thighs. Jodenny said, "Come here, Karl."

The koala cocked his head but didn't move.

"You don't even know if they're telling the truth," Myell said. "It could just be a way for them to sucker in our cooperation. Since when can we trust anything they tell us?"

"Since when don't you care about helping someone who's in trouble?"

"All these months, you and I have known Sam Osherman was out there somewhere. But we agreed not to help when we were on Kookaburra and we didn't do anything when we got back here. So how is that different?"

Her gaze didn't drop. "Because we believed the network was working. Because he took his chances by not listening to you. Sam knew what he was getting into."

"As did this team."

Jodenny swung her feet out of his grasp. "All we have to do is show up. Just go into a Sphere. If it works, they'll take it from there."

"If it works, they'll never let us be free of it. They won't let us walk away, like they did last time."

"If they're right, if somehow this entire network of ancient alien technology stopped working because of something we did, then we have a duty to assist any way we can. Won't you help at all?"

He took a deep breath. The cinnamon smell of the massage oil made his nose itch. "No."

"Then you're not the person I thought you were," she said, and left the room.

He let his head loll against a cushion. In the months that they'd been married they had never once gone to bed mad. But there had been nothing to fight about on the *Aral Sea,* and nothing really to disagree on since they'd landed.

"Jodenny!" he called out, but she didn't answer.

Myell told himself to get up and go make amends but he stayed on the sofa, instead, on the green sofa he'd picked out because she was too busy to help. The one he suspected she didn't like. He played Izim until he fell asleep. The next thing he knew the vid was off, a blanket was keeping him warm, and Jodenny was crouched before him in the dark, shaking him awake. She was in uniform.

"I have to go," she said. "I got called in."

Struggling out of a dream he couldn't quite remember, Myell drank in her sweet, floral perfume.

"What time is it?" he asked.

"You have a few hours," she assured him, and brushed her warm fingers along his temple. "Terry, I'm going to talk to them some more. Just talk. I want to be able to say my conscience is clear on the fate of nine people I never met."

He caught her fingers. "Can I stop you?"

"Can I stop *you,* when you set your mind to anything?"

"Just talk," he repeated.

"Just talk," she said. "I promise."

Jodenny arrived at work a few minutes before sunrise. The blue pyramid of Team Space headquarters included an enormous atrium full of trees, waterfalls, cafés, and comfortable furniture. Cleaning bots were finishing up with the blue and gold carpets as she crossed to the transparent lifts. Admiral Mizoguchi's command suite was on the sixth deck, where plastiglass windows overlooked the atrium's descending terraces.

"Thanks for coming in," Lieutenant Commander Chow said when Jodenny showed up. Chow had pulled midwatch duty and was due to be relieved by an officer who had called in sick.

"Not a problem." Jodenny's sleep had been fitful and uneasy. She'd dreamed of Sam Osherman fleeing through Spheres, in danger from some unseen menace. The call from Fleet had been a relief. "What's going on?"

Chow started going through a list. Admiral Mizoguchi was the area liaison for all the Fleet units located within the Kimberley region—a formidable lineup that included the basic training command, a half-dozen specialty schools, an airfield, a port operation, and intelligence, cryptology, and diplomatic units. The commands themselves had operational and administrative chains of command that made Mizoguchi just one of many higher echelons to report to, and Mizoguchi herself reported upward as well as sideways to other branches of Team Space. Jodenny and her co-workers were responsible for keeping her apprised, in charge, and capable of responding as needed to dozens of challenges a day.

"Ready for the morning brief?" Chow asked.

"Ready as rain," Jodenny said.

The briefing was short and succinct. Admiral Mizoguchi, a short trim woman with bright eyes, asked only a few questions. Afterward, Jodenny assumed the day watch and settled in at her desk.

"Thanks again," Chow said. "See you later."

Come midmorning, once business settled down a bit, Jodenny used her clearance as part of the admiral's staff to look up Anna Gayle in the Team Space Directory. Gayle was listed in the Research and Development branch with an office on Rathbone Street. Her contact information matched the one on the card she had given Jodenny, as did her picture.

Master Chief Paulie, who was the admiral's senior enlisted adviser, had an office down the hall. Jodenny knocked on her door and asked, "Can you spare a moment?"

"Sure, Commander." Paulie turned from her gib. Her office was a soothing oasis of blue and green, with pictures of her daughters on the vidded walls. "What can I do for you?"

Jodenny closed the door. "I wanted to check on someone who works in Research and Development. Beyond gib numbers and security photos."

"You could ask your agent to run a classified query. You've got the clearance."

"I don't think what I'm looking for would be in any database."

Paulie templed her fingers together. "Is this for personal reasons?"

"No," Jodenny said. "Strictly professional. But nothing to do with the admiral or her jurisdiction."

Paulie's gaze was inscrutable. "I'm not sure I can be of help."

"I don't want to get anyone in trouble, Master Chief. If I knew how to do it on my own, without drawing attention, I'd do it. But I think I'd cock it up. And then I'd bring attention to this office."

Paulie smiled. "That's your persuasive argument? You want me to help you so you don't embarrass the admiral?"

"It's worth embarrassing an admiral or two," Jodenny said solemnly. "It's worth a lot more than that. I'm just not sure who to trust."

"You can trust me."

Jodenny shook her head. "You don't have clearance for this."

"I have a top-secret clearance, Commander."

"I know, Master Chief."

Paulie played with her pen. "If you leave me the name I can make some informal inquiries, but I can't promise anything. I will need a promise in return."

"What kind of promise?" Jodenny asked cautiously.

Paulie was obviously choosing her words carefully. "If you do get involved in a matter over your head, that you let the admiral or myself assist you."

Jodenny figured that a promise like that contained a lot of leeway. She gave Paulie a slip of paper with Anna Gayle's name on it. Back at her desk, thrumming with nervous energy, not fully able to focus on her work, she glanced every now and then toward Paulie's office. Lunchtime came with no word. Early afternoon dragged by, nothing. Finally, when Jodenny's watch was nearly over, Paulie pinged her desk and asked her to step in.

"Dr. Gayle has an extremely high security clearance and a sterling reputation." Paulie tapped her fingernail on a printed sheet of paper. "She's been working for Fleet for four years, has a long trail of academic accomplishments, and is married to Dr. Robert Monnox, equally accomplished and respected. Does that help?"

Jodenny let out a careful breath. "It establishes her credentials. Thank you."

"Remember, Miz Scott. You're not alone in whatever this matter concerns. Can I count on you to ask for assistance when you need it?"

"Absolutely," Jodenny said.

Once she had turned the watch over to her replacement, Jodenny went to a public kiosk on Sydney Boulevard. Gayle answered the ping immediately.

"I hope you've agreed to help us," she said, her gaze direct and un-blinking.

"I've agreed to hear more," Jodenny said.

"May I send a flit to pick you up?"

"I'll come on my own." She told herself that Myell couldn't be-grudge her visiting Gayle's office. Checking out the department. Not agreeing to anything without consulting him.

And if he didn't agree?

Jodenny headed for the train.

On his way to work that morning, Myell got off the monorail early and walked six blocks along Water Street. A farmers' market had set up for the morning, vendors already selling fresh fruits and vegeta-bles. He maneuvered through the crowds and portable stalls, inhaling the aroma of breakfast crepes and waffles. A young Aboriginal girl unloading paintings from a flit nearly dropped some, and he stopped to help.

"Thanks," she said, as Myell eased the paintings to the ground.

"No problem." Myell eyed a large landscape in which a solitary gum tree held sway over a red plain. "You do these yourself?"

The girl ducked her head shyly. She was short and thin, her dress loose on her shoulders. "No, sir. My mom and aunties, they do them."

Another painting made him pause. A crocodile, gray-green and enormous, snarled on the banks of a river. Its teeth looked sharp enough to rip off Myell's arm.

"Not very nice, is he?" Myell asked.

"Crocs aren't nice or mean." The girl met his gaze with eyes as gray as the reptile's. "They just are, right?"

"I suppose," Myell said.

One last painting caught his eye. A lone black vulture whirled over a grassy plain, homing in on animal corpses lying below. Something about the painting made a rough chill go through him.

"Jungali," the girl said.

"What?" Myell asked sharply.

"Jungle cats," the girl said, indicating the corpses. "Lions."

Myell couldn't bear to look anymore. The market had grown too crowded, too loud. He hurried toward Supply School. The smell of the ocean made him nauseated. He went to his little basement office and sat there for two hours until Sergeant Etedgy knocked on his door, looking apologetic.

"Captain sent down some work for you to do," he said. Two ATs bearing boxes of loosely bound regulations followed Etedgy in. "He wants you to check the LOEPs on these and requisition any that we need."

The sailors put the boxes down on the deck. Myell didn't bother to point out that coordinating Lists of Effective Pages was a job any clerk could do. Instead, he offered Etedgy a bland smile. "No problem."

Once the sailors were gone Etedgy said, "I'm sorry."

"It's nothing to worry about."

"Not to be too frank, Chief, it's a shit job."

"But it's all mine," Myell said.

Kuvik had made the job more interesting. Half the books had split their spines, spilling their contents into jumbles of dusty, tattered paper. He must have dug deep in his closet to find them. No one consulted paper regulations anymore, not when databases could easily be consulted and cross-indexed again.

"Mine," Myell repeated, once he was alone.

Fifteen minutes before the first-period lunch, he went over to the mess deck and was first in line for the food. The faculty wardroom was empty and sparkling clean. Myell plunked his tray down at the center table and began to eat at a leisurely pace.

Two lieutenants arrived soon after and immediately went to a table in the corner. A gaggle of ensigns came in and claimed a rectangular table. Two chiefs who were part of Senior Chief Talic's clique came in with their trays, halted when they saw Myell at their table, reversed course, and chose to sit elsewhere.

Senior Chief Talic arrived next.

"You weren't invited to sit here," he said in a low voice over Myell's shoulder.

"I'm sorry, I didn't hear you," Myell said, loud and pleasant. "You wanted to welcome me to Supply School? Thank you, Senior Chief Talic. I'm happy to be here."

The ensigns and lieutenants looked their way and murmured among themselves. Talic put his tray down so hard that the silverware rattled. He took the seat opposite Myell.

"Did you have a good morning in class?" Myell asked.

Talic ignored him.

Myell pitched his voice louder again. "I asked if you had a good morning—"

Talic's glare was murderous. "It was fine."

"My morning was good, too," Myell confided.

Senior Chief Gooder, short and squat with the shoulders of a weight lifter, took the seat next to Myell and offered his hand. "My twelve-year-old daughter and her friends have a vicious little clique in school, but we're worse. Welcome aboard."

"Frank," Talic said, "you know what this is about."

Gooder shook out his napkin. "Yes, yes, standards, principles, pull the other one, why don't you? He's the only one at this entire command with a Silver Star on his uniform, so he must be doing something right."

Two other chiefs eventually joined them. They weren't as friendly as Gooder, but not as frosty as Talic. The table by the aquarium filled up with Captain Kuvik's secretary and other staff, some of whom gave Myell speculative looks. The conversation at the chiefs' table centered on Saturday's graduation, and some controversy over the AT who had been chosen as class speaker.

"Should have been based on grades, not personality," Talic argued.

"Best grades only means someone's good at taking tests," Gooder said. "Doesn't mean the person's articulate, or can hold the interest of a crowd."

"Tradition," one of the other chiefs said. "You're not going to convince Captain Kuvik to do it any other way than it's always been done."

"What do you think about tradition, Myell?" Gooder asked, a gleam in his eye.

Myell took his time answering. "Some are good. Some are outdated."

Talic jabbed a fork into the air. "Tried and true. It works. You don't go changing things on a whim, or because someone cries to their mommy, or because someone has a nervous little fit."

Myell wasn't about to point out that tradition was what had killed that chief-designee on Kookaburra. Everyone at the table surely knew the story. Dehydration, overexertion, a heart attack. It wasn't the first accidental death during a hazing ceremony but it was supposed to be the last. The initiation procedures for chiefs had changed radically after that, and had become "optional." Somewhere over at Fleet, Myell's former shipmates from the *Aral Sea* were no doubt still discovering that "optional" abuse was no less humiliating than the nonoptional kind.

"Only dead things are immune to change," Myell said. "Dead people, dead institutions, dead minds."

Talic's fork jabbed his way, but his gaze abruptly swiveled to the doorway. Myell glanced over his shoulder and saw Captain Kuvik carrying his tray in. He was accompanied by civilians in business attire.

"Captain hardly ever eats here," Gooder murmured, reaching for the salt. "Damn efficiency experts from Fleet. They come by to make life hell every now and again."

Talic seemed unwilling to continue his arguments about tradition with Kuvik in the room. He left, soon followed by the others at their table, leaving only Gooder to dally over his coffee. Gooder asked, "So, they really stick you down in the basement?"

"Any lower and I'd be in the foundation," Myell said.

Gooder grinned. "That's our captain for you. Don't worry. Your tour's three years, right? By the end of year two he'll have warmed up a degree or two. Might even let you teach a class."

"I doubt that."

"He's rigid, but usually fair. Listens to reason."

"Not on the subject of chief initiation," Myell said. "Or fraternization."

"So it's true? You married your lieutenant?"

"It's not exactly like that."

Gooder clapped him on the shoulder. "Nothing ever is."

After lunch Myell returned to his little office and spent the entire afternoon on his tedious task. To lighten up the silence of the basement he played music on his bee. He thought of Kuvik eating lunch with the so-called efficiency experts. Maybe they were really men from Fleet. Would Team Space transfer him anyway, force him to work on the Wondjina network despite his protests? He'd been told that the project was voluntary, but he couldn't be sure.

Stop being paranoid, he told himself.

At sixteen-hundred hours he still had several more days of work ahead of him. Myell left his office, started for the lift, then stopped when the overhead lights went off. He heard scuffling footsteps but was too slow to dodge the arms that grabbed him and dragged him backward. He kicked and yelled as adhesive tape was slapped over his mouth.

"We'll fucking show you what initiation means," someone said, a man's voice that he didn't recognize.

A hood was pulled over his head. It smelled musty and tainted with machine oil. He was hauled down the corridor. He couldn't be sure, not in the rush of panic, not as he fought to breathe past the tape and tried to break their strong hold, but he thought maybe there were three assailants. A door opened. Machinery hummed nearby. Air units, water heaters, the plumbing system. He fought as hard as he could, trying to squirm free, to yell, but they easily slammed him up against a support pillar. A fist drove into his abdomen.

"None of it's optional," one of his attackers said. A man, no one he could identify. "You call Fleet and tell them you want to go through initiation. Otherwise—" Another fist landed in his stomach. "Otherwise we'll be waiting for you every day, fucking teach you a lesson, you understand?"

They grabbed his hair and tipped his head back so tightly that he couldn't breathe.

"Understand?" the man said again.

Though Myell hated to let them win, he made a muffled sound of surrender.

"Good," he was told. "Be a good boy now. Work hard at it, why don't you, and maybe you'll get free on your own. If not, we'll send someone along in the morning to get you. Won't be the most enjoyable night you've ever spent, but you can use it to think about how much you'll enjoy initiation."

They tied him to the pillar with rope and left him there, breathing hard through his nose, pain like fire in his stomach. His legs were shaking so hard he thought they might give way. The attackers left without another word. Only the clang of the closing door told him he was alone. He pulled at the rope but the knots were solid, and already the muscles in his shoulders were beginning to cramp.

Think, he told himself. You can get out of this. They don't dare leave you alone like this.

But they did.

Anna Gayle's lab suite was in the basement of the Team Space complex on Rathbone Street. The lights were off, with information playing out in strong colors on a wallgib.

"This is a map of the Wondjina network stations that Team Space has visited," Gayle said. Her face was tight and smooth in the reflected light. "Eighty stations over the course of the last six years. There'd be more if they didn't make people so damn sick. We have a labeling system that helps keep track of where the loop originated and the station number."

Jodenny gazed at the map. "So Chief Myell and I traveled where?"

"On your first trip, you went through MRLM1—that's Mary River Lakeland Mother Station 1, the originating station. It's an express route, to MRLM2—that's Mary River Lakeland Mother Station 2—and back again," Gayle said.

There were two other people in the lab with them. Gayle had introduced them as Leorah Farber and Teddy Toledo. Toledo, helpful and earnest, built like a large refrigerator, said, "Express routes only go one or two stops and come back. Loops go a lot farther."

Gayle pointed at a circle of green lights. "This was your second trip, as you recounted it to the agents on Warramala. You got on at Warramala Sowbridge Mother 1 and went several stations on that loop, which runs one hundred and forty stations."

"We got very sick," Jodenny said.

"But you got back by transferring through other Spheres," Farber said. She was quieter than her partner, with a deeply somber expression. "Your husband claimed a serpent spoke to him and told him how."

Jodenny wasn't about to defend or explain Myell's Rainbow Serpent. If they hadn't taken a shortcut through the network, they'd probably be dead by now. Or still lost, like Sam Osherman.

"You said six years," Jodenny said. "Why couldn't anyone use them before?"

"There are fourteen sets of Wondjina Spheres here on Fortune." Gayle turned back to her map. "Tourists have been traipsing in and out of them for decades without triggering any tokens. Sure, there have always been urban legends, myths. People who claim to see spirits in them, or walk through one and end up back on Earth, or in heaven, or some pastel-colored astral plane. But only six years ago did we actually receive a verifiable report. An AT on Kiwi, visiting her parents on their farm, went sightseeing and wound up on a Kiwi express. Scared her silly."

Toledo said, "She'd been in and out of Spheres ever since she was a child. Never happened before."

Jodenny frowned. "I thought you have to be exposed to the system in order to travel in it. I saw one on the *Yangtze*. The next time I visited a Mother Sphere, I triggered one. Chief Myell was with me, so he was exposed then and could trigger them in any other Spheres he visited."

Gayle said, "Not every Mother Sphere seems to be active, and even those that are seem to go through periods when they're offline. But yes, that first AT was the only one who, to our knowledge, was not previously exposed. Why that token came for her, we don't know."

"Why do you call it a token?" Jodenny asked.

Toledo replied, "Someone thought the system resembles an old token ring computer network. Pre-Debasement technology. You've got fifty computers on the same network, and one token looping around between them on a fixed route. The computer that wanted to transmit information would grab the token, stick data in it, then send it on its way again so that other—"

"Yes, yes," Gayle said, interrupting. "As far as we know, there's only one ring at a time in any given Wondjina loop. When you step into a station that authorizes you, you have to wait for the token to come along. It might be a few seconds, it might be a minute, but if someone else is using it, nothing happens. That's the case up at Swedenville. We've done most of our experiments there."

"Is that where your husband's expedition left from?" Jodenny asked, returning her gaze to the map.

"No. They left from Bainbridge." Gayle keyed in a command, and a new map popped up. "We know from examining the token's diagram that it has thirty-four stations, none of which cross-references Swedenville or any other Spheres in the Seven Sisters. Like every other Sphere, it refused to transfer any automated probes—we tried DNGOs, we tried remote cameras, nothing. With the advances the medical division made, Robert thought thirty-four stations were well within reach for a human expedition."

Goosebumps rose on her arms. Jodenny resisted the urge to rub at them. "How big is the entire network?"

"Thousands of stations," Farber said. "Maybe hundreds of thousands."

Gayle shut off the wallgib and brought the overhead lights up to full illumination. "What we'd really like to pinpoint is the network's control station. The hub of it all, or hubs if there's more than one. You can grind a Sphere into dust and not find any type of machinery inside. How the tokens appear, what power source sends them spiraling onward—it's a mystery."

Jodenny asked, "You've destroyed a Sphere?"

Gayle gave her a patient look. "Hypothetical computer models. We would never destroy an archaeological artifact."

"But you did capture a token," Jodenny said. "You tried to transport it on the *Yangtze,* and it ended up destroying the ship."

She tried not to sound bitter about it. Hundreds of people dead. Her shipmates, her closest friends. The actual sequence of events was still an enigma to her. The Team Space agents on Warramala had insisted that no memory block had been installed in her mind, but Sam Osherman had told her otherwise. If he was alive, if she ever found him again, she intended to wrap her hands around his throat and throttle the truth out of him.

Gayle sat down. Her gaze, always direct, burned into Jodenny. "The field office on Warramala had no way of knowing what destruction the token would cause while transporting it. You can be sure that no one will try that again. Safety is our highest priority. That, and preserving the integrity of the network. We only want to understand what the Wondjina left for us. With any luck at all, it will help us understand them better. Bring us closer to who and what they were."

Myell would no doubt have something to say about that. Jodenny checked the nearest clock. He should be off work by now, on his way home. She hoped his second day at Supply School had been easier than his first one.

"All you want me to do is see if a Mother Sphere will respond to me?" she asked.

Gayle nodded. "If the system stays operational, if it's safe, we'll send a rescue team after Robert's group. If you'd like, I could get you on the team. With the new medical treatments, the sickness is no longer a problem. You could be part of an amazing adventure, Commander."

The offer was more tempting than she wanted to admit. Jodenny said, "What if the token doesn't come?"

"If it doesn't, we'll have to try something else. Can I count on your cooperation, Commander?"

Jodenny said, "When do you want to try?"

Gayle leaned forward. "Tonight. Tomorrow. You decide."

Her eagerness was a little unsettling. Jodenny said, "Let me call you in the morning."

She was halfway down the passageway, heading for the lift, when Leorah Farber came after her.

"Commander," Farber said. "A word?"

Jodenny replied, "I said I'd call in the morning."

Farber said, "It's about your husband. We'd appreciate his cooperation as well. I've tried talking to him and understand his reluctance, but this is an issue larger than individual concerns any of us might have."

The passageway was long but wide, filled with gleaming white floor tiles and windowless beige walls. A medbot sat on a perch high above, waiting for emergencies. Jodenny said, "His 'individual concerns' are pretty big."

"I know," Farber said. "But I've also talked to his commanding officer at Supply School. Captain Kuvik doesn't want him there. Doesn't believe he sets a good role model for the students or staff. Why should Chief Myell continue in such a hostile environment—"

"Wait," Jodenny said hotly. "Not a good role model? Winner of a Silver Star?"

Farber glanced pointedly at Jodenny's wedding ring. "It's not my opinion, ma'am. It's Captain Kuvik's. The fraternization issue, skipping initiation—these aren't taken lightly. But I promise you, here, in this project, no one will make an issue of it."

Jodenny shook her head in disgust. "If that's your entire sales pitch, Miss Farber, it's no wonder you didn't win him over."

She took public transportation home, mulling over Farber's words and rehearsing what to tell Myell about the project. She wouldn't even mention Gayle's casual offer to include her in the rescue mission. Better that he didn't even think that was an option. She wouldn't go gallivanting around the universe without him, anyway.

Jodenny tried pinging him from the monorail, but he didn't respond to his bee. He hadn't left any messages and Betsy reported that he wasn't home.

That was strange, but perhaps he'd gone to the gym and left his bee on a locker shelf. Once she was home and out of her uniform, Jodenny tried calling him again. No answer. She curled up on the ugly sofa with her gib, reading the news, watching the daylight fade outside. Karl snuggled between her feet, his ears twitching.

"Where are you?" she asked the ceiling.

Myell didn't answer.

Myell couldn't reach his bee. It buzzed more than once, and he imagined Jodenny's increasing worry on the other end. Sooner or later she would call the duty officer at Supply School to find out what time he'd left. The duty officer would report that he hadn't flashed his ID at the lobby security scanner on his way out. A search might commence. The idea of anyone finding him here, bound and gagged in the dark, was utterly humiliating.

He twisted and squirmed for the knots. Some large piece of machinery nearby started to hiss. Warm air blasted over him, and the dark terror of the hood over his head dissolved into a burnt-red desert that he hadn't seen since Warramala.

This landscape was different from the one he'd experienced then. A watering hole, large and unexpectedly blue, lay not far from his feet. A crocodile was immersed in it. Only the creature's head and snout showed. Its teeth were white like bone, its skin gray verging on black.

"I didn't have time for you," Myell said, shuddering.

The crocodile stared at him, its eyes flat and green. "Jungali," it said, though its mouth didn't move.

Myell tried closing his eyes, but they were already closed. Jungali was the nickname his mother had given him as a child. Was the name the Rainbow Serpent had used, in asking him to choose between the so-called real world and the Dreamtime.

"That's not me," he said.

The ground around the watering hole rippled, and another reptile tore free of the ground. It rose on its hind legs like a dinosaur might. Its breath smelled like burnt flesh, like something rancid and rotting left to dry under the sun. Thunderhead clouds boiled in the sky.

"Jungali!" the crocodile cried, and scurried out of the waterhole toward him. The dinosaur-thing attacked it with claws and teeth, and their ferocious struggles ripped through the air.

Myell jerked backward. The vision disappeared, replaced by darkness and the sounds of machinery, the cut of rope against his skin. Oxygen was becoming a problem. He forced himself to calm down, but it took several long moments before he could breathe steadily through his nose, and even longer before his hands were steady enough to get to work.

He finally managed to free himself, at the cost of torn and scraped wrists. The rest of the faculty and students had long departed the school, and the lobby was empty but for a bored-looking AT.

"Night, Chief," he said, as Myell passed through the scanners.

The air outside was fresh and mild compared to the basement. The after-work crowd had thinned. If he checked over his shoulder once or twice, that was caution and not paranoia. On the train ride home he worried how he was going to explain things. Jodenny would want to get involved, pull rank, pull strings, as she had on the *Aral Sea*. He didn't need to be rescued by his wife. He wouldn't allow a repeat of the bullying there to mar his time on Fortune.

His bee was silent, though. Maybe she'd given up trying to contact him. When the monorail drew close to Adeline Oaks, he pinged Betsy.

"Commander Scott is asleep," she told him. "Shall I wake her? She was eager to reach you."

"No," Myell said. "Leave her alone."

He trudged home from the train station in the darkness. She was dozing on the sofa when he let himself in. He hurried to their bedroom and closed the door behind him.

There were no marks on his face, except for irritation where the tape glue had been. His wrists wouldn't look pretty come morning.

Myell turned on the shower and climbed in under hot water. Only under its strong torrent did he allow himself to close his eyes, and lean against the shower wall, and let himself tremble.

Without meaning to, Jodenny had fallen asleep on the ugly sofa. When she woke the sky was full dark and the shower was running in the master bathroom.

She poked her head into the bathroom. "Terry?"

"You were sleeping," he said from behind the shower screen and a cloud of steam. "Didn't want to wake you."

Jodenny yawned at her mirror reflection. "I tried to reach you. Is your bee working?"

"It's been frizzing out all day. Sorry I was late—a few unexpected things came up."

"School was okay?"

Myell reached for a bar of soap. "Every day's something new. I'll get the hang of it. Did you eat?"

Jodenny thought of Farber's words. *Hostile environment.* She said, "I'm starving. Want to go to Mexwax?"

He didn't answer for a moment.

"Come on," she wheedled. "Quesadillas and tequila."

"Okay," he said.

Jodenny was glad. No doubt they both needed a little cheering up. She slipped into a little blue dress and was surprised when Myell ducked into his closet to pull on his clothes. Usually he dressed in front of her. He emerged wearing slacks and a black shirt, one of her favorites.

"You look great," he said, and kissed her cheek. His skin was still warm from the shower, his hair damp, and he had a little rash around his mouth. Jodenny touched it gingerly.

"Did you eat something you were allergic to?"

He looked at himself in the mirror. "Maybe. I didn't notice."

They took their own flit. Myell drove, refusing as always to put the car on autopilot. Traffic was light. A landscape of darkened stores, empty office parks, and carefully tended public parks slid by their windows, silvery in the moonlight.

"Did they tell you what you're going to be teaching?" Jodenny asked.

"They're still trying to figure that out. What about you? Your day was okay?"

She studied his profile. He had always been private, reticent, unwilling to complain. But she trusted that if he was having serious problems with Captain Kuvik or anyone else at school, he'd tell her about them. Farber's words had been meant to unsettle her, nothing more.

"I found out more about Dr. Gayle," Jodenny said. "She has a great reputation."

He nodded, his attention on the road.

"I spoke to her some more. I don't think what she's asking for is unreasonable."

Myell said, "You want to help."

"Yes."

His gaze didn't waver from the windshield. "And if I asked you not to? Because I don't think it's a good idea to become involved, and because I worry about your safety?"

Jodenny reached over and touched his arm. "Is your worry worth sacrificing nine lives?"

Myell didn't answer. Jodenny listened to the hum of the flit until they reached Mexwax, a sprawling adobe-style restaurant on a hill overlooking Kimberley's western suburbs. They were seated by a window with a good view, and their food came quickly. Jodenny's basil and ricotta enchilada was excellent. Myell only picked at soup and salad. She told him stories about herself as a young ensign in Supply School and the embarrassing gaffes she'd made. He smiled at all the right times and ordered two shots of tequila, though he barely touched the second.

Halfway through dessert she said, "Tell me what you want me to do."

Myell squeezed her hand. "You could never turn your back on someone in need. That was true when I met you, and it's true now. But I don't trust Team Space. Not about this."

She asked, "Are you seeing . . . you know. Things?"

He had told her that on the *Aral Sea* he had seen an Aboriginal shaman. During their trip through the Spheres on Warramala, he had seen a Rainbow Serpent. She didn't think about those visions too deeply or too often, because they seemed so illogical and fanciful, so entirely unlike him.

What could she say, anyway? She didn't believe in visions. She believed in *him*. As she hoped he believed in her.

Myell lifted his tequila and studied the depths of it. "A crocodile. In our kitchen."

She didn't know how to respond, so she made a joke. "I'm glad he wasn't in the bedroom."

Myell put the glass down. "I don't want you to help them, Kay."

The use of her old nickname made Jodenny's throat tighten. "I can't promise anything. Not yet."

He said, "You promised *me*. On Baiame. That we wouldn't get involved."

"Things have changed."

"I don't think they have."

They drove home in silence.

CHAPTER
SIX

Myell stayed awake long after Jodenny fell asleep. He stared at the ceiling and listened to her slow, steady breathing.

The little he'd eaten for dinner was still heavy in his stomach, or maybe that was the tequila, or maybe the lingering ache from being punched in the gut. He had managed to hide his wrists from Jodenny during dinner and while getting ready for bed. A small bump ached on the back of his head but he'd had worse, and mostly all he felt was a burning shame at being bound and blindfolded and gagged. If he hadn't freed himself, he would still be there, miserable and afraid.

He closed his eyes and saw the crocodile and dinosaur devouring each other, teeth rending flesh, blood in rivulets across the world.

Lying in the dark, his hand resting against her thigh, he tried to imagine success in forbidding Jodenny to help Gayle. *Tell me what you want me to do,* she'd said, as if it mattered. Myell's hand clenched. Of course his opinion mattered. But in the end, she had to do as her conscience dictated, or she wouldn't be the officer he'd married.

Woman he'd married, he reminded himself. Rank had no place in their bedroom.

He slept, his dreams a jumble of hissing pipes and coiling snakes and the crocodile, neck-deep in the watering hole. Jodenny was still sleeping when he left for work. He had to wear a light sweater over his khaki short-sleeved shirt to hide the marks on his wrists. At school, fifteen minutes before classes began, he went looking for Senior Chief Talic's office and found it on the third deck.

The office was small but well decorated with plaques and vids. Talic was on his way out when Myell blocked the doorway.

"Out of my way," Talic ordered.

"Fuck initiation," Myell said. "You want to threaten me, you do it by yourself, to my face, wherever you want. No more chicken-shit attacks in the dark."

"Are you crazy?" Talic asked, and tried to push past him.

Myell punched him hard across the jaw. That hadn't been part of the plan, but he took immense satisfaction watching Talic smash backward against a bookcase. A moment later Talic rebounded, his fists catching Myell in the ribs, and they crashed to the floor, cursing and struggling.

The fight didn't last long. The door swung open and Senior Chief Gooder and Sergeant Etedgy broke them up. Etedgy wrapped his arms around Myell and dragged him to a corner to calm down. Gooder pinned Talic up against the wall. Other chiefs were clustered in the doorway, and Gooder unceremoniously kicked the door shut for some privacy.

"What the hell is wrong with the two of you?" Gooder asked, red faced and breathing hard. "You want to get fired? You want Captain Kuvik to bust you down to able technicians?"

"He fucking started it." Talic spat out a bright wad of blood. "Came in here like a crazy person."

Myell had one arm pressed against his already bruised stomach. He too had blood in his mouth. "I'm finishing a conversation he started last night."

"Either of you need a doctor?" Etedgy asked, handing Myell some napkins from Talic's desk.

"They're fine," Gooder snapped. "Sergeant, you stand outside and shoo the crowds away. Get someone to cover Senior Chief's class. I'll handle these two idiots."

Etedgy left with a backward, worried glance. Gooder planted himself in the middle of the room and said, "One of you start."

"I told you." Talic was sullen. "He barged in here yelling gibberish."

Myell wiped blood from his lip. "He knows exactly what I'm talking about."

Gooder's gaze shifted to Myell's right arm. The sleeve of his sweater had ridden up, and the bruises around his wrist were livid in the overhead light. Myell pulled the sleeve down impatiently.

"I want to press charges," Talic said. "Assault. See how far a Silver Star gets him then."

"You want to press charges, too?" Gooder asked Myell.

Talic was indignant. "Against who?"

"No," Myell said. "I'm handling it."

"I can see that," Gooder said, dryly. "Come on, Phil. Let's take a walk. Myell, you stay here."

"He gets to stay in *my* office?" Talic asked, indignant, as Gooder steered him out the door. "What the hell—"

Left alone, Myell probed the inside of his mouth with his tongue, relieved not to find any loose teeth. He sat in the chair, suddenly cold, and was gazing blankly at pictures of Talic and his three towheaded children when a nurse from the clinic came knocking.

"Senior Chief Gooder asked me to check on you," she said. She was a brusque woman in her fifties or so, dark skinned, with braided hair and civilian clothes. "I'm Sally Clark, in charge of all cuts and bruises and assorted maladies that befall sailors young and old."

"I don't need medical attention," he told her.

"That might be, but I don't take orders from you." Sally put her medical bag down. "He said you fell down. Naturally clumsy, are you?"

Myell bit back a retort.

"You can make this easy or you can make this hard, but I've a job to do, Chief. You're not the first to fall down some stairs, walk into a hatch, or suffer some other silly accident. Look into this scanner, please."

He glared at her.

Sally didn't back away. "Sooner you do it, sooner I leave. Otherwise you and I will be here all morning."

Reluctantly he gazed into the handheld device. Sally made a tsking noise in the back of her throat. She took his pulse and blood pressure. Without asking permission, she rolled up his sleeves to see the rope marks.

"You do these to yourself?" she asked.

Myell rolled his sleeves back down. "None of your business."

"Hurts when you breathe or piss?"

"I think we're done now," Myell said.

She handed him a small tube. "That's antibiotic cream, with a bit of analgesic and skin sealant mixed in. Rub it on twice a day for any lacerations or cuts. For headaches, take whatever you normally do. Anything gets worse, come by and see us on the first deck."

She left without further instructions. Myell was left to sit alone until Senior Chief Gooder returned, this time carrying two cups of coffee.

"Captain's rightly pissed," Gooder said, handing one cup over.

The coffee smelled heavenly. Myell said, "He didn't want me here anyway. Where am I being transferred to?"

"Oh, you don't escape that easily. You're his for three years, he says. He'd be willing to string you up on the yardarm in the courtyard, except for Kenny Deeds."

"I don't understand."

"Custodian. Came to work this morning, found rope tied to some pipes in the basement. Right near your office, in fact. And the scanners say you didn't leave last night until well after working hours. Looks like someone's been pulling shenanigans."

Myell gulped the coffee. It burned his tongue, but he was glad for the distraction. "I have nothing to say about it."

"Nothing except you came in here fists flying, blaming Phil Talic for something. I'll admit, the man's stubborn. Not very personable. A stick-in-the-mud. But if you're looking to blame someone for a prank or two, I don't think he's your man."

"I wouldn't call it a prank."

"Would you call it an assault?"

Myell remained silent.

"He's denying everything, of course. Has a good excuse, too. Left here at fifteen hundred hours yesterday, went to the dental clinic. All right and proper."

Myell hadn't accused Talic of being there. He hadn't recognized the main attacker's voice, and wasn't sure if two or three other men had been with him. But Talic could have easily orchestrated it from afar.

Gooder sighed. "For the good of the command, he's not going to be pressing any charges. The two of you don't have to love each other, but any more of what you did this morning, you'll be sitting in the brig. You have a problem, you bring it to me. No one in this command goes it alone. Understand?"

"Yes." Now that the adrenaline of the fight had faded, he was beginning to feel sheepish about losing his temper. He really did know better than that, though he obviously hadn't proven it to anyone here.

"Come on, then," Gooder said. "I told the captain that to keep a proper eye on you, I need you up out of the dungeon."

Myell's new office was just down the passageway from Talic's. From his chair he had a view of the courtyard, where young sailors were marching in formation to and from classes. Within the hour a clerk from Etedgy's office was signing over a hand gib for him and telling him how to set up an agent. Another clerk hauled up the boxes of regulations that Myell still needed to catalog. He may have been promoted out of the basement, but he had no doubts he was still on Captain Kuvik's shitlist.

Or maybe not. Right before lunchtime, Sergeant Etedgy came by with another assignment.

"Captain said to put you in with the 510s," Etedgy said. "It's a study hall for those needing extra help. Usually we just set them up with Core tutorials and let them go at their own pace."

Babysitting. Myell could do that. But he couldn't quite face the ordeal of lunch in the mess. He made do with food from the vending machines. His esophagus was still smarting from a helping of spicy chili when he went in search of Classroom 510. It had nice views of Water Street, a dozen study cubicles, and a teacher's desk filled with old newspapers and fishing magazines.

He thought the room was empty, but some whispering led him to a pair of corner cubicles. Putty Romero was hunched over the gib of a young, fair-haired AT.

"But once you run your query, you don't need the additional parameters—" he was saying.

AT Tingley bit at her thumbnail. She was young, maybe eighteen, with a wide-eyed innocence that didn't seem to take umbrage at Romero's arm inching around her shoulder.

"AT Romero," Myell said, startling them both.

"Chief!" Romero said. His arm went back to where it belonged. "Didn't hear you."

"Afternoon, Chief," Tingley said, in a very soft voice.

"Speak up, Tingley," Myell told her. "I don't bite."

"My vocal cords just aren't very big," Tingley said, ducking her head.

Romero asked, "Is it true, Chief? You went and punched Senior Chief Talic?"

Myell didn't touch the bruise that he could feel by his eye. "Never you mind. What are you studying back here?"

"Data flow," she said.

"Louder, Tingley. They'll never hear you in the fleet."

"Data flow, Chief!" Tingley said, belting the words out. But then her face screwed up. "It's a makeup exam. If I don't pass it, I can't graduate."

"I told you," Romero said, "you're going to pass. We're both going to the *Kamchatka*. Who cares if Senior Chief Talic calls it a rust bucket?"

The bravado in Romero's voice was a far cry from the uncertainty he'd shown Myell the other day, but love could do that to a person. As for the *Kamchatka*, it was true that it wasn't very exciting duty, but someone had to do it.

"Tell you what," Myell said. "Let's concentrate on data flow, and worry about graduation later. If you want to go to the stars, AT Tingley, don't let anyone tell you you can't. Is that clear?"

She grinned. "Yes, Chief."

Romero nudged her. "Told you he's not like the other chiefs."

"So they say," Myell said.

J odenny slept in later than she expected. Myell had left her a note on the kitchen counter. "Love you," he'd written. She went for a nice five-kilometer run through housing with the paper folded inside her bra. At the top of Admiral's Hill, she jogged in place with the whole of Kimberley spread out before her. Her city, her home planet. She knew nothing of the missing scientists, where they'd come from, not even their names, but she could have grown up with one of them in the North Prosper orphanage, or passed them in the street, or known their siblings or met their children.

Love you, Myell had said. Nothing else.

And what if that crocodile he'd seen in their kitchen was a sign she couldn't ignore? That she should do what she could, do her duty, do her best.

Back at home, she called Anna Gayle on a secure channel.

"I'll help you at Bainbridge," she said. "Just to call the token. Nothing more."

"Excellent!" Gayle said. "Let's get you in for a medical screen and briefing. Civilian clothes, please. The less attention, the better. Will your husband be joining us?"

"No."

She spent several hours in Gayle's lab, donating tissue and blood samples, signing additional security clearances. Admiral Mizoguchi's office was contacted and asked to excuse her from work the following day. Permission was granted. Jodenny had no idea what kind of budget Gayle had to work with, but Team Space didn't seem to be skimping on workspace, manpower, or other resources.

Toledo and Farber were in charge of securing the Bainbridge Spheres from visitors. The monuments sat on a national park, not Team Space property.

"Just can't block them off without warning," Toledo said, rolling his large shoulders under his too-tight shirt. He dwarfed the chair he was sitting in. "Tourists get mad. And then they complain, and the gadfly press gets wind of it, and we don't need that kind of publicity."

"How will you do it, then?" Jodenny asked.

Farber didn't look up from her gib. "We're pretending to be filming a vid for a new virtual-reality game. Hush-hush, trade secrets, closed set."

"Do you know any of the missing team?" Jodenny asked.

"Good men and women." Toledo was snacking from a bowl of jellybeans on the conference table, assiduously picking out the purple ones with his large fingers. "Commander Gold, especially. He's in charge."

"I thought Dr. Monnox was in charge? Dr. Gayle's husband?"

Farber glanced up from her gib. Toledo picked up a red jellybean and juggled it from one hand to the other. He said, "Commander Gold was the mission commander. Dr. Monnox was the lead scientist."

Jodenny was done at Gayle's office in time to swing by Supply School. She hoped to catch Myell by surprise. Maybe they'd go to dinner again, or catch one of the live theater shows over in the Piccadilly District. She waited outside the main gate as a traditional ship's bell rang at sixteen hundred hours. Students and faculty streamed past. She saw Myell before he saw her, and admired how handsome he looked in his summer uniform. He was walking with two young able techs, teenagers really.

"Honey," he said when he saw her.

"I thought I'd surprise you—" Jodenny took a closer look at his left eye. The flesh around it was bruised. "What happened?"

"This is AT Tingley and AT Romero," Myell said, hurriedly introducing his companions. "This is Lieutenant Commander Scott, my wife."

"Ma'am!" Romero popped off a salute even though Jodenny wasn't in uniform. Tingley followed. Her lips moved, but her voice was too soft for Jodenny to hear over the crowd.

"At ease." Jodenny remained focused on the bruises. "Your eye?"

"My own fault," Myell said. "I was going to call you, see if you wanted to eat dinner out. Romero and Tingley are graduating, and they've never had Cuban *camarónes*."

"We don't want to be an imposition," Romero said.

Tingley bit her thumbnail and ducked her head.

Myell had a smile pasted on his face. "You can't go to the fleet without a hefty dose of garlic. It's good luck."

Oh, what a clever husband she had. Jodenny knew a diversion when she saw one, but she did love *camarónes*. The cantina off Water Street was a rowdy, crowded place filled with faux-wooden tables, colorful artwork, and robot parrots that flitted from one perch to the next. Music blared from a live band in the corner. Jodenny could barely hear anything Tingley said, but she could tell from shy smiles that the two able technicians were more than just classmates.

Myell was more effusive than usual, cheerfully relating tales from the fleet about what real supply sailors did. She had heard some of the stories, but not all. His experiences working in Supply Departments were vastly different from her own. She couldn't say that enlisted soldiers had more fun, but their shipboard culture was perhaps more colorful, their adventures on leave a little more grand than anything she'd ever encountered. Neither Tingley nor Romero had ever been off world, and both had plenty of questions about life down the Big Alcheringa.

"Well, Baiame's still backward," Myell said. "Warramala's all for fun and personal freedom. Mary River's duller than dirt, and Sundowner's full of all the smart ones. Universities on every block."

"Is that true, Commander?" Romero asked.

Jodenny signaled the waiter for another beer. "I didn't notice."

She wanted to haul Myell into a quiet corner and harangue him until he fessed up about the bruises, but had to wait through dinner and beers and more beers. When her patience ran out she sent Tingley and Romero back to their barracks in a cab. A second cab took Jodenny and Myell through the night streets of Kimberley and out toward Adeline Oaks.

"Tell me," she said, as he let his head fall back against the passenger seat. He looked more tired than she'd seen him in a long, long time.

He said, "Fight. My fault. Misunderstanding, maybe. Maybe not. But I swung first."

The thought of him brawling in the middle of Supply School made her wince. "What kind of misunderstanding?"

He gave her a crooked smile. "Do I have to tell? Or will you trust me to work it out on my own?"

Jodenny pursed her lips. "When we got married, we promised to work things out together."

"I know." Myell closed his eyes. "But I can do it alone."

She touched his arm. He winced a little, and she tugged up the sleeve of his sweater. Now she understood why he had kept it on all evening, even though the cantina had been hot. The bruising was ugly in the passing lights of other flits.

"That's not a misunderstanding!" she said.

He tugged his arm away. "It was a prank."

"A prank?" Jodenny heard the shrillness in her voice and tried to scale it back. "What prank? How could it be your fault?"

He glared at her. "Trust me or don't. Which is it?"

Jodenny folded her arms and turned from him. Her heart was thumping painfully fast. She had seen him bullied on the *Aral Sea*, had nearly lost him in the freezing darkness of a locked-down storage tower, and had watched him slide toward death on their trip through the Spheres. He was a damned fool if he thought this was about *trust*.

"I'm sorry," he said a moment later.

Jodenny shook her head.

They arrived home in silence. Jodenny used a yuro card to pay off the cab's automated driver. The house lit up as they stepped inside. Betsy had a few incoming messages for them, including more media queries for interviews. Karl wanted to be held.

"Scratch my ears," he demanded, and Jodenny obeyed.

"I have to take a shower." Myell disappeared into the bathroom.

When he came out twenty minutes later she said, "I told Dr. Gayle I'd help her tomorrow. We're going to the Spheres out at Bainbridge."

He rubbed a towel against his damp hair. A bathrobe concealed whatever other marks or injuries he hadn't told her about.

"I don't want you to," he said. "I'm asking you not to."

Jodenny folded her arms across her chest. "I trust her. And if you *trust* me, you'll leave it at that."

Myell gazed past her to the darkened living room and the vids glowing softly on the mantelpiece. Family and friends. Some lost, but never forgotten.

"It's not about trust," he said.

"Then what is it about?" Jodenny stepped toward him, part of her secretly pleased that he edged backward. If he needed her to challenge him, then she would do it. She hadn't expected that of marriage, but they'd barely known each other on the *Aral Sea*. Maybe they'd rushed into things before they were ready.

Relentlessly Jodenny asked, "Why won't you tell me what's going on at school? When did I become someone you couldn't tell the truth to?"

Myell's expression was a mix of bleakness and stubbornness. "When did I sign up to be interrogated and second-guessed? Do I ask you if you're helping because of Sam Osherman? Do I wonder if you want to go out there despite your promise because you want to find him, not some missing scientists?"

She wasn't going to be able to reason with him, not now, maybe not ever.

Karl ambled between them and made a soft querying sound.

"Do what you want," Myell said, and went into the guest bedroom. The click of the door behind him was as definitive and final an end to the discussion as Jodenny had ever heard.

CHAPTER
SEVEN

I t took Myell ten flights of stairs to realize what an idiot he was. The school gym had been crowded when he first arrived, but he'd snagged a training machine in the corner of the cardio room. News, movies, and other entertainment played out on the overvids. Beyond the plastiglass windows, sweat-sheened students were racing around a basketball court. Myell kept focused on his personal display, which relayed his progress up the stairwell of a hypothetical sky-scraper. He was sweating heavily and feeling the burn of protesting bruises, but the exertion kept him from brooding over Jodenny and whatever she was off doing.

The display pulsed a warning that he was exceeding his recom-mended cardio target. Myell slowed a little, aware of his heavy breathing and the sweat soaking through his T-shirt. The young woman beside him was going much faster than he was, though the age difference between them wasn't more than ten or so years. He told himself that planetside life was making him soft, and started pumping the pedals harder. He wasn't going to let a stupid machine limit his exertions.

But he was, it seemed, going to let his beloved wife go play around with the Wondjina Transportation System without him. His eyes went unwillingly to the clock. She might have already gone out to Bainbridge. Already there might be a gleaming ouroboros whisking more people out into the galaxy, playing around with a technology that none of them understood or could control.

His right calf began to cramp. He slowed down again. He leaned his arms against the machine's supports and sucked in air. Jodenny thought that what she was doing was helpful, and perhaps it was, for the missing members of the ill-fated mission. But Sphere travel was a perilous endeavor full of dangers that included the all-powerful Rainbow Serpent. He was sure of that, sure down to his bones, sure as the sweat soaking his clothes and socks.

Yet the Wondjina, whoever they were, had left their system behind to be discovered. Monuments of stone, empty and forlorn.

But not useless. Not dead. And Team Space was going to use them whether Myell objected or not.

In the men's locker room, he thumbed open his locker and groped for his gib. Jodenny answered on the third ring, tight lipped and stern.

"I can't really talk," she said.

"I'm sorry," Myell said. "For a lot of things. I want to help."

Jodenny gazed at him through the small screen. "Why the change of heart?"

"Does it matter?"

"Yes."

"I don't support what you're trying to do. But I support you. If this is what you really want, then I want it, too."

She dipped her chin a little. "You're sure?"

"More than sure."

Jodenny had to go offscreen for a moment, but when she came back she told him a flit would be by to pick him up in twenty minutes. Myell put the gib back in his locker, stripped off his sweaty clothes, and headed for the showers with only a towel and the dilly bag in hand. Superstitious, he told himself, but he didn't like to leave it out of his sight.

Five minutes under the hot water was enough to sluice him clean and ease the lingering cramp in his leg. When he returned to his locker the door was broken and hanging open. His gym bag, lunch, workout clothes, and uniform were all gone, and his gib was a useless smashed pile of electronics.

He stood there gaping, his face growing hotter by the moment, only peripherally aware of other men moving to and from their own lockers or the showers.

With only the towel around his waist, Myell went out of the locker room and along the basketball sidelines to the registration desk. The civilian employee at the desk gawked at him.

"You can't come out here dressed like that—" she started.

"Someone took my uniform," he said, struggling against fury. "I need someone to hunt down some clothes for me."

Her frown was a deep crevice. "I have to stay at the counter and Tommy's gone to lunch—"

Myell steadfastly ignored the attention he was drawing from athletes all over the gym. He'd stand there in his towel and drip water all day long, just to spite them. But the flit was due soon, and he wasn't going to call Jodenny to tell her that his things had been stolen.

"Are you sure you checked the right locker?" the clerk asked. A young civilian man emerged from the back office, a stack of neatly folded towels in his arms. She said, "Benny, would you go with this gentleman and see if you can find his things?"

"It's not there," Myell insisted. "I need to use your gib."

He tried pinging Senior Chief Gooder, but Gooder's agent said he was off base and unavailable. He tried Sergeant Etedgy next, but Etedgy was conducting a lunchtime training session.

"Sir, you really can't stand here half naked," the clerk insisted. "Do you want me to call Security and they can help you find your bag?"

She was entirely unsympathetic. Myell wanted to snap his towel at her face. Benny had gone to the locker room and returned with the remains of Myell's gib, a perplexed look on his face.

"This yours, sir?"

"I'm not a sir, and yes it's mine," Myell said, exasperated. "I dropped it."

"Hell of a drop," Benny said. "It was in the trash."

He didn't have time for any of this. He certainly didn't have time to file a report with Security. Myell considered leaving in just the towel, but then AT Romero came to sign in at the desk and asked, "Chief? Everything okay?"

"No, it's not okay." Myell dragged Romero to the side. "I need you to get me some clothes."

Romero offered his gym bag. "I've got some shorts—"

"Not quite my size," Myell said. He dispatched Romero off to the school store, and because he didn't even have his wallet, had to ask Romero to pay. Myell returned to the locker room and paced back and forth and tried not to count every passing second. Romero must have run all the way back, because he was red faced and sweating when he returned with a shopping bag.

"Don't have a heart attack," Myell told him.

"Senior Chief Talic caught me running, said I couldn't do that, had me do a hundred push-ups," Romero reported. "I'm not sure I got the right sizes or that the sneakers are going to fit—"

The school store was not known for fashion. Myell tugged on a jersey embroidered with the Supply emblem and a pair of black shorts. The sneakers were a little too tight, but he could live with them.

"You're a life-saver," Myell told Romero.

"Don't you want to tell Security what happened, Chief?"

"Not now," Myell said. "I need you to deliver a message to Senior Chief Gooder for me, can you do that? Tell him I had an urgent appointment outside of the building, and I'll talk to him first thing in the morning. It's very important."

A black flit was already waiting in the parking lot by the time Myell got there. He felt naked without his Team Space identification, but the young driver said, "Afternoon, Chief," and opened the back door for him.

The drive up to Bainbridge went more slowly than Myell had expected, thanks to midafternoon traffic in Kimberley and a road accident at one of the regional interchanges. The sedan's air-conditioning left goosebumps on the back of Myell's neck. The rolling landscape grew more mountainous, forest giving way to slopes and meadows. The driver stayed silent all the way up, but tuned the radio so that the afternoon news droned steadily in the background. As they drew near the Spheres he saw signs announcing their temporary closure.

"Security measures?" Myell asked the driver.

"They don't tell me much, Chief," the driver replied.

"What do you think's going on up here?"

The driver's voice was dry. "They're vidding a game. Izim Extreme, I hear."

They passed trailers and vans, and security guards dressed in casual clothes, and bits of vid equipment propped up in different areas. The three Spheres were just a hundred meters down the road, in a clearing surrounded by redwoods. Father, Mother, and Child. The stone triad that repeated itself through the Seven Spheres. The Father loomed largest, almost as tall as the redwoods around them. The Mother was exactly half its size, and the Child half again. Each Sphere had a single archway, darkness spilling out from inside.

Leorah Farber met the flit in a parking lot. She was wearing shorts and a T-shirt, with a ball cap tucked over her hair. She gave Myell's gym clothes a speculative look.

"Don't ask," he said. "Where's Commander Scott?"

"Just up here," she said, walking him toward the Spheres. Activity had picked up a little, with several of the fake vid crew retreating to the vans and other personnel, military by the look of them, securing the perimeter. "We haven't started yet. It should be fairly straightforward. Either the Sphere responds to you or it doesn't."

He said, "To my wife. I'm only here to observe."

Farber touched the headset under her ball cap. "On our way," she said to someone, and a moment later they met up with Jodenny and Teddy Toledo on a dirt path through the redwoods.

"Any problem getting away from school?" Jodenny asked, eyeing Myell's clothes.

"It's all fine," he assured her. She wasn't in uniform, either, but instead wore trousers and a shirt that made her look like any other member of the pretend vid crew.

Toledo, his green shirt already stained at the underarms, clapped his hands. "I've got a good feeling about this."

Myell's palms felt damp, and he instinctively reached for Jodenny's hand. She squeezed it briefly, gave him a smile, then let go as Anna Gayle met them.

"Chief Myell," Gayle said, offering him a brisk handshake. She was all business, he decided, very confident, not a single red hair daring to stray from the tight braid on her head. Slim, beautiful, hard: That was her husband out there somewhere, and she was determined to find him. Gayle said, "So very glad you decided to join us."

"I'm not joining you," he said. "I'm supporting Commander Scott."

Gayle's smile was bright and tight. "Same difference. We're almost ready, Commander. As you've been briefed, events will be direct and straightforward. I'll try activating a token, as will two others who've traveled in the network before. Each time we'll give the system ten minutes to respond. Then it will be your turn."

"I'll do my best," Jodenny said, though they all knew she had no control over it at all.

"We've got monitoring equipment set up inside, recording everything. The data's being fed up to that van," Gayle said. "You can watch from there if you'd like, Chief."

Myell squinted at the green van barely visible in the trees. "I'll stay here."

Gayle walked down toward the Mother Sphere. Myell sat with Jodenny in the grass by the side of the path. Farber and Toledo remained standing. The air was filled with birdsong and soughing wind, and a steady crunching sound from Toledo as he chewed on peanuts.

Ten minutes after entering the Mother Sphere, Gayle emerged with a flat expression.

"Nothing," she said.

Two other people whom Myell hadn't met came down the path and took their turns. The Sphere didn't respond to either of them.

"My turn." Jodenny stood up and brushed grass from her trousers. "No worries."

Myell rose with her and kissed her soundly. "Be careful."

"Always," she said.

"Good luck, Commander," Gayle said, her arms tightly folded over her chest.

Jodenny nodded at all of them, and went down to the Mother Sphere. She paused at the archway to throw Myell a questioning look. He forced a smile.

She walked inside, and was lost to his sight.

Jodenny didn't know why she was so nervous. Even if the token came, she wasn't going anywhere. The mission to save Dr. Monnox and Commander Gold would fall to others. But she couldn't shake off the memory of her last trip—the hard yellow light pushing them onward, ever onward, through dusty Spheres flung across the universe. The sickness ripping through her gut and head. The way Myell had looked when they finally returned to Warramala, his face slack and limbs cold.

Stepping into the Sphere was like plunging from day to night, despite the half-dozen large floodlights that had been erected in the interior. Darkness persisted high in the ceiling and at the base of the round walls. The place smelled cool and dry and musty. Nothing like the deep lushness outside, the redwoods that stretched like giants to the sky. This was a different giant, molded by the Wondjina, long before the trees outside had been saplings, or seeds, or even the idea of seeds.

"Radio check, Commander," said a voice on her headset, and she nodded for the benefit of the cameras.

"Loud and clear," she said.

She resisted the urge to rub the goosebumps on her skin. Instead she walked back and forth across the width of the Sphere, watching her boots make faint marks in the hard-packed dirt. She felt silly, walking around under remote scrutiny and waiting for a piece of alien technology to put in an appearance. What was Myell thinking, up on the path? She was glad he had come. Maybe when evening came they could find a nice, intimate restaurant, a place far from the crowds where they could talk and bask in just being with each other.

She knew after a few minutes that the token wasn't going to come for her. A relief, actually. If it wouldn't come for her, surely she wasn't in any way responsible for the system shutting down in the first place. Nor would she bear the responsibility of enabling more people to go off down the network on a second mission that might end in tragedy. But it was disappointing, as well, to find out that she wasn't special in any way. The token that wouldn't come for others wouldn't come for her, either.

Her radio clicked. Gayle's clipped voice said, "Thank you, Commander. You can come out now."

The sunlight was exceptionally bright outside, and Jodenny had to blink several times against the harshness. Myell and Gayle had come to meet her at the archway. Gayle nodded appreciation for Jodenny's attempt but her gaze was averted.

"I'm not discouraged," Gayle insisted. "I never expected immediate success. We can try the Spheres at Swedenville next. Still, while we're all here, I'm wondering if Chief Myell wouldn't agree to test his presence as well."

Myell kept silent.

Gayle said, "I understand that to you, this network is more than just ancient technology. More than machinery. There are severe political, economic, and religious implications if Team Space finds a way to make it a practical mode of transportation, and the repercussions cannot be underestimated. I wish I could see into the future and reassure you that the network will be put to only the most beneficial of purposes, and that all mankind will benefit. But we both know it's not in my power to do so."

Myell was still silent. Jodenny couldn't tell what he was thinking.

"But it is in your power to step into that Mother Sphere, Chief, and I'm asking you to do so. You know that my husband is out there somewhere. I believe he's alive. I believe he needs my help. To that end, I'll do everything I can to try and get this system working again. I'll beg you, if that's what you want. I'll get down on my knees right here. Because that's how badly I want to have him in my arms again."

"Dr. Gayle . . ." Myell sounded appalled. "Please don't."

Gayle's eyes started to glitter. "I believe you came here today not just because you wanted to support Commander Scott. I believe deep down that you want me to persuade you, that you truly want to help. It's a dozen steps from here into that Sphere. All you have to do is take them. Twelve steps, and you could enable my husband to come home again."

Jodenny watched indecision play out on Myell's face. Perhaps he had come out here just to be persuaded. It stung a little that Gayle could succeed where Jodenny had not, but then again, the stakes were much higher for Gayle.

Myell stared at the archway of the Mother Sphere.

"It won't work for me," he said, but not very strongly.

"Please try," Gayle said. "Please just try."

He looked hopelessly at Jodenny, but she couldn't help him. The decision had always been his to make. But she doubted that his convictions were strong enough to withstand the force of Gayle's grief and hope.

Myell said, "Only this once."

Gayle was instantly on her radio. "Chief Myell's going in. Make sure you're monitoring."

Jodenny squeezed his hand. "Thanks."

He kissed her hard, then disappeared into the Sphere.

"Thank you," Gayle said to Jodenny.

Surprised, Jodenny said, "I didn't do anything."

"You could have stopped him."

"You don't know him very well."

Silence from the Mother Sphere. Across the grass, a baby squirrel popped out of a fallen log, peered at them, then darted away again. Gayle's right hand, fisted at her side, looked so painfully clenched that she'd probably have fingernail marks in her palm for hours. The defeat of hope was such a difficult thing.

Then the loud, clear call of an approaching ouroboros blasted through the air, and that changed everything.

The horn cut through Myell as surely as a dagger.

He told himself he hadn't expected the system to respond to him. He'd said as much to Gayle and Jodenny. He was not special; he had in no way been singled out or chosen.

A lie, he knew. The worst kind. The kind told to oneself.

But Gayle had been right. He had come here knowing that they would ask, and perhaps wanting to be persuaded to try.

The scuffle of boots made him turn. Gayle and Jodenny came through the arch. Gayle shook his hand with a forceful grip and a wide smile.

"You did it, Chief," she said. "I'll always be in your debt."

Jodenny kissed his cheek. "Thank you."

A half-dozen Marines in gray camouflage uniforms entered the Mother Sphere, each loaded up with equipment, backpacks, and mazers. Leading them was a tall, muscular commander of Aboriginal descent. His hair was cut close to his skull, and his orders to the other soldiers were crisp and confident.

"Saadi, make sure your GNATs are ready to go. Collins, we might need that Blue-Q at the first station. Breme, Lavasseur, that anti-grav sled's got to get in position fast. Remember the window."

"You're leaving right now?" Jodenny asked, surprised.

"We can't take the chance it'll shut down again," Gayle said. One of the soldiers brought a backpack to her. She shrugged into it with practiced ease. "The mission leaves with that token."

Myell said, "But you don't know that the network will continue to work."

An ouroboros flashed into existence on the ground. The circle was larger than Myell remembered, the cool metal fashioned into a snake devouring its own tail. He could see the interior glowing faintly with symbols. The female soldier and one of the men steered a sled into its confines and took up position.

"It could stop," Myell said. "You might get one or two stations and the whole thing will shut down again."

Gayle spared him the briefest of glances. "That's why you're coming with us."

"No, you can't—" Jodenny started to say, but two of the Marines moved to Myell's side.

"Chief Myell, I'm Commander Nam," the Aboriginal commander said. "Effective immediately, you've been reassigned from Supply School to the Research and Development branch. You are ordered to accompany and assist this mission. You can go willingly, or you can go carried over our shoulders, but you are coming."

Leorah Farber and Teddy Toledo had joined them inside the Sphere—Toledo wide-eyed and gaping, Farber vocal in her disapproval.

"Dr. Gayle," she said, "this wasn't in the plan!"

"It was in my plan," Gayle said tightly.

"Mine, too," Nam said.

"No," Myell said. He wouldn't, he couldn't. "I'm not going."

"Let me be clear." Nam nodded to the soldiers, who grabbed Myell by the arms. "You don't have a choice."

Everyone was talking at once now—Farber and Toledo arguing, Jodenny protesting, Nam giving orders. The Marines tugged Myell toward the ouroboros. He thought about swinging his fists but he didn't want to risk Jodenny getting hurt. He cursed his own stupidity. Of course they had tricked and used him. Of course they had lied.

Jodenny watched helplessly as they took her husband away. She tried to join them, to leap forward, but Nam's other men restrained her.

Gayle and Nam joined the group in the ouroboros. Gayle said to Jodenny, "If all goes well, we'll be back soon. If not—well, if not, then perhaps we'll have been more successful than I hope."

Myell wasn't saying anything, but Jodenny could see in his face a thousand unsaid things—horror at how the situation had gotten out of hand, desperation at being dragged into the network against his will. Resignation, too. As if this had always been meant to happen. She remembered how they'd nearly died in the network, and realized she might never ever see him again.

"Can't you stop her?" Jodenny said to Farber.

Farber's gaze was locked on Gayle. "This is wrong, Anna. You're not going to find what you're looking for."

Gayle's face lit up in an unexpected smile. "I'll let you know."

Jodenny said, recklessly, "I'll follow you—"

Myell found his voice. "Don't. I'll come back. I'll come home. Remember that—"

A flash of hard yellow light took him, Gayle, Nam, and four Marines away before he could complete the sentence.

Jodenny sank to her knees on the ground, unable to stand on her own.

CHAPTER
EIGHT

Stale air. Flashes of artificial light, painful against his eyes. But not as painful as the dry heaves tearing from his stomach up his throat. In retrospect, he was glad he hadn't eaten lunch.

Urgent voices swirled over his head.

"GNATs deployed, Commander. Outside atmosphere cold but clear—"

"No sign of Commander Gold's team, no radio signals—"

"Time elapsed: forty seconds. Forty-five . . ."

"We have to stop here," a man said. "He needs to stabilize."

Gayle, sounding irritated, asked, "Why is he sick so soon, Ensign Collins?"

Collins answered, "This wasn't unexpected, after his reaction on Warramala. Commander Nam?"

Myell curled into himself further, aware of dirt and dust, and someone's hand on his shoulder. Bile burned at the back of his throat.

"You're sure he can't make the next one?" Gayle asked.

"Not without the risk of cardiac arrest, ma'am."

Nam said, "Haul out, then. We're stopping."

Gayle cursed. Strong hands reached under Myell's shoulders and more hands gripped his ankles. When they tried to lift him, he fought against the movement.

"It's okay, Chief," Collins said.

"He's fighting," said the woman at Myell's ankles.

Nam asked, "Can you sedate him?"

Myell gave up struggling. He was lifted and carried out of the ouroboros. They put him on the ground. Collins pressed some cold gel on the inside of Myell's right wrist, and some of the nausea began to pass.

Other voices in the dark were talking about GNATs, weather reports, recon information. Myell caught only part of the conversation. Eventually Collins and the woman carried Myell out of the Mother Sphere. The new planet's sky was black and clear, without any of Kimberley's city glow. A stream gurgled nearby and stars glittered above the branches of pine trees. The air smelled faintly salty.

"Make camp here," Nam ordered. "I want him ready to travel by morning."

Myell was eased onto a blanket. Several battery lanterns powered up, the blue-white light a comfort.

"Tents up, sir?" someone asked.

"Is the weather going to hold, Chief Saadi?" Nam asked.

"Too soon to tell, sir."

Nam said, "No tents. Not yet."

Collins, a dark-haired man with freckles across his nose, urged Myell to drink from a water bottle. Camouflage insignia on his collar indicated that he was an ensign, though he was clearly older than

Myell. Former enlisted, perhaps. Or maybe a late addition to the Medical Corps.

"You a doctor?" Myell croaked out.

"Medic," Collins said easily. "Feeling better? Your temperature's coming back up. I've given you a dose of Blue-Q."

Gayle, standing nearby, said, "So he's better. We can keep going?"

"Not until morning," Nam insisted.

Myell huddled in the bedroll as Nam set up a watch schedule. Sergeant Breme, the only female soldier, got the first watch. Sergeant Lavasseur, a lanky blond with a scar on his chin, would stand second watch. Chief Saadi, with his shaved head and intense stare, would round up with the third. Saadi controlled the remote-controlled GNATs and comm equipment, which he compulsively checked on the two gibs he carried with him.

"Fly, babies, fly," he was saying.

"Lavasseur, you're in charge of dinner," Nam ordered.

"Now, Commander?" Lavasseur asked. He had a strange accent. American, maybe. Must have come from Earth. "It's only fifteen hundred hours."

Breme jerked her head toward the dark sky. "Not here, it's not. Don't want jet lag, do we?"

Saadi consulted his gibs. "I've got multiple readings coming in. We've got a fix on several stars in the Rosette Nebula. The GNATs are still calculating the differentials—okay, here we go. This planet's a little bit smaller than Fortune, a little faster rotation, weather should hold, we should see sunup in about—oh, roughly, seven and a half hours. So it is *well* within time for dinner."

Lavasseur said, "Trip is going to mess up my circadian rhythm."

"Is that a complaint?" Nam asked.

"No, sir," Lavasseur said easily. "Just an observation."

Myell pulled the blanket tighter. He wished Jodenny were there. The look on her face as the soldiers had dragged him to the ouroboros was everything he had never wanted to see on her—anguish, helplessness, fury. She hadn't known Gayle's plan. Of course she hadn't known. He was the one who'd fallen for lies and tears. But if he hadn't volunteered to walk into the Mother Sphere, Nam or the others might have dragged him in anyway. The idea of choice had always been an illusion.

He slept, somehow, though his chest ached from missing Jodenny. When he opened his eyes again, a small fire was burning in a circle of rocks not too far away. Lavasseur had the watch. Gayle was sitting against a log and typing in her gib, her face bathed with its blue glow.

"Better or worse?" Collins asked, from somewhere behind Myell.

Myell rolled over. "Better," he admitted. "Thirsty."

Collins gave him a water bottle and rubbed more of the cool gel against his wrist.

"What did you call that stuff?" Myell asked.

"Blue-Q. Helps a lot. We've been receiving treatment for a few days now, but you haven't—"

"Ensign," Gayle said, a warning in her voice.

Myell pulled the blanket closer. The temperature had dropped while he was sleeping. "You knew the network would work for me."

"I had hopes," Gayle replied, without looking up. "It was hard enough to get you to consider cooperation in the first place. If I told you I wanted you to come along, you'd have run off screaming."

Myell said, "So you decided to drag me along anyway."

"In the service of Team Space."

"Team Space doesn't need this service."

Lavasseur, warming his hands by the fire, watched the two of them.

"We disagree." Gayle shut down her gib. "I don't expect you to be happy about it, but there's no turning back. The token carries us always forward, never backward. Your cooperation will ensure that we return as quickly as possible."

"My cooperation," he repeated.

"Passive cooperation," Gayle added. "Nothing is expected of you, Chief, other than you don't impede our progress. Think of it as a vacation."

Myell resisted the urge to vomit.

Collins said, "I suggest you get some sleep, Chief."

"I have to use the latrine," Myell said.

Commander Nam sat up in his bedroll. "I'll take him."

The last thing Myell wanted was help to the latrine from a commander. But he let Nam walk him down a narrow path toward the trees. Nam's flashlight led the way. Crickets and the occasional scuffling sounds of night animals reminded Myell of home, and home made him think of Jodenny. He finished as quickly as possible.

"Let's take a little detour," Nam suggested.

Nam steered him down a small hill to where the grass gave way to sand and the stream joined the sea. The roiling black mass of water was the source of the salty smell that Myell had been denying for hours. He shrank back, because if there was anything worse than the ocean it was the ocean *at night,* infinite dark roiling terrifying *ocean at night.*

Nam scowled at him. "What's wrong?"

"Nothing," Myell forced out, the word half strangled.

Nam thumbed his radio as if to call Ensign Collins but then stopped. He took Myell back up to a copse of evergreens. The view of the ocean was blocked, and they could see Lavasseur's distant figure sitting by the fire. Myell sank to the grass with his head between his knees.

"That wasn't in your file," Nam said. "Thalassaphobia."

Several moments passed before Myell could say, "Doesn't come up much when you're sailing the Alcheringa. Most people don't know there's a word for it."

Nam's gaze was locked on the dark woods. "My mother had it. Couldn't go near the ocean without throwing up."

Myell sucked in another deep breath. His head no longer felt full of salt and rotting fish smells.

"Dr. Gayle doesn't think you're going to cooperate." Nam's dark face was impassive. "I told her that of course you will. Whether you want to be here or not is irrelevant. This is a duty assignment like any other."

"I was brought on this mission against my will, at gunpoint," Myell said. "I wasn't given the chance to disobey. I would have taken the brig over this."

Nam made a snorting noise. "If you say so. Like it or not, you're part of a security project that will have ramifications for centuries to come. You feel some ownership and possessiveness, maybe a sense of entitlement. All because you tripped through the Warramala Spheres and had a hallucination about a talking snake."

Myell kept his gaze stubbornly on his knees.

"Let me tell you this, Chief. I don't know why the network stopped working. I don't know why it loves you enough to start sending tokens again. We've got nine people out here to rescue, nine people who are a hell of a lot braver than you or me. So you follow the orders you're given, you make sure those tokens keep coming, and we save that missing team. When we get home you go back to playing Izim and moaning about how unfair life is. Understand? Otherwise I'll have you sedated, and we'll carry your body through the stations until we get back to Fortune."

"Yes, sir," Myell said, his fists clenched. "I understand completely."

Sunrise arrived on the schedule Saadi had predicted. The landscape was pretty enough, a virgin pine forest sloping east toward the sea. The Mother Sphere stood alone, no other Spheres flanking her. Saadi and Gayle took vids, drew maps, and collected up the miniature GNAT satellites while Breme and Collins broke camp.

Lavasseur handed Myell a set of green fatigues in his size, along with boots, a flashlight, and a water bottle. Myell was glad enough to get out of his Supply School clothes that he didn't dwell on the fact that they'd stocked up on equipment for him. He kept the dilly bag around his waist, glad for the small, comforting weight.

"Why aren't we wearing protection?" he asked. "Doesn't anyone worry that the next station might not have oxygen, or be poisonous in other ways?"

"The rings don't transport organic material that's sealed up," Collins said. "Inorganic material, fine. Crates and clothes and equipment all go through. Dead things? Sure. They sent some dead mice in sealed gear through Swedenville. But never living humans in protective suits. And never any DNGOs or robots."

"There's got to be a pretty sensitive scanning system at work," Myell said. "To differentiate all that."

Nam said, "So it would seem."

Gayle was bright eyed and eager to start off, but she wanted to see if the token in the Mother Sphere would respond to anyone but Myell. She tried it, then Nam, then the Marines, but the ouroboros didn't sing out an approach until Myell stepped inside.

"Why only you?" Gayle asked Myell.

"I don't know," Myell said.

"Would you tell us if you did, Chief?" Lavasseur asked.

Breme poked him. "Shut up."

Nam, who'd been watching Myell, turned away.

The ouroboros was just large enough for all of them and the sled. Myell glanced at the glyphs carved inside the ring. Thirty-something more stops to go. He tensed and held his breath, which was silly. Transport through the ring never hurt. The aftereffects were the miserable part.

A hand closed on his arm. Collins said, "You should be fine, Chief."

Yellow flashed at them from all sides. The next station on the Bainbridge loop was as hollow and musty as any other he'd visited. To Myell's surprise, he didn't feel much worse for the wear. Saadi deployed GNATs past the Sphere's archway and took readings while Lavasseur vidded the interior. Breme kept a steady countdown for the token departure. They had assumed that the same amount of time would pass at each station: ninety seconds, give or take a split second.

"No radio signals," Saadi reported, watching his gibs. "Exterior looks like a swamp and it's raining out. No sign of Commander Gold's team. There are two Father Spheres outside."

Gayle, who was swinging her own gib back and forth, nodded briskly. She stepped out of the ouroboros's confines. "We need to check them out. Map their tokens."

"No," Nam said. "We keep going."

"Commander, we're tasked with learning as much about the network as we can," Gayle said.

Nam's gaze was unflinching. "We're not stopping at every station on this loop so you can gather data, Dr. Gayle. If the situation warrants, I'll be happy to let you do your digging."

Breme said, "One minute until we depart, sir."

Gayle showed no sign of stepping back into the ouroboros. "Team Space gave us a clear mandate, Commander. Search and recovery of my husband's team, but intelligence gathering as well."

"Commander Gold's team has been trapped out here for months," Nam said. "They're our first priority. If you choose to stop I'm not going to argue with you, Doctor. But this team and I are going forward. Hopefully you'll be here the next time a rescue team comes through. If one ever does."

Collins was studiously ignoring the argument. Myell had the distinct impression that it wasn't the first time Gayle and Nam had clashed, nor would it be the last.

"Thirty seconds, sir," Breme reported.

Gayle's glare didn't abate, but she stepped back into the ring.

The yellow light flashed again. The next Mother Sphere appeared around them. Myell felt nauseated and closed his eyes against an attack of dizziness.

"With all due frankness, sir, that one sucked mightily," Lavasseur said, putting his hands on his knees.

"It's probably the distance between stations," Collins said, looking queasy himself. "Greater the distance traveled, worse we might feel."

Breme said, "Look there. Equipment."

Four flashlights played over a tarpaulin and some small crates. "Haul out," Nam ordered, and they left the ouroboros to continue without them. Myell was happy to sit on the ground and rub the back of his aching head. Collins spread more of that miracle gel on his wrist. Already his skin there was blue, but it did help.

Lavasseur inspected the crates. "Serial numbers match Commander Gold's manifest."

Gayle nodded briskly. "Excellent."

Outside was a mountain slope of thin green grass, with clear blue skies and a nearby cliff that dropped a thousand meters into a rocky valley. Myell had never suffered from vertigo, but as he gazed out at the sweeping vista of green mountains and plunging ravines, he could heartily appreciate a fear of heights. The Mother Sphere looked like a giant marble, ready to roll down into oblivion with one push of a giant's hand.

"Jesus," Breme said, gazing at the valleys far below.

"Good place for hang gliding," Saadi said.

Gayle and Breme took a trip up the slope. Myell sat on the grass, happy for the sunshine after the gloominess of the Sphere. Saadi monitored his GNATs while Lavasseur conducted an inventory of what Gold's mission had left behind. Litter, mostly. A dead flashlight. Some freeze-dried ration cartons, empty. No notes. No messages for anyone who might come after them.

"No signs of a campfire, either, Commander," Collins said. "They didn't stay long."

Gayle and Breme came back down the hill. They'd found nothing of the missing team. Nam ordered them to move on. At the next station Lavasseur went down on his knees and vomited. Nam called a time-out for Collins to do a medical check on everyone.

"Thought this Blue-Q was supposed to make everything better," Lavasseur said sourly, as they sat outside in tall grass. A savannalike plain stretched out all around them. The air was hot and still under a cornflower-blue sky. The sun was almost directly overhead.

"It's not a cure-all." Collins went around to all of them, pressing sensors against their skin, collecting blood samples for later analysis, and dispensing more blue gel as needed. "But we'd be far worse off without it, trust me."

This Mother Sphere was flanked by two Childs. Gayle, who seemed to be tolerating ouroboros travel better than any of them, went off to investigate. With Nam's permission, Lavasseur stretched out with his pack as a pillow and dozed. Collins busied himself with his medical duties while Breme scouted the perimeter. Myell sat a short distance away.

Saadi, crouched nearby, was stowing his GNATs back into their cases. He said, "I hear you declined chief's initiation."

"That's right," Myell said.

"You think you can turn it down?"

Myell swatted at a fly. "Yes, Chief Saadi, regulations say I can."

"Shit on regulations. You're not a chief just because you put on the insignia."

Another fly tried to land on Myell's arm. "But you are a chief after you let someone force-feed you rotten eggs? After they make you crawl through shit and garbage?"

"Fucking lies, all of that," Saadi said hotly.

Gayle returned from the Child Spheres, a frown on her face. "I couldn't trigger a token in either one. We've never called them out in anything but Mother Spheres. But you, Chief Myell, reported that you and Commander Scott went through a Child when you traveled out of Warramala. I need you to try now."

Myell said, "No."

Gayle's gaze hardened. "What?"

He didn't move from his spot in the grass. "I refuse."

Lavasseur lifted his head. Saadi muttered, "Figures," and Gayle turned to Nam.

"You said he was onboard with this," Gayle said.

"Chief," Nam warned.

"I'll support anything that locates Commander Gold's team and gets us home," Myell said. "Exploring other Spheres isn't part of that. Not without proof the missing team switched loops. We start wandering off on other branches, we'll never get home."

"We're not wandering off!" Gayle said. "All I'm going to do is vid a token, if it comes. The glyphs will help us build a better map, might cross-reference back to Fortune or the Seven Sisters—it's absolutely imperative we accomplish as much as we can at these stations! Am I the only one who understands that?"

Nam studied Myell. "Dr. Gayle's request isn't unreasonable."

"I won't do it, sir," Myell said.

Gayle glared at him. "Yes, you will."

A scream from Breme ripped through the air.

Nam and the Marines jerked to their feet, mazers in hand. The grass to the west rippled and bowed as Breme appeared, running for her life, followed by four or five extremely large animals. Dark and fast, snarling viciously, predators used to catching and devouring their kill. Lions of some kind. Nam, Lavasseur, and Collins all fired their weapons. Two of the animals fell instantly, and the others scattered with yelps.

"Chase them down, sir?" Lavasseur asked.

"Let them be," Nam ordered.

Breme was shaken but unharmed. The animals had been killed instantly and lay sprawled in the grass where they had fallen. Four-legged, enormously large, with large fangs and thick pelts.

Saadi took vids, asking, "What the hell are they? Look at those fucking teeth!"

"Marsupial lions," Gayle said, crouched by the larger beast. "Extinct in Australia over fifty thousand years ago."

"You're sure?" Nam asked. "None of the Seven Sisters harbor any extinct species."

"We're far from the Seven Sisters," Gayle replied.

Collins took samples of skin, fur, and blood. Saadi suggested cutting off paws for souvenirs, an idea that Nam nixed. They left the lions to rot in the sun and headed back to the cool dimness of the Mother Sphere. Looking back over his shoulder, Myell saw a lone vulture home in on the corpses. More would come, with beaks to pluck out eyes and claws to rip flesh. Just like in the painting in the farmers' market on Water Street, where the girl had called him Jungali.

The Mother Sphere was dark and comforting, but even as he stepped into the ouroboros, Myell could hear the vulture outside squawking in victory.

At the eighth station out of Bainbridge, Breme began vomiting violently.

"We have to stop, sir," Collins said.

Collins and Lavasseur carried her out of the ouroboros. Myell tried to help Saadi with the sled, but the other chief said, "Leave it, it's mine."

"Let him help," Nam ordered.

Snow was spilling through the open archway. Their breath frosted in the air as they waited for Saadi's GNATs to collect data. "Winter wonderland out there," Saadi reported. "Looks like an alpine forest. Dusk or thereabouts, and below freezing. No sign of other Spheres."

"Below freezing, snow, forest, dark," Nam said. "We're better off in here."

Gayle said, "If Chief Myell stays in here, he'll keep triggering the system. I don't want to risk overtaxing it."

Myell waited for them to order him outside, to freeze in the snow by himself. Instead, Nam had them break out thermal sweaters, winter parkas, gloves, and other equipment from the sled. A well-prepared expedition, Myell thought. When they stomped outside, snow was piled high on the north side of their Mother Sphere. Bare ground lay exposed on the south.

"Get the tents up," Nam said. "Saadi, you're in charge of the fire."

Collins was still busy treating Breme, so Myell pitched in helping Lavasseur erect the tents. The winter landscape was quiet and silvery-white from the light of a moon. Every one of the Seven Sisters had a satellite moon, just like back on Earth: a fundamental of Wondjina design, people said. Moons were necessary to maintain tides. Oceans, those blasted things, didn't rise and fall much on their own. The moon currently hanging low in the trees had different markings than the ones Myell knew back on Baiame and Fortune, but was comforting nonetheless.

"Don't listen to Chief Saadi," Lavasseur said quietly, while they worked on the last tent. "About that chief's thing, that is. I had a friend, back on Earth. He went through it. Said it was all bullshit."

"Most of it is," Myell said.

Lavasseur pulled the tent zipper open. "They ever pick me for promotion, I'm going to tell them exactly where to shove their initiation."

Myell's boot brushed against something small lying on the ground. He stared at it for a moment. Sourness rose in his throat and coated his tongue.

"Commander Nam?" he called out. "You should see this."

Nam came over. Soon they were all staring down at what Collins and his gib had identified as a human finger bone. More bones were scattered on the ground or under the edges of snow. The largest was a rib. The creepiest, to Myell, was part of a lower jaw with three teeth still embedded in it.

"Animals must have dragged off the rest," Lavasseur said.

"No clothing," Gayle remarked. "No bits of uniform, rubber from boot soles, or metal insignia."

"Can you identify the victims?" Nam asked Collins.

Collins replied, "I'm working on DNA profiles, sir."

Gayle shoved her hands deep into her pockets. The skeletal remains could belong to her husband. Nam looked equally tense. Myell shuffled in the cold air and tried not think about the gruesome discovery he'd made back on the *Aral Sea,* a blue-white corpse crusted with ice.

"Lavasseur's right about animals," Nam said. "Everyone keep an eye on the perimeter and your scanners. I don't want to be surprised by anything like those lions."

Another long minute passed before Collins said, "There's two different sets of remains here, Commander. Dr. Jiang and Dr. Meredith."

Nam asked, "Can you tell when they died?"

"No, sir," Collins said.

Gayle picked up the jawbone and examined it with cold scrutiny. "If they deceased on arrival, Robert wouldn't have left the bodies out to decompose. Susan and Eric were friends. The team must have buried them, and animals dug up the corpses."

"Commander Gold would have covered them with rocks, given the frozen ground," Nam said.

"We don't know that it was frozen when they passed this way," Gayle retorted.

Collins took the jaw from Gayle, treating it with a reverence she hadn't shown. "Ensign Holt is the finest field medic I know. No one on the team should have died because of the token, not unless he lost all his medical equipment and their supply of Blue-Q. These bones have chew marks on them. They could have been attacked while alive. Like those lions that chased Breme."

Nam tasked Lavasseur and Myell with searching the snowy forest around the Spheres for more remains. The going was slow. Their scanners picked up rocks and branches and dead leaves that gave false readings as clothing. They kept vigilant for wolves and bears and any other large animals that might come their way. The work and cold tired Myell more than he cared to admit. He cast occasional glances back at the camp, where Breme was moved into one of the tents to recuperate and Gayle was working on her gib by a blazing warm fire.

"Lavasseur, report," said Nam's voice over their radios.

"Nothing, sir," Lavasseur reported. Despite the winter gear, his teeth were chattering.

"Come on back, the two of you, and get some hot coffee."

Myell was happy to oblige. In addition to coffee, Collins had broken out their meal rations. Though it hadn't been long since lunch, they were still trying to eat small meals on the schedule of whatever world they were visiting. A package of self-heating chili went a long way toward making Myell feel warm again.

"Is the temperature going to keep dropping during the night?" Nam asked Saadi.

Saadi was already deploying more GNATs. They rose into the trees like sparks from the fire. "There's a high-pressure front coming in from the north, but it's pushing air that's not too much colder. We should be comfortable in the tents with the heat packs."

"You don't sound too confident," Nam said.

"It's not that, sir," Saadi said. "I'm having trouble with astronomical calculations."

Myell tilted his head back. He could see plenty of stars, but no recognizable constellations.

Nam poured himself more coffee. "Is it your equipment?"

"No, sir. The bugs are fine. But they're not getting a fix. I'll keep working on it."

After dinner, Nam sent Lavasseur and Myell back to the snowy woods. They didn't find any bones or clothing, but on the fringe of their search area Lavasseur found something much, much larger.

"Down there," he said, pointing down a steep slope.

A Father Sphere lay in a ravine about two dozen meters below, a great gray hulk in the moonlight. Part of its surface was smashed in. A Mother and Child lay nearby, apparently intact but coated with snow.

"Dr. Gayle'll love it," Lavasseur said.

Lavasseur radioed in a report. Within moments Nam and Gayle were traipsing through the woods toward their position. Gayle wanted to climb down the slope immediately.

"Damaged Spheres are rare," she said. "If we could find out what happened to it, whether it was natural or from other causes . . . and we can see if the other two are working."

Myell steeled himself for another argument but Nam forestalled it by saying, "No one's going down there in the dark. We'll assess the climb in the morning. Everyone back to camp."

Gayle muttered something under her breath. They all trudged back through the snow to the beckoning fire. Saadi had been working on his calculations while they were gone. He reported that sunrise would be another eight hours. The GNATs had told him that they were in the northern latitudes of the planet, but they still hadn't identified any of the stars.

"We might be completely out of the Milky Way," Gayle said eagerly. "The first interstellar travelers to do so."

"M81, M31, M10—shouldn't matter. I've got everything loaded here," Saadi said, and went off to consult more equipment.

Nam hadn't said anything about Myell's earlier refusal to explore other Spheres on the planet of marsupial lions. Surely the matter wasn't settled. Myell could feel Nam's gaze on him every now and then, a frowning assessment. Nam split the night watches between Collins, Saadi, Lavasseur, and himself. Breme and Gayle shared one tent, and Myell got to be in the tent with a rotating roommate. He fell asleep with Saadi in the adjacent sleeping bag and woke when Collins took his place.

"You could freeze your ass off out there," Collins said, rubbing his hands together. "I'm going to shoot Saadi. Not much colder, he said."

Myell rubbed his eyes. He'd been dreaming of Jodenny and Karl back at home, and the way Jodenny smelled when she was sleeping beside him. "Maybe the GNATs are malfunctioning."

"Sure. Whatever."

"Breme okay?"

Collins slid into the sleeping bag that Saadi had vacated. "She'll be fine. I'm actually surprised that the Blue-Q is working as well as it is. We didn't get much of a chance to test it, what with the system down."

"You don't think traveling through the tokens killed Dr. Jiang and Dr. Meredith."

Collins lifted up one elbow, punched his small pillow, and settled down again. "We're still alive, and our Blue-Q is no different than theirs. Ensign Holt and Commander Gold wouldn't endanger anyone by pushing through if they were sick. Neither would Commander Nam."

Myell stared at the tent walls. Firelight outside cast a reddish glow.

"Nam's a good man, you know," Collins said. "He's a lot of things. Completely committed to finding Commander Gold's team. We all trained together at Swedenville. Could have been this team that went on the Bainbridge loop first, but they drew the lucky straw. Nam's not going to let anyone stand in the way of finding them."

Myell didn't answer. After a while Collins's breathing evened out. Myell waited for sleep, waited some more, waited as long as he could, but finally he crawled back into his parka and snowpants and boots and left the tent. Lavasseur and Nam were sitting by the fire, mazers close at hand.

"Wolves," Nam said. "GNATs picked them up. A dozen of them traveling in a pack, two kilometers north."

One of the wolves cried out, and the other animals answered in a long group howl. They sounded a lot closer than two kilometers. Myell took up residence by the fire, though Nam didn't see fit to give him a mazer.

"Did Chief Saadi get his astronomical fix?" Myell asked.

Nam shook his head. "The data doesn't make sense. Some of the stars almost match, but the constellations aren't where they should be."

Myell gazed skyward at the smattering of stars visible through bare trees. "Those marsupial lions you killed. On Earth, they've been gone for fifty thousand years. We know that Fortune and the rest of the Seven Sisters are as old as Earth, share similar fossil records and evolution of species. None of these planets appear any different. So what are fifty-thousand-year-old lions doing running around?"

"You've got a theory?" Nam asked mildly.

"Stars drift and constellations shift," Myell said. "Maybe enough, over the millennia, to confuse the GNATs."

Nam warmed his hands by the fire. "You think we're traveling in time as well as space."

Lavasseur choked on his coffee. "Is that possible, sir?"

"Anything's possible," Nam said.

The wolves howled again, closer.

"Maybe we should head out, sir," Lavasseur said. "If those things killed Dr. Jiang and Dr. Meredith—"

"We can handle a pack of wolves," Nam said.

He wouldn't want to retreat, not with the chance of more bones lying under the snow. But Myell doubted that they could hold off a dozen wolves without injury.

"Everyone else could take shelter in the Mother Sphere," Myell said. "I can stay out here."

Nam studied his gib, tracking the wolves. "Not necessary, Chief."

The wolf howls woke the others, who emerged from their tents sleepy-eyed and anxious. Even Breme, who looked much better than she had when they arrived. For the rest of the long, uncomfortable night they sat huddled around the fire, listening to the circling wolves, making do with heated blankets and gallons of coffee. Myell must have slept, somehow, because after a long space of time with no thought at all, he opened his eyes and saw Nam looming over him.

"We're off to explore those other Spheres," Nam said. "Dr. Gayle found evidence of Commander Gold's team. You're coming along."

Breme, Saadi, and Collins were left to guard the camp and mind the equipment. Gayle and Lavasseur were already out at the hillside, their breath frosting in the clear morning air. Sunlight bouncing off snow dazzled Myell's eyes and the exposed skin on his face tingled.

"There," Gayle said, for Nam's benefit. "Cables and a harness. Someone climbed down there."

The cable was military-issue, coated with a thin layer of ice. It snaked down the incline toward some bushes, where the yellow safety harness was snagged. Nam and Lavasseur freed it and tested its strength.

"I'll go first," Nam said. "Dr. Gayle, Chief Myell, you're next. Sergeant Lavasseur, keep an eye out up here."

Nam descended slowly. Gayle waited impatiently for her turn and told Lavasseur to lower her faster. Lavasseur rolled his eyes and disobeyed. When the harness came back up, Myell pulled the straps absurdly tight.

"Afraid of heights, Chief?" Lavasseur asked.

"Afraid of plummeting to my death," Myell answered.

The incline was sharp and jagged. He was glad for his gloves and uniform, which protected him from the sharp bite of rocks and brush. Disturbed snow showed him the path Gayle and Nam had taken. Slowly he descended, trying not to get his boots caught between jagged outcrops. When he reached the bottom of the gully, he heard Gayle happily chattering on.

"Imagine what could have happened here," she said. "A force that smashed through the rock and wrecked the token."

He followed her voice to the broken Father Sphere. Half of it was crushed in, but the archway was intact. The wind smelled like ash and the walls, in places, looked seared. Daylight fell through breaches in the ceiling and landed on piles of snow-covered stones. At the Sphere's center, an ouroboros jutted out of more snow. It was twisted and misshapen.

Gayle patted the dull metal. "If we can bring this back with us, it'll be the treasure of the century."

Nam frowned. "Bring a token through another token? Sounds like the kind of thing that doomed the *Yangtze.*"

"Not the same situation," Gayle retorted.

Myell drifted away from their argument. The gully was full of crooked trees and boulders. It sloped downhill and then leveled off. The shin-high snow was easy to stomp around in. The Mother Sphere lay several meters away and didn't appear damaged. He didn't go into it. The smell of smoke persisted on the wind, making his nose itch. A forest fire, he thought, but in winter?

Then he rounded the Child Sphere and froze in place.

A few meters away, a fire burned against the Child's exterior. Red flames licked at a pile of kindling. A small creature was crouched next to the fire, warming itself. It had two thickly muscled arms and legs under green leathery skin. The head was bulbous, almost like a dinosaur's. Two eyes, nose holes, large teeth. Tufts of hair stuck out on the back of its head and it had feathers—no, it *wore* feathers, a cloak of white and gray thrown over boots and trousers.

Myell didn't move, didn't dare breathe.

Lying on the ground nearby was another of the creatures, much larger. It was unmoving and coated with snow. The smaller creature went to it, patted it fretfully, then went back to the fire. It made a second trip, patting again, making a faint whining noise. Mourning it. The larger alien—parent? mother?—was unmoving, and there was a black pool underneath it that might have been frozen blood.

Myell had encountered the Rainbow Serpent during his journey out of Warramala but never any aliens, no true-to-life other species. If Team Space had a standard operating procedure for first contacts, he didn't know it. Myell shifted his weight from one foot to the other. It would probably be best to get Commander Nam or run like hell—

The small alien snapped its head up, alarmed, and flattened itself against the Sphere with a little cry.

"It's okay," Myell said. "I'm not going to hurt you or anything."

It put its clawed hands over its eyes and trembled.

Myell opened his arms in what he hoped was a reassuring gesture. "No, really. It's okay. I'm probably more scared of you than you are of me."

The alien made a peeping noise.

"Or maybe not," Myell said. "Are you alone? Can you speak?"

The alien child—because it was a child, Myell decided, a youngling of some kind—lowered its hands and tilted its head. It was intelligent, certainly. Alone in this frozen wilderness, with only the corpse of its parent for company.

"Chief Myell," said Nam's voice from behind him. "Move very slowly. Back away."

Myell risked a glance over his shoulder. Nam had his mazer out and trained on the alien. Gayle's mouth and eyes were wide with surprise, but she had erred on the side of caution and was hiding, in part, behind Nam.

The alien child sniffed the air but didn't cower at the sight of more humans.

"I think it's on its own," Myell said. "The parent died."

"I don't care if it's the saddest orphan in the galaxy," Nam said. "Move. Very slowly."

Myell tried to inch backward but lost his balance on underfoot ice and went down to the snow with a thump. The child cried out and darted to the corpse for safety.

"Don't shoot it," Myell said.

Nam tracked it with his mazer but didn't fire.

"We need to capture it alive," Gayle said. "Bring it back to Fortune."

Nam keyed his radio. "This is Nam. We've got Yips in the ravine, two of them, one possibly deceased. Chief Saadi, send your GNATs to my location. Breme, secure the camp."

"Yips?" Myell asked. "What's a Yip?"

The child patted the corpse again, tugging at its clothing. A moment later it made a chirping noise and extended its right hand toward Myell. The hand had four fingers and a thumb, and claws extended out from the knuckles. The creature offered a clump of dark material that Myell couldn't easily identify.

Gayle said, "It's a peace offering. Take it, Chief."

"Dead flesh," Nam said. "Some offering."

The alien child must have sensed their disapproval. It withdrew the gift and swallowed the flesh with one large gulp.

A challenging cry cut through the air—angry, fearful. Myell turned to see a third alien striding out from the distant woods. It was much larger than the child, probably twice its size, with a dark cloak and a silver helmet. It had a weapon in one clawed hand, some kind of rifle that spat out red bolts like drops of burning lava. It screeched and made clicking noises, and raised the weapon toward them.

"Run!" Nam ordered.

Gayle sprinted away, nimble despite the snow. Nam grabbed Myell's arm and jerked him upright. The adult continued to advance with screeches and more dripping lava. Nam shoved Myell toward the Mother Sphere and said, "Take cover!"

Once inside, Myell fell to his knees. Gayle was already there, hands on her knees as she gulped in air. Nam fired at the alien from the archway. Myell took a quick peek and estimated it was about thirty meters away, moving quickly through the snow.

"We're under attack," Nam radioed to the base camp. "Copy me? Two Yips, one of them armed—"

The adult fired again. This time the lava shots merged into a tight, hot beam that slammed into Nam. He collapsed immediately. Myell grabbed for his mazer but it fell outside the Sphere, and more lava bolts made it impossible to retrieve. The air smelled burnt and hot, ready to fry his skin.

"The token!" Gayle said, and he heard the sweet call of an inbound ouroboros. She scrambled to her feet. "It's our only chance!"

"We'll be lost," Myell said.

"Otherwise we'll be dead!"

The ouroboros arrived. Nam was unconscious, maybe dead. Myell dragged him backward into the ring. The adult alien appeared in the archway, weapon aiming for Myell's chest, screeching out a protest—

Then the yellow light took them, and Myell was happy for the void.

At the next station Myell dragged Nam out of the ouroboros. The Sphere was dark and hot around them. Gayle followed and went to her knees, vomiting thinly into the dirt.

"Commander," Myell said. "Wake up."

"The token." Gayle turned to it and starting counting glyphs aloud. "Twenty, thirty, forty, forty-five—I don't recognize any of these symbols—that's almost like Mary River Oakdale, but not quite—"

Nam was breathing, but his face and limbs were slack. Myell rubbed his breastbone and slapped his cheeks until his eyes opened into little slits. Behind them, the token departed with a flash of yellow.

Gayle said, "Goddammit."

"Wh'we?" Nam mumbled.

"What?" Myell asked.

"Where we?"

"Not sure yet." Myell watched Gayle walk to the archway. Sunlight outside, hot air. No more snow. "How do you feel?"

Nam didn't sit up. Drool had accumulated at the corner of his mouth. He swiped his lips clumsily with the back of his hand. "They follow us?"

Myell sat back on his heels. "You call them Yips. Why?"

Nam squinted at him. "Where's Dr. Gayle?"

"Did you know there were aliens in the network?"

Nam squeezed the bridge of his nose. "Gayle. Go with her. Who knows what's out there."

Myell wanted to argue more, to demand answers, but he hauled himself to his feet and passed under the archway. The marshland surrounding them was cracked and baked from drought. Dried-up creeks stretched out in all directions, punctuated by eucalyptus and gum trees. Insects buzzed in the scrub bushes that surrounded the Mother Sphere and the two Children that flanked it.

Gayle was stomping around, glaring at everything as if personally affronted.

"No equipment whatsoever," she said. "My gib, the Blue-Q, all of our resources—back at the base camp."

"Who are the Yips? And why didn't you mention the fact that we might run into them?"

Gayle gave him a narrow look.

"Focus, Chief. We have more important things to worry about right now."

Myell's fists ached. He unclenched them and rubbed them against his thighs. It was ridiculous to keep his winter coat on and he wrenched it off, and dropped his thermal sweater next to it.

"Don't look so aggrieved," Gayle said. "You knew there was intelligent life out in the network. You spoke to a snake, didn't you? So if there happen to be some Bunyips running around, that's no surprise."

"*Bunyips?*" Myell asked. "What kind of name is that?"

Nam appeared in the Mother Sphere archway, clutching it for support. His pallor was awful. "Old urban legend."

"Not an urban legend. A folk myth," Gayle said. "A creature in the Australian bush rumored to have feathers and scales and a terrible screech."

Nam squeezed his eyes shut against the brilliant sunlight. "Not a myth any longer."

Myell thought of the alien child proffering dead flesh. "What about everyone else? Do they know about them?"

Gayle stopped pacing and pulled off her coat. Her T-shirt was already damp with sweat. "Will you stop considering yourself a victim of some conspiracy? You didn't need to know."

"Is the rest of the team safe?" Myell asked icily.

Nam started sliding down the archway as his knees buckled. "They can protect themselves."

Myell went to Nam's side. He lowered the commander and helped him out of his winter gear. He gave him water from his own bottle. Gayle went off to investigate the interiors of the two other Spheres. Flies buzzed in the heated air, and Myell swatted to keep them away.

"We have to go back," Nam said, eyes still closed.

Myell said, "There were forty or fifty glyphs on that token. We'd never survive a loop all the way around."

"Can you get us back?"

"How?" Myell asked.

"Talk to your snake friend."

"It's not my friend." Myell hadn't seen the Rainbow Serpent or accompanying shaman since he and Jodenny returned to Warramala. "I wouldn't even know how."

"You can't improvise?"

Myell scowled. He was keeping an eye on the interior of the Mother, waiting to see if the Bunyips—really, what a name—followed.

"Why were they there?" he asked, thinking aloud. "Camped out. For a while, judging by the snow on the dead one. Two adults and a kid."

"Stuck," Nam said. "Trapped when the system shut down. You're still the only one who can call a token. Which means the rest of our team is trapped back in the snow until we get back to them."

Forty or more stations to get back, and no Blue-Q to ease the way. Myell swatted at more flies. The horizon to the west was hazy and gray, and a shift of the wind brought him a hot, bitter smell.

"That's smoke," he said, standing.

"Muck fire, maybe," Nam said.

"No GNATs to tell for sure."

"Not much of anything," Nam said. "Inventory?"

"Winter gear, some emergency hand warmers, three flashlights, three bottles of water, three radios, and whatever's stashed in your and Dr. Gayle's pockets. Your mazer fell before we were transported."

Nam opened his eyes reluctantly. "Unarmed, no equipment, no food. Not exactly the rescue mission I'd planned."

The flies were feasting on Myell's neck. He swatted and squashed some, and gazed out at the dried-up marshland.

Nam said, "Evidence of intelligent aliens was found at several different stations on loops out of Kiwi and Warramala. Fire pits, crude shelters, animal carcasses that showed evidence of tools. There were three confirmed sightings of creatures that walked upright and wore feather cloaks. One exchange of hostile fire. Two of our own were killed. Then a team working on Kookaburra captured a token and tried to ship it back to the research facilities on Fortune. They thought the risk was small, and it was important to get a handle on this technology if we were going to be facing hostile species. You know this part."

"The *Yangtze* blew up when it tried to enter the Alcheringa," Myell said.

"The disassembled token activated. Someone—something—was trying to come through."

"Jodenny didn't see anything," Myell said, but even as the words came out of his mouth he knew they were wrong. Jodenny's memories had been tampered with. Blocked. Sam Osherman had said that Team Space had done it, though others had denied it.

"She did see something, didn't she?" Myell asked. "She saw one of them. That's what you're telling me."

"Team Space thought it prudent to block that information."

"Tamper with her brain, you mean. Osherman saw it too, didn't he? Son of a bitch."

Nam put a hand out to the Sphere and pushed himself upright. "Saadi, Collins, the others—they didn't know much more than to be prepared. And so we all are."

Gayle returned with a disgruntled air. "I can't trigger any tokens. You'll have to try, Chief. Unless it interferes with your personal idea of what this mission is about."

Nam said, "Dr. Gayle. There's only the three of us, and he's the only one who can make the Spheres work. I think a little civility is in order."

Gayle's mouth formed an unhappy little line. "Fine. Chief Myell, will you *please* try to save our asses by triggering a token?"

Nam rested outside while Myell went to try. The first Child responded almost as soon as he entered it. The token came bearing sixty glyphs. Gayle recognized number thirty as a remote spot on Kiwi.

"Too far," she said. "Even if we got there safely, it's a thousand-kilometer hike to civilization. Then it would take us months to ride the Alcheringa back to Fortune."

They checked on Nam, whose eyes were closed again. His skin was clammy under Myell's touch and his pulse a little fast. In the second Child, the arriving token had only two glyphs on it.

Gayle said, "An express. I don't recognize the destination. Could lead to more Spheres, could be a dead end."

The air outside was growing thicker with the smoke from the muck fire. The sky had darkened and grit made Myell's eyes sting. Gayle gazed at the Mother Sphere and said, "We'll have to keep going on the loop. Hope that the next station holds more promise."

"Not today, we won't." Myell bent low to Nam. "The commander's too sick. We don't have any Blue-Q or medical equipment to revive him if he gets worse."

Nam proved he wasn't asleep by saying, "Don't be ridiculous. Fire's coming." The words were slurred, almost indistinct.

Alarmed, Gayle said, "I agree. We can't stay here."

"We'll retreat until the fire's out, then come back," Myell said. "These Spheres aren't going to burn down. I'm sure they've been through worse over the centuries."

Nam swatted at Myell's arm. "Go ahead without me."

"That's not even an option, sir. You're going to have to walk."

Nam cursed, Gayle argued, but Myell told them that they were wasting time. The fire was growing closer. Unless they planned to be incinerated in its path, they had to move *now.* Finally Nam let Myell help him up to his unsteady feet and Gayle shut up and they started east, skirting the marsh, fire and smoke chasing them.

The air was baking hot, Nam's weight heavy against Myell as he tried to maneuver both of them across the unsteady ground. Gayle led the way in grim silence, keeping an eye out for snakes or crocodiles or other predators. Home on Baiame had been less desolate, but the wide open space with no sign of civilization was familiar to Myell, the sense that the world was endless and forever, horizon to horizon, with nothing between a man and the madness of the wide open. Black vultures flew east over their heads, eager to escape the inferno, but one bird took an interest in the human party and circled downward with increasingly loud cries.

Gayle said, "Kill it, won't you?"

Myell asked, "With what?"

Nam, his breathing labored, only grunted.

The fires pushed them eastward. The hillside became more dense with gum and dried-out creek beds and scrub bushes. Myell was soaked with sweat, aching from exertion, but strangely enough his skin bothered him the most. He itched all over. Even his tongue itched, which was odd. Gayle was scratching her arms so often that welts had started to appear.

Myell asked, "That Blue-Q. It's addictive, isn't it? We're in withdrawal."

"It's a small price to pay," Gayle said.

"How bad will it get?"

Gayle shrugged.

They were hiking above the valley now. The landscape fell away, rugged and harsh but beautiful in its own strange way. Jodenny would like it for a day hike, as long as the day ended with a reliable flit to carry them back to modern civilization. Thinking of Jodenny comforted him a little, but he was already starting to fear he might never see her again. It would just be him and Gayle and Nam lost on this outback planet, doomed to wander forever and never find their way home.

"Done," Nam finally said. He sagged so abruptly that Myell nearly lost hold of him. They were several kilometers east of the fires, which were now smudges on the horizon. It wasn't an ideal spot to make camp, not with dry, loose ground sloping toward gullies, but Nam had reached the end of his endurance and even Gayle looked exhausted.

They drank from their water supplies. "Better in you than in a bottle," Nam muttered, but Myell rationed himself strictly. Gayle curled up on the ground, her head pillowed on her arms. She didn't volunteer to go off and hunt down dinner for everyone. Myell considered the odds of stoning or catching a wild animal. He wished he'd thought to stuff his pockets with ration bars that morning.

Though he was bone-tired, someone needed to keep watch on the fire and for wild animals. It was late afternoon, the sun burning somewhere low in the smoky west. Gayle and Nam slept. Myell forced himself to walk a perimeter line, to throw rocks at an improvised target, do anything he could to stay awake. Darkness came, and soon afterward rain started dropping from the sky. The others woke immediately.

"Thank God for small miracles," Gayle said as she played her flashlight over the ground and up into the sky.

Myell welcomed the wetness. He let it soak into his skin and onto his tongue. Nam, beside him, rolled onto his back and spread open his arms as a father would to a child. But then the water started pouring down.

Lightning arced in a hot blue flash across the sky. Thunder rolled across the clouds a few seconds later, a long, low, rumbling explosion.

"We can't stay out here!" Gayle said.

"We have nowhere else to go!" Myell said.

More lightning slammed through the air above them. The shock of it made Myell's heart jump. Automatically he pulled into himself, hoping to become as small a target as possible. Rain soaked down, hammering and pummeling. A punishment. He'd never been caught outside like this, never been lashed by the elements. Sound and light blistered through the air, diminishing his will and turning him to spineless flesh.

Nam pressed against him. They both huddled into the mud with their hands laced over their heads. Gayle yelled against the thunder, her words unintelligible. Railing against the unfairness of the universe, perhaps. Even with his eyes closed Myell could see the lightning bolts, hot against his eyelids. Electricity sizzled through the air and was followed by deafening booms that made his teeth ache. The urge to flee nearly made him scramble to his feet, but that would be suicidal. *Stay away from storms,* his mother had always told him. *Stay low. Stay low . . .*

He tried picturing the Rainbow Serpent, appealing to it for help. Mud and water pushed against his mouth and he choked, spat out. Jodenny would kill him if he drowned. The softening ground sucked at him, trying to swallow him whole. Quicksand? And still the thunder and lightning chased each other across the nighttime clouds, a terrible game of one upmanship that had him trembling so wildly that he feared pissing his own pants.

Nam tugged at his arm and yelled something, but Myell's ears had dulled from trauma and he couldn't make out the words.

"Easing up!" Nam shouted, and Myell risked a glance skyward. The rain was still torrential, but the storm itself had passed its peak of fury.

"I hate this!" Gayle said from nearby. "We should have kept going on the loop! Stupid goddamned chiefs—"

So she'd been cursing Myell all this time, not the universe. He found that funny. So funny that he began to laugh. The laughter made him slide a little in the mud. But his amusement ended when the ground below slipped away, carrying him like a river.

"Chief!" Nam screamed, and grabbed for him.

The grab missed. Myell slid away.

Rocks gouged into his hips and legs as the hillside collapsed. A slow, inexorable tide carried him down several feet, twisting and turning him. He covered his face, hoping mud wouldn't bury him alive. But the ride didn't last long before he thudded to a stop. He tilted his head back, rain still hitting hard, then lurched to his knees and feet in a pit of cold mud.

He found his flashlight and played it around. Walls of rock, a narrow channel, strange shapes. He thought at first they were ghosts. Eagles and crocodiles, and something like a whale, or a large shark. White and yellow outlines painted in ocher. Petroglyphs.

Exhausted, sodden, shaking with cold, Myell nevertheless thought the paintings were beautiful and strange, wondrous.

He glanced up, searching for Nam or Gayle, and saw light gathering in the sky. Boiling white light. How very strange. The light became burning lines and curves shaped like the snout of a crocodile, like a twisting long tail. More beautiful than any real creature, and more deadly.

The lines collapsed, the crocodile diminishing to a tiny point that exploded outward, downward, a directed explosion of heat and sound that blasted through Myell and turned the entire world white.

CHAPTER
ELEVEN

I know what I saw," Nam said.

For the third time, Myell said, "It must have been a trick of the light, sir. Of the storm."

Gayle, who was busy examining the petroglyphs on the cave walls around them, spared a glance over her shoulder. "No entry or exit wounds. Besides, if he *had* been hit by lightning, he'd probably be dead."

Nam didn't look persuaded. Myell rubbed the side of his head. His head felt full of static, but he wasn't about to admit that. He'd woken up from a sound sleep feeling muzzy-headed and sore from tumbling along in a mudslide, but he had no obvious injuries or burns and no memory of being struck by lightning, as Nam claimed.

Gayle was right. If he'd truly been struck by a bolt of enormous electricity, he'd probably be dead. Or close to it.

Daylight spilled through the cave opening. Outside, a steady rain kept falling in the gulley. Thunder rolled in the distance and the water drummed against mud and into puddles. The cave wasn't very deep but it was elevated, making it a dry and safe haven. Gayle was ecstatic over the paintings that covered the outside gully and rapturous over the ones inside the cave. Eagles, crocodiles, whales, and other animals stretched from floor to ceiling, yellow and red and white and sometimes blue, a cornucopia of artwork, a zoological spectrum caught in stone.

"See how they layer over each other? How the style evolves slightly?" Gayle pointed her flashlight at an example. "There's centuries of work here. Generations of painters. It's not the kind of discovery that will thrill the military, but I know people who would die to see this. If only I could show them . . ."

Myell reached for his recently refilled water bottle. He ignored the grumbling in his stomach. Nam, gazing out at the rainy day, said, "We better get going. Back to the Spheres."

"Going?" Gayle asked, her voice shrill. "We can't go anywhere."

"We stay here, we'll starve," Nam said.

She turned back to the wall. "I'm not going anywhere until the weather clears. Go hunt something down and cook it."

Myell raised an eyebrow. Nam said nothing. He seemed recovered, but his eyes were bloodshot and his hands shook as he drank from his water bottle. Myell had wanted to start a small fire, but they had no chemical sticks or kindling and Gayle forbade anything that might damage the paintings, such as smoke.

"I can go looking," Myell offered. "Try to catch something."

"Ever hunt down your own dinner before?"

"Used to catch lizards back on our farm." Myell didn't mention that he'd always released them afterward.

Nam said, "Right now I could eat a crocodile."

The word *crocodile* struck deep inside Myell, spasming a muscle that was already sore and stretched. He sucked in a sharp breath.

"Chief?" Nam asked.

"Nothing." The memory of a crocodile in the sky flashed through him, too quick to hold on to.

Nam examined his boots. "It's natural to be a little confused after being hit by lightning."

"I wasn't hit by lightning," Myell said.

Gayle said, in exasperation, "Shut up, the two of you. Don't you have any idea how significant this find is? We're millions of light-years from Earth and there are Aboriginal paintings on the wall. You two are just sitting there like logs."

Nam said, carefully, "Maybe this *is* Earth."

She shone her flashlight on his face. "Are you crazy?"

Myell gazed out at the rain. A spider was perched in the cave's mouth, one leg flexing in the air.

"We haven't seen any constellations," Nam said, quite reasonably. "We know there aren't any Spheres on Earth now, but we could be thousands of years in the past. Chief Myell here thinks the Wondjina Transportation System moves through time as well as space."

Myell shrugged. "That was just speculation."

"What speculation?" Gayle demanded. Her light shone into his eyes, and he waved it off.

"Those marsupial lions," Myell said. "Saadi's GNATs not getting a fix on the stars. I was thinking aloud."

Gayle sighed rather dramatically. "Don't think too hard. There's no evidence we traverse anything but distance."

"Then who painted these walls?" Nam asked. "Interstellar Aboriginals?"

She said, "I hope we find out."

Nam studied his boots some more. Despite his Aboriginal heritage, he hadn't shown any interest in the cave paintings. Myell, for his part, was still numb with surprise over the Bunyips. Aliens with guns. Jodenny, having seen one. Compared to that, petroglyphs weren't much to get excited about. Unless . . .

"Are they recent?" Myell asked. "Are the painters still around?"

Gayle said, "I don't know. My gib's broken, and I don't have any other way to test the paint."

Myell's belly rumbled with hunger. He imagined his stomach shrinking up, folding into itself, lines of white shrinking to a distant point—

"Chief?" Nam asked.

"I'm fine." He pushed himself upright. "I'll be right back."

He stepped carefully out of the cave and into the rain, skirting a low outcrop of rock to the spot they were using as a latrine. He kept an eye out for crocodiles, Bunyips, and Aboriginals, but the landscape was desolate and empty. Water ran down his neck and under his uniform. He wondered if one of them would catch cold out here, if sickness or exposure would claim them before starvation did. He eyed a patch of dead shrubs and dug up some weedy-looking plants by the roots.

When he returned to the cave, Nam said, "Going to eat those?"

"Thinking about it," Myell said.

"Poisonous, probably," Gayle said.

He wasn't in a hurry to find out, hunger pains be damned. The rain outside slanted down harder and the thunder grew louder. Nam said, "We'll give it until morning. Then, weather or not, we'll have to head back."

Gayle made a noise in her throat and resumed her studies.

Nam nodded off with his chin against his chest. Myell stretched out stiff muscles, drank more water, and joined Gayle in examining the back of the cave. She was using a small ink pen to take notes on her arms, because her paper notebook had been ruined by water. Her handwriting was very fine. On her upper arms she'd drawn copies of swirls and symbols.

"What are these?" Myell asked, pointing to seven odd figures on the wall. "Men with kangaroo heads?"

Gayle said, "Therianthropes. Ancestor gods believed to have entered the rock, merged with it, and left their imprints behind."

"And these people over here?" They were elongated and sticklike, but wearing robes and headdresses. Some of them carried arrows or spears. They were beautiful and strange, and made him shiver.

Her tone was cool. "Remarkably similar to the Bradshaw paintings discovered in northwest Australia. Those were believed to be fifty thousand years old."

Myell almost touched the paintings, but one stern look from her quelled his hand. He spread his fingers a few centimeters over a white handprint and eyed a fine black boomerang.

"Sorry you can't vid it?" he asked.

"Of course I am. That's a stupid question."

"You couldn't show your colleagues anyway. Top-secret mission and all that."

Gayle moved sideways and continued to write on her left arm. "One day it'll be declassified."

"And you'll be ready to tell the world."

"Is there something you need, Chief? Otherwise I prefer to work in silence."

Myell eyed the kangaroo men again. "Jodenny told me you wanted our help to find your husband. I don't see how studying cave walls helps you do that."

Her lips pursed. "Expert on heartache, are you?"

"Yes," he replied.

She stepped away from him. "Robert would be fascinated by this. He'd want me to find out as much as I can, in the short time allotted."

"Allotted, or created?"

"I have no idea what you mean."

Myell took a step her way. He enjoyed that she was discomfited. It was a look that suited her.

"That rope and harness," he said. "Commander Gold's team never went down into that ravine. You put them out there so there'd be a reason to investigate the other Spheres."

"Maybe you *were* hit by lightning, Chief. You're delusional."

"Am I? That harness wasn't very weathered."

"But there was ice on the cable."

"A wet cable will get icy overnight."

She smiled. "So I snuck out of camp during the middle of the night, when it was dark and wolves were out, just to loop a cable around a tree and throw it down the slope, so that we could go down there and discover the aliens that probably killed Dr. Jiang and Dr. Meredith. I'm pretty clever, aren't I?"

Myell said, "I think you'll do anything you can to further your knowledge of the network. You've already proven yourself a liar."

"Chief," Nam called out. "Dr. Gayle."

They went to where he was standing at the cave mouth. He was staring out into the gray afternoon. "There's someone out there."

"You're sure?"

"Up on that ridge."

Myell couldn't see anyone. Gayle shook her head. Nam said, "I'm going to check it out. The two of you stay here, and try not to kill each other."

Myell wished their radios worked, but they'd been ruined in the storm. He watched Nam go down the gully and start up the incline. The threat of mudslide was still imminent, and he held his breath as Nam steadily ascended, his figure growing fuzzy in the dusk.

"You should go after him," Gayle said.

"He said to stay here."

"Lot of good that will do if he tumbles down the hill."

Myell hesitated, unwilling to disobey an order. Gayle said, "Fine, I'll do it," and went out into the rain.

Left alone, Myell rubbed the sleeves of his uniform. The fabric had dried out on its own, as it was designed to, but he still felt damp. A crack of thunder made him withdraw into the cave. The painted animals appeared to shift and change, ever so slightly, at the edges of his vision. He turned a sharp eye on a yellow kangaroo.

"No funny stuff," he said. His dilly bag weighed heavily against his leg. "I'm not in the mood."

Rain poured down. The cave was deeper than it had first appeared, folds of rock hidden in darkness. He swung his flashlight over the recesses. Painted animals stared back at him. The stick people, with their long legs and arms, remained locked in stone. He imagined men kneeling in this cave with ocher and brushes, painstakingly setting down the stories and symbols of their lives. Stories and legends, victories and losses. The world would spin and seasons pass, storms rage, generations die off, but still the stories would remain.

Myell turned and saw an Aboriginal crouched in the cave mouth, spear in hand, teeth bared in the dim light.

His heart lurched, but annoyance quickly overrode the first cold wave of fear. "I said no funny stuff," Myell snapped. "I don't have time for visions right now."

The Aboriginal cocked his head but said nothing. He was a young fellow, sturdy, midnight black. Feathers and seashells were entwined in his long hair. Swirls of yellow ocher decorated his torso from throat to waist, and wavy lines flowed from his shoulders to his wrists. He had a dilly bag like Myell's, but no clothing. A shark's tooth hung on a cord around his neck. His penis, large and flaccid, hung between his well-muscled thighs.

Myell edged backward. "Shit. You're real, aren't you?"

The Aboriginal took that as an invitation to speak, and replied with a series of words that Myell couldn't understand at all.

"If this is your cave, I'll be happy to leave," Myell said.

Shark Tooth—the name seemed as good as any—took his long, sharp spear and drew quick lines in the dirt. A head, two arms, two legs. He jabbed at the drawing, pointed to Myell, and spoke several long words.

"That's me?" Myell gestured at the lines and at his own chest. "Me?"

A grunt. Shark Tooth drew another line in the dirt. He clapped his hands together and made a rumbling sound, then stabbed the spear in the shape meant to represent Myell.

Myell said, "I wasn't hit by lightning!"

Shark Tooth leaned back on his haunches, quite satisfied with his artwork.

Myell edged along the cave wall, inching by Shark Tooth and his spear with deliberate slowness. "Sorry for disturbing the place. We didn't touch anything. Nice to meet you."

He got no farther than the cave entrance before he spied Nam and Gayle up on the ridge. Relief was quickly replaced by disappointment. More Aboriginals flanked them, a tribe of young men carrying spears and knives.

Shark Tooth shouted out something long and triumphant, and the warriors cheered.

Snow and ice blanketed the landscape outside the conference room, bleak gray and white as far as Jodenny could see.

The room itself was small, well heated, and full of standard Team Space furniture, including a long oval table of faux wood and swivel chairs with blue cushions on them. The walls were vidded lime green. In the two hours that Jodenny had been sequestered there, she'd paced a small track in the beige carpet, had memorized exactly how many steps took her from one wall to the next, and knew exactly how many white ceiling tiles comprised the overhead. An able technician had brought her juice and a sandwich on a tray but hadn't been able to answer any questions. The two guards standing outside the door didn't have any answers for her either.

"You're to stay here, ma'am, until someone comes for you," they said, whenever Jodenny opened the door and asked.

She told herself that Myell was fine. That he could endure a trip through the Spheres without her. That Gayle might be a lying bitch but the Marines were trained in survival techniques. All they had to do was stay on the ouroboros loop, and they'd return to Bainbridge sooner or later.

Jodenny stared out at the snow-swept land. Bainbridge was a three-hour birdie flight away, and she damn well didn't appreciate the way she'd been taken here instead of, say, Kimberley, where she could even now be kicking up a fuss. Compass Bay was a small base set up for ocean and atmosphere monitoring, with only a small staff and limited resources. No civilians lived within several hundred kilometers, and the only way in or out was by launch field.

If they thought they were just going to leave her here, let her stew in worry while Myell was off being dragged around the universe, then they would be sorely surprised. Jodenny already had plans to call Admiral Mizoguchi the minute she got near a comm. Failing that, she had other paths to try. She was still a decorated hero of the *Aral Sea*, and had a queue full of unanswered media inquiries. Any of those reporters would be delighted with a scoop on Team Space's most secret project—

But even as she contemplated her options, Jodenny knew she couldn't reveal the secret of the Wondjina Transportation System to the general population. She'd end up in the brig for a good twenty or thirty years for violating her security clearance. Being in jail wouldn't help Myell at all.

Being stuck out here, in the cold armpit of nowhere, wasn't helping him either.

The door clicked open. A Team Space captain with gray bushy hair and a beak-shaped nose came in. Despite her anger, Jodenny stiffened to attention.

"Sir," she said.

He said, "At ease, Commander Scott. Sit down."

Jodenny took a seat across from him. Behind the captain, Leorah

Farber and Teddy Toledo filed in and took up positions standing against the wall. Both had changed into business attire, and Toledo as usual looked too wide for his shirt. The captain had brought a single piece of paper with him, covered with handwriting so tiny that Jodenny could not decipher it upside down. The row of ribbons on his uniform was easily three times as large as hers, and his Alcheringa patches covered one entire sleeve. He wore no nametag.

"I'm Captain Fisch," he said, meeting her gaze dead on. "Here to straighten out a few misconceptions and decide where to go from here."

Jodenny said, "With all due respect, sir, would that be the misconception that Chief Myell volunteered for the mission he was dragged onto *by force,* by Marines holding *weapons* on him?"

She was proud of the way her voice stayed level. Fisch didn't blink at the accusation, nor did he look surprised. Jodenny thought Farber grimaced, but she wasn't looking at her straight on and couldn't say for sure.

Fisch replied, "You think what Dr. Gayle and Commander Nam did was wrong."

"Yes, sir," she said flatly.

"You too, Miss Farber," Fisch said, without turning.

"Sir," Farber replied. "I would have advised against it, if I'd been told."

"Mr. Toledo?"

Toledo's cheeks turned pink. "I was very surprised, sir."

"In retrospect, both Gayle and Nam should have been removed from the project," Fisch said. He leaned back in his chair and laced his fingers together. His keen gaze hadn't shifted from Jodenny's face. "Both are too emotionally involved. Gayle is eager to be reunited with her husband, and Commander Nam has a relationship with Commander Gold."

"Relationship?" Jodenny asked doubtfully.

"It developed while they were training in Swedenville," Fisch said. "They were very discreet."

Toledo coughed a little.

Jodenny didn't care if Nam and Gold were the most discreet lovers in the entire Seven Sisters, but she refrained from saying so.

Fisch's chair creaked as he shifted his weight. "As it so happens, Commander Nam did have authorization to go with the mission the moment a token was activated, regardless of who triggered it. It was our hope that whoever activated it would volunteer to accompany the rescue team. If not, the commander was authorized to conscript anyone he needed. Miss Farber, Mr. Toledo, your department wasn't briefed on that. It was on a need-to-know basis."

Jodenny wished she were outside, in the tundra, where the icy air would cool her rising temper. She knew she had to be very careful, lest she end up in the brig.

"Sir," she said, "Chief Myell has concerns about using the network. He has the right to refuse a direct order from Team Space without having a weapon pointed at his face."

A frown pulled at Fisch's mouth. "Do you really think, Commander, that your husband would risk a court-martial for refusing a direct order? That he wouldn't want to save the lives of those missing people on Commander Gold's team?"

"He wasn't allowed to choose."

"That wasn't my question."

Deflated, Jodenny shifted her gaze to the tabletop. She stayed silent.

Fisch asked, "Do you trust him, Commander?"

"Sir?"

"Do you trust your husband?"

Her temper started to rise again. "Yes, sir."

Fisch nodded. "Do you trust that he'll do his best to keep that token coming, if the lives of two teams depend on it?"

She remembered the surprise on Myell's face when the ouroboros arrived. "I don't believe he has control of it. There's no guarantee the network will keep running. It could stop tomorrow, and he wouldn't be able to do a thing about it."

"But you don't know," Fisch said.

"None of us know, sir," Farber said from against the wall. "That was my whole argument in keeping Chief Myell out of the network. He's too valuable to risk."

"What we know is that we're a damn sight closer to rescuing Commander Gold's team than we were yesterday," Fisch said. "Whether Chief Myell can control it or not, the system seems to like him. He has a strong incentive to come home to you, Commander Scott. And he has a penchant for coming up like a daisy even when covered with shit, judging by his military records both official and unofficial."

Jodenny would have argued, but Fisch wasn't done.

"The question is, what do we do with *you* in the meantime?" he asked.

"I have my own job, sir. In Kimberley," she said.

His eyebrows lifted. "No one believes you're going to go meekly back to your desk and do your duty like a shy ensign, Miz Scott. Your penchant for bending orders and jumping ranks to get what you want is well known, and fairly effective. Odds in the betting pool are three to one that you'll try to go back to Bainbridge on your own. Four to one that you'll go to other Spheres, maybe up at Waylaid Point. You trust your husband, Commander, but you also might be tempted to go out there and join him. Save the day."

She didn't know whether to be appalled or flattered that people were taking bets.

"The question is, if you were me, what would you do with you?" Fisch asked.

She took her time answering.

"Temporarily reassign me here in Compass Bay, sir," Jodenny said. "Far from everyone and everything. Take away my comm. Put me to work in some tedious job no one else wants."

Toledo shuffled from one foot to the other. Farber said nothing.

Fisch replied, "Not a bad idea. Unfortunately, you know how to fly a birdie, you have the charisma to swindle a comm link out of some unsuspecting sailor, and after a day or so you'd probably do both."

Jodenny asked, "Work from home back in Adeline Oaks?"

Fisch tapped his fingers on the table.

"Work from somewhere else?" she asked.

"Not work," Fisch said. "Think of it as a *vacation*."

Jodenny muttered to Farber, "I hate everything about this."

Farber nodded. The birdie was full of civilian passengers, half of whom were clutching their armrests in fear. The other half were chattering in excitement and peering at the bright blue world of Fortune as it fell away from the vidded viewports.

"And I currently hate you, too," Jodenny said to Farber.

Farber said only, "I understand, Miss Spring."

Ellen Spring. A stupid name if Jodenny had ever heard one. She would never remember to respond to it. Did she really look like a civilian librarian? Like someone named *Spring*? The name rankled. More than she wanted to admit.

Captain Fisch had insisted on the fictitious cover story for her. "Passenger records are public, and we don't need any intrepid reporters tracing your temporary reassignment," he'd said. "You'll go as a civilian, you'll conduct yourself as a civilian, and in two weeks you'll be back to find the rescue went well and Chief Myell's safe and sound. In the meantime, we'll all be happy that you're staying out of trouble."

Sitting on the birdie, Jodenny scowled at the memory and elbowed Farber's arm off the armrest.

"There she is," Farber said, adjusting the vid. "The *Kamchatka*."

Jodenny didn't look. The *Kamchatka* was one of a half-dozen freighters that regularly transited the Little Alcheringa between Fortune and Earth. The duty was tedious and unglamorous. The ships were old and built for capacity, not grace or speed. The *Kamchatka*'s captain was probably some bitter old officer only a year or two from retirement, saddled with a crew who couldn't score better assignments elsewhere.

"That's our ship, Mommy Kate," said a young girl across the aisle.

One of the women traveling with her said, "That's it, sweetie. Home sweet home until we get to Earth."

Another woman in the same row said, "You aren't scared, are you?"

"Yes, she is," said a girl sitting nearby. "She's scared of everything, Mommy Alys."

Jodenny counted four young girls traveling together, all of them blond and fair skinned. Neither Mommy Alys nor Mommy Kate looked like the biological mother, but it was hard to say for sure.

It seemed a shame for such a healthy family to leave Fortune for the debased and ruined Earth, and Jodenny wondered if the mothers were missionaries. She couldn't imagine giving up the clean air of Fortune for the gray ashy skies of Earth, not without a damn good reason.

An old woman sitting behind Jodenny said, "It doesn't look very big."

"Large enough for a hundred crew and twice as many passengers," said the old man with her. "Don't worry. You'll find a drinking buddy or two."

The woman said, "Bastard," but she didn't sound vehement about it.

"Yes, but I'm your bastard, aren't I?" he replied.

Jodenny squeezed her eyes shut. She'd supervised sailors in the middle of divorces, sailors in acrimonious relationships, and it always appalled her how cruel married people could be to each other. She and Myell hadn't even had a serious argument yet, though they'd disagreed about Gayle's experiment, and gone to bed angry—

She should have listened to him, of course. Should have run from Gayle at first sight. Maybe things would be different now. Maybe not.

Thirty-four stations. A minute or two transit between each station. Just over an hour to make a complete loop, but of course they would have to stop for rest and food, and exploration, and who knew what kind of trouble they'd get into on far-flung worlds while they searched for Commander Gold's team.

"Do you trust him?" Fisch had asked, as if that had ever been in doubt. She believed Myell would do what was expected of him, that he would conduct himself with honor and courage, and that he would do everything he could to fulfill his promise to come home.

But the Sphere technology was unknown, Gayle and Nam harbored their own agendas, and the worlds they were visiting might be awash with lava, swept by dust storms, rocked by earthquakes. A thousand things could go wrong, and Myell was all alone. No, of course not, not alone. But solitary and quiet by nature. Uncomplaining. If he got sick or hurt he might not make a fuss, and they might overlook him.

She told herself that he was more than capable of taking care of himself and had been since he was eighteen and a runaway from an abusive home life. Besides, Nam wouldn't be in charge if he weren't at least competent.

Still, her eyes felt suspiciously watery. What kind of example was she setting as a military officer?

But today she was a civilian, and maybe a civilian woman could get a little teary-eyed at the prospect of not knowing where her husband was, what kind of danger he might be in, and if he'd ever return.

"We're here," Farber said, as the birdie docked with a clamping noise. "I won't tell you the trip will go fast, but maybe it won't be as long as you think."

Every minute will be an hour, Jodenny almost said, but that was too melodramatic.

The docking lounge was a long, low compartment that badly needed fresh paint and a carpet cleaning. The green plastic chairs were scratched and dented. Warning vids on the wall listed prohibitions against bringing weapons or alcohol onboard. One by one the passengers had to file through security checkpoints, which Jodenny found annoying. They'd already been screened back on Fortune. Two security techs, both of them sergeants, checked passenger identification and ticket status.

The family with the two mothers and four children were the Frasers. The bickering couple who had been sitting behind Jodenny were an elderly couple named the Zhangs. Jodenny's gaze slid over the other travelers, noting a businessman furiously typing on his gib, two women with government-issue briefcases, and an Aboriginal man wearing a black suit and a white minister's collar. Most seemed patient at the long wait to pass through the checkpoint, though the Fraser children talked eagerly about exploring the ship and the Zhangs were bickering about their cabin.

"It won't be big enough for all those smelly socks you brought," Mrs. Zhang said.

"Or for your extensive shabby wardrobe," Mr. Zhang replied.

"Next," one of the techs said, and Jodenny stepped forward.

"Ellen Spring." Jodenny placed her thumb on an antiquated scanner and stared into a retinal device. Part of her hoped that the ship's database would access Team Space records and flag her true identity, but Captain Fisch's people would have already thought of that wrinkle.

"Occupation, Miss Spring?"

"Librarian," Jodenny replied.

"Business or pleasure trip, miss?"

"Pleasure," she said tightly. "First time."

The sergeant cocked his head, as if something about her features was familiar. Jodenny knew that vids of her had been on the civilian news channels and in the military media outlets. Celebrated survivor of the *Yangtze*, savior of the *Aral Sea*.

Recognize me, say my name, she urged silently.

"Cabin D-25," he said, instead. "Take the lift over there up three decks and follow the signs. Here's your PIC. That's a Passenger Information Card. Keep it with you at all times. It's how you pay for meals and anything else you purchase onboard. If you lose it, you'll have to get a new one."

Jodenny took the card. "Thanks so much."

"Sometime after launch we'll be having a safety drill," he said. "Your lifeboat assignment is on your PIC. Stay calm and follow directions, and you'll be fine. Also be sure to read the emergency information on the hatch in your cabin. That's what we in Team Space call a door."

She almost said, *And you are what we in Team Space call an idiot.*

Jodenny waited for Farber to pass through Security. They took the dim, oily-smelling lift to D-deck. The passageway had four burned-out overhead lights and the signs, once polished, were smeared with fingerprints and grime. Their cabin was a well-worn compartment with two single bunks, two lockers, and a shower unit that leaked into a dark, foul-smelling drain.

"It's moldy," Jodenny said. "Captain probably hasn't conducted an inspection in months."

"Which bed do you want?" Farber asked.

One bunk had a rattling air vent over it, but the other had a vent that was completely blocked. Jodenny preferred the rattle. She shoved her bag of civilian clothes into the locker and said, "There. All unpacked. I'm going to find some coffee."

"I'll come with you," Farber said.

"No," Jodenny replied. "I refuse to have you shadowing my every step for the next two weeks. Captain Fisch gave me direct orders. I may not like them, but I'll follow them. It's bad enough we have to share a cabin. I'm not going to let you control everything I do or everywhere I go. Understand?"

Farber's face flushed. She took a step forward and put her hand flat against the hatch.

"Just so we're clear, Commander, I'm not the one who lied to your husband and then dragged him off into the network. I'm not the one willing to sacrifice everyone and everything to find a control station that may or may not exist. My little girl turns five years old next week. I had to call her and tell her Mommy can't be there for the party we've been planning for a month. The last place I want to be is on this crappy ship babysitting you for the next two weeks. So if I want a cup of coffee, I'm going to get a goddamn cup of coffee."

Jodenny nodded a little. "So you do have some feelings in there. I was wondering about the stoic act."

"Yes," Farber said grimly. "I have feelings."

"Good. Now we know where we stand. Let's get this trip over with."

Farber let her hand fall from the hatch. "The sooner the better. Find us that coffee, Ellen."

CHAPTER THIRTEEN

The *Kamchatka*'s passenger galley was antiquated and dingy, with a dirty brown overhead and several cheerless tables and benches bolted to the deck. Jodenny decided that the Food Service Officer should be ashamed of himself or herself. Couldn't manage a fresh coat of paint or new floor tiles? The crew galley was probably no better, and the ship's wardroom was probably an embarrassment. Jodenny scanned a row of prominently displayed pictures and saw that the Food Officer was a young ensign named Fila Sadiqi. Ensign Sadiqi wore a head scarf and a dour expression, as if she knew exactly how terrible her facilities looked.

A dozen passengers were already in line, food and drinks balanced on gray plastic trays. Steam drifted out from the kitchen, where a tall, red-faced cook was supervising two DNGOs.

"Miserable machines!" he was bellowing. "Can't even boil an egg without blowing a gasket!"

The DNGOs, two old class IIs, spun in midair and made little squeaks.

Jodenny eyed the battered coffee urn dubiously, but siphoned some into a cup and took a cautious sip.

"How bad is it?" Farber asked.

It was easily the best coffee Jodenny had ever had on a Team Space ship. Dark and complex, not too bitter, richly roasted, with a caffeine kick that already delighted her tired brain.

"Like burnt sludge," she told Farber.

Farber moved on, grumbling, to get some tea.

The cold case held a surprising mixture of sushi, fresh wraps, dark green salads, and luscious-looking desserts. Jodenny rapidly reassessed her opinion of Ensign Sadiqi. She grabbed a cucumber roll and sweet-potato chips and went to the self-service checkout. Her PIC card recorded the cost. Two of the older Fraser daughters were using another machine, but a whiny beep-beep-beep indicated that they were having problems.

Ensign Sadiqi herself came out of the kitchen, making a tsk-tsk-tsk sound. She was the shortest officer Jodenny had ever seen, and had probably scraped by the Team Space minimum height requirement.

"Silly machine," she said, scolding it with a wagging finger. "So temperamental. So unhappy."

The Fraser daughters giggled.

Sadiqi fixed whatever problem ailed the scanner and sent the children off on their way. Jodenny, fascinated by the tiny officer, said, "Great coffee."

"Thank you, ma'am," Sadiqi said brightly. "It's a special blend, with very carefully requisitioned beans. Welcome aboard the *Kamchatka*."

Jodenny and Farber ate at one of the bolted-down tables. The Fraser daughters had brought a deck of cards with them and began a game Jodenny didn't recognize. The Zhangs arrived, made disparaging comments about the food, then fell into rapture over helpings of spicy tofu and rice. Other passengers wandered in and out, some of them stopping to socialize, others off to inspect the recreational facilities.

"There's a pool and a gym," Farber said, reading the back of her PIC. "And a library. A bar called the Hole in the Wall that serves crew and passengers."

Jodenny gazed at the countdown vid on the bulkhead. Fourteen hours until the ship left orbit. Another day or so to the Little Alcheringa drop point. Four days in transit. Nothing compared to the months it took freighters on the Big Alcheringa to transit between the Seven Sisters. Once at Earth, they'd discharge cargo and passengers and take on new ones, then make the return trip.

"And this is Ellen Spring," Farber said, jerking Jodenny's attention back to the table.

Farber was talking to a tall, dark-haired lieutenant with bright blue eyes and dimples in his cheeks. "Mark Sweeney," he said, offering a handshake. "Passenger Liaison Officer, among other things. Welcome aboard. First time to Earth?"

"Yes," Farber said. "For both of us."

Sweeney's smile deepened. He folded his arms over his chest, casual and relaxed. "It's an eye-opener. Nothing like terra firma, home sweet home, cradle of humanity. Don't believe anything anyone else says."

Jodenny asked, "What does a Passenger Liaison Officer do?"

"Passenger complaints, duly noted. Passenger compliments, gratefully passed up to Captain Balandra. She'll be leading our happy cruise down the Little A. New to space travel?"

Farber said, "Brand new."

"And you, Miss Spring?" Sweeney's gaze was direct and earnest, and one she recognized. Passenger Liaison Officer in more ways than one. Not that he didn't deserve an active social life, stuck on this milk run back and forth to Earth. Once she might have even been inclined to reciprocate the interest, but those days were long behind her.

She replied, "I've never been on a ship like this before," which was true.

"We've got a tradition here in Team Space, for sailors on their first trip down the Alcheringa. Turns you from a newbie to a welcomed member of the club. Civilians are invited to participate as well. Interested?"

Jodenny knew all about the shellback ceremony. A day of merriment, sticky substances, arcane rituals, good-natured humiliation. As a young ensign she'd participated, and been no worse for the wear. But ever since Myell had been faced with the prospect of chief's initiation, she'd rethought her position on so-called welcoming ceremonies.

"No, thanks." Jodenny picked up her tray. "I'm going to go check out the gym."

"I'll show you where it is," Sweeney volunteered.

"I can find my way."

"It's easy to get turned around on a ship this size."

Jodenny said, "I'll manage. Good day, Lieutenant."

The passenger gym was one deck down. Though the bulkheads were scuffed and the floor mats well worn, the treadmills were modern enough. The adjacent swimming pool was closed for maintenance. Jodenny headed for the library, and found a small compartment with overflowing bookshelves and some comfortable furniture. Not a bad place to hide out if—*when,* she admitted—the cabin she shared with Farber grew too small for comfort.

She ran her finger along the spines of some mystery novels, trying to figure out which ones Myell might like.

In one of the passenger lounges, a friendly game of farkar had taken up the attention of four adults. Business travelers, or maybe investors. An elderly couple with a small black lapdog were watching a movie on the wallscreen. Retirees, maybe, on their way home after many years on Fortune. Two teenagers sitting on a chaise-longue shared a gib back and forth, their gazes shy and brief.

It surprised Jodenny that such a range of people would actually be heading back to Earth, to the debased land, but she didn't dwell on it.

Instead she went back to cabin D-25 and started counting the hours until launch.

At T-minus-two hours, the overhead comm clicked to life.

"This is your captain speaking," a woman said. She sounded confident and assured, utterly in charge. "I regret to inform you we've had an engineering delay. Launch countdown is on hold. Enjoy your evening, and I'll be back to give you an update come morning."

Lying on her bunk, Farber said, "That doesn't sound good."

"It's not," Jodenny replied, from where she'd been doing sit-ups and push-ups on the deck.

Farber sighed and went back to reading her gib.

"Don't you think you should check in with your department? In case Commander Nam's team has returned already?" Jodenny asked.

"I called them after dinner. There was no word."

Nam's team had been gone long enough to go all the way around the Bainbridge loop if both the network and Blue-Q gel were working properly. Obviously something—illness, accident, discovery of the missing team—had prompted them to step off the loop.

Jodenny showered, brushed out her hair, and put on a jersey and slacks.

"Going somewhere?" Farber asked.

"You said there was a bar. I'm on a reconnaissance mission."

The decor of the Hole in the Wall was no better than anywhere else on the ship, and the dark interior felt more claustrophobic than anything else, but the beer was cold enough. Jodenny sat at the long plastic bar and eyed some off-duty crew. Admin types, not engineering. Some passengers were conferring around the dartboards, and others were playing eight ball.

"Think we'll be launching come morning?" she asked the bartender, a stocky civilian with a bristly red beard.

He had his gaze on an overhead, where a soccer game was under way. "Doubt it."

"Engines break down a lot?"

"Pieces of shit that Team Space won't upgrade. This is no ship to be on if you're in a hurry."

Jodenny nursed a growing resentment. Longer they dallied in orbit, longer the trip would take, longer she would suffer not knowing where Myell was, how he was faring.

Two sailors passed behind her, giggling, in love, and one accidentally jostled Jodenny's arm.

"Sorry," the male sailor said. His eyes widened. "Miz Scott, it's you!"

Jodenny recognized AT Putty Romero at once. With him was AT Tingley. Myell's students at Supply School. She slid off her stool, her back to the bartender, and steered the two young sailors toward a private booth that smelled like faux leather.

"So nice to see you again," she said, with forced cheer, until she got them seated. "Listen. I'm not me. I'm assigned here under a different name, understand? You can't call me Commander or ma'am. That's a direct order. As far as you know, I'm a civilian named Ellen Spring."

"Why, ma'am?" Tingley asked, her voice as soft as ever.

"Long story. And don't call me *ma'am*. What are you two doing here? Shouldn't you still be in school?"

"We graduated," Romero said. "Big ceremony, all the brass were there. And look! We got married."

He held up his ring finger. Tingley held up hers as well, her face bright. Gold knots gleamed in the bar's low light.

"We thought it would be easier to get a cabin together," she said. "But we didn't even get one! Everyone below the rank of E-5 sleeps in open bay. It's not very nice."

Open-bay berthing had been abolished on the Big Alcheringa, but the *Kamchatka* was old and Team Space probably didn't want to pay for a retrofit.

"It doesn't matter," Tingley said. "This is our honeymoon, either way."

Jodenny had seen too many impulsive marriages on ships, too many young people who didn't think things through before they legally entangled their fortunes. She wasn't going to think much about her own honeymoon brochures still sitting at home in Adeline Oaks.

"Chief Myell didn't make it to the ceremony," Romero said. "Is he okay? I know what they did to him at the gym."

"What did they do?" Jodenny asked.

Her tone of voice made Romero look uneasy. "You know, taking his stuff. Trying to hassle him for not going to chief's initiation. Everyone knows that's why Captain Kuvik gave him the jobs no one else wanted."

Funny how Myell hadn't mentioned that part.

"And then that fistfight—" Tingley started, then fell silent.

It took some persuasion on Jodenny's part, but soon she had the story of the fistfight, the locker-room theft, and, even worse, the rumors of an assault in the basement. Neither Tingley nor Romero was clear on what exactly had happened, but most people blamed Chief Talic for some kind of prank.

"He kept denying he had anything to do with it," Romero reported. "Maybe, maybe not. He's kind of old-fashioned. You didn't know, did you?"

"Sorry," Tingley said, sympathetically.

Jodenny didn't want sympathy. It wasn't their fault if her very own husband neglected to tell her crucial details of his day. She wished she could reach through the nearest ouroboros and shake him by the shoulders for being so secretive.

I didn't want to worry you, he would say, as if that excuse meant anything.

Abruptly she rose. "Congratulations on your wedding," she said. "But remember, this isn't your honeymoon, it's your first duty assignment. Duty first, personal lives second, right?"

"Yes, ma'am," Romero said.

Tingley nodded earnestly.

Jodenny went back to the cabin and stayed awake, staring up at the rattling fan, for most of the night.

At oh-seven-hundred the comm clicked. A man's cheerful voice said,

"Wakey wakey. All hands rouse out. Morning has commenced. Today's weather will be sunny and dry. Beach attire is authorized for those lazing about the pool. Crew members to duty stations, and passengers are reminded to eat a healthy breakfast. Launch countdown is now T-minus-two hours and counting. Thank you and have a nice day."

"What the hell was that?" Farber asked, and switched on the cabin's overhead light.

Jodenny used her arm to shield her gritty eyes. "Morning call. A tradition that's been thankfully abandoned on the Big Alcheringa."

"Every morning he's going to do that?"

"Every morning."

Farber muttered something unintelligible and locked herself in the head.

They were about to go to breakfast when Teddy Toledo came by, carrying a rucksack and wearing a chief's uniform. Jodenny stared at the patches and ribbons he'd appropriated to decorate it. She supposed he looked the part, with his short hair and overall fitness, but the idea of him impersonating a chief made her unaccountably itchy.

"Brought you what you wanted from your house," Toledo said, unmindful of her stare. He put the sack on her bed. "Think I got everything. Oh, and something else."

The sack moved on the bed. Karl the Koala poked his head out and made a faint mewling noise.

"How cute," Farber said dryly.

Jodenny scooped Karl up and let him cuddle in her arms. He smelled like clean bedsheets and eucalypt leaves. "You should have left him at home."

"It was pretty insistent," Toledo said.

"Scratch belly," Karl said, and tugged on Jodenny's shirt.

Farber asked, "Why the launch delay?"

"Valve problems," Toledo said. "Apparently nothing new around these parts. Word is, Team Space squeezes as much profit as it can out of the Fortune-to-Earth run, keeping what they make on cargo and passengers and putting as little as possible back into maintenance."

Farber blanched. "That makes me feel safe."

"Ship's safe enough, just not very pretty," Toledo said. "Captain Balandra has a good reputation with the crew. Chief's wardroom's happy enough. Should be a fast trip to Earth and back."

"Once we actually get going," Jodenny reminded him.

Breakfast was an excellent buffet of pancakes, waffles, fruit dishes, and omelets. Afterward all passengers were asked to return to quarters for launch. Farber gripped her chair with both hands during the countdown.

"Have you *ever* been in space before?" Jodenny asked her.

"Not so much," Farber said.

Three, two, one. The transition out of orbit was a little rockier than Jodenny expected, but still a marked improvement over doing nothing at all. She vidded a picture of Fortune and felt stomach pangs as it retreated into the distance. Down there somewhere was Bainbridge, and a Mother Sphere that held the key to Myell's return.

"You better be here when I get back," she murmured.

She switched off the vid and let the screen stay dark.

It took about an hour for Farber to get violently spacesick. One of the ship's medical assistants swung by with some medication. He said, "No worries. Happens a lot around here. Good thing we've got gravity, eh? Otherwise the vomit would—"

"Yes, thank you," Jodenny said.

"I'm never going into space again," Farber said as she lurched off toward the head.

Jodenny grabbed her exercise clothes and left Farber to her misery. On the way to the gym she passed the passenger lounge, which was crowded with the Fraser family, the bickering Zhangs, and the business travelers with their farkar game. After five kilometers on the treadmill, she showered off, grabbed lunch from a vending machine, and sought out the library. The deskgib there had a connection back to Fortune. She was still able to access the Supply School's public site and read the profiles on Captain Kuvik and Senior Chief Talic.

Kuvik had an impressive biography and a stern, commanding photo. Talic's record wasn't as impressive, but he had made ten Alcheringa runs and been awarded three commendation medals.

Bastard, she thought, just as the gib fizzled out and died. She tried the power button and thumped its edges, to no avail. When she pulled out the unit to check the connections, someone behind her said, "You could get electrocuted doing that."

The speaker was a kid about twelve years old, with long brown hair framing his thin, frowning face. He was short and skinny, all elbows and knees, and he was wearing long brown shorts that had black stains on them.

"I won't electrocute myself," Jodenny said. "There's a built-in safety."

"Safeties fail." He scratched his nose. "You should put in a maintenance request instead of rip apart the console."

"I'm not ripping it apart. Who are you?"

"Malachy. Who are you?"

"Ellen." Jodenny slid the gib back into place and tried the interface again. "See? I fixed it."

"It'll just break again. Nothing on this ship stays fixed for long."

He said it with an unhappiness that spoke of long experience. Jodenny asked, "You're sure?"

"My mom's assigned here. I make this trip a lot."

Jodenny was accustomed to crew having families on the Big Alcheringa, where a full loop took a minimum of nine months. She'd thought the short runs to Earth would enable more people to leave their spouses and kids behind.

She turned to the gib, hoping he would go away. He lingered by a bookcase, chewing on a hangnail.

"I have some work to do," she said.

Malachy asked, "Are you a technician? Most civilians don't know how to fix gibs."

Jodenny replied, "I'm only a passenger. With work to do."

He continued to linger. Jodenny decided he was probably a lonely kid, no one to play with, neglected by his mom. Socially inept. Not athletic. Some caring adult maybe needed to take him in under their wing, but that caring adult would have to be someone else.

"You could work in your cabin," he said. "Unless you didn't want your roommate to see what you were doing."

"You could work in yours and stop bothering me," she retorted, and after a moment he went away.

She concentrated on the gib for a full moment before her guilty conscience nudged her out of her seat. She found Malachy sitting at a corner table, meticulously drawing on a tablet. He was using his right hand to shape images and his left to manipulate color, texture, and pattern.

Jodenny said, "That's beautiful."

He didn't turn from the tablet. "I'm working."

She sat down at the table. "I'm sorry. I was rude."

The corner of his mouth turned up in an unhappy little quirk. "People usually are, when they first meet me. I get on their nerves. Then they meet my mom, and they're all nice again."

"Why is that?"

"She's the captain."

Malachy Balandra. Well, then.

Jodenny said, "I'm still sorry, and that has nothing to do with your mom. This trip is making me a little unhappy."

"You don't want to see Earth?"

"It's a little more complicated than that." Jodenny eyed the drawing. "Is that a dinosaur?"

"No."

"Some other kind of reptile?"

"It's a Komodo dragon." He eyed her crookedly, came to some kind of internal decision, and slid closer to her chair with the tablet in tow. His knee bumped against hers. "They're extinct on Earth, but you can find them in the Seven Sisters."

"Are you a naturalist?"

To her surprise, he pulled the tablet back. "No. I like science."

Jodenny wasn't sure what he meant, but before she could ask he said, "I have to check in with my mom," and dashed off with the tablet in his arms.

She returned to her side of the library, mulling over Kuvik and Talic again, wondering if she could persuade Myell to file a complaint against Supply School when he returned. Part of her wondered if Captain Fisch's group hadn't encouraged some kind of harassment to make Myell more amenable to the Sphere project. She typed up notes on what Tingley and Romero had said, then put a password on the text and tried assigning it to her passenger account. The gib asked for her PIC, but Jodenny couldn't immediately find it.

She patted her pockets. She'd used the card to access the gym and the library. It had been poking her hip while she was fixing the gib. Jodenny checked under the table, traced her route to Malachy's table, and inspected under the chairs there.

She remembered him pulling his chair closer, the almost imperceptible brush of their knees touching.

The little bastard had stolen her card. Captain Balandra's son was a thief.

Space was limited on the *Kamchatka,* and officers and chiefs worked out of their cabins. Jodenny tracked down Lieutenant Sweeney in officers' berthing. His hatch was open, and he was sitting at a desk covered with paperwork.

"Miss Spring," he said, pushing it aside. "Delighted to see you. Enjoying your trip?"

"I need a new PIC," she said. "The quartermaster said I had to get you to authorize it."

"Bureaucracy, rules, regulations. Have a seat."

Jodenny preferred to remain standing rather than sit on his bunk. "No, thanks. I've been sitting all day."

"Tell me about it." He reached for a form. "If it's any consolation at all, you're my second customer today. Those little cards are easy to lose."

"I didn't lose mine. It was stolen."

His smile faded a little. "Really? You're sure?"

"I had it one moment, and a few minutes later it was gone."

"They're easy to drop."

"Mine disappeared after I met a boy who said he was Captain Balandra's son."

Sweeney bent over his form and filled it in with a pen. "Malachy's a great kid. Did he show you his artwork?"

"He did," she said, and waited.

Sweeney checked off a small black box and initialed a line of text. The air vents in his cabin didn't rattle, but they made a high-pitched whine that was almost, but not quite, too faint to hear. The second locker had an ensign's nametag on it, and the desk was precisely arranged.

"Here you go," Sweeney said. "Take this back to the quartermaster. Any suspicious charges show up on your account, just let me know."

"Are you going to tell the captain, or shall I?"

Two ensigns passing by outside cast curious glances into the cabin. Sweeney scratched the side of his head, pursed his lips for a moment, and closed the hatch.

"Malachy Balandra is a mixed-up kid with a mom who's trying her best," he said. "There's nothing you can tell her about him that she doesn't know already. If you want a direct apology from her—"

"Not from her," Jodenny said. "From him."

Sweeney gave her an intent look. "You're a librarian, right? You must deal with kids all the time."

"Did you read up on my passenger info, Lieutenant?"

He blushed. "I check everyone's."

Jodenny doubted that. "Kids who screw up aren't going to stop screwing up if you coddle them."

Sweeney leaned back against his locker. "Let me guess. You got in trouble as a kid yourself. Then you found a role model and straightened up and became a better person."

She arched her eyebrows. "Is that your official Team Space response?"

"I'll talk to the captain," he said. "Malachy's going to deny it, like he has every other time. She'll apologize, and worry some more about him. You'll disembark at Earth and go about your business, and never think of us again. Would you like to have dinner with me?"

"No," Jodenny said, opening the hatch. "I'm committed to someone else."

"No wedding ring."

It hung on a silver chain around her neck, tucked deep inside her shirt. Jodenny said, "Don't need a ring," and left him with that.

She was halfway to the quartermaster's when she realized what he had said.

"When are we coming back?" she demanded of Farber when she reached their cabin.

Farber was lying in her bunk, still pasty-faced and miserable. "What?"

"We're not booked for the return trip on this ship, are we? Lieutenant Sweeney thinks we're getting off at Earth. Captain Fisch promised me two weeks, no more—"

"Relax." Farber fumbled for her vomit bag. "We have seats on the *Yellowstone*. It's a bigger liner, scheduled to return sooner than the *Kamchatka*. Don't you think you could trust me a little bit?"

With that, Farber threw up. Karl made a squeaking noise and burrowed under Jodenny's blankets in distress. Jodenny fetched Farber a glass of water and said, "You want to see the doctor again?"

Farber said, "No. I just want to die here in privacy."

Jodenny took that as permission to leave.

On second thought, she took Karl with her.

Everyone loved Karl.

"Oh, how cute," the Fraser daughters cooed when Jodenny visited the passenger lounge. They each wanted to hold him and cuddle him and stroke his fine golden fur. They cried, "Moms! Can't we get one?"

Mommy Alys was a bit reserved on the idea, but Mommy Kate promised to think about it. "Where did you get it?" she asked Jodenny.

Jodenny replied, "He was a gift."

"All you ever give me are lice," Mrs. Zhang said, pinching her husband's arm.

"What more do you deserve?" he asked, rubbing the spot.

The lounge was a long rectangular compartment with several sofas, wallvids, game consoles, card tables, and even an old-fashioned pool table. Malachy Balandra was playing Izim. He slunk out the door before she could confront him. She thought about following him, but he was fast on his feet, and knew the ship a whole lot better than she did.

"That's the captain's son," Mommy Kate said, following her gaze. "Seems like a good kid."

"Seems like," Jodenny agreed blandly.

Sitting at the farkar table were the four business travelers Jodenny recognized from the night before. They introduced themselves as Lou Eterno, Louise Sharp, Baylou Owenstein, and Greg Smith, who said, "I get to be an honorary Lou. Hullabaloo, to be exact."

"Join us in a game and you could be another honorary Lou," Baylou said. "You can be Lu-lu."

"No, thanks," Jodenny said.

But a short time later Lou Eterno excused himself to go read, and three remaining Lous recruited Jodenny to play a game of pool.

Jodenny eyed the table. "I don't know the rules."

"Neither do we." Louise Sharp raised a glass of beer. She was a tall woman with magenta hair and dangling gold earrings. "Hit things into pockets. That's our plan."

Hullabaloo said, "Be my partner. I'll show you how to do it."

"What are we playing for?"

"Jellybeans," Louise said. "The high stakes chocolate-bar wager comes later."

Jodenny sized up a pool stick, rubbed the end dutifully with chalk, and followed Hullabaloo's friendly instructions. Her aim was okay, but twice she hit the cue ball so hard that it jumped off the table.

"Got a little pent-up frustration there?" Louise asked, not unkindly. "Hullabaloo, go get the girl a drink."

"I'm fine," Jodenny said.

Two hours and three beers later, she and Hullabaloo had lost all their jellybeans. Hullabaloo didn't seem to mind. He was her age, maybe younger, with a smile aimed most of the time at Baylou, who seemed to enjoy the attention. Karl was busy napping on the sofa in the lap of the youngest Fraser daughter, who was watching a movie.

"Thanks for bringing him," Mommy Alys said. She'd been watching the game from a nearby stool. "We promised the girls a dog when we get to Earth."

"You're not going on vacation?" Jodenny asked.

Mommy Kate, curled up in a corner chair with a book, said, "Moving."

"Permanently?" Jodenny didn't mean to sound so surprised, but debased Earth hardly seemed fit for a young family. Then again, it didn't seem like a suitable vacation spot, either.

"As long as they'll have us," Mommy Alys said, and dropped a sweater atop the sleeping child.

The overhead comm clicked, and an emergency klaxon began to wail. Jodenny's fist tightened on the pool stick so hard that she was surprised it didn't snap in two.

"Attention, all passengers and crew," Captain Balandra said. "This is a emergency evacuation drill. Please consult your passenger information cards or the nearest crew member and report to your evacuation pods. I repeat, this is a drill, but your participation is mandatory."

"Bloody rules," Louise Sharp said, downing the rest of her drink.

Jodenny had forgotten the mandatory drill. Her PIC directed her to C-deck, pod 7. Not a far distance at all. The Frasers were also heading that way, as was Hullabaloo. Sailors stood by at every lift and ladder to direct traffic. It was all very orderly and calm, and the gray-green emergency pod was well outfitted with survival gear and medbots.

The officer in charge, a portly man named Chief Reed, made sure all twenty occupants were belted in and understood their responsibilities in case of a true emergency.

"This part of the pod is my area," he said. "Passengers aren't allowed to touch it. We're fully automated, no steering wheel or navigation controls, but through this console I can talk to our onboard computer, and the computers aboard the *Kamchatka*, and communicate planetside."

"Have you ever had to launch?" one of the Fraser girls asked.

Chief Reed patted her head. "Never, my dear. No emergencies are allowed around here. This ship has the best safety record in the fleet."

Jodenny kept her gaze on the bulkhead and bit her lip. She knew what it was like to hear General Quarters klaxon for real, to smell burning flesh and fuel, to feel her lungs sear and heart trip-hammer in terror. But she was past that now. She was calm and collected.

"Ellen?" said Hullabaloo, from beside her. "You're going to break my arm."

She realized that the armrest she'd been using was human, not plastic. "Sorry."

"I've made this trip a dozen times. Trust me. They just do this because regulations say so."

The drill lasted thirty minutes. Afterward, the Frasers asked Jodenny to join them for dinner. All she wanted was to crawl off to her cabin and recuperate. First she had to collect Karl from the lounge, where she'd left him curled up in the sofa cushions. But the little robot wasn't there. Jodenny searched under all the furniture and behind the vending machines. She remembered Malachy Balandra lingering earlier. The little weasel. She went up to senior-officer berthing on B-deck. A sign warned that the area was off-limits to passengers, but the captain's cabin wasn't hard to find.

She buzzed the hatch, and Malachy answered with Karl in his arms.

"What do you think you're doing?" Jodenny demanded.

"He was in the passageway!" Malachy protested. "I saved him from being stomped or getting lost."

"Who is it, Mal?" asked a woman's voice from inside.

Malachy opened the hatch wider. Captain Balandra was standing in the middle of the suite, signing off a gib held by a young ensign. Balandra was tall, sturdy, and olive skinned, with a sweetheart-shaped face and neatly coiled dark hair.

"This is the bot's mom," Malachy said, handing Karl over.

"Such a cute pet," Balandra said pleasantly. "Now I'm going to have to get him one when we return to Fortune. Miss Spring, is it?"

"Ellen Spring, ma'am," Jodenny said.

"Enjoying your trip so far?"

Karl nuzzled against Jodenny's neck. She said, "It's been educational."

Captain Balandra laughed. "I'll take that in a positive way. Mal tells me you were able to fix one of our library gibs. I'd like to say our Maintenance Department would have been right on that, but thanks for taking the initiative." To the ensign she said, "That's all, Mr. Ingstrom. Back to the bridge for you."

"Ma'am," Ingstrom said, and edged past Jodenny.

Balandra gazed frankly at Jodenny. "Know you, don't I? Your face is awfully familiar."

"I get that a lot," Jodenny said.

Malachy tilted his head, as if memorizing her features.

"I'm having some passengers over later to enjoy the drop into the Little Alcheringa," Balandra said. "Can I interest you in some wine and cheese, at around twenty-one hundred hours?"

Farber would be irate if Jodenny took up the captain's invitation. For that, if no other reason, the offer was tempting. But Jodenny said, "Sorry, I have another commitment."

"Maybe dinner some evening, before we reach Earth?"

"Maybe," Jodenny said. "Thanks for watching Karl. Good evening, Captain."

She intended to experience the shift from normal space into the Little Alcheringa from the safety of her cabin, but Hullabaloo and Baylou came by and nagged her into coming down to the Hole in the Wall. Passengers and crew alike had crowded into the bar, shouting to be heard over the music. Dancers bumped and gyrated on the dance floor and beer sloshed freely over the rims of glasses everywhere.

"Bit frantic about it, aren't they?" Hullabaloo asked. "Trying too hard to be merry."

"What do you mean?"

Baylou said, "Didn't you hear about that ship? The one that blew up off Kookaburra when it tried to enter the Big A? It was in the news last month."

Jodenny took a steadying gulp of beer and said, "Thought that was separatists. You know. The Colonial Freedom Project."

"That's what they want you to think," Baylou said.

Hullabaloo said, "Don't listen to him. He's a little nervous himself."

"Nothing's going to go wrong," Jodenny said.

The wallvids were programmed to show Fortune's system. Fortune was still visible, but only as a small blue and green orb. She thought about her little house in Adeline Oaks, and about Myell out there somewhere in the network, and about all the *Yangtze's* dead, and raised her glass.

A countdown appeared on the overhead, bright white letters on a sea of blue. The crowd took up the chant.

"Ten . . . nine . . . eight . . ."

They were all shouting now, good-natured, maybe a little frightened, but Jodenny was suddenly happy to be with them and not locked up with Farber in the cabin. Most of this group had long forgotten their school lessons about Jackie MacBride, the first captain to pilot a ship along the Little Alcheringa. But Jodenny raised a glass and made a second toast to Jackie and her crew, lost astronauts from Earth who'd changed the course of humanity with their discovery.

"Just like New Year's Eve," Hullabaloo said, eyes glittering.

"So kiss me, you fool," Baylou said.

Jodenny saw Ensign Fila Sadiqi in the crowd, her long hair streaming down her shoulders as she danced in the arms of the galley cook. AT Romero and AT Tingley were perched on stools at the bar, their arms wrapped around each other.

". . . three, two, one!"

The ship shifted, ever so slightly. The wallvid went blank, as expected. No stars shone in the Alcheringa. The crowd cheered and kissed and Jodenny sighed in happy relief. The beer in her glass went down smooth and cold, and she turned to order another.

Then the *Kamchatka's* engines shuddered and failed, and the entire ship plunged into darkness.

The Aboriginal warriors spent the night talking and singing around a campfire at the edge of the petroglyph cave. Myell couldn't understand a word of their quick language, but he very much appreciated the dinner they provided—soft chewy tubers and little brown things he couldn't quite identify.

"Baked grubs," Nam said.

Myell wasn't very hungry after that.

Gayle spent hours trying to communicate. "Gayle," she said, laying her hand flat on her chest. "I'm Anna Gayle. My name is Anna Gayle."

The natives laughed at her efforts and poked at her fair skin and blond hair. Nam watched carefully, tensely. Maybe waiting to see if things would get out of hand. Myell didn't think the Aboriginals posed any risk to Gayle's virtue, but he kept watch as well.

Shark Tooth was fond of his drawing on the floor, and referred to it several times during the evening. Nam said, "He must have seen the lightning hit you."

Myell squeezed the bridge of his nose. "I wasn't hit by lightning."

The rain continued overnight. Myell spent a restless night listening to the Aboriginals snore. Two of Shark Tooth's men kept watch, preventing any attempts at escape. Come morning, Shark Tooth led the way out of the cave and up the gully. Already the landscape was changing, turning green. They walked toward the morning sun blistering in the eastern sky.

Nam said, "You wanted to meet the locals, Dr. Gayle. I guess you're going to get your chance."

Shark Tooth's men began to sing as they walked. After several hours the plateau transitioned to a lush rain forest of tree roots that entangled their feet, mud that sucked at their legs, rot and moss everywhere, nettle plants that Shark Tooth's men beat back with sticks. For hours they continued east with no breaks for food or rest.

"How far are we going to go?" Myell asked.

Nam said, "As far as they take us."

Bright birds fluttered in the canopy of leaves overhead. Myell wished he were a bird, light and quick, so that he could fly back to the Spheres and end this misadventure. Jodenny would love to be part of such a momentous occasion, this meeting of civilizations. But even she might find the heat and pace daunting, the prospects ahead a little frightening.

"We should have tried to escape when we could," Nam said, swatting aside an oversize palm frond.

Come midafternoon, the rain forest abruptly gave way to ancient brown cliffs and the most terrifying view of an ocean Myell had ever seen. His legs froze up. All he could see was unlimited blue, the rising and falling water that stretched from a rounded bay and reached to forever. Salt water, billions of liters of it, heaving and frothing—

Nam's hand closed on Myell's arm. "You'd better walk over here," he said, and blocked the view with his own body.

But not seeing the ocean made things even worse, because Myell could still hear it smashing on the rocks and spires and smell the salt and rot.

"Chief." Nam slapped his cheeks lightly. "Stay with me, here."

Gayle and the Aboriginals were walking north along the cliff line. Shark Tooth turned back to investigate the delay. Myell tried to suck in a steadying breath but his throat was too tight, his chest an aching block of frozen muscle.

Nam forced his chin up with the tip of his finger. "There's no ocean over there. You hear me? No ocean at all."

"There's a *huge* fucking ocean there, sir," Myell managed to say.

"I'm your commanding officer, and I say there's not. So move your ass, Chief. This nature hike isn't over yet."

Myell managed to take one small step, then another. It helped that Nam's grip was still tight on his arm, and that there were plenty of dusty feet around to concentrate on. By the time Myell felt ready to walk on his own they were at a village set back a hundred meters from the cliff's edge. The salty smell was still prevalent, but now mixed with pine and smoke and burning meat and the sweat of unwashed bodies.

The village itself consisted of thirty or so leaf-thatched homes sharing gardens and pigpens. Naked children ran freely about, laughing and shouting. Adults wearing slightly more clothing rose from their chores and closed in on the returning group. Myell lost sight of Nam. Voices jabbered at him and fingers poked his white skin.

"Commander!" he yelled out, panicking.

"Stay calm!" Nam shouted back from somewhere behind him. "They're not going to hurt you!"

Easier to hear than believe. Easier to start swatting people away than stay still and endure. Hands pinched and probed, and bodies pressed close. He was going to drown in an ocean of people. Then Shark Tooth intervened with a bellow, brandishing his spear until the villagers pulled back. The next pair of hands that grabbed him belonged to Nam.

"They do love you." Nam glared at the crowd. "What's your secret allure?"

"I don't know." Myell tried to catch his breath, but he was shaking too hard.

Shark Tooth ushered them to an open-air structure where a palm-frond roof rose over the beaten sand of the floor. In the center was a squared-off area protected by large, rough stones and fallen logs. A stream of bare-breasted women with feathers in their hair brought food and other offerings—mango fruits, dried fish, small woven baskets, gourds of fresh water, totems carved from wood.

"We're honored visitors," Gayle said.

"Some of us more honored than others, maybe," Nam said.

Gayle tried to talk to their captors. Nam watched but didn't participate. Myell stretched against one of the logs, glad for the fresh breeze and the dimness under the thatched roof. His legs ached from the long march and a little rest seemed like a good idea. After a few minutes he opened his eyes. Darkness had come on. A large bonfire blazed in the sand far from the buildings.

"No dinner yet," Nam said. "If these are my ancestors, they need some hospitality training."

Myell rubbed the back of his head. "That almost sounded like a joke, sir."

Nam said, "Don't get used to it."

"Where's Dr. Gayle?"

"They took her."

He sat up. "You didn't stop them?"

"She wanted to go," Nam said grimly. "Thinks she can communicate with them, heaven help us."

Six of the native women approached, shy and giggling. They carried basins of water and roughly woven towels.

"Washing-up committee." Nam's hands clenched. "I hope this isn't the part where we get prepared for the ritual sacrifice."

The cleansing consisted of having their feet and hands washed, rubbed with oil, and decorated with ocher. The thick, swirly designs made Myell's skin itch. After the washing, they were escorted out to the bonfire. Dozens of logs blazed upward from a tall pyre. Ten or so old men and women had arranged themselves in a semicircle nearby.

Gayle was sitting on her haunches in the sand before the elders. White feathers had been tied to her hair and multiple strings of seashells hung around her neck.

"Been making friends?" Nam asked.

"Been trying," Gayle said, her eyes on the oldest of the male elders. "I think he's their chief. The others defer to him."

Shark Tooth approached and crouched before Chief Elder, who put a hand on his head. The villagers around the fire, sixty or seventy men and women and children, observed in silence. Gayle climbed to her feet. The only sounds now were the wind and the crackle of flames, the distant roar of the ocean, and the occasional cry of a baby who could not be hushed.

Chief Elder spoke a long monologue of syllables that shifted and climbed over one another. Shark Tooth turned and motioned for Myell to step forward.

"Do as they say, Chief," Gayle cautioned. "Everything."

"I thought we didn't know what they were saying," Nam said.

Myell was presented to Chief Elder with a flurry of words. Shark Tooth's arms and hands made great sweeping motions from the sky as he spoke. He imitated thunder and then fell wildly, as if struck by lightning. The crowd murmured in appreciation, and Chief Elder gave Myell a speculative look.

Shark Tooth stood up. While he brushed dirt off himself, a tall figure moved through the parting crowd. It wore a silver helmet over its head, and a long white feathered cloak swirled downward from its broad shoulders.

A Bunyip.

"Christ," Nam said.

The alien's skin was scaly, its black eyes narrow. It opened its jaw to reveal rows of razor-sharp teeth. The villagers murmured in appreciation. The Bunyip didn't seemed interested in Nam, but it stared at Myell. The clawed knuckles and scaly fingers flexed widely, their points dark with mud or blood.

"Their god," Gayle said. "You've challenged him by surviving that lightning strike."

"That's terrific," Myell said.

Nam said, "Stay calm."

Gayle continued, "The locals aren't afraid of it. It may have been here a long time. On the other hand, we're total strangers. They could kill us if we're perceived as a threat."

The Bunyip turned to Chief Elder and spoke. Its chirps and cries were translated into the local language through a silvery box hanging around its waist. Chief Elder replied, his voice rich and loud. After more exchange, a young boy brought forward a cage of leaf fronds. Shark Tooth extracted a small green gecko and let it dangle by its tail.

Gayle said, "Small reptiles often symbolize evil. They'll want you to vanquish it."

"Vanquish how?" Myell asked.

Shark Tooth handed the squirming gecko to Myell. Its legs and forearms scrabbled frantically in midair.

Shark Tooth gestured toward Myell's mouth and spoke several words.

Gayle said, "They want you to eat it."

Myell thrust the gecko back toward Shark Tooth. "Absolutely not."

Gayle came to his side and rested her hand on his forearm. Her voice was low. "Chief Myell. Swallowing it will demonstrate to the villagers your strength and courage. It'll raise you up in their eyes. Elevate all of us."

"No," Myell said.

Her expression sharpened. "If you don't, you could be endangering us all," she insisted. "Commander?"

Nam hadn't taken his eyes off the alien. "I suggest you open wide, Chief."

Myell held the gecko higher. He remembered Koo, the gecko that briefly had been his companion on the *Aral Sea*. She had enjoyed darting around the terrarium on his desk with her head held high and her tail curled up. Rumor had it that inductees in chief's initiation were made to swallow goldfish. A gecko, its arms and legs and tail scrabbling for purchase, would be a lot more difficult.

But he could do it, if he needed to.

If he wanted to.

The gecko totems in his dilly bag weighed heavily against his skin, so warm they nearly burned.

"No." Myell dropped the creature to the sand. The gecko darted toward the trees and disappeared within seconds.

The crowd hissed at him, their tongues between their teeth. Gayle said, "You shouldn't have done that, Chief," and Nam made a disapproving sound.

"I won't do it," Myell told Shark Tooth.

The boy with the basket produced a second gecko, and Shark Tooth handed it by the tail to the Bunyip. The Bunyip swept it high into the air and dangled it over its cavernous mouth. The crowd murmured in anticipation. Myell's stomach twisted.

The gecko dropped into the Bunyip's mouth.

The crowd cheered.

The Bunyip held one clawed hand high in triumph.

"If that was the first test," Gayle said, "you failed."

Chief Elder spoke again. Shark Tooth smiled and repeated the instructions. The Bunyip bowed its head and began stripping off its helmet, cloak, and boots. Myell watched dumbly until Shark Tooth poked his arm and tugged at his clothes.

"Oh, come on," he protested. "Naked?"

"We won't look," Nam promised.

He told himself that stripping bare in this seaside village in front of total strangers wasn't so bad. No worse, surely, than the communal showers in Team Space barracks. But he could feel the hotness in his face as he left his uniform, boots, and underwear in the sand. A quick glance at the Bunyip proved that it too had external genitalia. Myell didn't want to know more than that.

Shark Tooth motioned to two young girls, who brought forth more ocher. Additional designs were painted on his back and stomach. He stood still, trying to ignore their close presence and bare breasts and the tickle of their fingers. He took several deep breaths and thought about supply regulations. About Senior Chief Talic's sequencing lecture. The bonfire was a blaze of heat and light in the corner of his vision.

"How you doing there, Chief?" Nam asked.

"Fine, sir."

After the body painting was done, Shark Tooth led Myell and the Bunyip to an enormous tree that towered over the clearing. The trunk was smooth wood with thick knobs and dozens of branches. The branches arced off in crazy curves, heavy with fronds and vines. Myell could hear birds or small animals moving in its dark depths—snakes, maybe, or owls, or even monkeys. He tilted his head back and saw a few stars through the thick cover.

Shark Tooth spoke and motioned.

The Bunyip grabbed the lowest branch and started climbing.

"Good thing you're not afraid of heights," Nam said.

Myell swore under his breath. Eating geckos. Stripped naked. And now he was supposed to climb a tree, bare-assed without even a flashlight?

"I want hazard pay," Myell told Nam. He reached up for the branch and hoisted himself up. "A lot of it."

The climbing wasn't hard, actually. The branches were closely spaced and thick enough to support his weight. The darkness hampered him, though, and the ropy vines were slippery. The Bunyip, already a few meters above him, didn't seem to be having the same problems. It climbed swiftly, making clicking noises as its claws dug into the wood. If this contest depended on being the swiftest, Myell was probably going to lose.

Without warning the Bunyip made a grunting noise and stopped. Myell immediately halted. He peered upward but couldn't see much. He shifted against the trunk and brushed his right hand across a large, leathery frond. Almost immediately his skin began to burn as if seared by drops of acid.

"Jesus," he muttered. A stinging tree. Jodenny had been victim to a stinging bush during their trip out of Warramala. In the starlight his palm was already turning pink. He jammed his hand under his left armpit, but the burning eased only a little.

The Bunyip made another noise and began climbing again. Myell followed, being extraordinarily careful not to touch anything but the bark. As the fronds grew thicker and closer he had to shimmy his bare shoulders sideways, or pull his long legs close. Despite the cool air, sweat broke out on his back and neck. Far down below he could see Shark Tooth holding up a burning torch. Red light playing off Nam's concerned face.

"How's it going?" Nam shouted up.

"I hate this tree." He didn't actually mean it. Then, suddenly, he did. The tree seemed alive—not in the botanical sense, but instead as a sentient, menacing being that didn't want supply chiefs climbing its branches. Animosity rolled out of it in waves like tiny gnats. The muddy green smell of it intensified, became acrid. The vines writhed in an unnatural breeze. Myell hoped it hated the Bunyip as well, that the hostility wasn't personal.

The Bunyip slowed down as it too tried to climb close to the trunk without touching the offending fronds. Its bulk and size worked against it. Within a few minutes, Myell found himself close to its scaly heels. He didn't particularly want to pass it, and didn't get the chance. When the Bunyip saw him it smashed its leg down and hit Myell's shoulder, trying to dislodge him.

"Hey!" Myell shouted. He teetered off balance, grabbed at the nearest branch, felt a stinging race across his left thigh. "Shit."

"Chief?" Nam called up.

Myell gritted his teeth. His hand still hurt, but not as badly as the welt rising on his leg. He clung to the trunk and shivered. "Nothing. Son of a bitch."

The Bunyip made a sound like a huffing. Myell couldn't be sure, but he thought it was laughing at him. Asshole. Then the laughing choked off in a yelp. The alien lost its balance, crashed down past some branches, and then dropped like deadweight past Myell. Sickening cracking noises followed it down to a heavy, thumping landing on the ground.

Nam yelled, "What happened?"

"I don't know!" Myell replied. "Is it dead?"

Soft velvety rain began to fall against Myell's shoulders. He glanced up, startled, but the stars still shone over the tree's height. The raindrops landed on his skin and began to scurry with tiny tickling legs.

"Oh—" he started, and then shut his mouth, his eyes, against an army of tree spiders. He buried his nose against the crook of his arm and clung desperately to the trunk. The tiny creatures raced across him like the scratching of a million little fingernails. He could feel them crawling between his legs, down his flanks, trying to squirm into him—

He nearly began screaming then, and would surely have lost his balance if not for the sense of the tree changing its mind about him. It murmured words that made no sense and reached long sinuous vines toward him. Gently the vines brushed the offending creatures aside. With his eyes closed he saw no such thing, but after a moment the scratching faded and disappeared, leaving him naked but unmolested.

Thank you, he thought. No answer came in the darkness. The tree's presence had faded, and maybe had never really been there at all.

"Chief!" Nam sounded frantic. "What's going on up there?"

"Nothing," he forced out. "I'm coming down."

He descended as quickly as he could, earning stinging welts on the soles of his feet and his ass. He dropped from the lowest branch to the ground and huddled there, shaking, as the sizzle blazed across his nerves. When something cool and wet touched his leg he looked up and saw Shark Tooth with a bowl full of creamy pale salve.

Nam crouched down low beside him, a hand on Myell's shoulders. "What the hell happened?"

"Tell you later," Myell said. "More of that stuff, please. Where's the alien?"

"Over there," Gayle said.

He gazed at the Bunyip, which was far from dead. It was pacing an area near the tree, obviously agitated at having fallen. One of the village women tried to offer it salve for its wounds, but it brushed her off.

"So much for that," Nam said. "Hopefully that's the last of this nonsense."

But there was one more challenge to go.

N o," Myell said. "Not in a million years."

The hour was very late. A moon hung over the ocean, silvery red and distant. It cast a long wide path on the water, and the waves looked full of blood.

Chief Elder spoke again. The Bunyip gazed across the ocean with its teeth showing. Myell, dressed once more in his uniform but not his boots, tried not to stare at the rounded bay below, the rocky islands and mounts and shadowed places. The ocean crashed ashore, hammered sand against rocks, and drained away with a cascade of roars. Death lay down there, death in the most gruesome fashion, and he had to breathe hard to keep from panicking.

Gayle said, "It's really not that far down."

"I'm not diving off a cliff," Myell said with absolute certainty.

Chief Elder spoke a few harsh words. Shark Tooth motioned to his warriors, who seized Gayle and put spears to her throat.

"No," Myell repeated, speaking directly to Chief Elder. "I can't. I'll swallow a gecko. I'll go back up that fucking tree. But I'm not diving into that ocean."

"I'm a very valuable scientist," Gayle said to the warriors. "You really don't want to hurt me—"

She was marched back toward the main part of the village. Nam, who hadn't been touched, gazed steadily at Myell.

"I can't order you to do it," he said.

"And I'm not going to," Myell said, tired and sore and still hurting despite Shark Tooth's medicine. "Find someone else."

He limped off to a little frond tepee near the cliff's edge. The Bunyip had its own shelter, ten or so meters away. Separate lines of well-wishers had formed to bring gifts and offerings, and through word gestures ask for benedictions.

Nam had been allowed to sit with Myell. The shelter was ceremonial, wouldn't hold up under a good storm, but at least it diverted some of the cool ocean breeze.

"How are the burns?" Nam asked.

"Not so bad."

Myell accepted a string of shells from a pretty young girl. She bowed her head and he reluctantly touched it. She moved to the Bunyip's line, apparently eager to get its blessing as well. "You're a good swimmer," Nam said.

"I'm okay," Myell said. In pools. In ponds. In bodies of water that didn't have large deadly creatures circling in their depths. He gave Nam a sideways look. "That's in my file? That I'm a good swimmer?"

"It says you're not so bad."

Another villager approached Myell, carrying a jug of what smelled like wine. Jungle hooch. Myell took a swallow, felt it burn its way into his chest, and passed it to Nam.

Nam drank a healthy gulp, his eyes going wide.

"Enough of that, maybe, and you'll have no trouble going over the side?" Nam asked.

Myell stared glumly at his own hands. He couldn't see the ocean, but its nearby presence lay like an enormous weight on his skull and chest—a heaving, rolling, smashing weight. "If I drink myself unconscious, maybe. Then you can push me over."

"I won't push," Nam said.

Back at the bonfire, villagers were dancing in circles and passing around large conch shells. A ritual of some kind. Great party, he supposed. The cliff dives would probably come at dawn, when the gory results would be visible to all.

"My mother also had a phobia about insects," Nam said. "Used to turn her shoes over before she put them on, just to make sure nothing had crawled inside while we slept."

"We did that on our farm," Myell said.

"We lived in the city. In a fifth-floor apartment."

Across the divide between them, the Bunyip shooed away the last of its well-wishers and crouched on its hind legs with its face toward the horizon. It closed its eyes and breathed deeply, its chest expanding and contracting.

Myell suggested, "You could push *him* over."

"Maybe you should get some sleep," Nam suggested.

The villagers were settling down now. Some went back to their huts, but others stretched out on the ground in clusters of two or three or more, family units, lovers, grandparents with grandchildren. They stroked one another's backs and whispered words and gazed up at the sky. The constellations here were unfamiliar, but Myell could figure out his own patterns in the bright, distant stars: a shark, a stingray, a jellyfish. The sky was just a different kind of ocean.

"You'd do it, wouldn't you? Jump without hesitation?" Myell asked.

Nam handed over the wine jug. "This isn't about me."

Myell leaned back. He imagined himself standing at the edge of the cliff, arms stretched overhead, the breeze buffeting him as he peered down into the churning, heaving water that would suck him in and swallow him up. He could swim, yes, but he couldn't swim in that. And so he would never go home, never hold Jodenny again, never smell her skin and feel her heart thrum under his outstretched palm.

He tried to sleep, to close his eyes and think of Jodenny, but the ocean roared and hissed nearby, keeping him terrified.

When the horizon began to brighten he considered fleeing into the jungle. As an alternative he dug around in his vest and came up with a pencil. Unfortunately he had no paper. Nothing at all to write on. He searched the gift pile, hoping for parchment or tree bark or anything at all.

"All the technology in the universe." Myell's voice was hoarse in his own ears. "I'd trade it all for one piece of paper."

The horizon started to turn gold. The Bunyip rose from its crouch with fluid ease. Villagers came forward for the final challenge. Shark Tooth came and beckoned Myell to his feet. Myell's legs felt weak, and he had the appalling urge to find a large rock and crawl under it.

Nam stood with his fists tensed, but if he had any ideas, he wasn't sharing them.

"Will you tell Commander Scott that I thought of her until the end?" Myell asked, appalled at the tremble in his voice. "That I love her?"

"You'll tell her yourself," Nam said fiercely.

Another joke. Who knew Nam was such a comedian? Because even if he survived the plunge, he wouldn't survive the water and rocks. Myell went to the cliff's edge and waited several meters from the Bunyip. He couldn't look down. The ocean, the damned terrible ocean, spread as far as he could see.

Chief Elder approached. A dozen drums started beating like thunder.

"I'll do it," Nam said to Chief Elder, stepping forward and barring Myell. "I'm in charge. I'm responsible."

Chief Elder made a sharp, quick motion. Warriors grabbed Nam by the arms and pulled him back from the cliff's edge.

"Don't do it, Chief," Nam ordered. "It's suicide!"

The drums beat faster, louder, drowning out reason, demanding action. The sun ascended over the horizon with a blast of light and the villagers began cheering.

The Bunyip lifted its arms and pitched over the edge.

Myell couldn't. He was breathing too hard, his knees were knocking together, his thoughts were fragmenting into tiny shiny pieces that made no sense at all. He was too frightened to make his body move one way or the other—

But he did it anyway, he dived, dived over the crumbling edge, threw himself into goddamn nothingness, away from the safety of land into a long, frantic fall toward the rocks and froth of the bay below.

CHAPTER
FIFTEEN

I t's been eighteen hours!" Mr. Zhang said angrily. "How long does it take to fix a valve?"

Agreement swept through the passengers assembled in the galley. Jodenny, standing near the empty buffet with Farber and Hullabaloo, sensed mutiny in the air. Not true mutiny, not the passengers rising up to unseat the captain and crew, but certainly anger and frustration. She suspected that there would soon be several strongly worded letters of complaint to Team Space.

Lieutenant Sweeney, who'd been given the thankless task of keeping the passengers updated, rubbed at the side of his head.

"The Engineering Officer is working as hard as he can," he said. "The problem is not simply a broken valve. The malfunctioning parts

are ones we normally don't carry spares for, and can't be manufac-
tured onboard. But that doesn't mean we can't work around them. In
the meantime, the batteries are supplying all essential services and
could do so for months, if need be. I realize it's inconvenient, but
we're still going to arrive on time. Engine thrust has nothing to do
with speed in the Little Alcheringa."

"Is that true?" Hullabaloo asked Jodenny.

"Absolutely," she said. "If we can't thrust and maneuver once we're
back in normal space, Demos Command will send a tug to see us into
orbit."

Farber said, "No more fancy sandwiches. Nothing too hard about
that."

Jodenny agreed. True, the *Kamchatka* was a bit dimmer with only
emergency lighting in the passageways and cabins. Showers had been
restricted to cold-water dousings only. All entertainment units were
offline. The gym was closed, and meals had been reduced to cold rations only. Even the coffee was cold.

But the ship still had air, gravity, climate control, and comm systems. The trip might be a little inconvenient for the passengers, but
certainly not life threatening.

The same couldn't be said for the moments just after the lights had
gone out, when there'd been a near panic in the Hole in the Wall. Pa-
trons started pushing toward the exits so frantically that some people
fell underfoot. Jodenny was shoved from behind, but Hullabaloo
caught her arm and kept her from falling. Then he too was pushed,
and the air grew hot and claustrophobic, and Jodenny remembered
fire and smoke, screams, burning flesh. After a few seconds, battery
power switched on. Sharp commands rang out from some of the
crew.

"Keep calm!" Ensign Sadiqi shouted out, climbing to the top of the
bar. "Don't panic!"

Chief Reed, who was in charge of Jodenny's lifeboat, likewise
yelled out, "It's all right! Everything's under control!"

Jodenny told herself they were fine as long as the GQ didn't start
shrieking. It was useless to deploy lifeboats in the Little Alcheringa.

Transit speed depended on mass, and evacuees would die of dehydration or oxygen deprivation long before their lifeboats reached Earth.

"I need everyone to calm down," Chief Reed repeated, climbing onto a chair. "Probably a little glitch, the engines will come back on soon."

But the engines hadn't come on soon. Hadn't come back yet, hence this briefing with many of the passengers crammed into the galley and Lieutenant Sweeney looking as unhappy as everyone else.

"We paid a lot of money for this trip," someone said from the back of the room.

"Are we going to get refunds?" someone else asked.

Jodenny idly wondered if she was a curse. First the *Yangtze* disaster, then the assault on the *Aral Sea*, now the *Kamchatka*'s engineering woes.

"You'll have to take up any refund requests with Team Space passenger office," Sweeney was saying, which was just about when Jodenny lost interest in the conversation. She headed for the exit and happily stepped out into the cooler air of the passage. So many bodies crammed into one space irritated her. Hullabaloo and Farber were close behind her.

"Fancy a drink?" Hullabaloo asked. "The bar's open. Beer's probably warm, though."

"I had enough beer last night," Jodenny said.

"I don't drink," Farber said.

"Suit yourselves." Hullabaloo headed off.

Farber asked, in a low voice, "You think Sweeney's telling the truth?"

"Don't see why not."

"Are people going to get refunds?"

"Not even if they hold their breath and turn blue," Jodenny predicted. "They paid for passage. They didn't pay for passage in comfort."

"I'm going to go find Teddy," Farber said.

Jodenny went upladder to D-deck. Several passenger hatches were open and people were lingering in the passageways, driven to sociability by the shutdown of the entertainment units in their cabins. Karl, entrusted to the care of the Fraser daughters, was batting a small yellow ball between his paws. Jodenny patted his neck as she stepped by. Louise Sharp, her magenta hair as brilliant as ever, was sitting on the deck outside D-18. She shuffled a deck of oversize cards between her hands.

"Hey, Lulu," Louise said. "Come keep me company."

"I was going to try to nap," Jodenny said.

"Oh, sure, like sleep's more interesting than me." Louise gave her a crooked grin. "Sit down and rest your weary dogs."

"Dogs?" Jodenny asked.

"Dogs. Feet. Earth slang."

Jodenny sat and leaned her head against the bulkhead. It was nice to rest her feet, after all. "You've been there often? Earth."

"We make this run about twice a year, checking on company investments. It's not half the cesspool people make it out to be, though I wouldn't exactly call it hospitable in most places. Ruined cities and burned-away ozone do that to a world. Makes the naturalists cranky."

"The who?" Jodenny asked, thinking of Malachy Balandra.

"Big movement. Back to nature, anti-technology, all that, but they need the tech to clean up the mess left from the Debasement. What brings you there?"

"I'm on vacation. Wanted to see something different."

"Different, it is." Louise flipped a card down on the deck and said, "Ah, the wallaby. Change is coming soon."

"What are those?"

"Aboriginal tarot cards."

Jodenny examined the card more closely. It was old and frayed at the edges, but the artwork was intricate and carefully inked. "I thought tarot cards were European."

"Well, like everything else European, they found their way to Australia," Louise said. "Hocus-pocus cockeyed bullshit, all of it, except when it isn't."

She tossed another card down on the deck. It showed a brown and orange koala clinging to a gum tree as storm clouds raged overhead. "See there? Turmoil. Not surprising. The future shapes the present, you know. Something up ahead of us is significantly different than what's behind us."

Jodenny didn't want to think about the future unless it specifically involved reuniting with Myell. "You don't seem like the mystical type."

"I believe in the great unknown, and the great unknowable. And a martini every evening after work." Louise shuffled the cards. "I'll do a reading for you."

"I don't really need one."

"Free of charge. Keeps me in practice." Louise put four cards down on the deck in the shape of a diamond. "Romance, Finance, Career, Fortune. First card: Will our dear Ellen find true love?"

Two male passengers stepped over Jodenny's outstretched legs on their way down the passage. It was cool in the ship, the heating elements only on half power, and she rubbed her bare arms.

Louise turned the romance card over. A dark figure, arms and legs akimbo, stared up at them.

"The Lightning Man," Louise said, impressed. "Very powerful. And you already know him, don't you? His feet are flat on the ground, not on tiptoes, indicating certainty. He cares for you very deeply."

Jodenny tried to keep her expression blank. Her wedding ring burned on its chain around her neck.

Louise said, "Thing about the Lightning Man is that he's very powerful, but also very dangerous. Doesn't know his own strength. Brings destruction, and in the aftermath, rebirth. You jeopardize yourself by keeping company with the likes of him."

"I don't know who you're talking about," Jodenny said.

Louise's mouth quirked. "If you say so. Whoever he is, you'll probably see him soon. Lightning Men, they tend to stick around whether you want them to or not. Next question: Will Ellen be rich?"

Louise overturned the second card. A blue and white seal swam through golden waves.

"Congratulations. The seal indicates you'll have all you need. Maybe you're going to win the lottery. Or you could be rich in other ways, money notwithstanding. Next comes Career. Will Ellen achieve great professional success?"

A great white egret stared up at them with black eyes.

Louise was silent for a moment.

"Determined, persistent, strong," she finally said. "When you set out to do something, you do it."

"Not always," Jodenny said.

"What did you say your job was?"

"Librarian."

Louise twirled a curl of magenta hair between her fingers. "Thing is, it's inverted. See? Upside down. Compromised. Subject to the power of the next card: Fortune. Go ahead and turn it over."

Jodenny touched the card gingerly and then flipped it. A Rainbow Serpent curled around the card's surface, gleaming gold and bronze, yellow and white. She could almost smell its hot, rotting breath.

"The Creator." Louise's gaze narrowed. "First among all in the Dreamtime, the land that was and is and will always be. But it's reversed, too. Your connection is through someone else. Your Lightning Man, perhaps?"

The passageway was getting more crowded. The meeting in the galley must have broken up. Jodenny put her hand on top of the Rainbow Serpent and then swept up the other three cards. Let Louise do readings for other passengers. Let her peer into artwork on their behalf and presume to know anything at all.

Jodenny said, "There's no Lightning Man, and no Snake. I have to go."

Louise cocked her head. "Go where? We're all trapped here until we get to Earth."

Jodenny started to get up anyway. Louise peeled one last card from the deck and put it facedown on the deck. Louise asked, "What about this ship? What's our fate going to be?"

She turned the card over. It showed a crocodile, its jaws wide and tail high.

Despite herself, Jodenny asked, "What does that mean?"

Louise took her time answering.

"Undecided," she finally said. "And it's also inverted. A bad sign. Things don't look so good."

Rubbish, Jodenny almost said. She left Louise with her cards and headed back to her cabin. The prospect of staring at bulkheads didn't make her happy at all. She climbed downladder instead, bypassing the galley for the library. It was more crowded than she'd expected, with several passengers tucked into the comfy chairs and either reading or doing puzzles by flashlight. She detoured by the passenger lounge, found that too crowded as well. She was heading for Toledo's cabin, hoping he might have an update, when AT Tingley caught up to her in an E-deck passageway.

"Commander," she said. "I've been looking all over—"

"Miss Spring," Jodenny corrected, with a quick look around. No one else was in the passageway, but eavesdroppers were never far away. "What's wrong?"

Tingley took a deep breath. "It's Putty. He got in a fight and they put him in the brig and it's not his fault, he was trying to get my ring back!"

They had no privacy while standing right there in the passageway. Jodenny spied a unisex head and towed Tingley inside. The stalls were empty, and the thin red light from the emergency light left most in shadows.

"Tell me what happened," Jodenny said.

"My wedding ring! I took it off this morning when I was washing up and left it on the sink shelf by accident. Everyone else was already off to breakfast. So then an hour later I remembered, and I went back, but it was gone. Someone told Putty this kid Malachy was hanging around berthing, and he was seen in the bathroom, and he picked it up."

Jodenny squeezed the bridge of her nose. Junior sailors on the *Kamchatka* shared not only berthing but a communal head. She could easily imagine Malachy Balandra slipping in after everyone had gone off to their daily duty assignments.

"Putty didn't know he was the captain's son!" Tingley said, unshed tears beginning to glimmer. "He went off to find him, and they got in a fight, and the kid's still got my ring, and Putty's going to be charged with fighting, and what are they going to do to him?"

"Someone actually saw Malachy Balandra take the ring?" Jodenny asked.

Tingley nodded emphatically. "Bobby Shu saw with his own eyes!

But now he won't swear to it because he doesn't want the captain mad at him, and Putty didn't even punch first, the kid did that."

That was a little hard to believe. Malachy didn't seem like the violent type.

"What is it you want me to do?" Jodenny asked.

"Talk to the captain! Or to Security. Can't you? Because they can keep him in the brig until we get all the way back to Fortune, and he'll just hate that, he hates little places, and then he'll have to get a lawyer, and Team Space doesn't like him anyway—"

"Take a breath," Jodenny ordered. "Deep breath. In and out through your nose. You're going to hyperventilate."

Tingley did so, and wiped at her eyes.

"I'm not a sea lawyer," Jodenny said. "As far as anyone on this ship knows, I'm not even a lieutenant commander."

"But you know him!" Tingley said. "You can stand up for him. No one else is going to do that."

Myell had been thrown in the brig once, accused of a crime he hadn't committed. Jodenny hadn't known him at the time, but she knew it hadn't been good for him. She tried to imagine being nineteen years old and assigned to a ship for the first time, and being convicted of a crime for trying to recover your wife's wedding ring.

She said, "I'll go talk to them."

"Thank you, ma'am!" Tingley threw her arms around Jodenny and hugged her in a decidedly unprofessional way. She pulled back almost instantly, her face flushed. "Sorry. I didn't mean to do that."

"We're on a ship with no power and your husband's in jail," Jodenny said gruffly. "I guess you're allowed a hug."

"Thank you, ma'am," Tingley said, and dragged her sleeve across her nose.

"Just don't let it happen again," Jodenny said, and went off to talk to Security.

Falling off a cliff took forever.

One thousand, two thousand . . .

Wind rushed at him. The dark and ominous sea expanded beyond the edges of his vision. The sharp rocks below waited for him with hardened teeth and jagged claws. Myell saw his death, clear as the sky: his body slamming into stone, bones cracking and splintering under the strain, his lungs punctured and skull shattered like an egg.

Three thousand, four . . .

The terror of the cliff had been replaced by a strange, cold calm. No sense worrying about the inevitable. In a few seconds everything would be over, and if anything lurked beyond the blackness of death he'd find out.

Still, calm notwithstanding, he scrabbled for some kind of purchase in the air, anything to grab on to, anything at all.

Five thousand, six, the pull of gravity, the onrushing rocks, awareness that the Bunyip had already gone into the water and had not surfaced, the fleeting lament *Jodenny,* and he hit.

Cold. Shockingly cold, and dark, and his mouth and nose and lungs and chest and body were full of water, a torrent of it flooding into him, making breath and life impossible. In terror and desperation he tried to suck in air, air that didn't exist, his chest muscles paralyzed, his lungs turned to stone, and his heart beat wildly out of control in a battle that was already lost, already far beyond his control.

He didn't remember sinking, but here he was deep in salty blackness, unable to see, unable to focus, his limbs heavy and fingers slack, freezing cold, bitterly cold, no sense of up or down, no way back to the surface, all lost, so lost, and when seaweed brushed against his lips he couldn't even recoil, because the water carried him and drowned him and he was dimming, all of him was dimming, and going into the darkness.

Come, a woman's voice said, a voice like a song. *Open your eyes.*

Impossible, but he did it anyway. His vision was a blurred landscape of black and dark blue and there, a woman's silvery face. She shimmered in the darkness like a beacon. Her eyes were tiny burning fires of green, her smile full of sharp gray teeth. Her hands slid over Myell's arms and up to his throat and cupped his face, oh so cold, and slimy like a fish.

Come and live, she coaxed.

Her lips brushed his. Her tongue slid into his throat, a violation that brought blessed air. Myell choked, gasped, and bolted upright on a damp bed of rock. Around him, the walls of a sea cave shone green with luminescent plants. He clutched his throat, sure that he couldn't breathe, but air flowed freely down into his chest, where a residual ache told him that he hadn't dreamed the ordeal. He had jumped from a cliff into the ocean and lived to tell the tale.

Unless this was some odd kind of afterlife, an afterlife that was wet and salty and cold, and in which he was naked again.

Shivering, he clutched at a coverlet of seagull feathers that had been wrapped around him. The feathers smelled moldy. He inspected his arms and legs, looking for injuries. A few scratches, a bruise or two. The welts from the stinging tree had faded. But something was missing—

His dilly bag was gone.

He patted the coverlet, searched the bed of rock, scanned the floor. No sign of it. Silly to be sentimental about a cloth sack, but the loss cut him anyway.

You've got bigger problems, he told himself.

He staggered upright, paused to let his spinning head settle down, and limped stiffly toward a low archway of rock. A large crocodile in the doorway snapped at him with teeth like knives.

Myell jerked back several frightened steps. The crocodile's tail twitched, long and heavy, but it made no moves toward him. He glanced around for some kind of club or stick, anything that could be used as a weapon. The sea cave gave him nothing.

"She won't eat you," a woman's voice said.

Myell turned back to see a young woman standing beside the crocodile. The woman had dark hair that curled in luxurious waves to her hips, and a silvery-white face that seemed familiar. She wore a scrap of fabric around her waist. A string of fish bones and palm fronds hung around her neck.

"She's just curious," the woman continued. "She thinks Nogomain who pretend they are birds must have spent too much time in the sun."

All the questions Myell wanted to ask jammed up in his throat. The woman stepped farther into the chamber, her dainty feet pale against the wet rock. Her lips were blue in the glowing light.

"I don't think you're Nogomain yet, and you would make a terrible bird." She advanced on him with delicate steps. The tip of her head reached only to his shoulders. "Still, you're welcome here. At least until you tire of fish and salt and the sharks who circle you even now."

She put one hand on his chest. Her fingers were short and stubby, her nails green. Her bare, firm breasts were covered with translucent scales, and the nipples were black. She gazed at him steadily, her eyes betraying nothing.

"Who are you?" he asked.

"Names are secrets," she said. "You can call me Free-not-chained."

"Are you . . . human?"

She laughed. "Are you?"

Free-not-chained turned away before he could answer. She glided from the cave as if the rocky wet floor were made of ice. Myell followed very carefully, eyes on the crocodile. It let him pass unmolested. Free-not-chained led him through more narrow, low caves. In some the luminescent walls faded to faint glows, leaving him stumbling. In others, open pools of seawater lapped at rock, and silvery fish splashed at their surfaces.

Free-not-chained's destination was a wide, high chamber where sunlight broke through large gaps in the ceiling and walls. He could hear birds cawing and the wind whistling, and see chunks of the distant blue sky. The cavern floor was littered with birdshit-stained rocks and women like Free-not-chained basking in pools of sunlight. Crocodiles slept among the women, curled up like pets.

"He lives," one of the women murmured, opening her eyes at Myell's arrival.

"He's only a man," another said, arching her spine and licking at her fingers.

Free-not-chained showed him a flat expanse of damp sand and bade him to sit down. "He's Jungali," she said, which made goosebumps run down his spine.

"Where did you hear that name?" Myell demanded. His mother had given him that secret nickname. The Rainbow Serpent had called him by it. But no one else, not even Jodenny, knew it.

"Whispered by the gods," Free-not-chained said. "Murmured in awe and fear."

She gave him a cup of fresh water. Though he didn't expect to be thirsty after inhaling half an ocean, he finished all of it with slow, even swallows. When she offered him bits of raw fish, he shook his head.

"What about the Bunyip?" he asked. "The creature that dived into the sea when I did."

"Stranger," said one woman.

"Interloper!" said another.

Free-not-chained leaned against an old, scarred crocodile. She stroked its tail with one hand and gave Myell a long look from under her black eyelashes. "He swam to shore. They took him. They celebrate him as the Lightning God, in error. We kept you."

Myell pulled the seagull feathers tighter. "Why?"

"So curious," said one of the others, and rubbed her legs languidly against each other.

To Free-not-chained he said, "I am thankful that you saved my life. But I need to get back to my friends. Will you take me?"

She licked her lips. "Not curious. Denying. But your friends, they will come soon to take you to the Nogomain."

"Who are the Nogomain?" he asked. "I don't know that word. Are they gods? Like the Rainbow Serpent?"

None of the women answered. Free-not-chained continued to stroke her crocodile. Sea spray shot over the rocks above them, sending down water drops that chilled Myell's skin.

"I have a wife," he said. "I have to go home to her."

Free-not-chained closed her eyes. The other women also seemed to doze. Some of the crocodiles stayed awake, their eyes flat and watchful. Myell edged to his feet, tiptoed past tails and claws, and tried to avoid the clamp of jaws around his ankles. Sweat trickled down his neck and made the feather coverlet stick to his skin. It wouldn't be so funny to survive a cliff dive only to be devoured by wild reptiles, but he was their Jungali, whatever that meant, so maybe they wouldn't rip his limbs apart, wouldn't snap his bones and chew up his organs.

At the far end of the chamber was a jumble of boulders that twisted up to the sky. He'd never been much for rock climbing, had never even attempted it beyond a few tries in shipboard gyms, but he could see footholds and handholds. The rocks were rough and sharp, and sliced into his palms and bare feet as he ascended.

Blood, he thought. A great way to attract a crocodile's attention.

He did his best not to look down and instead focused on each purchase and heft upward. The coverlet fluttered around his ankles and feathers clung to his knees. He abandoned it for expediency's sake. Bare-assed was not his favorite way to brave an incline of mercilessly sharp rock, but it wouldn't matter one way or the other if he fell to his death.

Despite the cool air he was soon sweating. He couldn't climb steadily upward but instead had to zigzag and double back at times when the rock proved too steep. He imagined that at the top of the climb he'd find Jodenny, warm clothes, a hot meal, and an ouroboros, in that exact order, but the list was depressing because of its improbability, and so he concentrated instead on not slipping and crashing to the ground below.

He did look down, at one point, and was startled to see that all the women had vanished, and in their places were more crocodiles: crocodiles with red eyes and green nails, crocodiles lolling with their tummies turned to the sun.

Myell climbed higher.

The surface finally came within reach, and he hauled himself into a dazzling, overwhelming jumble of rock and sky and clouds. For a moment all he could do was sit and shake and tremble. Impossible task number one, accomplished. Then he lifted his head and saw ocean in every direction. The caves were part of an underwater reef and islands whose jagged tips rose above the tide and currents. He couldn't see the mainland. Even if he dared swim, he didn't know which direction to swim in, which way to safety and shore.

He sat back, already feeling the sun burning his skin, unable to contemplate a climb back down into the crocodile pit. He had no fresh water, no food, and no hope to cling to.

No clothes, either.

If only Jodenny could see him now.

He was still sitting there when a long wooden canoe curved into view with two women inside it. The first had dark skin and white hair, her face marked with scars. The second was a young woman of Asian descent whom Myell had last seen on the *Aral Sea* several months earlier, and who he'd presumed was dead.

"Hi there," Able Technician Ishikawa said with a smile. "Can we give you a lift, Sergeant?"

"Chief," he said dumbly. "I'm a chief now."

Ishikawa gave a mock salute. "Chief. I'm glad they promoted you."

Myell considered several responses to that, but went with the one most obvious. "You're not real. Neither of you."

Ishikawa's smile grew wider. "Real or not, maybe you'd like a ride to somewhere with a few more amenities?"

He considered the boat, the waves, the sea. His legs were still shaky from the climb. He tipped his head back and let the sun warm his face. "Nope."

"He's crazy." That was the second woman in the canoe, the woman he didn't know, speaking with an accent that he couldn't quite place.

"I'm not kidding. We've got a nice place for you to sleep, good food, tree houses, gods . . ." Ishikawa said.

Myell cracked an eyelid at them but didn't commit.

Ishikawa added, "Or you can stay here until the tide comes in," and that did the trick.

He'd been in a few situations more humiliating than climbing naked down the rocks and into their canoe, but at the moment he couldn't think of any. Ishikawa handed him a red-and-blue woven blanket. He pulled it over his shoulders and tucked it under his ass, but still felt exposed. The boat rose and fell with the waves, twisting from side to side. He tried not to look at all the water.

"I should ask you the normal questions," he said to Ishikawa. "Who, what, everything."

"All good things in good time," she replied. "This is my sister Silrys."

Silrys began paddling. "You're Jungali," she said over her shoulder, and she didn't sound like she approved.

Myell pulled the blanket tighter. "I wish people would stop calling me that."

The women exchanged looks he couldn't read, which annoyed him more than anything else had that day. But he lost his grip on his irritation as the canoe started across the water. Oddly enough, plunging into the ocean from a terrifying height hadn't cured his phobia. He closed his eyes and tried to breathe steadily, an exercise that was supposed to calm him, but the back of his throat began to burn and he knew, with certainty, that he was about to vomit.

"Chief, here." Ishikawa pushed a jug into his hands. "Drink. It helps me. I always get seasick."

The liquid was thick wine that tasted like honey. He slit his eyes open and saw that they were still surrounded by water, by the treacherous and merciless sea, but they were headed for a large, sloping island not too far away. He nursed Ishikawa's brew and ignored the dizzying motion of the canoe.

"Sharks," Silrys said, sounding very casual about it.

Fins sliced through the water off their starboard bow.

"No worries," Ishikawa said, and patted Myell's back.

They reached the hilly island without being besieged by sharks, dolphins, whales, or other monsters of the deep. Ishikawa helped Myell from the canoe and past salt-crusted rocks. The alcohol had left him a little tipsy. The shoreline was rough. No scenic beaches here, no curving ribbons of sand.

"Nice place you've got," Myell said, keeping a tight grasp on Ishikawa's wine jug.

The rocks quickly gave way to sea grass, then to a forest where a canopy of green leaves tinted the sunlight. There were no houses or other shelters immediately visible, but as the two women took him farther from shore he began to see rope bridges up in the trees, platforms made from hewn logs, thatched huts nestled in branches. Colorful birds flitted from tree to tree and women's faces peeked down at him—sunburned faces, dark-skinned faces, young faces, faces of old women.

"This is our village," Ishikawa said.

Myell tilted his head back. "You live up there?"

Ishikawa said, "Mostly."

The tree houses grew more numerous and complex. Most were clustered in concentric rings around a Child Sphere sitting by itself in a dirt clearing. Unlike other Spheres that Myell had seen, this one was covered with Aboriginal paintings that mirrored the ones they'd discovered in the cave. Crocodiles and birds, animals and reptiles of all kinds, and one lone, large figure that looked like a man or a god holding arrows in his hand.

Flower offerings, bits of food, and carved wooden totems surrounded the Painted Child, whose dark archway called to Myell like no other Sphere had ever done.

"Up here, Chief," Ishikawa said, steering him toward a ladder fastened to one of the trees. "I know you're not afraid of heights."

Not normally, no. But as Myell tipped his gaze up the tree, he thought about spiders and stinging fronds.

"I think I'll stay here," he said. He slid to the base of the tree with the jug and blanket for company.

Silrys glowered down at him. "He's drunk."

"Am not," Myell protested, and swallowed more wine.

More women appeared around him, some of them barely clothed, a few of them muttering disapprovingly. Some of them giggled. Small boys and girls poked at his arms or hung seashell strands around his neck. The sunlight through the trees dazzled his eyes. The blanket scratched his skin. He began telling Ishikawa, with earnestness and great detail, how he'd been promoted to chief and then turned down initiation and now some other chiefs hated him, and officers too, and Commander Nam. But halfway through the story he fell asleep, and when he next woke up he was in one of the tree houses. Green leaves and colorful birds and brown rope bridges surrounded him. The sun had fallen far in the sky, and someone nearby was roasting spiced meat.

"There you are," Ishikawa said as he stirred.

Myell sat up groggily. The tree house was a single room outfitted with weavings and sea treasures and wooden carvings. His bladder was close to bursting. Ishikawa handed over a clay pot and turned her back until he was done.

"There's water in that jug over there," she said. "No more hooch for you. Dinner should be ready soon."

Myell peered at the tree huts and bridges and platforms. "What is this place?"

"Island of the Amazons," she said.

"You're kidding."

She smiled. "Well, that's what some of us call it. I don't think you could pronounce the local word for it. Home sweet home."

Myell pressed the palm of his right hand against his right eye, wishing Ensign Collins were nearby with his medkit. Then again, he'd survived worse hangovers.

"Do the villagers back on the mainland know you're here?"

"The People? They have rumors. Folk tales. We try to keep our distance."

"How'd you get to Team Space?" he asked.

"I grew up here. When I was old enough, I was sent to Fortune—as were many others—to look for the man called Jungali. I joined Team Space, hoping to find him along the Seven Sisters. So there I was, on the *Aral Sea,* and fate put me in your department. It all worked out."

Myell's headache was easing. "It almost didn't. Commander Osherman ordered you to tell the ship's bridge that Lieutenant Scott and I were trapped in that cargo tower. We nearly died."

"The Rainbow Serpent came to me, told me who you were, said you had your own path to follow. Honest!" Ishikawa crossed her heart. "He told me to come back here. And so I did. Now you're here, too. That's destiny for you."

"It's something," he agreed. "But just because my mother picked a strange nickname for me doesn't mean I'm the man you're looking for. Who told you about that nickname, anyway?"

Ishikawa put her small hand on his arm. "The Snake."

He sighed.

"Your mother gave you the name Jungali because the Rainbow Serpent whispered it in her ear while she slept. You were chosen for this a long time ago. The Nogomain need you. Garanwa needs you."

"I'm afraid to ask. Who are the Nogomain? Who's Garanwa?"

Ishikawa brushed her hands on her knees and stood up. "Yambli will tell you. She gets to tell all the good stories. Silrys is our leader, but Yambli's like our grandmother. She wants to see you."

He glanced down at himself. "Maybe you could find me some clothes first."

While she was gone Myell watched the tree village and the children who dashed across the rope bridges without a care. Mothers were cooking meals in carefully tended stone ovens, and someone was playing a didgeridoo. A traditionally male musical instrument, if he remembered correctly. Yet he didn't see any men besides himself, which led to the question of who had sired all the kids.

Ishikawa returned with a brown woven shirt and a red skirt.

"We don't have any trousers," she said. "Sorry."

He eyed the skirt judiciously.

"Yambli sent it herself," Ishikawa said.

When he was presentable, Ishikawa led him across the nearest bridge. Myell didn't like the swing and buck of it, but it held their weight easily. Across platforms and huts and more swaying bridges they went, the chatter of women in the air. The sun was lower now, streaking the sky red, leaving the forest in deepening darkness. Bugs tried to feast on his arms and legs.

"Here, smear this on," Ishikawa said. "Insect repellent. The good stuff, too. Imported from Fortune."

At last they came to a large hut. The inside glowed yellow from the light of oil lamps. The single room held several hand-carved chairs and rugs woven from palm fronds. Tree-bark masks hung on the walls, their mouths and eyes wide, their faces decorated with shells, flowers, and paint. Seven or eight women, including Silrys, were in attendance around the oldest person Myell had ever seen.

She was tiny and shriveled, with gray hair cropped close to her skull. Her dark skin looked fragile and bruised. Her right arm was bent awkwardly against her chest and the hand was a tightened knot, useless. Her legs were like a bird's, sticking out from under a blue blanket. But her eyes were still lively, and her mouth stretched wide in a smile when she saw him.

"Jungali," she rasped out.

The other women stared at Myell, not all of them so welcoming.

"Sit here," Ishikawa said, and showed him to a spot very close to Yambli. Myell sat cross-legged, careful not to expose himself under the ridiculous red skirt. Most of the other women sat as well. Somewhere nearby, incense was burning. It smelled like lavender and salt.

"Chief Myell," Yambli said. "I am so pleased to be meeting the son of my daughter."

"Your daughter?" he asked, startled.

She raised her good hand and said, "All are my daughters."

White streaks of light flashed from her fingers and spread across the ceiling. Tangled lines, twisted, the roots of a vast eucalyptus tree, and he was at the tail end of one of the tiniest threads, and she was farther up the convolution, and the whole tree itself pulsed with energy, ancient and enormous power.

Yambli said, "Your mother came from Australia, the lost People of the northern coast, the same as my mother, and her mother before her. That's how we measure families here: through the mother, always. The People of the land are the same way. They believe you to be the next incarnation of the Lightning God."

Myell blinked. Yambli's house reassembled itself around him. The other women were gazing at him with careful eyes. Yambli herself smiled toothlessly.

She said, "The People were taken out of Australia and through the Egg several generations ago, by the Nogomain. The Nogomain serve the Wondjina. We serve the Nogomain. You are Jungali. Favored by the Rainbow Serpent, destined to join the Nogomain. We've been searching for you for generations. Since Garanwa told us to. When you step through the Egg, you'll be part of them."

Yambli coughed, a dry and raspy sound. Ishikawa pressed a teacup into her hand. The incense smell was very strong.

"The Egg," Myell said. "The Child Sphere below?"

Silrys stepped forward, her expression grim. "Garanwa is the last of the Nogomain. He needs Jungali's help. To take his place in the First of all Eggs, and to keep the interlopers from taking the helm. The ones you call the Bunyips. He calls them the Roon."

Myell wished he had Ishikawa's wine jug again. He gazed at the women's faces and saw fervent belief, irrational hope, skepticism. The lavender and salt smells were very strong now, and the insect repellent made his skin itch. He was sitting in a skirt in a hut in a village of women who wanted him to help the gods.

"Your wife," Yambli said. Her smile was long gone. "She saw the Roon. She knows the threat. Bring us to dust, they will, unless Jungali stops them."

Myell stood up. "Look. I'm sure you're all great people and you mean well, but I'm not the one you're looking for. I'm sorry."

Yambli stretched her useless hand to him. The skin on it was withered and sagging, and the bones underneath looked too thin to bear weight.

"I'm sorry," he said, and lightly touched her fingers.

The world dissolved into chaos.

Light and dark, everywhere mixed, vibration and not-vibration, cacophony and silence in swirl, and he was without shape or form, but his mind soared through the world like a bird, or a spear thrown by an unseen warrior.

"The beginning," Yambli whispered in his ear.

The chaos separated into brown land and blue sky, and sun so bright that he feared blistering his nonexistent eyes. His physical body was a memory, fleeting and inconsequential. He barely missed it all. He was free (Free-not-chained, he remembered, giddily) and nothing would ever bind him to Earth again. It was paradise and perfection and power that could never be tamed.

Around him, balls of light dropped to the ground like shooting stars, and where they landed, the land humped and moved. The humps rose into shapes like crocodiles, birds, gum trees, dark warriors. The beginning, he understood. The newly created shapes trekked across the flatland, over hills raising themselves from the dust, over lakes springing in great gushing geysers, over rivers mingling and twisting together in shining blue paths.

He swooped in lower, his nonbody dipping and lifting, laughing in spirit if nothing else. The ground reached and pulled him into an embrace that left him in the shape of a gecko, a gecko crawling forward through an enormous world of rocks and blades of grass. He felt less joy, now, dwarfed to insignificance, the stomping dark feet of children making the ground shake around him. He darted through the brush and an ocean bay opened up beneath his vantage point: a bay of shimmering blue, a wooden ship sailing into it with great white sails made in England, white men come to claim and steal land—

Abruptly Myell lost the shape of a gecko. He was a man now, an Aboriginal standing on the shore with the men of his tribe, their fists wrapped around spears that were no match for pistols. He was decorated with feathers and sticks in his thick hair, and his skin was painted with ocher. Sweat itched between his shoulder blades. The English ship was drawing closer. The world was about to change forever.

But before the ship reached shore, the great Rainbow Serpent curled down from the sky and dropped a stone egg. From the egg emerged the Nogomain and their shaman, Garanwa, who bade the People to journey to the stars.

To this land, where the People would be safe.

"But what do I have to do with any of this?" Myell asked, with a mouth that had no lips, no voice.

The Serpent swallowed him whole.

CHAPTER
SEVENTEEN

Night on the island of women. Myell felt drunk again, though he hadn't had any wine. Torchlight streaked across his vision like the burning trails of comets. He was a planet spinning its way through a void, but the void was full of palm trees and beautiful women, and dirt between his toes, and children singing.

"I'm going to be sick," he said to Ishikawa.

She pulled him to a fine wooden chair carved from a tree trunk. "Sit down."

The party swirled on without him. Flower petals drifted down from above, soft like rain. Myell caught some and crushed them against his face, thinking of Jodenny's perfume. The archway of Painted Child had been decorated with garlands and wreaths. The darkness inside soothed him, steadied his vision.

"You want me to go through there," he said.

"It's what you were born to do," Ishikawa said.

He leaned back in the chair—the throne—and let his head loll. The women's music was bright and fast, no more didgeridoos here. In harmony they sang words he didn't know. The little boys of the village banged on drums made of skin and wood. Whenever Myell closed his eyes he saw white trees and red landscapes and Jodenny, calling to him.

"My wife," he said.

"Lieutenant Scott understands duty," Ishikawa said. "She of all people would want you to do what's right."

He corrected her. "Lieutenant *Commander* Scott."

Ishikawa's hand pressed against his. "You'll have the power of the entire network in your hands. Your control, your will. Otherwise the power of the First Egg will fall to the Roon."

The Roon. The Bunyips, with their white feather cloaks and silver helmets and clawed hands. Fantastical and strange. Surely creatures from a dream, or a nightmare.

Ishikawa's voice was close to his ear. "You're always going to do the right thing, Chief. It's just the way you are. So you might as well walk into that Egg and face what needs to be done. Stop the Roon."

Damn her for making sense.

Myell stood up, straightened the red skirt tied around his waist, and stepped toward the Painted Child. If he could dive off a cliff, he could do this. Embrace his destiny, whatever it was. Be their Jungali, at least until they realized that they had the wrong man. It wouldn't be the first time he'd been mistaken for someone better than he was, but maybe it would be the last.

The music stopped and the drums fell silent.

He kept walking, aware of Ishikawa trailing a respectful distance. He almost asked her to accompany him but that would be selfish, unfair. He had no idea what lay ahead. Some paths could only be walked alone.

Myell saw Yambli watching him, her eyes bright. Beside the old woman, Silrys stood with a frown. She didn't believe in him at all, which was strangely comforting.

I don't believe in me either, he wanted to say. *But I'll try.*

A small boy stepped in front of Myell to give him a bouquet of flowers. Feeling absurdly like a bride, Myell took the flowers and patted the boy on the head. Jodenny had carried flowers during their wedding. The ceremony had been short and efficient, both of them still recuperating from injuries, well aware of the risk of fraternization charges and retaliation, but worth the danger. If anyone had ever told him he'd marry an officer, he would have laughed at the idea.

The flowers in his hand were red, not white. Tropical and wild, not carefully cultivated and cut from a ship's hydroponics bed. They smelled like wild honey, and the dirt on their roots, and the fresh green of their stalks.

The Painted Child called to him, beckoned.

Jungali. Save us all.

"Chief?" Ishikawa asked.

The words came out on their own, unbidden. "I can't."

Panic crossed her face. "Of course you can."

"I can't leave her." His head felt clearer, his knees steadier. He hadn't realized how hard they were trembling. Myell clutched the flowers closer to his chest and gave Ishikawa a quick kiss on the cheek. "I'm sorry. It's selfish and wrong, but I made a promise. I'm going home to my wife."

He walked off into the jungle, taking the red bouquet with him.

Myell walked through the jungle toward the moon. When he found a clearing he slept with his arms pillowed beneath his head, and when he woke the sun was up and Silrys was sitting next to him.

"You're a surprise," she said. "I'll give you that."

She had water and fruit for him, and he was famished enough to accept both. As he chewed he said, "You're not here to persuade me to go through the Child Sphere. You don't think I'm the guy for the job anyway."

She said, "All my life, I've been taught the importance of finding the man named Jungali. Garanwa commanded it, and he's our god."

"Jungali has to be a man?" Myell asked. "Kind of sexist, isn't that?"

Her gaze narrowed. "The Nogomain picked. We didn't."

"This Garanwa. What's he like?"

"He was a boy, once. Now he's something else."

The fruit, some kind of mango, left Myell's fingers sticky. He wiped them on his skirt. "So you send women out to go looking for Jungali. Ever go yourself?"

Silrys's gaze was on the trees. "For fifteen years I lived on Mary River, waiting for a sign that didn't come."

"That's the thing about signs," Myell said, not unkindly. "Sometimes they're right, sometimes they're wrong. Some of your people think I'm destined to join the Nogomain. The villagers back on land thought I was the reincarnation of their Lightning God. Did you know there's one of those—what do you call them?—Roon among them?"

Silrys's face creased with a frown. "Yes. It's been trapped there for several months, as have all who've tried to use the Eggs. It calls itself a god. It studies the People, learns their habits."

"You think it's dangerous. The whole species."

"Garanwa fears nothing, but he fears them," Silrys said, in a hushed voice. "He tells us little about them other than that they are interlopers. That they don't worship the Wondjina. But they mean to cause great destruction."

Myell pushed down the lump of shame in his chest. "I'm not your man."

Silrys said, "You bear the name. The Rainbow Serpent has curled around your legs. Garanwa allows you, and only you, to use the Eggs. I've been stubborn and wrong in my disbelief."

"I have to go." Myell stood up and, after a moment's reflection, picked up the wilted red bouquet from the ground. "Thank everyone for their hospitality, okay? I'm sorry if I disappointed. But one man, against an entire alien species? It was never going to work in the first place."

He started through the jungle toward the beach. The path was worn well enough for him to follow, but the foliage was thicker than he remembered, the going a little tougher. He wiped sweat from his face—damn, but the day was hot—and tried not to cut his bare feet on anything sharp. He fought his way past low-hanging branches and stepped over vines and decided that what he really needed was a vacation in a *city* somewhere, concrete and glass and every imaginable amenity.

The aroma of salt and seaweed grew stronger on the breeze, but when he stumbled clear of the forest Myell saw a wide stretch of sand instead of the rocky beach he remembered. The ocean was a bright, glinting carpet of blue and green. He hated it.

Yambli was waiting for him, standing thin and fragile in the sea grass. Ishikawa was with her.

"Chief," Yambli said, and held out a hand.

"Ma'am." Myell was wary of touching her, but he and Ishikawa helped her to sit on a long, salt-crusted piece of driftwood.

Yambli wagged her fingers at Ishikawa. "Leave us. The chief and I must speak alone."

"But, Grandmother—"

"Go," Yambli insisted.

Ishikawa retreated to the trees, her arms folded in worry.

Myell squatted down low to be at Yambli's eye level. "I can't stay here. I have to go back to my wife. And to my friends, trapped in the network."

"Who can stop Jungali?" she asked, with affection. But her head was cocked, as if she was listening to something just out of his hearing range. A song from the sea, maybe, or somewhere beyond it.

"Why does Garanwa need someone to help him against the Roon?"

"He is the last remaining Nogomain," she whispered. He strained forward to hear her more clearly. Yambli said, "Only one, the boy named Burringurrah, and like me he is very old."

Ocean waves pounded ashore and drained away, an inexorable pattern.

"I can't help," Myell said. "I'm sorry."

He tried to pull away, but Yambli's hand closed on his fingers with a crushing grip.

"There's only the one," she said fiercely, her rheumy eyes locked on him. "Only the boy. The Roon would steal the First Egg and try to destroy the Rainbow Serpent himself. Will you stand with them or against them? Will you be the inheritor? Take the helm, or let the boat go unruddered?"

She released her grip and covered her face, sobbing dryly.

On Yambli's orders, the women brought Myell a canoe. Long and low, it had an elaborately carved bow shaped like a bird's head. Well made. Solidly built. It would fetch a good price back on Fortune, maybe at a boat show or Aboriginal corroboree. The paddles were sturdy, and he'd paddled before on lakes and in rivers, so he didn't think it would be too hard to paddle on open sea.

The ocean, as always, would be a problem. He was trying hard not to think about that.

They were gone now, Yambli and her followers, leaving him to the sea and sky. Silrys had given him some tips on how to navigate the waves and currents. His plan was to aim for the coast and pray for the best. He didn't have a life preserver, a kit for patching holes, or weapons for defending himself against sharks. He was probably doomed.

"Or am I?" he asked the crocodile that had been sitting in the surf eyeing him for the last fifteen minutes.

The crocodile opened her jaw and then snapped it closed again. Myell thought the creature was Free-not-chained, though he couldn't be sure.

He said, "Destiny, here I come."

Waves broke on the beach, lapping at the edge of the canoe. Myell peeked at the roiling, wild, and unfriendly ocean, his nemesis. He wasn't hyperventilating yet, but he could feel his breaths beginning to shorten, his palms growing cold and wet, and soon he would vomit, and then his heart would explode from anxiety.

"Hey," Ishikawa said, from farther up the sand.

Myell shielded his eyes against the sun. "Come to tell me how I'm destined to join the Nogomain and ruin the Rainbow Serpent's plan for all mankind?"

"Something like that." Ishikawa approached, her skirt flapping in the breeze. "I wanted to give you a gift. A belated wedding gift, as it were."

The knife was small but sharp, with a fine wooden handle inlaid with seashells. "Thanks. I'm sure Commander Scott will like it."

"This one's from Yambli. She says you lost your last one."

He accepted the gift of a small, woven dilly bag. Inside it were small wooden carvings of a crocodile and a gecko. The totems made him blink several times. The wood was golden and lustrous, warm to his fingers.

"Thank you," he said. "Can I order you to come with me, to return to your duties?"

"I serve the Nogomain before anyone else." Ishikawa leaned forward and kissed his cheek. "Take care of yourself, Sergeant."

"*Chief,*" he said.

She grinned and retreated, and he was alone again.

Before he could think of a dozen different reasons to delay, he pushed the canoe into the water and jumped in. He banged his shin on the side so hard that little drops of blood welled up on the skin like sweat. The canoe rocked, the paddle nearly slipped from his grip, and the waves push-pulled, push-pulled him toward the beach and back again. Free-not-chained slid off the sand and disappeared into the surf, abandoning him to his fate.

Myell thought maybe he wouldn't be so nervous if he could see bottom, but the land beneath the water quickly dropped off, leaving him with only sunlit blue and the deeper depths of green, and fish darting under the canoe's bow. Silrys had advised him to circle west around the island and stick close to shore. He alternated paddling to port and starboard, trying to find a rhythm for it, failing miserably. The waves kept him off balance and the breeze buffeted him from all sides.

This is not the ocean, he told himself. Just a really huge lake.

A river with no banks, perhaps.

The largest bathtub ever. It needed only a rubber duck or two.

He steadfastly tried not to look any farther out into the water than he had to, afraid that he might see shark fins or whale humps or something else intent on devouring him. The island fell away on his right. Ishikawa, Silrys, and Yambli were standing at the edge of a sandy point, watching him. Ishikawa and Silrys raised hands in farewell. Yambli clutched her staff and tipped her face to the sky.

He waved, just once, and kept paddling.

More small islands appeared, a string of them, and in the hazy distance were the cliffs that he and the Bunyip had plunged from. He kept the islands to his right and continued paddling. Waves kept trying to sweep him to shore, currents under the canoe tried to pull him out to sea, and the canoe's bow kept swinging left. Paddling at sea was ridiculously harder than paddling on a still lake.

He was lonely for the sound of another human, any human. The wind, the smash of waves against the hull, and the birds' irritating squawking were all eating at his brain. One of Myell's old friends back on the *Aral Sea* had been in a rock band, but none of the lyrics came when he tried to remember them.

Terror was edging up on him again, the ocean everywhere, the water and the waves and darkness pressing in. He sucked in deep breaths, tried to keep paddling, and pretended that Jodenny was in the bow.

"Well, Yambli did say you were a conjurer," Jodenny said, her long, pretty hair fluttering in the wind. She was wearing white shorts and a blue bikini top. Her skin was pink from the sun. "You can conjure up me or anyone else you need to talk to."

Myell replied, "She asked if I were the *inheritor,* not conjurer. And something about a helm. Besides, I don't need to talk. I need to be distracted."

"Distraction's not what you need at all. You need to stay focused."

"I'd prefer a beer."

Jodenny smiled. "Not in this neighborhood, partner."

Something white glided through the waves to his left, too quickly gone to identify. Myell started paddling faster, though already his arms and shoulders were beginning to ache.

He said, "Wish I were home with you."

"What makes you think I'm pining away at home, waiting for my man to return from sea?" Jodenny leaned back, basking in the sun. "Would you have stayed home, if our positions were reversed?"

The shark fin reappeared, closer to the canoe. Myell tried to judge the distance to the nearest island.

"I can't save you and everyone else, too," he said.

She smiled ruefully. "Save yourself first. You're the one with a shark off your bow."

He was trying not to think of that. He had the knife that Ishikawa had given him, and the paddle. If the canoe sank under the shark's jaws or weight, he'd likely be injured in the process. More sharks would come at the scent of blood. As a preemptive strike he could maybe bash the animal's head in with the paddle, but he had no idea how hard a shark's skull might be.

"Ideas?" he asked tensely.

Jodenny peered over the bow. "Let sleeping sharks lie."

Myell kept paddling. The shark circled, came back, glided closer. The far cliffs were like a mirage, dancing at the edge of his vision and never drawing nearer. He fell into a quick, rhythmic stroke, but paddling against the currents was exhausting.

"I'm thinking of the mountains for our honeymoon," Jodenny said. "Mountains and snow—"

Then she was gone, bikini and all, and the shark bumped the canoe with its snout.

"Shit, shit." With the paddle in one hand, Myell yanked out the knife. If he could stab it in an eye, or some part of its neck—

The shark rammed the canoe, sending him hurtling over the side.

He surfaced quickly, choking on vile-tasting seawater, the knife in hand. The canoe was floating nearby, capsized but not sinking. Not yet. The shark glided by. Long, lethal, playing with him. Toying with dinner before eating it.

Myell could swim, seawater be damned, but he had no place to swim to, except the overturned canoe. He treaded water carefully, slowly, his legs terribly exposed. The shark could easily rip one off as an appetizer. He was sure he'd lost control of his bladder. Was urine a repellent? He told himself he wasn't going to die, here in the ocean, without ever saying goodbye to Jodenny.

"Nice shark." His voice shook. "Nice little fish."

The shark slid by him, so close that he could almost feel the sand-paper of its skin, so quickly that it was maybe a phantom of his imag-ination. Yes, he'd conjured one up, as he'd conjured Jodenny—

The shark reversed course and barreled toward him. Another large shape slashed through the water and attacked first. Free-not-chained clamped her mammoth jaws around the shark and gouged at him with her razor claws. The water around Myell exploded with the force of the two creatures thrashing and smashing. He swam away as fast as he could, making for the overturned canoe, but in his panic he lost his sense of direction, and blood splashing into his face blinded him.

Not his own blood, not yet. The animals snapped and grappled with each other, Free-not-chained grunting, the shark's tail slapping the water as it fought. Myell choked on the bloody water, spat it out in terror, flailed as he felt himself sinking. His hands fell on the hull of the canoe. He hauled himself on top of it anyway, a meager refuge. His arms and legs were shaking uncontrollably. Instinct told him to try to swim for shore, but he couldn't move.

Swim, Jodenny said in his head.

The shark clamped its teeth around Free-not-chained and shook her like a rag doll. Myell couldn't tell how badly she was injured, but surely she couldn't last much longer.

Swim! Jodenny ordered.

Myell pushed off the canoe and started kicking. The waves and un-dertow and tide tossed him like driftwood. He kept his arms and legs moving as quickly as possible, trying not to suck in more salt water. The ocean was everywhere, in his ears and mouth and stinging his eyes, soaking into his skin like he was a pickle, or maybe he was just another creature of the sea now, in a mindless struggle for survival.

He could still tell up from down, at least, the dazzling sun hot in his eyes when he turned his head upward and coughed out water. Yambli's vision came to him, the creatures forming themselves out of land and sea in the eternal Dreamtime. And maybe he was doing that, maybe he was forming himself out of the water into man, or man going back into the water, and had been forever, and would be until the seas of this planet had dried up and left the ocean plains bone dry.

Stroke, stroke, keep kicking, and now a bump against his leg, a bump he could hardly ignore. He sucked in air the wrong way, choked, wheezed in breath. He was drowning.

Another bump, rough skin under his hands, and he pushed the shark away.

"Stubborn," a woman's voice said.

Myell flailed in surprise, and felt himself pulled into Free-not-chained's embrace. She was strong and cold and naked in his arms, her dark hair streaming around her, bleeding bite marks on her shoulders.

"You're injured," he said.

"In body, not spirit," she said.

She was a stronger swimmer than he was, even with the shark wounds. Her embrace was both comforting and disconcerting. Her feet were kicking, and with one arm she was pulling them along, the other wrapped around him. He was faceup, his limbs lax, his heart still pounding furiously.

"What are you?" he asked.

"The crocodile who dreams she's a woman," Free-not-chained said. "The woman who dreams she's a crocodile. You already knew that."

"Why help me?"

"We serve the same gods." Her voice was sibilant in his ears, soothing beneath the waves. Her hands cupped his cheeks, and her fingers were surprisingly hot. "Listen to the ocean the way I do. Hear it."

Birds, waves, wind, the frantic emptiness. Myell coughed up more water. "I'm listening."

"Not with your spirit."

This was hardly the ideal circumstance to start meditating. Then again, Myell didn't think she was going to let him drown. Didn't think he could be any safer than in the arms of a woman-reptile who could kill a great white shark.

"Close your eyes," Free-not-chained whispered.

He closed them. The eternal ocean persisted. He heard the wind pushing the waves up and down, the birds swirling, fish jumping, and beneath the surface there were newly arrived sharks chomping on the remains of Free-not-chained's victim, and whales circling beneath the sharks, and shrimp making noise, fish making noise, too, and the soft whish of anemones opening and closing their delicate fingers.

The sounds merged into a long, sustained sigh, the exaltation of a god, the wind of the Dreaming as it rolled on over everything, as it carried the world on its shoulders.

Free-not-chained turned him, her hands on his hips, her lips on his mouth, the world splitting between his legs as he entered into her, and the Dreaming, and all there was. His face burned under her touch, his cheeks on fire, his whole body tensed and aching.

Then she released him so that he was floating in the sea on his own, buffeted by the waves, the undertow. She retreated into the ocean with a flip of her crocodile tail. Before he could panic at being on his own, his feet touched sand. Myell hauled himself up onto the shore near the yellow cliffs and collapsed in the sand, all boneless and drained.

A long time later, he pulled himself upright and went to find lunch.

Putty Romero was in the brig for almost a full day before Jodenny succeeded in seeing him.

The first time she tried, visiting hours were over. The second time she went, after breakfast the next day, Romero was in an "interview" and unavailable. The third time she went, right after lunch, the sergeant on duty tried to dissuade Jodenny from getting involved.

"It's military business, Miss Spring," he said. Like the rest of the ship, the security office was lit only by emergency lights. The sergeant's eyes glinted red. "Nothing for passengers to worry about."

"I'm not just a passenger," Jodenny said. "I'm his aunt."

That was the story she and Tingley had agreed on, at least.

A little white lie was permissible, under the circumstances.

"Family or not," the sergeant said, patience wearing thin on his sharp face, "it's military business."

"Yes, you said that. Still, I think the passengers have a right to know there's a thief onboard. No matter who his family is."

The sergeant's face twisted up. He disappeared into the back of the office. Jodenny heard murmured voices. A tall chief with a bushy mustache stepped out and put his hands flat on the counter.

"Miss Spring," he said. "I'm Chief Prescott."

Jodenny said, "Nice to meet you, Chief. I've left three messages in your queue since last night. Did you receive them?"

Prescott was several centimeters taller than Jodenny, with a runner's physique. He peered down at her and said, easily, "You may have noticed that we're having a few problems with the ship. Sorry to say, it's not been an easy cruise. But rest assured, AT Romero's case is being handled as best we can."

"He punched the captain's son," Jodenny said. "How impartial can anyone be if they work for her?"

Prescott's hands lifted, spread. "We have safeguards in place, I promise. Regulations and rules."

"One of which is that an accused sailor has the right to counsel, a chaplain, and visits from family," Jodenny said. "TEAMSPACEJA-GINST 14.01.2. There's no chaplain onboard, there's no legal-service office for sailors, and his wife and I are his only family."

Prescott's fingers wagged a bit. "His wife's been in to see him."

"And now I want to see him, too."

"You know a lot about regulations, do you, Miss Spring?"

"The ship has a library, Chief Prescott."

"So it does." Prescott pursed his lips, thought for a moment, and then nodded. "Come on back. The brig's this way."

As far as brigs went, it wasn't much. Two small compartments with locked hatches, a conference area, and a holding area where another guard kept watch. Very dim, and somewhat cold. Romero was escorted out by a female RT armed with a mazer. His expression was glum until he saw Jodenny.

"Aunt Ellen!" he said.

They were seated at the conference table, and the female RT seemed determined to stay, until Jodenny said to Chief Prescott, "14.01.03, sub-paragraph 2?" and Prescott took her out of the room with him.

Romero leaned across the tabletop and said, urgently, "I didn't do it! Well, I did, but I didn't mean to."

Jodenny said, "What have they told you?"

"That if I sign a few forms, I'll get fined and be on probation and there will be a service-record entry, but it won't affect further promotions. But I don't care about getting promoted. I'm getting out when my enlistment ends."

She had certainly heard that before. From Myell, in fact.

"If I don't sign," Romero continued, "then I can have a hearing, but it won't take place until we get back to Fortune, and I have to stay in the brig for two or three more weeks, and they're trying to blackmail me, aren't they?"

"I wouldn't use the word *blackmail*," Jodenny said carefully. "You do have the right to a hearing, and to legal counsel."

"You could be my legal counsel!"

"I'm not a lawyer," she said, appalled.

"But you don't have to be! A lawyer, that is. Anyone can be your counsel. Hanne looked it up in the regulations."

"AT Romero, I'm getting off this ship at Earth. All the captain has to do is schedule your hearing for after that."

His expression fell into pessimism. "You think I should sign their forms. Plead no-contest."

"It would be the easy thing to do," Jodenny said. And if Romero really wasn't concerned about ever advancing in rank, that was good, because no matter what they told him on the *Kamchatka,* the promotion board wouldn't look kindly on a no-contest assault charge. "You're sure he took the ring? Maybe it fell down into the drain. Someone maybe pulled a practical joke, telling you it was the captain's son."

"Bobby Shu wasn't fooling," Romero said tightly. "Everyone knows the kid's a thief."

"You have to be careful of what everyone knows," Jodenny said.

"Does that mean you won't help me?"

"I'll do what I can," she said. "Don't sign anything yet."

Jodenny tried tracking down Romero's division chief, but the man didn't return her calls. She didn't want to talk to AT Shu yet, not without more information. The ship wasn't large enough to have a full-time legal officer, so that collateral duty had gone to Lieutenant Sweeney.

"Figures," Jodenny said, and went off to officer berthing.

He raised his hands when she appeared in his hatchway. "Whatever it is, I didn't do it."

"AT Romero. You have to drop the charges."

Sweeney leaned back in his chair and crossed his legs at his ankles. "Do I?"

"You know that it's the only fair thing to do."

He picked up a piece of paper and squinted at it. "You're saying this as impartial Aunt Ellen?"

Jodenny looked for a place to sit down. His bunk was the only option. She remained standing. "Putty just graduated from Supply School last week. The same night, he got married. This is his first ship, we've lost all engine power, and someone steals his wife's wedding ring. Maybe he could have handled it better. But no, he punches Captain Balandra's son, who shouldn't have been down in crew berthing in the first place, and who we know to be a thief."

"He says he wasn't in berthing yesterday morning."

"You have surveillance cameras all over this ship."

"We're on battery power," Sweeney reminded her.

"The cameras are designed to work on battery power," she retorted.

Sweeney leaned back farther. His chair creaked. "You know a lot about spaceship design."

"I know common sense. Why punish Romero for what Malachy did?"

"Romero punched the kid," Sweeney reminded her. "Broke his nose. The ship's doctor fixed it right up again, but that's not the point."

Jodenny said, "If you ruin Romero's career now, he'll never be a good sailor. If you let Malachy get away with theft, he'll never be a good man. I can't believe Captain Balandra wants either of those things."

"Neither does she want the crew thinking you can hit someone when you don't agree with them. She takes fighting very seriously."

Jodenny tried a different tack.

"She can't hold a captain's mast or award nonjudicial punishment. He could appeal on the grounds that she's not impartial, and Fleet would have to review the case back on Fortune. Meanwhile, news leaks out to the media, and suddenly something that could have been taken care of very easily is a public relations stain for the military and for Captain Balandra herself," Jodenny said. "For the good of the service, if nothing else, this needs to be resolved here and now, and fairly."

"What do you consider fair?" Sweeney asked.

Jodenny pursed her lips. "First off, the return of AT Tingley's wedding ring."

"Assuming it can be found. Next?"

"AT Romero attends an anger-management seminar, and does a week's extra duty as assigned by his division officer. No entries in his service record or performance eval."

Sweeney laced his hands over his chest. "Three weeks."

"Two."

"Fine. Anything else?"

"Malachy Balandra is restricted to quarters until the ship returns to Fortune."

Sweeney snorted. "Captain might not go for that."

"She will," Jodenny predicted. "She knows as well as anyone that it's bad for her command if the kid continues to run amuck."

"You're sure you're a librarian?" Sweeney asked.

"Sure as rain," she said.

She didn't hear anything more for the rest of the day. Tingley pinged to say that Romero was growing despondent and talking about signing the no-contest agreement just to get out of the brig.

"Don't you let him," Jodenny said. "What he does affects his career and yours now. I'll talk to Lieutenant Sweeney."

Tingley promised and hung up. From her bunk, Farber said, "What's all that about?"

"Nothing," Jodenny said.

"Ellen," Farber said.

The hatch was open and the dim passage again full of passengers. The air both inside and outside had begun to smell rank. Jodenny didn't mind the odors, though she would kill for a hot cup of coffee.

"A sailor asked me for some help," Jodenny said.

"What kind of help?"

"Doesn't matter."

Farber said, "You're supposed to be keeping a low profile "

"I'm low," Jodenny promised. "Very low."

She didn't sleep much that night, worried over Myell on the Bainbridge loop. She dreamed he was lost at sea, floating on a raft surrounded by water dragons. He was dying of razor-sharp thirst and bone-racking hunger. When she woke, she thought about Putty Romero locked up in the brig, slowly going nuts. At breakfast in the cold, dim galley, she eyed other passengers in sweaters and coats and thought how many problems Captain Balandra already had, Putty Romero notwithstanding.

At noon, with thirty hours or so until the drop into Earth's solar system, Lieutenant Sweeney came looking for her.

"We've got a meeting," he said.

"When?"

"Now."

Jodenny followed him up to the C-deck conference room, a small square of a compartment barely large enough for a table and six chairs. Captain Balandra and Malachy were already there, the latter dressed in a white shirt with all the buttons done up. His face was pinched and unhappy, but no unhappier than his mother's.

"Miss Spring," Captain Balandra said. "Please sit down. You too, Malachy."

A security tech arrived a moment later with Romero in tow. Romero's nervous expression eased when he saw Jodenny, but he paled at the sight of Captain Balandra.

"Sit," Sweeney told him.

Once the hatch was closed, Captain Balandra said, "This is my attempt at informal mediation. I shouldn't even be trying it, and if it backfires I'm the one to blame, but Miss Spring here has suggested it's in the best interests of all concerned that we settle this quickly, fairly, and without prejudice."

Romero stayed silent. Wisely silent. Malachy stared at the tabletop. Sweeney had a bright, interested look in his eyes.

"Does anyone have any objections to discussing this?" Captain Balandra asked.

Jodenny said, "It depends, ma'am, on where the discussion leads."

"I'm not sure where it'll end up," Captain Balandra said, "but I know where it starts. AT Romero, if you agree with the two weeks of extra duty and counseling class that your aunt recommended, as well as the stipulation of no service entry or performance-evaluation note, then we're done regarding the assault complaint. I never want to see you involved in a fistfight again, either of you, is that understood?"

Malachy nodded. Romero glanced at Jodenny for confirmation, then said, "Yes, ma'am."

Captain Balandra grimaced. "As to the wedding ring, Malachy says he didn't steal it."

"He did!" Romero burst out.

Jodenny put her hand on his knee. "Calm down."

"I didn't," Malachy protested. His eyes were wide and watery, but his chin was set. "I was in berthing, and yes I saw it, but I didn't take it. Taking something that's in plain view isn't stealing, anyway, it's—"

Captain Balandra said, "Malachy, enough of that."

"I didn't take it," Malachy said miserably.

Romero made an impatient noise. "You stole other things."

"Which is, strangely enough, why I'm inclined to believe him now," Captain Balandra said. "Show them."

Malachy pulled the box toward him and opened the lid. "This is a locket I stole while Mrs. Grindle was swimming during our last trip to Earth," he said, laying it carefully on the table. He reached inside again. "These are the PICs for Miss Spring, Jenna Fraser, and Mr. Zhang, all of which I stole on this cruise. These are eyeglasses from someone who was in the library before we left Fortune. This is . . ."

He went on, a dozen or more carefully tended treasures laid out for inspection. AT Tingley's wedding ring was not among the items.

"That's everything," Malachy said, finally. His voice was very small. "I never take from the crew. I didn't steal her ring."

Romero said, "It doesn't prove anything. He could just be hiding it somewhere else."

Jodenny agreed, in principle. But Malachy's misery was obvious, and she saw no particular reason for him to keep hiding the ring unless it was out of spite for Romero, who'd broken his nose.

She said, "It was AT Shu, wasn't it, who said that he saw Malachy take the ring? He could have taken it himself."

Sweeney said, "We already asked him. He denied it."

"He wouldn't do it," Romero said.

"You've known him for how many days?" Jodenny asked.

"He was the first person to welcome Hanne and me aboard the ship," Romero said. "He helped us get oriented and find things and he wouldn't have any reason to take it."

"And if he did take it, he surely would have gotten rid of it by now," Jodenny said. "Still, the captain of the ship can authorize a search of his locker."

"I'm not going to do that, not yet," Captain Balandra said. "Lieutenant Sweeney, talk to him again. Check to see if there are other items gone missing from crew berthing since AT Shu checked onboard."

The comm pinged. The bridge needed Captain Balandra's attention, and the meeting ended as abruptly as it had started. Jodenny regretted that Tingley's ring hadn't been recovered but still held out some hope. She was glad that Romero's punishment for fighting wouldn't be too onerous, but wanted to make sure he understood that it could have been worse.

"You don't get to hit crew or passengers you don't agree with," she said afterward, as they celebrated Romero's release with cold snacks in a corner of the galley.

He raised his right hand. "I swear, Auntie Ellen, I'm never going to fight again."

He seemed sincere about it, though entirely too comfortable with calling her Auntie Ellen.

Tingley snuggled closer to Romero's side. "Do you really think Shu took my ring?"

"I think you might never know," Jodenny said. "But rings can be replaced, as much as it pains you. Your good name, and making sure Malachy's not wrongly blamed, even if he did steal other things—that's more important."

"Chief Myell was right about you," Tingley said.

Jodenny lifted her coffee. "Right about what?"

Tingley gazed at her admiringly. "He told us that maybe the *Kamchatka* wasn't the best ship in the fleet, and maybe we wouldn't like it, but that the crew was more important than metal bulkheads. And then he said we might not like the crew, either, but there would be some people in the chain of command that we could trust to do what's right. He said that person might even be an officer."

Jodenny's cheeks grew warm. "Well, that was nice of him."

Romero added, "He said that's what happened to him on the *Aral Sea*. He found you. Then he married you. Which is what made us think it was a good idea to get hitched before we left Fortune."

She wasn't sure Myell would be happy to hear that part, but hoped she'd get to tell him soon enough.

With only twenty-four hours left until they dropped into Earth's system, the *Kamchatka*'s engines throttled to power and the overhead lights blazed on. Jodenny, alone in her cabin when it happened, heard cheers in the passageway. The comm clicked on and Captain Balandra thanked the Engineering Officer for his hard work. Jodenny headed on down to the Hole in the Wall, where three of the four Lous were already leading a celebration.

"Always knew they'd fix the old girl up!" Hullabaloo said, slapping the nearest bulkhead.

Baylou kissed Hullabaloo and raised a toast. "To full power and hot water!"

Even the bickering Zhangs found smiles and a compliment or two about the Engineering Officer.

Everywhere she looked, Jodenny saw couples kissing or embracing. More than she'd noticed before—the days of inconvenience had inspired a bit of romance. Myell's absence was like an enormous chunk carved out of her stomach and chest, leaving nothing but airlessness, imbalance.

"What's the matter?" Louise Sharp asked, her magenta hair obscuring one eye.

Jodenny shook her head.

After a while Louise, Hullabaloo, and Baylou took her up to the galley, which was open for a special hot midnight buffet. Jodenny didn't think she could eat, but they plied her with food and some warm beer, and took her down to the passenger lounge to play pool, and she didn't stumble back to bed until the wee hours.

When she woke with a raging hangover, Farber said, "Have a good time?"

Jodenny pulled a pillow over her head. Karl nestled his golden chin against her arm and gave a sigh.

By the time they were due to drop, her headache had abated to a manageable state and her stomach no longer felt in utter revolt. The wallvids in the passenger lounge were keyed to exterior feeds so that the assembled crowd could watch Mars, Demos Command, and Earth appear when they slid out of the Alcheringa.

"I don't think I'm up for another party," Hullabaloo said from where he sat curled up on the sofa.

Baylou patted his arm. "Maybe a sedate one."

The comm squawked. "Alcheringa drop in five, four, three, two, one . . ."

The entire ship shifted back into normal space, and the passengers applauded.

Demos Command appeared first, the massive space station like a giant cobweb with a shiny blue heart. A sliver of Mars hung behind it, not as red as Jodenny had expected. Earth was the brightest dot in a background of stars.

"Zoom in on the old girl," Baylou said. "Home sweet home."

The edge of the wallvid came equipped with a manual zoom control. Someone adjusted the focus so that Earth hung white and brown against the darkness. Gray sooty clouds covered much of the globe. Jodenny knew the atmosphere hadn't always been that way. The Debasement had done that. Then a green bulbous spaceship slid out from behind the curve of Earth. Its hull was pockmarked green metal, with no portholes but many strange knoblike protuberances. It had large thrusters sticking out its backside, but no glow of engine thrust. The overall shape was ungainly, no sleek lines or sweeping curves. The size was hard to judge. She figured it was several times larger than the *Kamchatka*. Maybe even bigger than the *Aral Sea,* which carried several thousand people.

The crowd in the lounge had fallen silent.

Hullabaloo finally asked, "What the hell?"

Another ship slid into view, and then a third. Three enormous ships, hanging in Earth's orbit.

Her skin ice-cold, goosebumps rising across her neck and down her spine, Jodenny said, "Aliens."

The village of the People was bustling with activity when Myell walked into it. He supposed he looked absurd in a half-torn shirt and red skirt, but the trek up a switchback cliff path hadn't provided much opportunity to improve his wardrobe.

At first no one noticed him, but then people began to murmur, someone else laughed, and children squealed. Two men approached Myell warily. Myell stopped walking. The men stared at him, their eyes wide.

One of them fell to his knees in the dirt and bowed down.

The other yelped and ran away.

Myell scratched his head. His hair was stiff from salt, and his scalp itched. He was sunburned all over, especially in places that never normally saw the sun. He hadn't worried about it before, but he hoped the People would let him get some sleep before they made him dive over a cliff again.

He was still standing there when the Bunyip, the Roon, came striding toward him.

It was larger than he remembered, tall and wide and bedecked in its fine helmet and cloak. The green skin on its head and arms gleamed in the sun. Its claws looked sharp enough to tear an animal, or a human, into bite-size pieces.

Myell wanted to flee but he was too tired, so instead he held his ground.

The Roon stopped and considered him with a tilted head. Spoke in clicks and whistles. But the voicebox it carried had apparently been damaged, and no language emerged from its speaker. A crowd formed around Myell, respectful and awed, and Shark Tooth pushed to the front of it. He cupped Myell's face in a strangely intimate way and thumbed his cheeks.

"Chief Myell!" That was Nam, jogging his way. "Thank Christ. What happened to your face?"

Myell touched his cheeks. He felt raised ridges, like welts.

"Looks like you got tattooed," Nam said.

Shark Tooth was speaking enthusiastically, the Roon was talking in its own language, and the noise of the crowd was growing louder. Myell said, "Maybe we could sit down?" and the next thing he knew, Nam had steered him into one of the huts. The interior was cool and dim, and Myell drank gratefully from a large jug of water.

Several children peeked inside, giggling and gawking, as Nam said, "We'd given you up for dead."

Myell waved his hand. "It's never that easy, sir. What's happened with the Roon?"

"The what?"

"The Bunyip."

One of the village women brought in a plate of kiwifruit, shelled nuts, and hot bread. Nam said, "Dr. Gayle's trying to talk to it, heaven help us all. When it climbed out of the surf and you were presumed drowned, the villagers weren't too keen on letting us go. For a while I wasn't even sure they would let us live."

Chief Elder arrived in the hut, a small entourage in tow. They all peered at Myell's face and argued about something. Myell wished he had a mirror so he could see what the fuss was about. Tattoos, Nam had said. He blamed Free-not-chained's hot hands, and wondered what marks she'd left.

After the elders departed it was Gayle's turn. She arrived dressed in a native skirt, with seashell bracelets rattling on her wrists.

"What happened to you?" she demanded of Myell. "Where did you get those clothes?"

"Where did you get yours?" Myell asked.

Nam said, "Forget fashion. What happened after you dived off that cliff?"

Myell hesitated. "Maybe there's somewhere more private?"

"Don't be ridiculous," Gayle said. "None of the natives understand a word we're saying, and I've made minimal progress with the Bunyip. It can't even make half the sounds we do, never mind understand them."

Myell rubbed his neck, hating the scratch of salt and grit. "We could take a walk instead."

"I don't understand your paranoia," Gayle said.

Nam said, "He wants to take a walk, let's take a walk."

But the People had other ideas. A celebration had already commenced outside, and Myell was escorted to a seat of honor among the elders for several hours of singing, dancing, clapping, drum beating, didgeridoo playing, and the ceremonial roasting of a sad little pig. Nam sat nearby, silent but watchful. Chief Elder presided over the telling and dramatic reenactment of many tales, none of which Myell understood. On the other side of the bonfire, the Roon played some kind of pebble game with Gayle and two children. Its gaze drifted more than once to Myell.

"You don't trust it," Nam said, passing along a plate of charred pork.

Myell eyed the charred meat and passed it on to Shark Tooth. "Neither do you."

"You called it something. Roon?"

"That's what they call it. The people who fished me out of the ocean."

"The ones who tattooed you?"

The ridges itched when Myell touched them. "I don't know who did that."

The men of the tribe rose to dance. Shark Tooth pulled Nam and Myell to their feet. Nam said, "No, really, I'm good," and Myell also tried to decline, but they were swept into the foot-stomping, thigh-slapping crowd. The women cheered and clapped. Nam's evident mortification, a Team Space commander dancing with the mostly naked natives, cheered Myell up. He would have taken more delight, but at that very moment his right ankle turned beneath him and he started to crash to the ground.

The Roon caught him. Its grip was careful but strong. Its teeth were so close that Myell could see slivers of pig caught between incisors and smell its meat-scented breath. The alien held him upright while the dancers spun around them and Nam pushed his way over.

"Put him down," Nam ordered.

Gayle, standing at the alien's elbow, said, "He's just examining him. He won't hurt him."

The Roon's flat gray eyes narrowed, but it gave no indication of understanding them. Myell shuddered as it leaned even closer. The alien's nose holes widened as it sniffed Myell, actually sniffed him, as if he were an appetizer or maybe even the main course.

Nam didn't have a mazer, didn't even have a knife, but he grabbed the nearest scaly arm as if to physically wrestle the Roon. The grip on Myell released, and he fell to his ass on the hard ground.

"Told you!" Gayle said.

The Roon made several clicking noises and retreated a few steps.

Nam kept a wary eye on Myell and said, "You okay?"

He rubbed his ankle. "Only wounded my pride."

The Roon walked off. Gayle followed. The drums, already loud, grew in volume as women dancers joined the men. Children lit torches to illuminate the encroaching dusk, and Myell let Nam help him up.

"Let's take that walk," Nam said.

Afterward, as they sat on the edge of the village swatting bugs, Nam said, "You have the strangest adventures."

Myell squinted at the distant firelight. The singing and dancing hadn't abated, even if the guest of honor had disappeared. He didn't feel adventurous. He was tired, hot, and still covered with sea salt. The only part of the story he'd omitted was Free-not-chained and her band of crocodile women. He could push Nam's credulity only so far.

Nam slapped at an insect on his neck. "That Sphere, on the women's island—it'll take us to this Nogomain? Garanwa. The one who wants to stop the Roon. The one who needs your help, maybe take his place?"

"Allegedly."

"You should have gone through," Nam said. "Taken the chance while you could."

The second-guessing stung in a way that Myell hadn't expected. Before he could object, however, Nam added, "We can't go there now—the risk's too great that the Bunyip, Roon, whatever you call it, will follow. We can't ever let it gain control of the network and all the Spheres."

"You've got a plan?" Myell asked.

"Keep you away from it," Nam said. "It's obviously interested in where you've been. We'll have to leave on our own, get back across the plain, without it noticing."

"Sounds impossible."

"I'm working on it," Nam said.

They went back to the hut that Nam and Gayle had been sleeping in. Shark Tooth came around, urging them back to the party, but finally accepted Myell's bleary-eyed refusal. A young girl brought a basin of fresh water and Myell happily rinsed himself and the clothes he was stuck wearing. Nam sat outside, keeping an eye out for Gayle or the Roon.

Myell had no idea what time of night it was, but as he lay down on one of the pallets he told himself he'd just close his eyes for a short while. He wished Jodenny were there to lie with him. She would curl over him, her legs twined with his, her breath warm on his cheek. Sometime later he woke, muddy-headed and exhausted, to the sound of men arguing outside the door. More precisely, Nam was haranguing Shark Tooth.

"This high, long hair, tiny waist, talks a lot? How far could she go?"

Shark Tooth's reply was all in his native tongue, and explained nothing.

Myell hauled himself to the doorway. "What's wrong?"

"Gayle's missing," Nam said. "I don't see the Roon anywhere, either."

The party had ended, with only embers glowing in what had been the central bonfire. A few last stragglers were heading off toward their huts. Shark Tooth was coated with sweat and dust and looked ready to sleep off the feasting, but Nam was insistent.

"Where does it sleep?" he demanded, making shapes in the air that were meant to resemble the Roon. "Where does it go when it's not here?"

Myell rubbed his gritty eyes. He too tried sign language, simple words, pantomimes, until Shark Tooth abruptly nodded and called out across the village. Two of his men appeared, wobbly on their feet, wine drying on their chests.

Shark Tooth gave them orders. The men stumbled off, and Nam said, "Maybe now we'll get somewhere."

They got nowhere. Neither Gayle nor the Roon was anywhere to be found. Shark Tooth grabbed some torches, handed them off to Nam and Myell, and led them into the jungle on a narrow footpath. The going was tricky, the insects merciless, and they had to wrest their way through brush and moss and mud. Their flashlights made the going only a little easier. Snakes slithered out of their way and other animals moved in the undergrowth.

"Keep an eye out for crocodiles," Nam said as they crossed a small stream.

After twenty minutes of hiking, they came to a clearing where a large, low shelter of vines and twigs had been erected and roofed with palm fronds. The work of someone with a lot of time on his hands, Myell thought. Someone who had painted ocher symbols on a door fashioned from branches. The symbols looked like a greeting of some kind, or maybe a warning.

Shark Tooth called out, but the Roon didn't appear. A knife in hand, Nam pulled open the unlocked door. From inside came the stink of rotting meat and something sweet, like candy.

"Good lord," Myell said.

His torch illuminated dozens of dead birds strung from the shed ceiling. Exotic birds, red and yellow and blue, some of them with their feathers half plucked, some partially dissected, others fully intact. One or two stirred on their vines, as if still alive. Other animals were pinned to the walls or crammed into glass cases—wallabies, bats, frogs, even a koala. They suffered from rotting fur, empty eye sockets, splayed legs, and pinned wings. Death and decay, nothing but it, and it seemed like the specimens had been collected out of cruelty, not curiosity.

Shark Tooth's men muttered unhappily among themselves.

Nam said, "Goddammit."

Myell tried hard to breathe through his mouth and not his nose. "It slept here? Lived here?"

A long, low pallet lay against one wall, along with some baskets from the People's village and a pile of gnawed-over bones. The bones were too long to be from birds, too thick to be from fragile mammals. In fact, one looked like a human femur—

Myell lurched outside to the clearing.

Shark Tooth and his men came out making warding gestures and spitting into the dirt. Nam emerged last and asked, "If it's not here, where else would it take her?"

Myell shook his head. "Not to the women's island. Gayle didn't know about that."

"The Spheres," Nam said. "Maybe it thinks she can help it get home."

Myell tugged on Shark Tooth's arm, performed more pantomimes, and drew pictures on the ground. Shark Tooth finally seemed to understand, but took them back to the village first for water skins, easy-to-carry food, and farewells.

Chief Elder, roused from sleep, made a long speech and kissed Myell on the head.

"Yes, yes," Nam said impatiently. "Enough of the farewells."

The moon was arcing down in the western sky. Myell guessed it was four or five hours until dawn. He hadn't had much sleep lately, but Nam had probably had even less. Shark Tooth and two of his men led them south along the cliff in reverse of the journey they had made a few days earlier, and far below, waves crashed and drained against rocks. Nam kept himself between Myell and the ocean, insulating him from the view.

"It's not so bad anymore," Myell assured him, though it was a relief when they turned into the jungle.

The going was slow. The landscape pulsed with nocturnal animals and insects, and occasional screeches, flapping noises, and scuffling left Myell unnerved. He couldn't help but remember the dead birds swinging in the Roon's hut, with their tiny claws open and grasping. He and Nam should have torched the place, even if it risked a larger conflagration.

Myell stopped abruptly, his hands on his knees.

"What's wrong?" Nam asked.

He shook his head.

"Hold up," Nam said to Shark Tooth. The Aboriginals stopped hacking through the brush.

Myell blew out as large a breath as possible and resisted drawing more air in. Yambli believed he could stop the clawed, cruel Roon. Believed it was his destiny. As if one man could possibly do anything against the tide of an alien species that plucked eyes from koalas and offered the dead flesh of its own as a gift.

Nam said, low and calm, "You're worrying me, Chief."

"It's nothing," Myell said, an enormous lie.

They resumed walking as soon as Myell could make his legs go forward. Sips of water and a steadfast refusal to think further than the next step kept him going until dawn. By then they had reached the floodplain, which stretched gray-red under the lightening sky. The rains had brought more greenery to it, but crossing it would be as difficult as the last time.

Shark Tooth waved his hands around and gestured toward the trees, and Nam said, "I think we're stopping for a while."

Myell said, "We can't afford to. The Roon already has a head start."

"If it's gone, it's gone," Nam said. "We can rest for a bit."

Myell needed no further encouragement. He swallowed down some nuts and dried fruit that Shark Tooth offered, and fell asleep in the shadow of some trees. In his dreams a flock of birds cried out soundlessly, their throats cut open. The frantic fluttering of their wings brought him awake with a jerk, and he squinted at the sun overhead.

"We're moving again," Nam said.

The hike was miserable, though he was glad that he'd put aside his boots and socks before the cliff dive and Nam had saved them for him. The skirt chafed at his knees until he rolled it higher. Shark Tooth and his men cheerfully slung rocks at lizards and talked among themselves, while Nam plodded steadily forward and Myell tried to keep pace. He drank from his water bottle in moderation, trying to keep from dehydration. Worse was the sunburn spreading on his face and arms and legs.

"Are we going to march right up to the Spheres?" Myell asked. "It might not give her back without a fight."

"I'm still trying to figure out why it took her in the first place," Nam said.

Dark gray clouds rose up in the west, thunder and lightning cracking inside them. Myell slapped at bugs on his arms and sipped water and wasn't surprised when the first cool drops of rain hit his face. They pushed on across the ancient landscape as the water bled down into the dried-out marshlands and sent geese fluttering across the horizon.

Shark Tooth stopped, gesturing, pointing across the horizon, and Myell saw the Spheres. He was absurdly grateful, despite the danger ahead.

Nam said, "Tell them to turn back. I don't want to get anyone killed."

Myell tried the best he could, but either his pantomime skills had faded during the hot day or Shark Tooth was being deliberately obtuse.

"Iiwariniang," Shark Tooth said, or something like that. "Iwaringdo."

Nam also tried to get them to go back, to no avail.

Myell wiped rain from his face. The drops were coming down faster, harder, and he didn't like the increasing proximity of the lightning.

"I'll go in," Nam said. "Leave you here with them. See if I can talk to it, see if Gayle's still alive."

"Then it has two hostages," Myell said.

"Better idea?"

"I go in, trade myself for Gayle, send her out. It's not interested in you, but it likes me."

Nam squinted at him. "Not going to happen."

"You can't save both of us, sir."

"I can damn well try. Don't make me give you an order, Chief."

Myell held his gaze. "Don't make me disobey one, Commander."

Shark Tooth murmured something, slapped both their arms, and started jogging toward the Mother Sphere. Nam said, "No, wait!" and Myell tried to stop him, but the Aboriginals splashed gleefully through puddles, called and shouted out and made a ruckus, and any chance they might have had of arriving quietly was ruined.

Not that it mattered much. Gayle came to the archway, waving her hand eagerly. "There you are! Come in out of the rain."

The Roon appeared behind her, large and expressionless, but not bearing any kind of weapon. The Aboriginals hovered but didn't move forward. Nam held Myell back several meters from the arch-way. Water poured down as the sky darkened even more, but they couldn't get any more wet.

"What the hell are you doing?" Nam demanded of Gayle.

"It wanted to come out here," Gayle said. "We're beginning to reach real understanding through pictographs. I drew the Spheres, it drew the token. It wants to communicate."

"It wants more than that," Myell said.

The Roon watched them, silent.

Gayle grimaced. "It's an anthropologist, don't you see? It's not a soldier or a general or anything other than a scientist stranded here when the system shut down."

"You can't be that blind," Nam said.

"You can't be that obtuse," she retorted. "It's alone, without equip-ment, trapped here for months. The worst that can happen is that we take it to the next station. That's such a crime? But if we can commu-nicate, if we can establish trust—"

Something moved in the corner of Myell's vision. He started to yell, but the second Roon was too damned fast. It rose out of the grass, grabbed Myell, and yanked him close.

"Chief!" Nam yelled.

"It won't hurt him!" Gayle called out. "I think it's his mate."

The Aboriginals made unhappy noises, but they didn't raise their spears. Nam held out his knife but didn't approach. Squeezed tight, the claws sharp against his throat, Myell didn't fight or antagonize it. He felt himself dragged backward and tried not to stumble. The sec-ond Roon pulled him into the dim, dry confines of the Mother Sphere.

"It's all right," Gayle was saying. "They're just desperate, like us."

The two Roon conferred in clicks and whistles. Myell's breath was going short, his vision dimming, at the pressure on his throat.

"It's going to kill me," he said.

Gayle motioned to the female. "You need him. Please."

The male Roon kept talking, clicks and whistles and shrill little sounds. The female hauled Myell tighter, her breath foul. He didn't know what they were arguing about. He told himself he'd do the same thing, if he and Jodenny were stuck somewhere for months on end—do anything, desperate, frantic, ruthless, to get home.

The call of an approaching ouroboros made both Roon fall silent.

Languid calm enveloped Myell. The next station might be the Roon home world, or it might be another floodplain, or snow planet, or somewhere completely different, but the token was coming . . .

Nam and the Aboriginals appeared at the archway. Nam had taken someone's spear and looked ready to hurl it.

"They're not going to kill anyone," Gayle said. "They want to get home, like we do."

"Not with him," Nam said.

The ring appeared, solid and beautiful. The female Roon dragged Myell in, and the male joined them. The male hesitated, then motioned to Gayle and Nam.

"Don't," Myell said, the calm evaporating. "Stay here."

"And be stranded?" Nam stepped forward.

Gayle was already ahead of him. "Not a chance."

Shark Tooth raised a hand in farewell. "Jungali," he said, and the others echoed. Their voices grew louder and more fervent: "Jungali, Jungali, Jungali—"

The ouroboros whisked them away.

The yellow light was different than before. Harder, hotter. Something was wrong with it. The next station appeared like a snapshot, no time for Myell to assimilate their surroundings, and then they were swept forward again. Another station materialized. But the light pushed them onward, and the next Sphere was just a blur, and Myell was aware of Nam trying to say something in the milliseconds, of the Roon chittering in alarm. The tattoos on his cheeks burned like acid. Too late he realized that they were a marker, a signal, a trap—

Then a Sphere unlike any other coalesced and stayed permanent. Myell fell to his knees. He was aware of the Roon clutching each other, Gayle vomiting on herself, Nam gasping for breath.

Soothing blue light played over them, a beam of some kind, and all the wrong parts within Myell righted themselves, all the wild chemistry in his body realigned.

"Where the hell are we?" Nam asked.

Myell focused on the room the ouroboros had left them in—room, not Sphere, large and high-domed with multiple archways leading out of it. The tiled dome glowed a soft, soothing shade of blue. The walls were smooth, curving sandstone, the floor hard dirt. He smelled the faint aroma of flowers in the air. Lilacs.

"It's the hub." Myell rubbed his temples. "The Sphere that controls all the others. End of the line."

CHAPTER TWENTY

We know this much," Toledo said, his chair squeaking as he shifted his weight. "They arrived twelve hours ago, coming in from the other side of the sun—Demos Command didn't pick them up until they were passing Venus. Three of them. Went straight to Earth, took up orbit, haven't made a peep on any radio frequency. Don't answer hails. Don't try to communicate with anyone, it looks like. Haven't fired any weapons, haven't sent down any ships. They're just sitting there. At the same time, instrument-based radar down on Earth has gone crazy. Nothing can fly. Anything with a navigational computer on it has been rendered useless, and that includes land-, ocean-, and satellite-based missiles."

Jodenny felt cold all over. "Earth is defenseless?"

"Even if anyone down there could launch missiles, we're talking fleas against dinosaurs here," Toledo said glumly.

Farber, her vomit bag close at hand, asked, "Why are we still on course for Earth?"

Toledo shifted again. The chair protested. "Because that's what the Admiralty ordered."

"There's no place else to go," Jodenny replied. "It's a straight, empty run from the drop point to Earth."

"We could change course for the asteroid mines or Martian colonies," Farber said.

"It's possible the aliens don't know they're out there," Toledo replied. "No one wants to reveal their presence if that's true. I've heard that any Team Space ships in flight have been ordered to hold position. We're talking passenger ships on their way to the moon, cargo ships outbound to Mars, the Survey Wing birdies over at Jupiter and Saturn. Even some fox fighters training off Venus. No one's going anywhere. Except us."

Farber leaned closer to the gib, almost blocking Jodenny's view. "But we don't have any weapons. Just a handful of birdies."

"We have ourselves," Jodenny murmured. "Thrust and maneuverability, and engines that can be set to overload."

Incredulous, Farber said, "What can we do? Ram them? With a ship full of civilians?"

"If it comes to that," Jodenny said grimly.

The ships on the deskgib continued their orbit of Earth. Jodenny watched for a few more hours but didn't learn any more than she already knew. She forced herself to go off in search of food, anything that would silence the growling in her stomach, but that was a mistake. The galley was full of noise and fear, passengers with nothing else to do but worry.

"I always believed there were aliens out there," she heard one man saying. "Just not that they'd come gunning for us."

Hullabaloo, Baylou, and Lou Eterno called Jodenny over to their table. Reluctantly she went over with her sandwich and coffee and took the space they made for her.

"Any news from the bridge?" Hullabaloo asked.

"Why would I know?" Jodenny asked.

Baylou gave her a speculative look. "Heard you have friends in high places."

Jodenny glanced past him to the wallvid. "Not that high."

"I keep telling you. If they meant to wage war, they would have opened fire by now." Hullabaloo reached past Jodenny for a salt shaker. "Earth would be rubble. We'd all be little charred bits of bone and flesh, drifting through space."

So much for eating. Jodenny pushed her food away and said, "No one knows. Don't start planning for the worst."

"What do you think they look like?" Lou asked. "Bug eyes? Furry? We've got a betting pool. I think they have two heads."

She appreciated his levity. "Never saw one, couldn't begin to guess—"

But then her hand jerked, and coffee sloshed over the rim onto her hand. She was barely aware of heat and wetness. She lurched to her feet. She *had* seen one. Standing in the middle of a destroyed laboratory, an ouroboros encircling its clawed feet, a feather cloak around its scaly shoulders. The thing was maybe as surprised to see her as she was to see it. Around them, the General Quarters klaxon screamed and clanged, and Sam Osherman was saying, "Go! Get out of here!"

Hullabaloo put his hand on her arm and tried to restrain her. "Ellen? What's wrong?"

"Nothing," she mumbled. "Leave me alone."

She fled the galley, blindly climbed the nearest ladder, and made it to her cabin without being aware of the actual steps. Once inside, she locked the hatch and slid to the deck with her arms wrapped around her knees. The chemical memory block had dissolved. She could remember everything now, every part of the *Yangtze* disaster. Her body shook and tears slid down her face and she hugged herself hard, missing Myell so keenly that she couldn't breathe, wishing he were right there beside her.

An alien, on the *Yangtze*. No wonder Team Space had blocked her memory. They hadn't worried so much about her learning the secrets of the Wondjina Transportation System. They'd been worried about the aliens, about sentient or hostile life somewhere in the network.

Jodenny slowly peeled herself from the deck. She needed a shower, something to wash off the stench of fear and despair, but settled for curling up on her bunk with Karl. The koala snuggled against her side but she was still cold, very cold, and no robot could ease that chill.

Fucking aliens. Fucking Team Space, knowing it all along.

She squeezed her eyes shut. Jem, Dianne, all the lost dead of her first ship. She didn't sleep, not with their faces and voices so present in her thoughts, but awareness of the cabin faded away. When a keening sound cut through the air she thought she was dreaming. She jerked upright and watched, in dulled surprise, as a green ouroboros appeared in the space between her bunk and Farber's. This one wasn't shaped like a snake eating its tail, but instead like a crocodile. A large, hungry crocodile with sharp eyes. Knowing eyes.

Jodenny sat up. Karl rolled aside, yawning, and went back to sleep.

"No," Jodenny said to the ring. "I can't trust you."

It spun lazily.

She said, "You could be a trap."

Something small moved within its shadow. A tiny green gecko climbed up the inner rim, reached its summit, and gazed at her with head erect. The entire ouroboros lifted ever so slightly, then descended again.

Geckos and crocodiles. Totems and gods.

"Will you take me to Terry?" she asked. The gecko flicked its tail, and the ouroboros brightened like a little green sun.

"Oh, hell," she said, and stepped inside.

Nam and Myell put several meters of distance between them and the Roon.

"Keep away from them, Doctor," Nam said.

"Stop being ridiculous." Gayle wiped her mouth with the back of her hand. "They need our assistance."

The two aliens stopped comforting each other and took an interest in their surroundings. The room had multiple archways, but no signs or maps indicated where they might lead. The dome, several hundred meters above, was as distant as the sky. The glowing walls were soothing, the air cool and fresh. The ouroboros didn't move on, but remained resting on the dirt floor.

"You're sure this is the control station?" Gayle asked. "How do you know?"

He shrugged. Myell couldn't explain it, didn't want to try. "I just do."

"There," Nam said, pointing past Myell's shoulder. "Look."

Part of the wall began to slide down, revealing an eyelid-shaped viewport to outer space. A thick swath of stars ran across the sky, glittering, brilliant, close enough to almost touch. Myell had spent many nights on Baiame staring up into the nighttime sky, had visited the Seven Sisters in all their glory, but had never seen the cosmos so breathtaking, so gorgeous.

"Jesus," Nam said.

The Roon clicked and whistled.

Myell walked slowly toward the view, aware of a faint tingle in the dirt. He stopped, stepped again. His Team Space boots were a hindrance.

"What are you doing, Chief?" Nam asked.

Myell chucked the boots aside and peeled off his socks. The dirt was cool and slightly moist under his toes. "You don't feel that?"

Nam gazed doubtfully at the ground.

Myell concentrated on the tingling. Not like static electricity, not like any kind of electricity, and it had a taste. Faintly bitter, but not unpleasant. He followed it, barely aware of Nam trailing behind, and Gayle and the Roon behind Nam.

"You're sure this is a good idea?" Nam asked.

The path led into another domed room, similar to the first, but the walls were yellow and the open viewport revealed an enormous red nebula of stars. A cluster of gum trees grew in the center of the room, ringed by small shrubs with red flowers. The air smelled wetter, tinged with sweet fragrance.

"I think we're on a space station," Gayle said, gazing at the nebula.

"The views don't match," Nam said. "They're probably vids, maybe artwork."

The yellow chamber had several archways of its own. The path beneath Myell's dirty feet curved and crossed over other tingling lines, each distinct. The one he was following made him feel small and quick, camouflaged, four-legged . . .

He stopped and said, "It's a gecko."

Nam was frowning deeply. "It's a what?"

"Gecko line," Myell said. "Songline."

He started following it again. Gayle said, "But songlines are just myths, and you're not an Aboriginal."

Nam said, "Don't ruin the mood, Doctor."

The gecko songline continued on through more beautiful chambers, some of them filled with blue or white light, some dim and soothing. Some had viewports onto more galactic wonders—a hot red planet here, a cluster of asteroids there—and some had only the graceful curved walls reaching up, ever up. Trees and flowers grew everywhere now, tropical rain forests re-created and thriving, and thick carpets of green grass swept Myell toward more archways, always more archways.

Gayle said, "We're going to get hopelessly lost."

"Worry more about your friends," Nam said.

The two Roon trailed behind them, conferring with clicks and whistles. Myell didn't spare them any of his attention. The gecko line crossed a kangaroo, a wallaby, a crocodile. The crocodile pulled him along, inexorable as the current of a stream, until they reached a chamber unlike any of the others. It was rectangular, not circular. The light was blue-white, like a summer's day, and the ground was more mossy than grassy. Orange and black towers of rock, no taller than Myell's shoulders and similar to beehives, formed mazes around small ponds and tiny streams.

Gayle touched one of the rock piles, and it began to crumble under her fingers.

"Silica." She peered under her fingernails "Algae, maybe lichen."

On the most distant wall hung an enormous mural that measured ten meters high and twice as long. Myell approached it warily. The fabric was organic and stitched together in large patches. Tufts of fur poked out from under the edges. Skin cloaks, sewn together. Large-scale paintings like petroglyphs covered the canvas, but instead of cave animals he saw swirls and whirls, lines, zigzags, arcs.

The Roon began to chitter in excitement. Myell tore his attention from the skin cloak to watch a small man approach from one of the archways. No, not a man. A boy, or what had once been a boy a very long time ago. The not-boy had taut brown skin and a swollen, bald head. He looked as fragile as the beehives, and older than anyone Myell had ever met.

The not-boy wore no clothes, only a white crocodile painted on his torso. His genitalia were shrunken and misshapen. The Roon hissed at him and raised their clawed hands. Nam's hand went to the empty place on his belt where his mazer usually hung.

"You brought the interlopers," the not-boy said, his wide, milky white eyes fixed only on Myell.

Myell said, "I'm sorry. It happened that way."

Gayle stepped forward and asked, "Who are you?"

The not-boy stared only at Myell.

"Garanwa," Myell said, uncertain at first, but growing more confident. "Of the Nogomain. Last of the Nogomain. Is that it?"

Garanwa lifted his trembling right hand toward the skin cloak. The designs brightened and hummed, as if gaining power.

"Chief?" Nam asked, sounding nervous.

"We're trying to get back to our people," Myell said. "They're stuck back on a planet a few stations away from where we started. There are other people, too. A team that went before us. We came to rescue them. Then we can go back home and leave the network alone. That's all we want."

Glyphs on the skin cloak began to glow white hot. A silver-green ouroboros shaped like a crocodile dissolved into existence nearby, encircling Collins, Saadi, Lavasseur, and Breme. They were all still dressed in winter gear, with snow on Saadi's shoulders and frost on Breme's goggles.

"Commander!" Collins said.

"What the hell—" Saadi started.

The crocodile ring flashed away, and returned several meters away with a different crew inside—six men and women whom Myell didn't recognize, but who wore Team Space gear and were tanned and dirty, as if they'd spent many weeks in the field.

The second team saw the Roon first. "Lizards!" one of them yelled. Instantly two of them pulled mazers from their holsters. Two others raised hand-made spears. Saadi, Lavasseur, and Breme were only a split second slower.

"Stand down!" Nam ordered.

Garanwa stalked away, leaving them to their confrontation.

The gecko and crocodile ring left Jodenny in the middle of a dark chamber. She couldn't see the walls or the ceiling, but the floor at her feet was sky blue and vast, as if she were standing on top of a world.

"Hello?" she asked. She turned in a circle. "Is anyone here?"

A Great Egret twice her size walked out of the darkness and dived into the floor. Its wings spread with majestic power as it swooped and sailed beneath Jodenny's feet. It had graceful curves and a long neck, with white feathers and black feet. Clouds and sun rolled by under Jodenny, and she had to sit down or fall over from dizziness.

"You're not real," Jodenny said.

The glass floor dissolved and plunged her into the clouds. She shrieked. Flailed for any kind of handhold. Plummeted, wildly, onto the back of the egret. It had become exceptionally large, and she very small. She clutched its white feathers and tightened her legs around it and closed her eyes against the dizzying landscape.

"Put me back!" Jodenny ordered.

"Where have you gone?" the Great Egret asked, its voice clear and high. "Are you lost?"

The bird flew and flew. Jodenny forced one eye open and immediately regretted it. Far below her was a black ocean churning and crashing with great white waves. Above her, the blue chamber was a field of stars and planets, a great dizzying progression of the cosmos.

"You're a dream," she said through chattering teeth. Icy air buffeted her. "You're not real."

"Then why are you talking to me?" It sounded amused.

"I'm talking to myself!"

"Then say something interesting."

Hallucination or dream, the joy of flight slowly seeped into Jodenny. Skimming the ground in flits was fun enough, soaring into orbit in a birdie even more so, but never before had she so keenly felt the wind lifting and dropping her, the sun hot on her face, the clouds like wisps of cotton candy that twirled around her fingers and trailed up her arms to her shoulders.

"What do you want from me?" Jodenny asked, her voice muffled in the soft white feathers of the bird's neck.

The Great Egret swooped through the sky, clouds parting around them, other birds appearing and disappearing, their cries distant and comforting. Rivers of wind carried them along. The ocean below crashed up against a red landscape of desert and rock where shadows swirled and whirled, and connected to one another in a pattern that looked older than time, older than the wind itself.

"Not yours to tread or rule," the Great Egret said. The bird dipped lower, its voice deepening. "Nor theirs."

The wind slowed. The sky began to smell of smoke. Jodenny's eyes focused on an army of figures moving over the surface of the red land: helmeted, towering, reptilian creatures with claws. Like the kind she had seen on the *Yangtze*. They kicked at the landscape, smashing and overturning every stone.

"Roon," said the bird. "The Interlopers."

"Why are you showing me?" Jodenny asked.

"Only the Lightning Man can stop them," the Great Egret said. "You must let him do his job."

Jodenny buried her face in the bird's feathers. "No."

"It is his destiny—"

The Great Egret cried out sharply. Bright red blood blossomed under its feathers. Jodenny's heart trip-hammered and she clutched the bird's neck frantically as they dropped limply out of the sky. She was falling, worse than falling, plummeting, both of them, and though Jodenny told herself *just a dream, just a goddamn dream*, she couldn't help but scream as the wind sucked at her clothes and hair, and she was still screaming when she crashed.

CHAPTER TWENTY-ONE

E veryone put down your weapons!" Nam ordered.

"Step away from them," Commander Gold said to Gayle. He was a slim man, with bright green eyes and months of beard on his face. His uniform was torn, his hands dirty. His mazer was aimed directly at the larger Roon's head. "Get away *now*."

"No," Gayle said. "They're unarmed. They're not going to hurt us."

Myell waited, breathless, ready to duck if mazer shots started flying.

"Chief Saadi, Sergeant Breme, Sergeant Lavasseur," Nam said, his voice steady. "I'm giving you a direct order. Drop your weapons."

Nam's team lowered their mazers. Gold's team waited for word from their commander.

"Byron?" Gold asked, flicking a gaze toward Nam.

"Drop them," Nam said. "You can always kill them later."

Gayle asked, "Where's Robert? Why isn't he with you?"

Myell slipped out of the room, intent on following Garanwa. The little not-boy had a lot of explaining to do. The adjacent chamber, dark and woodsy, was full of archways and vines and greenery, but Garanwa wasn't there.

Myell stared down at the dirt and grass, trying to see with his eyes. That failed, so he tried to feel with his feet instead. After a bit of shuffling he found the gecko songline, and followed it into a long low room of black divans and cushions. The viewport here was the floor itself, which was like a thick pane of glass hovering over stars and two blue-gray moons.

Should keep looking, he told himself, but languor made him stretch out on the nearest divan. He didn't remember closing his eyes but when he opened them Garanwa was there, his misshapen face like a moon in the dimness, his swollen fingers on the side of Myell's head.

"The helm needs to be steered," Garanwa said.

Myell murmured a protest, or thought he did, but was soon asleep again.

When he next woke, Lavasseur and Saadi were somewhere nearby, arguing.

"That's the thing about alien spaceships," Lavasseur was saying. "What if this is really the engine room? You could be pissing on a nuclear power rod or something."

The room they were arguing in had water flowing into round bowls set at waist level. If there were other water sources or drains, they were well hidden. Iridescent tiles, blue shading to pinks and yellows and purples, covered the walls. The air was moist and smelled like newly fallen rain.

From the doorway, Myell said, "Looks like a bathroom to me, but if you're wrong, it'll be interstellar war."

The other two squinted at him.

"Kidding." Myell gazed for a moment at the walls, at the wavy designs barely visible beneath the tiles, and waved his hand at an appropriate spot. "Use these controls."

Benches slid soundlessly out of the walls, each one equipped with more bowls and drains. Water jets overhead trickled to life, then grew stronger.

"How'd you do that?" Saadi asked.

Myell pointed, but they insisted that they couldn't see any designs.

"Well, wave your hand at this spot here when you're done," he said.

"Nice skirt, Chief," Lavasseur said.

He gave them an obscene gesture and went back to bed.

The next time he woke, Saadi and Lavasseur were asleep on their own long cushions. Three other people from Gold's team were sacked out as well. Myell used the bathroom and then shamelessly raided the backpacks that had come with Nam's team. Properly dressed in Saadi's spare pants and Lavasseur's green T-shirt, he went in search of breakfast or Garanwa, whichever presented itself first. He found Breme and another sergeant sitting on the floor outside the sleeping room, pens and pieces of notebook paper in hand.

"I don't think those rooms are close together," Breme was saying. She lifted her head. "Good to see you, Chief."

Myell yawned. "Good to see you, too. What are you doing?"

"Trying to make a map of this place," said Sergeant Highcastle. She tucked wisps of blond hair behind her ears. Her uniform was threadbare at the knees. "It's a big old maze. The rooms don't line up."

"You follow the lines in the floor," Myell said.

"What lines, Chief?" Breme asked.

"Take your shoes off," he said.

The women did as told, but no matter how precisely he showed them where to stand, they insisted that they couldn't feel any kind of power under the dirt. When Myell started to follow the gecko line out of the chamber, Breme put a hand on his arm.

"Commander Nam said we should stay with you, make sure you don't get into any trouble," Breme said.

He was almost, but not quite, affronted. "Where's everyone else?"

"Exploring," Breme reported. "Or sleeping, or guarding the lizards. We're on shifts."

"Anyone find any food?" Myell asked hopefully.

Highcastle sighed. "I'd kill for some chocolate."

Myell set off following the gecko songline with his two escorts in tow. Three chambers away, in a green room with a stream running through it, they found a stone table heaped high with breads, nuts, fruits, and some tuberous vegetables that reminded Myell of the food in the People's village. The aromas went straight up his nose and down to his stomach.

"Thank you, thank you, thank you." Highcastle reached across the table and started grabbing food. "Three months of meal rations and local fruits and whatever we could kill, and I'm just about starved."

Breme was watching Myell carefully. "You going to eat, Chief?"

He pushed aside some hunger pangs. "I'm going to look for Garanwa. Little guy, about this high? I'll be back soon."

Reluctantly they rose to follow him again.

"At ease," he said. "Stay here, wait for the others."

Breme said, "But Commander Nam ordered us to stick with you."

"And I'm ordering you to stay here," Myell said. "I need to do something alone."

"Belay that," Nam said, from the archway of the room. With him was Commander Gold. Nam said, "You're not going anywhere. Sit and eat."

"But—"

"Sit," Nam said, and Myell sat.

From the other side of the table, Commander Gold said, "Chief Myell, thank you for all you've done in rescuing us."

"It wasn't me." Myell slid a glance at Nam, who was busy spreading red jam on a piece of bread. "It was everyone."

"That's not what I heard," Gold said.

More of Gold's team joined them. Lieutenant Vao had short red hair and a nasty-looking sunburn. Ensign Holt, their medic, had grown a long, wild beard.

"Three months in the field," Holt said, stuffing himself with grapes and chunks of watermelon. "Damn nice thing to have indoor plumbing again."

Lieutenant Vao asked, "Is this really a space station? In orbit somewhere?"

All eyes turned to Myell.

"I don't know," he said. Then, to divert attention, he asked Gold, "Everyone from your team is safe?"

Gold's goodwill faded. "We lost two of our people to the lizards."

"We know," Nam said. "We found the bodies, remember?"

"That's right." Gold ran his thumb along the tough skin of a lemon. A muscle pulled in his cheek. "You told me."

Lieutenant Vao said, "And later, Dr. Monnox."

Myell stopped eating. "Dr. Monnox is dead?"

Gold tore into the lemon's skin. "Six weeks ago. We were hunting bison, got too close. He was injured."

Neither Vao, Holt, nor Highcastle added anything to the story.

"How is Dr. Gayle taking the news?" Myell asked Nam.

Nam shrugged one shoulder.

Holt reached across the table for a loaf of dark bread. "We've been stuck five stations away from home for forever. Damn Mother Sphere wouldn't make a peep. Planet was nice enough, if you like prairie dogs and locusts and tornadoes. Built us some sod houses. Ate what we could kill. Then that crocodile ring appeared out of nowhere and brought us here."

Vao shivered. "Why? Why this big reunion?"

To make me happy, Myell thought. *Because I wanted it.*

Gayle arrived. She didn't look like she'd been crying, or that news of Monnox's death had affected her much at all. Myell doubted that was true. He felt bad for what he'd said to her in the petroglyph cave about not really wanting to find her husband.

"The token that brought us here is gone, and we haven't been able to trigger another," she reported. Her voice was flat. "The crocodile ring in the control room is also gone. Garanwa won't say so, but he must control them through that skin cloak."

"I told everyone to stay away from him," Nam said.

Gayle reached for a pitcher of water. "He approached me, actually. He calls himself a Nogomain. That's an Aboriginal Australian god who gives spirit children to mortal parents."

"Is he the only one?" Nam asked.

She replied, "He won't say where the others are, or what happened to them. They might have died off, they might have left this place voluntarily. But he clearly said he needs someone to help him run the network. A replacement. Chief Myell, it seems."

Myell concentrated on peeling a banana.

Gayle said, "I think he'll consider other candidates."

Nam said, "Such as you?"

"It's obvious Chief Myell doesn't want to do it," Gayle said.

"He won't have you," Nam said.

"You want it yourself," Gayle retorted. "You want to grab it and use it for military purposes only."

Commander Gold slammed a fist onto the table. "Have you seen those fucking lizards? Seen them kill?"

Nam leaned forward intently. "We're talking about control of the Spheres, maybe of the Little and Big Alcheringa as well. Of course it has to be in military hands."

Gayle didn't look intimidated. "We live in a democracy, Commander. The freely elected government of Fortune and the Seven Sisters have a vested interest in this."

"Interest, yes," Nam said. "Authority, no."

Myell had enjoyed a brief surge of pleasure that Garanwa wanted *him,* no one else, but it left a sour taste in his throat. Now he pushed back from the table and said, "I need to take a walk."

"We'll go with you," Nam said.

Myell understood he didn't have a choice. Nam and Gold both came with him, leaving breakfast to the others.

"I'm going to put a guard on that cloak, make sure she doesn't try experimenting with it," Nam said.

Gold said, "She's upset about her husband. I didn't tell her he died slowly of sepsis. Holt tried every drug we had. Monnox wasn't a bad guy, you know. Opinionated, stubborn, but pulled his weight."

Myell kept his focus on the ground. More chambers, more vistas, the cosmos unfolding. The scenery was amazing. The maze, unending. The songlines beneath the floor wove and unwove patterns that he could follow for the rest of his life, if he let himself be drawn into them.

After several minutes of walking Gold asked, "Why does it seem like the rooms keep rearranging themselves?"

Without looking up, Myell said, "It's recursive. It exists all over time, all over the place, many places, and keeps folding back in on itself."

Nam stopped him, frowning. "How do you know that?"

"I just do," Myell said. "I think Garanwa must have told me while I was asleep."

"Because he needs you," Nam said.

"You know that I don't want the helm, Commander."

Gold asked, "What's a helm?"

Myell stopped, perplexed. "The helm of the boat. Of this station. He said that, when we first met him."

Nam folded his arms. "No, he didn't."

Gold stayed silent.

Myell said, "Whatever it is, I don't want it. You know that."

"I used to know what you wanted, Chief," Nam said. "Now I'm not so sure. What if it's true that you're the only one who can take control of the network? Are you going to walk away from that responsibility?"

Nam was too close, too stern. Myell almost pushed him away. How much did Team Space want from him? He'd been dragged on this mission against his will. He'd endured lightning and storms and crocodiles and alien soldiers. He'd dived off a cliff, leaped into a goddamn *sea,* in the crazy name of duty.

Gold put his hand on Nam's arm and said, "I have confidence that Chief Myell will do what he needs to do. Can you take us to Garanwa? I think it's time we asked a lot more questions."

Myell let the gecko songline lead them to the room with the beehive rocks. Garanwa wasn't there, but the skin cloak was alive with swirls and dots and dashes in Aboriginal colors. He recognized it now as a map to all the Eggs, the Spheres, spread across the galaxy like stars.

"A thousand worlds," he murmured. "The Nogomain made them to please their gods, the Wondjina. They made them for us, to explore."

Gold tilted his head back. The cloak colors played out over his gaunt face. "But we can't use them. We get sick."

"We're not supposed to use them. Yet. Until we're ready." Part of Myell was growing increasingly alarmed that he knew these things, that the knowledge was there in his head. But the information felt natural, as if he'd always known it. As if he'd been carrying it around for years, in a secret compartment in his brain that Garanwa had unlocked with a curl of his swollen, unseen fingers.

He shook himself, tried to snap himself into focus.

"Earth to start with," Myell said, pointing to part of the cloak and hoping it made as much sense to them as it did to him. "Then Fortune and the other Sisters. Earth was our crib, the Sisters are our playground."

The skin cloak rippled and shifted, the swirls tightening and unspooling again.

"When the Nogomain deem us ready, they'll let us through the Spheres to the other worlds," Myell said.

Gold touched Myell's arm and stood in his line of focus. "They already let us through, Chief."

"There were mistakes." Myell touched part of the design, and watched as tiny ripples flowed out of it. "Garanwa only meant for a few to go through, a chosen few. Yambli's people. They were searching."

Nam said, "For you."

The ripples deepened, hummed, and then dissipated.

"What about the lizards?" Gold asked. "Where are they?"

Myell concentrated on the map, trying to find the Roon world. "Explorers. Not Nogomain. They know of the Wondjina gods, despise them. They seek control of everything. What they can't control, they'll destroy."

Gold turned to Nam. "That's it, then. We should head back home, warn them."

"We have to secure this place first," Nam said.

"If they reach Fortune—"

"That could be hundreds of years away. Thousands. Think, Tom. This is the prize. This station, and whoever controls it." Nam turned to Myell. "Can you control any part of the network now, Chief?"

"No," Myell said automatically. But that wasn't exactly true. He could feel something in him, a strange unknown pulse, and he thought that if he focused very hard, if he reached out and pushed, he might be able to manipulate the network after all.

"No," he repeated.

"Yes," Garanwa said, from the archway. His dark skin looked mottled and flaky, as if it were sloughing off. His white eyes had taken on a tinge of yellow. "You were chosen to take the helm, Jungali. By the Rainbow Serpent himself."

"He doesn't want it," Nam said. "I'll do it. I volunteer."

"Commander—"

"Byron—"

"Shut up, both of you." Nam stepped toward Garanwa. "You need someone. I'm here."

Garanwa didn't hesitate. "You were not chosen."

"On our world, in our species, we choose, not get chosen," Nam said. "We make our own destinies. We don't elevate people into positions because of their genes or favor from the gods."

Garanwa stayed silent. Gold, his face ashen, dropped his gaze to the floor.

Myell said, "You may think I was chosen by the gods, but I'm as ordinary as anyone else, and I can't do what you want me to do. I have a wife who I love more than anything. We have a life together, and I won't abandon her."

"I never thought you would," Jodenny said, from the archway behind him.

CHAPTER TWENTY-TWO

Jodenny had woken from a dream of flying through the clouds and crashing to the ground in a smash of feather and bone. Afterward she wandered for what seemed like hours through strange chambers of light and forests, searching for the Great Egret. Then she heard Myell's voice, and it led her to a strange, mossy room of orange and black rocks.

Myell's hair was a mess, red tattoos marred his face, and his feet were bare and dirty. Beside him stood Commander Nam, and another man she didn't know, and a small shape that she paid no attention to, because Myell was all that mattered.

She threw herself against him and squeezed hard enough that something made a cracking noise in her shoulder. She drank in the smell of his skin and hair and the dried sweat on his neck. He felt thinner than usual, as if something vital had been sucked out of him.

"Hi there," Myell said, clutching her frantically hard. "Oh, God, hello."

She kissed him soundly. His lips were chapped and warm and hungry. When they broke apart she put her hands on his tattooed cheeks. The tattoos were ridged, red swirls.

"You've been busy," she said, her vision blurry.

"Commander Scott," Nam said. "Meet Garanwa."

Jodenny wasn't interested in meeting anyone. She wanted to stay there all day in Myell's arms and let the universe take care of itself for a change. But then she turned her head and saw a small, twisted figure that reminded her of a boy, if a boy could be so old and still be alive.

Garanwa bowed his head, but said nothing.

Myell said, "I'll tell you everything," and started tugging her away.

"Chief!" Nam said. "Where are you going?"

"Give them a minute," said the man beside him.

Jodenny followed Myell through more chambers, some of them with the most extraordinary views of the galaxy she'd ever seen, much better than anything in a planetarium, better even than the real experience of visiting the Seven Sisters. Though there were no signs or markers anywhere, Myell walked quickly, confidently, as if he had the whole place memorized.

"Where are we?" she asked.

"Doesn't matter," he said.

They reached a room of black divans where the floor was filled with stars and moons. Team Space gear and sleeping bags were strewn about haphazardly, but the divans were empty. Myell pressed her down, one hand sliding through her hair, the other working to peel off her shirt. Need and hunger rolled out of him, demanding, insistent. Jodenny tried to respond, but she could still see Garanwa's yellow-white eyes, and here they were on an alien spaceship, *alien*, and no amount of passionate kissing could make her forget the circumstances.

"Terry," she protested, even as her traitorous hands pulled him closer, "maybe this isn't the right place."

"It's all we have." His words were muffled against her skin. His lips found her breasts. "I need you."

"The alien," she insisted, even as it grew harder to string together words.

"He won't watch," Myell promised.

He pinned his weight against hers, his hands roaming freely, igniting her, and maybe it was true that she should celebrate the moment, this reunion. Misgivings fled. His fingers stroked her thighs insistently while his hot mouth worked her nipples. Her sense of time evaporated under his weight and heat, until she was muffling her cries into an official Team Space sleeping bag.

When they were done, she felt boneless. He looked dazed and sweetly spent, content to nuzzle her neck.

"I missed you," he said.

She caressed the long, strong muscles of his back. "Tell me everything."

Myell kissed her cheek. "You first."

"Hmmmm," she replied. "Well, I helped Putty Romero get out of the brig."

"I fell off a cliff."

"And landed on what?"

He rested his head against her chest. "The ocean."

She fingered his soft brown hair. "I met four people named Lou."

"Why are you wearing your wedding ring around your neck?" he asked, tugging on it.

Jodenny slipped it off the chain and put it on her finger. "I was supposed to be traveling incognito."

"Did that work?"

"I guess." She gently traced the tattoos on his cheeks. "These coming off?"

He sighed. "I hope so."

She waited for him to say more, but his breath evened out and when she rolled him over he started to snore. Jodenny was too curious to sleep. She slipped out of his arms and cleaned up in a room filled with sinks. She returned to watch Myell. In the starlight the facial tattoos seemed to glow and almost move. A noise disturbed her, and she looked up to see Ensign Collins in one of the many doorways.

"Sorry," he said. "I need to get my gib."

Jodenny watched him retrieve it from his vest and followed him out of the room. "You don't seem surprised to see me."

"No, ma'am. Commander Nam told us you were here."

"Tell me everything that's happened to your team since you left Fortune."

"Ma'am." Collins shifted from one foot to the other. "Don't you think the commander better tell you?"

"I want to hear it from you, Ensign."

Collins hesitated, then gestured for them to sit on the dirt-covered ground. Jodenny was pleased that she could keep Myell in sight. Collins told her about the marsupial lions, discovering the dead scientists under the snow, and being separated from Nam, Myell, and Gayle.

"The commander radioed in they were being attacked," Collins said. "Then there was nothing. We tried to find them, but there were only campfire remains, tracks into the woods, and a dead Bunyip."

"Bunyip?"

"Chief Myell calls them Roon. They look like lizards."

She remembered the vision the Great Egret had shown her. The alien on the *Yangtze*. A lasso of steel tightened around her lungs, squeezing out all her air.

Collins said, "Commander, are you all right? You look like you're going to faint."

Not faint. Scream. She scrambled to her feet. "Where's Commander Nam? I need to talk to him *now*."

Collins radioed Nam, who said he was in the room with the view of the comets, which was next to the room where the food was, and that they had discovered some kind of power source.

"I think I can get us back there," Collins said. "Place tends to go all screwy when you're not looking."

Jodenny was loathe to wake Myell, who was deep asleep and

looked exhausted. She kissed his forehead, then followed Collins through the maze and forests and even over a clear-running stream until they reached a fabulous vista of twin comets. Nam, Saadi, and two others, Commander Gold and Lieutenant Vao, had removed a panel from the dirt-covered floor. Glass conduits glowed green and yellow in the space below.

"Chief Myell kept saying he could feel some kind of current," Nam said. "This might be it."

"There's something more important you should know," Jodenny said, and told them about the spaceships around Earth.

"No one has seen the aliens on those ships," she said. "They're not showing themselves. But what are the chances it's yet another species?"

Nam's expression hardened and his lips thinned and he asked her a dozen questions, as if she were lying, or inventing the whole thing.

"You don't believe me?" she asked.

Nam gazed down at the glowing conduits, the bright rivers of light. "I believe you."

Commander Gold, sitting on the ground with his arms folded, said, "You should have let me shoot them."

Saadi said, "I say we kill them now."

Jodenny gave Nam a puzzled look.

"We have two of them prisoner," Nam said. "Under guard and not going anywhere. We can't communicate with them. Don't know what they want."

"They want Earth," Vao said. "Can we stop them? This space station, or whatever it is? The alien? Can't he do anything?"

"Maybe if someone takes the helm," Collins murmured.

Nam's chin lifted. Gold glanced up, hopeful.

"What do you mean?" Jodenny asked.

"The alien is dying," Nam said. "Garanwa. He wants someone to take over."

Saadi said, "Your husband."

"No," Jodenny said.

"He said he doesn't want the job," Nam said, as if that meant anything at all. Didn't they know Myell? Hadn't they learned a thing about him?

"I need to go talk to him," she said.

But when she went looking, he was already gone.

Myell woke alone. At first he thought Jodenny had been a dream, a sweet brief fantasy before everything went permanently dark. But the physical evidence of their lovemaking was no illusion, and as he cleaned up in the shower room he could smell her skin, and the shampoo she'd used in her hair. He leaned against the tile wall, letting hot water stream over his shoulders. He needed to send her home to safety. Needed to send them all.

Swirls and lines faded into the tile walls, glowing images in blue and green, a beautiful tapestry tracing and retracing itself into existence. He touched them through the falling water and felt a faint tingling. *There,* he realized. Fortune. And over there, glistening wet, his home world of Baiame. All the Seven Sisters, their Eggs. More Eggs, here, and *here,* and the whole map unfolded, spread open under his eyes, the Thousand Worlds of the Nogomain, and he was their steward, their helmsman—

Myell slammed his hand against the tile and disrupted the images. Pain spiraled up his wrist and into his arm.

"I'm not," he said. "I refuse."

But when he closed his eyes he saw a hundred thousand Roon marching across a blistered countryside, their helmets blood red in the setting sun.

Once he was dressed again he sat on the divan where he and Jodenny had lain together and studied the galaxy beneath his toes. A whole universe out there, and he was just a very tiny part of it, his own needs and desires dwarfed. He could see Earth, if he tried. Earth, with ships of green surrounding it. So much fear there, so much uncertainty.

He squeezed both temples with his fingers, trying to drive the images away. Garanwa had done this to him. In his sleep, in the dark, in his dreams.

But that didn't change the fact that the Roon were interlopers. That only one man could stop them, could steer them away.

Barefoot, damp, with swirls and whirls pulsing in his vision, he followed the gecko songline through sweet-scented rooms of flowers and trees to the chamber where the skin cloak hung.

"Chief?" Lavasseur was keeping watch, and like many sentries seemed bored at the task. "Is everything okay?"

Myell kept his gaze on the cloak. A thousand worlds. Multiple Eggs on each of them. A network larger than any of them had ever imagined. His to control. Jodenny would not be happy. Where was she? He thought she had come, that they had been together, that he'd listened to her heartbeat and tasted her mouth, but now she was gone, leaving him empty. His head began to hurt.

Lavasseur clicked on his radio. "Commander Nam? I think you'd better come."

"I can send you home," Myell murmured. "Back to Fortune. Do you want that?"

"Hell yes," Lavasseur said, as if Myell had just offered him buckets of gold. "Right now?"

"Right now," Myell said.

A crocodile ring appeared on the ground behind Myell. He didn't have to turn around to see it. He commanded it. Commanded all of them through space and time . . .

He was inside Garanwa, inside the once-a-boy, running naked across the hard dirt of the outback in gasping terror, fleeing those who would kill him. His tribe. His kin. He fled, stomach churning, lungs laboring—

"Chief?" That was Nam, peering at him, slapping his cheeks. "What's going on?"

—and they were chasing him with sticks and spears for his failure, for his cowardice, but the sky opened up and the Rainbow Serpent flicked its tongue—

"See if you can find Commander Scott," Nam said to someone.

Myell focused on him. "I can send you back. To Fortune. You can warn them about the Roon."

Nam jerked his head toward the crocodile ring. "Through that?"

"Sounds like a good deal to me, sir," Lavasseur said.

Commander Gold, standing behind Nam, asked, "How can you, Chief? Do you know how the controls work?"

"They're not controls." Myell's head was beginning to ache in earnest now. He was surprised that his brain wasn't leaking out his ears. "Where's Jodenny? I need—"

He went to his knees, unable to stand on weakened legs. The sound of his heartbeat thudded in his ears like a drum. *Sick,* he thought. *Dying. Not him. Garanwa. The not-boy . . .*

"Easy now." Collins crouched next to him with his gib. "Deep breaths, Chief."

"What's wrong with him?" Nam asked.

"Pulse is high, blood pressure is skyrocketing—I need my medkit, sir."

"Commander!" That was Gayle, arriving with Garanwa in her arms. The not-boy was gasping for breath, clearly in distress. Gayle's face was blotchy red from exertion. "We need help here."

"What did you do to him?" Nam asked.

"Nothing! He was in the passageway outside, couldn't walk—"

Gold took the not-boy from her arms and laid him out on the ground near Myell. Nam radioed for Ensign Collins to bring the medkits, and for everyone else to fall back to the skin-cloak room.

"And keep your eyes out for Commander Scott," he said. "She doesn't have a radio."

"Sir, should we leave or bring the aliens?" That was Breme's voice, crackling loudly.

Nam said, "Bring them. Be quick about it."

Garanwa's head lolled to the side. Through darkening vision Myell saw the not-boy's eyes wide open, drawing him into . . .

the Serpent's embrace, the whisper, "You will be the helmsman," the Eggs planted inside him . . .

"Chief, I need you to lie down," Collins was saying, but Myell shook his hand off.

"We don't have much time," Myell said. "Get into the ring now if you want to go home."

Saadi moved toward the crocodile ring. "For once I'm not going to argue."

"Wait," Nam ordered. "Why now, Chief? Why the hurry? We have to find out more about this station, the network—"

"There won't be a station." Myell tasted hot salty liquid against his lip, and wiped at blood trickling from his nose. "When he dies, this place dies."

Nam asked, "How do you know?" and that was just it, Myell couldn't explain, but he *knew*.

"Go, please," Myell said. "I'll follow."

Nam met his gaze for a long moment, judging his truthfulness, before turning to Gold.

"You take them," Nam said.

Gold's eyes widened. "Not without you."

Garanwa gave out a loud gasp. Collins, bending over him, said, "I don't think the alien's going to last much longer, sir."

"They need you," Nam said to Gold.

Gold shook his head.

The station rumbled from somewhere deep within, a growl of distant but sustained thunder. Some of the beehive towers started to crumble. The ground and walls suddenly lifted up and lurched sideways, a violent upheaval that sent Vao and Saadi stumbling to the ground.

"What the hell—" Nam asked.

"The whole place will come apart!" Saadi said.

The shudder subsided, but Myell knew the respite would be brief. The tremor would return. The whole place would collapse to ruin and ash, and there was nothing he could do to stop it.

"You have to hurry," he told Nam.

"Tom, please," Nam said to Gold, and took his face between his hands, and kissed him hard.

When they broke apart, Gold said, "You better be right behind me."

Nam unexpectedly grinned. "Count on it."

More of Gold's team arrived. Nam ushered them into the ring alongside Saadi and Lavasseur. Myell gathered the wild power in his head and sent them back to Fortune. Emerald-green light flashed, dazzling his eyes. He didn't know how he was doing it, only that he could, that he could send anyone to anywhere—

Nam clicked on his radio. "Breme, Holt, Highcastle, where are you?"

Holt replied, "I think I'm close! But the rooms keep rearranging themselves."

"We can't find you!" Breme said. "We're in the room with the stream in it—"

Gayle said, "I'll go find them," and dashed out before anyone could stop her.

The pain in his head was making it hard to stay conscious. Myell rocked back and forth, his vision gone hazy, his breathing harsh in his own ears. "Easy, easy," Collins was saying, but there was nothing easy about this, not with the world ending in red agony. But still he managed to bring the crocodile ring back. It shimmered and hummed against the ground even as the rumbling returned, and more beehive towers of rock crumbled to dust.

Collins, his attention split between Myell and Garanwa, said, "I'll stay here, Commander."

"There's nothing you can do for either of them," Nam said. "Go back home, Ensign."

The chamber lurched and shook, great sections of the ceiling buckling under the stress. Too soon, too soon; Myell couldn't take the helm. But he didn't have a choice. In his head he could see Breme and Highcastle, lurching along a passageway, frantic for rescue. He sent them a ring and the ring took them home. He saw Holt, lost in a room of vines and trees. Another ring, another green flash. He tried to find Jodenny but of her there was only a blur of white, of feathers like a bird—

Garanwa gave out a last shuddering gasp and went still.

Energy bolted out of the corpse, an explosion of hot frantic power, and lightning tore Myell's world to shreds.

I hate this place." Jodenny hoped that the Great Egret was listening. "Hate it! Do you hear me?"

No answer. Jodenny had left the room with the starry floor and found the room with food in it, but she didn't want fruit or bread or strange-looking vegetables. She picked the archway to the far right and followed it into a dark chamber with a blazing comet overhead. No sign of anyone, not Myell or Nam or anyone from the teams.

"What do you want from me?" she asked, fists clenched. Surely someone in charge here was screwing with her, making her deliberately lost and confused and frustrated.

No answer came from the dirt or walls or even the comet, which sailed across the universe in a streak of silent fire.

She pushed herself on through another archway, then another. When the station began to rumble and buckle beneath her, she feared not for her own safety but for Myell's. Whatever forces ruled this place wanted him alive. Needed him alive. Wanted to steal him from her. She said, "Leave him alone, you bastards," just as the ground tilted crazily and roared and she lost her balance. She landed hard on one arm, feeling something in it snap.

Pain knifed through her just as hot light exploded out of nowhere. Scorching and blue hot, it crackled across the adjacent chamber. The air came alive around her, sparking and tingling. The accompanying clap of thunder slammed through her like the volley of cannons. She couldn't hear, couldn't see, couldn't think . . .

Then all fell silent and dark. She wasn't even sure that she was still alive, but the gritty taste in her mouth as she gasped for air had to mean something.

Jodenny sat up. Pain sang along her right arm, wrist to elbow, bright and hot and demanding of attention. She wanted to vomit. Her ears felt numb but were quickly recovering, and blue-white imprints danced in her vision. The station had stopped rumbling, which she hoped was a good sign, but most of the ambient illumination had disappeared and the air smelled like char and ash. Legs wobbly, coughing out dirt, she found her footing, tried not to move her broken arm, and lurched to the archway of the beehive room.

At first she thought Myell was dead.

Nam, too. And Collins. All of them, sprawled on the ground and unmoving. Jodenny fell to her knees and touched Myell's face ever so carefully. His skin was blistered and burned. His lips were slightly parted, and his faint breathing had a whistling sound to it. She didn't want to touch him further, didn't want to aggravate any injuries or cause him more pain, but it was a torture not to tug his head into her lap, to keep from pressing her head against his shoulder.

Collins stirred. Nam sat up with a groan. Under the dim, flickering light they looked as ghastly as Myell. Beside Collins was a shrunken gray thing that she realized was Garanwa's corpse. It was shriveled like a dried fruit, and the lips were so retracted that she could see a half-dozen rotted teeth. The beehive towers of rock throughout the room had toppled or shattered, leaving the air thick and bitter.

"What happened?" Collins asked.

"Lightning Man," Nam murmured, one hand pressed to his head.

Behind them, a green crocodile ring faded into existence. It glowed with an uneven light, as if it was barely sustaining itself.

The ground rumbled, an aftershock or a preamble of more devastation to come.

Collins started crawling toward Myell. He spared a glance for the crocodile ring, asking, "Last chance to escape?"

"Or a one-way trip to nowhere," Nam said.

"Is your arm broken?" Collins asked Jodenny.

"I think so." She touched Myell's brow with the fingers of her left hand. "Is he . . . he's burned. You all are."

Collins had a gib, but it was a blackened, useless shell and he tossed it aside. The far-off rumbling increased, moving closer. Jodenny imagined a rock crusher or some other mammoth machine jawing toward them, devouring everything in its path.

"We have to get out of here, sir," Collins said.

"Not until I know the others are safe," Nam said. "Breme, Holt, Gayle . . ."

Jodenny understood. He was the commander of this mission, responsible for his team. Their lives were more valuable than his own. But she had no such burden of command. She hooked her left hand under Myell's armpit.

"Help me," she told Collins.

Together, using her one good arm and his two fully useful ones, they dragged Myell to the crocodile ring. He was heavier than Jodenny remembered. Deadweight. He made a faint protesting noise, a mewl of pain, but they could do nothing for him but escape, and hope for help wherever the token took them.

Nam got to his feet, his gaze on the archways. He tried his radio but it was as dead as Collins's gib. He shouted out, "Gayle! Breme!"

No one answered. The only sounds were their own breathing, and the growing sound of thunder, and Myell's increasing distress as he regained consciousness.

"Easy," Collins said, as they tugged Myell over the ring's edges. He himself didn't enter the ring, but instead glanced back at Nam.

"Go," Nam ordered.

"Another ring might not come," Collins said.

Myell gasped and arched against the ground, his spine stiffening, his arms twitching. Jodenny bent close to his face and whispered, "Ssh, I'm here. It's going to be okay."

A lie, obviously a lie, but he quieted at her voice. Twin drops of water landed on his cheeks. Jodenny wiped at her face, surprised to find tears there. Though Myell kept his eyelids closed, his mouth opened and he tried to speak.

"Ssh," she said again. "Don't talk."

His cracked lips kept moving. Jodenny bent close, trying to make sense of his hoarse, broken whispers. When she looked up, Nam was giving them both a deeply etched frown.

"He says you have to come." Jodenny's voice choked in her throat. "Don't kill yourself."

"I'm not killing myself," Nam said fiercely.

Collins said, "Commander, please."

Myell stiffened again, letting out a sharp cry.

"The ring won't leave without you," Jodenny said.

"Breme!" Nam shouted out again. "Gayle! Holt!"

No answer, only the unseen beast drawing nearer. The lights in the damaged dome went dark, flickered on again, then started to rain down sparkles of green and white. Tiny specks of light, falling like stars. Cradling her broken arm, Jodenny shielded Myell before any could land on him. Three or four fell onto her exposed skin and melted like snowflakes.

Nam let out a long growl of words that might have been, "God-damn heroics," and joined them in the crocodile ring.

Jodenny closed her eyes against a bright green flash.

The next thing she saw was the overhead of the *Kamchatka*'s infirmary.

Easy, now," Farber said from nearby, as Jodenny tried to sit up. "You're not ready for that yet."

Jodenny agreed. Her mouth was sandpaper dry, her right arm had a twinge of pain in it, and she couldn't quite remember why she should be in bed. Nevertheless, she pushed herself up from the pillow. The infirmary room started spinning around her, and she would have sagged back down again if not for Farber's steadying hand and the sight of Myell lying in the next bed over.

Memory flooded back. Garanwa and the space station and the lightning.

"You're fine. The doctors fixed you up," Farber said. "Both of you, as best they could."

For the first time Jodenny noticed a security tech in the small room with them. He was armed, and stationed inside the hatch, not outside, which didn't bode well.

She would worry about that later. Jodenny got herself standing, her bare feet cold against the deck, and lurched across the small space separating her bed from Myell's. He was curled up on his side with his face to the bulkhead. Sleeping. His skin was no longer burned and the facial tattoos had faded to ghostly imprints. Under his eyelids, his eyes moved back and forth quickly.

"Commander Scott!" A thin, wiry doctor had entered the room while her attention was on Myell. "I'm Dr. Ruiz, ship's Medical Officer."

He didn't appear old enough to be out of medical school, but Jodenny shook his hand anyway.

"You know my name," she said, with a glance toward Farber.

"Oh, yes, we had to scan your embedded dog tag to access your medical profile. We ran Chief Myell's tag too, and luckily the next-of-kin information is all up-to-date. You'd be amazed how many people forget to do that when they get married," Ruiz said. "You can see we healed up the burns, we rehydrated him, blood pressure down, that's all good. Do you know what exactly happened to him? I've been told he was hit by lightning. Twice. That would be amazingly bad luck."

Farber asked, "Wouldn't it have killed him?"

"Not necessarily. A lot of people get hit by lightning, and many of them survive, often with some disabilities—" Ruiz abruptly stopped, eyeing Farber and the security tech. "I'm sorry, Commander. Your husband does have the right to medical privacy. Do you want to speak alone?"

"Yes," she said.

"Sorry, ma'am," the security guard said. "I'm not authorized to leave."

"The captain has some concerns," Farber added.

Ruiz wrung his hands. "Team Space is very clear on the issue of medical privacy."

Jodenny sighed. "I give you permission to go on."

"Usually we're talking frontal-lobe injuries, the neural circuits all fried up. Moodiness, sleep problems, memory problems, and depression are all common. Was he evidencing any of that?"

"He was tired," she admitted, stroking the side of his face.

Ruiz nodded. "We'll know more when he wakes up. His frontal lobe is scanning fine but there's an unusual amount of dreaming going on, from what we can tell."

"Can we just wake him?" Jodenny asked.

"They've tried," Farber said.

Jodenny tried, too. His breathing didn't change, his eyes kept moving, his hands remained warm and relaxed in hers, and he kept sleeping.

Ruiz said, "Let's see how the next few hours unfold. As for you, Commander, we patched up your broken arm with the bone knitter and it's as good as new. You're clear to be discharged, unless you have any medical complaints."

Farber said, "I think she's still a little woozy."

"I am not," Jodenny retorted, too sharply. Her vision went blurry on the edges. "Not much, anyway."

Ruiz suggested she stay under observation for a bit longer. She was happy to do so if it kept her close to Myell. After Ruiz left, Lieutenant Sweeney came knocking at the hatch.

"Sorry to disturb you," he said, his gaze frank and curious. "So this is your husband? When you told me you were married, *Ellen,* I didn't quite believe it."

Relegated back to her own bed, Jodenny pulled the blanket up higher. "Traveling incognito wasn't my idea, Lieutenant."

"I presented Captain Balandra with a copy of our sealed orders," Farber said. "None of that is at issue, though she was irritated at being deceived. The real problem is the Bunyip ships still in orbit around Earth."

"They're called Roon," Jodenny said.

Farber's gaze narrowed. "So Commander Nam says. How, exactly, was that ascertained? Did you talk to them?"

Sweeney turned to the security tech. "You can go and wait outside. I'll call if I need you."

The tech left, an unhappy look on his face.

"I didn't talk to them," Jodenny said. "They haven't done anything while I was away?"

Sweeney asked, "How long do you think you were away?"

Jodenny squinted at the overhead as she calculated. "Six hours, maybe."

"The ship's scanners registered a power surge in your cabin." Sweeney folded his arms and rocked back on the heels of his boots. "An emergency team was sent. Thirty seconds later, before they arrived, another power surge registered. They opened your hatch and found you, Chief Myell, Commander Nam, and Ensign Collins all lying on the deck. Nam and Collins are up and about now. You two, not so much."

Jodenny glanced at Farber. "I was only gone for thirty seconds?"

"So it would seem," Farber said. "Where did you go?"

"More importantly, can we use that transportation technology to stop the aliens?" Sweeney said.

Jodenny gave Farber a raised eyebrow.

"We told them about the tokens," Farber said. "The captain and her officers. Considering the situation, I thought security clearances were a moot point."

Myell made a faint noise of distress. Jodenny put her hand on his forehead. His skin was warm, too warm, and his eyes were still moving quickly.

"You want us to shut up?" She squeezed his hand, but he didn't squeeze back.

Sweeney said, "Captain wants to know if those so-called tokens can be used to evacuate civilians to Earth, or transport people between ships."

Farber cleared her throat. "Commander Nam thinks your husband can control them."

Jodenny smoothed Myell's hair back from his temples. "I don't know if that's true."

"You'll have to tell her yourself," Sweeney said. "She wants to talk to you. Down here or up in her conference room, makes no difference. As soon as possible. Before the aliens start attacking."

Jodenny kissed Myell's forehead. His skin tasted like the soap they'd used to clean him up and was soft to her touch.

"Get me a uniform," she said.

C an these so-called tokens be used to board the alien ship?"
Captain Balandra asked from the head of the table.

The furrows in Balandra's forehead indicated that she probably had a headache. Jodenny empathized. She herself was grateful for the sturdiness of the conference-room chairs. Her legs were still wobbly from the walk up from the infirmary. The conference room was standing-room only, crowded with Balandra's senior staff.

"Why would we want to, ma'am?" Farber asked. "We don't know anything about the conditions inside those ships. Just because the Roon can roam freely in climates conducive to us doesn't mean vice versa. We don't have any way of communicating with them, so even if we boarded, we couldn't negotiate."

Balandra said, "We wouldn't be there to negotiate, Agent Farber."

Toledo, sitting at the far end of the table, said, "Even if Chief Myell could somehow summon a token, we don't know anything about their shielding technology. We already know their interstellar capabilities outmatch ours. Their science might be centuries ahead."

Balandra said, "You two aren't holding back any intelligence information, are you?"

Both Farber and Toledo looked offended. "No, ma'am," Toledo said, and Farber said, "We've told you everything we know about previous Roon contacts. We know nothing about their civilization, their capabilities, their goals."

It annoyed Jodenny to no end that Farber and Toledo had known there were aliens out there, known Myell might be facing them, known Jodenny had seen one on the *Yangtze,* and had said nothing. She supposed it was a grudge she could settle later, if they all survived.

Balandra leaned back in her chair and gazed pointedly at the wallvid, with its relay of Earth and the Roon ships. "We're not at war. Yet. But if it comes to it, I'd like be able to beam over there, or whatever you want to call it, in one of those tokens. Carrying whatever kind of bombs we can rig up."

Jodenny put one hand on the smooth brown surface of the tabletop. "Ma'am, with all due respect, this is all conjecture. We don't know what exactly happened to Chief Myell on that station. We don't know if he has some special way of controlling the network, if that alien passed on special information." Her voice faltered, but she persisted. "We don't even know if he's going to wake up."

Nam was sitting beside her. His burns had been healed up, and he had showered and dressed in a new uniform. He said, "For all we know, those ships are just the advance scouts for a larger fleet. The important thing to do is let Fortune know what's happening and give them time to ramp up defenses. An automated probe will take months to get through. Only a ship our size can make it back with any speed. We need to head back to Fortune."

One of Balandra's officers asked, "Abandon Earth to its fate, sir?"

"Save the Seven Sisters," Nam replied. "We're a lone cargo ship with few weapons. We have no hope against the Roon. Earth itself has no hope. Nothing with a navigational computer can launch from Earth. Team Space doesn't have much to throw at them, and did I mention we're up against a species that crossed a galaxy to get here? Fortune needs to be warned."

Toledo said, "They used interstellar propulsion to get here. We've seen them in the Wondjina network, so they know about the transportation capabilities of the Spheres. But they might not know anything about the Alcheringas and the Seven Sisters. If we loop back, we'd lead them right to the drop point."

"They've surely picked us up on their sensors by now," Nam said. "All they have to do is trace our course back."

"We don't know what they've noticed," Balandra said. "We don't know what Chief Myell can do. We don't have much in the way of weapons. A commando team might not be able to destroy one of their ships. But maybe we can cause enough damage to give them second thoughts."

"Or retreat," someone added.

"They're not going to retreat," Nam said. "They came all this way for something."

The argument continued, voices swirling angrily around Jodenny's head, but she was thinking about the vision that the Great Egret had shown her. Roon marching across the countryside, turning over stones. Over and over. Looking for something. For what?

Balandra said, "The Admiralty has ordered us to resume full speed on course for Earth. If nothing else, we're to gather intel on the Roon carriers that might be useful later."

The officers were too disciplined to erupt in protest, but several drew in sharp breaths or shifted unhappily on their feet.

Nam said, "We're a passenger ship with no defense capabilities."

"I know, Commander." Balandra rose from her seat. "I know. We'll be at Earth in twenty-two hours."

When Jodenny returned to the infirmary, Putty Romero and Hanne Tingley were sitting hand in hand on Jodenny's bed and talking to Myell despite his unresponsiveness.

"—And you should have seen her, Chief, she was like a real lawyer," Tingley was saying when Jodenny stepped in. "Hi, Commander. Hope you don't mind."

"The doctor said friendly voices might help," Romero added.

Jodenny touched Myell's right hand. He didn't even twitch. At least his eyes had stopped moving. "Has he done anything?"

"Said a few words," Romero reported. "Talking in his sleep."

Tingley added, "Something about crocodiles. And steering a helm, whatever that means."

The young couple didn't stay long. Hullabaloo and Baylou came by a short time later, but Jodenny didn't let them into the room. She thought Myell would be annoyed by people staring at him like he was on display.

"Anything we can get for you?" Hullabaloo asked.

Jodenny shook her head.

She spent most of the afternoon sitting at Myell's bedside. He didn't stir when she rubbed his breastbone with her knuckles. Didn't respond when she kissed him.

"Always stubborn," she said, tracing his jaw with the tip of her finger. "Ridiculously stubborn. You tell Garanwa to take his helm and shove it up his scrawny dead alien ass, all right? First we go on our honeymoon. Then you can think about saving the universe."

By the time Nam dropped by, Jodenny's back ached from sitting in place and her stomach was cramping from emptiness. Nam had a cup of steaming coffee in his hand. The smell made her perk up.

"Get your own," Nam said. "I'll stay with him."

She hesitated. Someday, maybe, she'd forgive him for dragging Myell off at Bainbridge, orders or not. But she didn't think he'd earned it yet. Myell hadn't seemed to hold a grudge, though. According to what Farber and Collins had told her, the two of them and Anna Gayle had survived trekking across the wilderness on one planet. They'd even been held captive at the hands of Aboriginal villagers. Jodenny didn't trust Nam to put Myell's welfare above that of Team Space, but surely he couldn't wreak too much havoc while she went to get some food.

"I'll be right back," she said, and kissed Myell's forehead.

The galley was mostly empty when Jodenny arrived. Meals on the *Kamchatka* had been reduced to basics again, mostly soup and sandwiches and a few desserts. She picked out a spinach wrap and a large cup of coffee. At the cashier station she realized she had lost her PIC again. Ensign Sadiqi came to her rescue.

"Is it true, Commander?" Sadiqi asked. "You've met the aliens?"

"Is that what the rumor mill is putting out?"

Sadiqi nodded unhappily. "And that they mean to destroy us."

"They mean something, Ensign. I don't know what."

They mean to destroy us, she thought as she ate at a corner table. That didn't sound right. *They mean to enslave us. They mean to march over the width and breadth of the Earth.* She gulped at the coffee, glad for the hot bitterness. *They mean to just visit, that's all, say a friendly intergalactic hello.*

She pushed aside her food, her appetite forgotten, and headed back to the infirmary.

"Ellen!" a voice called out, just as she reached the nearest downladder.

Jodenny paused to let Louise Sharp catch up to her. Louise's magenta hair was disheveled, and dark circles of exhaustion rimmed her eyes.

"You look terrible," Jodenny said.

"Thank you, *Commander,*" Louise snapped. "Scott, is it? Your real name?"

"I was traveling under orders—"

Louise waved her hand. "Doesn't matter. I've been reading cards for the last twelve hours. Cards about you, your so-called husband, those aliens—"

"He *is* my husband—"

"Not the point." Louise pulled her tarot cards from her pocket, shuffled them for a moment, and then extended the deck. "Pick up the first one."

Jodenny sighed. "I really don't have time—"

"Try," Louise ordered.

She turned the card over. A stern-looking sea captain stood at the bow of a sailing ship as it entered a tropical bay.

Louise let out a sharp breath. "Captain James Cook and the ship *Endeavour*. First landing of the British in Australia, way back when. The year seventeen hundred and seventy. You know the story?"

Jodenny shrugged impatiently.

"Doesn't matter," Louise said. "Now, watch."

Another shuffle of the deck, the first card upturned again. James Cook.

"Coincidence," Jodenny said.

Louise mixed the cards again. Offered the deck. Jodenny touched the top card, hesitated, then flipped it. Cook and his ship and paradise, about to be spoiled.

"It doesn't mean anything," Jodenny protested.

"All night long. Captain Damned Bloody Cook. You know what happened to the Aboriginals after the British came? They were destroyed. Their culture, their way of life, their history—"

"Put the cards away and get some sleep, Louise."

Jodenny climbed upladder to B-deck, pushing away thoughts of Cook and conquest, images of Roon marching across the world. When she stepped into Myell's room she saw him sitting up in bed with Nam in the chair beside him. Myell was poking at a bowl of peaches with a grimace on his face.

"You're awake," Jodenny said, stupidly, because of course he was, and nothing could henceforth go wrong, and relief made her lightheaded.

But then he lifted his head and gazed at her as if she were a stranger. No trace of recognition, no flicker at all of familiarity.

Her heart clenched.

"He's a little confused," Nam said, sounding remarkably casual. "Isn't that right?"

Myell's focus slid to Nam, then back to the bowl of peaches. "B-b-bad," he complained.

Jodenny stepped forward carefully. "What's bad?"

He poked at the fruit clumsily with a fork. His movements were off, uncoordinated. She didn't remember Dr. Ruiz saying anything about motor-control damage. She peered into the bowl and saw thick syrup accompanying the peaches.

"Do you want something else?" she asked. Her voice sounded like it was a long way away and belonged to someone else, someone calm and detached.

Myell dropped the fork, tried to recover it from his lap, and accidentally knocked the entire tray over. Nam caught it deftly, but not before the peaches went slithering to the deck in a plop of liquid. Myell covered his eyes with one clumsy arm and made a shamed noise.

"No problem," Nam said.

Jodenny looked away.

Dr. Ruiz soon arrived to begin a battery of tests and scans. Myell didn't recognize either Jodenny or Nam, as it turned out. He couldn't say his own name. He had a vague idea of the date, but it was off by several weeks. His answers to Ruiz's questions were stilted, sometimes stuttered. He said he wasn't in pain, but the deep line between his eyebrows told Jodenny otherwise.

"You don't have a headache?" she asked, trying to smooth the line.

"N-n-no." He shied away from her touch.

That stung. Jodenny withdrew her hand and sat on it. Myell gave her a quick, bashful look and tensed as Dr. Ruiz put a gib in his hands.

"Can you read that first line for me, Chief?"

He stared at the letters.

"A few words?" Ruiz prompted.

Myell thrust the gib back at him.

No reading ability. Poor hand-and-eye coordination. Stuttering. They got him to his feet but the effort clearly exhausted him, and he managed only a few shuffling steps before his strength ran out. Jodenny told herself that it was all temporary. Fleeting inconveniences. She didn't believe he'd been struck by actual lightning, not once and certainly not twice. Something like lightning; something that damn alien controlled.

Once back in bed, Myell lay panting from exertion with his face scrunched up. She wanted to touch him but, mindful of his earlier protest, held back.

"I think some rest is in order," Ruiz said. "Eat and drink. We'll do more tests in the morning."

Farber came by, her face set in a stony mask, and called Nam out. Neither came back. Jodenny concentrated on getting Myell to eat some soup. Myell was petulant. He swallowed some of it, then closed his teeth against the spoon she wielded. He wouldn't meet her gaze, and kept glancing anxiously at the hatch as if waiting for Nam to return.

"Fine," she said in exasperation. "Don't eat. Waste away. It's not going to get you out of doing the dishes after I eat. You're still going to do half the housework, mister."

He slid her a sideways glance, then looked to the hatch again.

"See this?" Jodenny wagged her finger and wedding ring. "You're still mine."

Another sideways glance, as if she were becoming more interesting by the moment. But then he started trembling, his arms and legs jerking. His eyes rolled upward. Jodenny yanked the soup out of the way and hit an alarm. A med tech hurried in, followed by Dr. Ruiz.

"He's seizing," Ruiz told Jodenny. "Not entirely unexpected."

It was unexpected to her. Jodenny backed away while Ruiz and the tech did their work. She couldn't watch too closely. For a brief, panicky moment she feared that this was what their life together would be, from now until death. Him in a bed, unable or unwilling to communicate, suffering seizures and bedsores and who knew what else, while she took care of him and died her own quiet death for years on end.

Assuming the Roon didn't kill them all first, of course.

She bit her knuckle to drive away selfish thoughts and went out into the passageway. To her surprise, Toledo was lingering out there with Karl in his arms.

"Didn't want to disturb you," Toledo said, hefting the koala. "Thought maybe this little fellow might cheer things up."

Karl came willingly into Jodenny's arms and nuzzled her neck. Toledo's thoughtfulness made her blink several times. "Thanks."

"How's he doing?"

"Not so good. Any news on the Roon?"

"Still eyeing Earth like it's the main feature on the buffet table." Toledo stared at the bulkhead as if he could see through it to Myell. "Your chief's going to be fine, Commander. He's a tough guy."

Karl nuzzled Jodenny's neck. She said, "I suppose."

Toledo offered her a rueful grin. "Oh, there's no doubt about it. Married you, didn't he?"

He gave her a salute and went off. Jodenny cuddled Karl until Dr. Ruiz came out and said, "We're all set in here, Commander. I expect him to sleep for the rest of the night. Like I said, seizures aren't uncommon. Hopefully they'll abate with time."

"And if they don't?" she asked.

Ruiz squeezed her arm. "Worry about that later."

Jodenny rejoined Myell. He was indeed sleeping, his face slack and his breathing steady. Karl clambered down her arms and nestled into the sheets. One of Myell's hands moved automatically to cup his golden fur. She found herself irrationally jealous.

"Don't get too comfortable," she told Karl.

The koala yawned and went to sleep, leaving Jodenny to contemplate both man and robot. Her family, for as long as it lasted.

CHAPTER
TWENTY-FIVE

Jodenny woke with a start when soft hands began fondling her breasts. She almost lashed out, but in the dim light of the infirmary room she could see Myell leaning over her, wonder and amazement on his face.

"Kay?" he asked. "Jodenny?"

She barely remembered taking off her boots and curling up on the second bed. Sleep had come hard and fast. Still groggy, she reached up and touched his cheek.

"Are you back?" she whispered.

His mouth descended on hers with a gentle kiss that grew greedier, harder. Jodenny wrapped her hands around his head and pulled him closer. Relief flooded through her, accompanied by a surge of fierce possessiveness. *Mine,* she thought, and against his mouth she said, "You're never going away again."

He fumbled awkwardly, trying to join her on the narrow mattress. Jodenny urged him down to the deck instead, and yanked down the thin blankets as cushioning against the hard metal. She pinned him under her weight, kissing him again, running her hands over his bare arms and under his infirmary pajamas. He squirmed a little, ticklish. His hands on her back were clumsy, pawing instead of caressing, but she didn't care.

"Missed you," she said.

His lips and breath were warm against her throat but he made no sound.

"Terry." She cupped his face and searched his dark eyes. Saw recognition, but also confusion. "Talk to me."

He blinked at her and then said, crustily, "Lost."

"Who's lost?" Jodenny asked.

He swallowed hard. "Lost e-e-everything."

She sat up, pushing her long hair over her shoulder. The infirmary was cooler than she remembered and smelled like bitter medicine. Jodenny gripped Myell's nearest hand and massaged the side of his head.

"You haven't lost everything, Terry. You've got me. Do you remember who I am?"

His lips parted, hesitated. "Lieutenant?"

Her stomach churned. "Is that all?"

Myell's hand tightened on hers and he suddenly smiled. "Wife."

"Yes." She kissed his forehead. "Where are we?"

Myell shifted his gaze to the bulkheads. "Not *Aral Sea.*"

"No, not there."

He yawned so wide that she thought she heard his jaw pop. Jodenny snuggled against him on their nest of blankets. She kept her hand flat on his chest and listened to his breathing even out, deepen, turn to a faint snore. She didn't sleep. At oh-six-hundred a med tech came in with Myell's medication and stepped back in surprise.

"Do you need help, ma'am?" he asked.

Jodenny said, "No. We're just resting."

Ruiz came by a bit later and was encouraged that Myell had spoken and taken some initiative. Jodenny woke him, and together she and Ruiz got him back into his bed. Myell seemed groggy, and shied away from the light Ruiz shone into his eyes.

"Bad headache?" Ruiz asked.

Myell squinted at him. "S-s-s-mells bad."

"The light smells bad?" Ruiz looked intrigued. "What exactly does it smell like?"

Nam appeared at the hatchway and beckoned to Jodenny. She adjusted her uniform, scrubbed at her blurry eyes, and joined him in the passageway.

"The Roon Carriers have started deploying more of their scout ships down to Earth," he said grimly. "Several dozen are hovering over South America, Africa, Australia. Each of them is five times the size of the *Kamchatka*. No skirmishes yet, but people are starting to panic."

"What do you want me to do?" Jodenny asked.

"Not you," Nam replied.

Jodenny shook her head. "He doesn't even know where we are, Commander. Terry's not your one true hope."

"I don't have any others," Nam replied, and slid past her.

Ruiz was finishing his examination and seemed pleased enough. "The antiseizure medicine's doing its job. Some retrograde amnesia's not unexpected. The stutter is improving a little. Never ran into synesthesia before—that's when he said the light smelled bad—so we'll see how that plays out."

"Is there anything I can do to help?" Jodenny asked.

"Just do what you've been doing, Commander."

After Ruiz left, Myell said to Nam, "You were th-th-there."

Nam asked, "Where, Chief?"

"Village."

"Yes, in the village," Nam said. "Do you remember?"

Myell dropped his gaze to his fingers.

"It's important that you try," Nam replied. "Remember the Roon? The aliens? They're here at Earth. We don't think they're here to make friends."

Jodenny watched carefully, but Myell only picked at a hangnail.

For several more minutes they both tried prompting him, but Myell's memory was extremely sketchy. From the village he remembered a bonfire, seashells, a gecko. Of Garanwa he claimed to know nothing. He said he remembered living with Jodenny in Adeline Oaks, but couldn't give them the address.

"How about this?" Nam asked, and pulled a small cloth bag from his pocket. He shook the contents in his palm. "Do you remember these?"

Jodenny had seen Myell's dilly bag before. This one looked smaller, darker. The small wooden shapes inside were also different.

"Where did you get that?" she asked.

"He had it on him when we got here," Nam said.

She asked, "Why didn't you give it back before?"

"I was having it tested," Nam said. His voice held no apology. "Nothing but wood and cloth, it turns out."

Myell had his eye on the carvings. He said, "Mine."

"Yes, yours," Jodenny said, irritated at Nam. She plucked the gecko and crocodile from his palm, tucked them into the bag, and gave it to Myell. He curled up on his side and closed his eyes.

Jodenny pulled the blanket up over his shoulders.

"We need more information," Nam said, fists clenched.

"He can't give you more than he has," she replied. "I'd appreciate it if you left now. Sir."

After Nam was gone, Jodenny washed up, left instructions with the staff that Myell wanted no visitors, and went in search of Farber and Toledo. They were in Toledo's cabin, watching the live vid.

"What are the Roon doing?" Jodenny asked.

Toledo surrendered his chair to her. "See for yourself."

Jodenny skimmed through several channels of media feeds. Earth had never had a central government, not even before the Debasement. The hodgepodge nations that had survived the devastation were responding in different ways to the Roon deployments. The Asian Alliance was in observational mode. The Americanadians had launched some primitive missiles that bounced off the Roon scout ships like pebbles. The United North Kingdom had fired weapons as well, just as ineffectively. The Roon hadn't retaliated, which Jodenny thought was a good sign.

Toledo said, "Most of the ships seem to be mapping the oceans, or scanning it for something. They've only landed in a few places. They stay a few minutes, take off again quickly. They're looking for something."

Farber crossed her arms tightly. "Cross thousands of light-years in search of what?"

Buried treasure, Jodenny thought. The stuff of adventure myths. But she thought of Captain Cook, dispatched from England to explore the South Pacific. He hadn't been looking for gold or silver. He'd been in search of knowledge, and the world of the Australian Aborigines had changed—had nearly been destroyed—because of it.

Jodenny turned to a news channel coming out of New Sydney and listened to a young reporter with blond-and-black-striped hair. A Roon ship was over the Great Barrier Reef, a coral landmark that had been killed off during the Debasement.

"What are you thinking, Commander?" Toledo asked.

She sat back. "Nothing good. How are the crew and passengers?"

"Crew's holding steady," Toledo said. "Passengers aren't happy at all. They've started a petition."

Farber added, "Led by Mr. and Mrs. Zhang."

"A petition for what?" Jodenny asked.

"Guaranteed safe passage to Earth," Toledo said. He shrugged. "Keeps them busy."

Jodenny returned to the infirmary. Myell was sleeping with Karl curled up against him. She sat and stared, memorizing all over again the line of his nose, the graceful arc of his eyelashes, the little scar over his eyebrow. She'd never asked him how he'd gotten that, or why he kept it. He started to wake up, and she made sure that the first thing he saw was her.

"Hey, sleepyhead," she said.

He tried to touch her face, but his hand was still clumsy. Thickly he said, "They're here? R-r-roon?"

"Do you remember them?"

"Inter-lopers," he said. "Get up."

With her help he rose off the pillows, and after a moment of rest he swung his feet to the floor. His gait was unsteady and he gripped her shoulder tightly, but he made it to the hatchway and seemed determined to keep walking.

"Where are we going?" she asked.

"S-s-see them," he insisted.

The medical lounge at the end of the passageway had a wallvid in it. Myell collapsed onto the sofa, his pajamas damp with sweat. Jodenny turned on the feeds, sat beside him, and watched his expression as more media reports came in.

"Do you remember them?" she asked.

His nose wrinkled. "Lizards."

She took his closest hand and massaged it in hers. "Do you remember Garanwa?"

He leaned closer to the screen and ignored her question. Dr. Ruiz walked by, saw them, and stopped to observe. Jodenny said, simply, "He wanted to see the aliens," and Ruiz pursed his lips thoughtfully before continuing on.

"We think they're looking for something." Jodenny rested her head on Myell's shoulder. "Do you know what it could be? Did Garanwa tell you anything?"

He covered his face with both hands and didn't answer.

They sat there until the comm clicked and Captain Balandra's voice said, "Attention all passengers and crew. As you're aware, we will soon be entering Earth's orbit. The aliens have shown no signs of interest in us, nor have they made any threatening overtures. We intend to approach one of their ships, reconnoiter, and perhaps establish communications.

"I can't predict how successful we'll be, nor how this mission will end. I will tell you that Team Space is committed to your safety and my goal is for us to return safely home in the very near future, wherever home may be. Given the danger of this situation, however, I am asking all nonessential personnel to report to their lifeboats, and for essential crew to go to General Quarters. There will be no alarms sounded. Please proceed in an orderly and careful fashion to your lifeboats and duty stations. That is all."

All very polite and clear, Jodenny thought, but she had no idea how she was going to get Myell to a lifeboat, or if he could even make the trip. The medical staff, however, already had evacuation procedures in place. Ruiz and an orderly brought over an anti-grav wheelchair. Myell was cooperative and seemed to understand what they were doing, but wouldn't leave without Karl.

"He'll be okay," Jodenny said.

Myell tried to get out of the chair.

She said, "Fine, I'll get him," and went back to Myell's room. Karl wasn't in the covers or under the pillows. Jodenny got down on the deck, and saw him hiding under one of the beds.

"Come on, Karl," she said.

He scratched himself.

"I'm serious!" Jodenny said. "Get out from under there."

It took another long minute of coaxing to get him out, and she was still disgruntled when she carried him back to Myell.

"I'm sorry we ever got you," she told the bot.

Myell's face fell in dismay.

Jodenny said, quickly, "No, I'm not," and kissed the koala to prove it. She kissed Myell too, and earned herself a small smile.

"Commander, this way," Ruiz said.

They evacuated to one of the medical lifeboats, which was larger than the others Jodenny had seen. Myell was made comfortable in a blue reclining chair. Two other patients from the infirmary were likewise cared for—a pregnant passenger in early labor and an able tech with an injured back. Counting additional crew, there were fifteen people in the boat. Jodenny wasn't surprised when Commander Nam showed up at the hatch.

"You're not assigned to this lifeboat, Commander," Dr. Ruiz said.

Nam jerked his head toward Myell. "He's my responsibility until we get back to Fortune."

Jodenny let Karl curl up in one of the underseat nets and gently rubbed Myell's arm. The trip had tired him out, and he was dozing. She asked Nam, "Do you really think the Roon will fire on us?"

"I hope to God not," Nam said. "I've seen their hand weapons. Don't even want to think of their shipboard armaments."

She waited for the sound of weapons fire, of damage and explosions. There was only the steady hiss of the air-circulation system and subdued conversation from the crew.

"How long do you think we'll be here?" one of the med techs asked.

"Hours," another answered.

A third let out an unhappy noise. "Better here than crashing down to Earth in flames."

"There aren't going to be any flames," Nam said, severely.

They watched on the vids as a Roon carrier grew closer. Jodenny wished Balandra would give updates over the comm, but the captain was probably a little busy. Nothing on the exterior of the Roon hull appeared to be weaponry, but there were several landing bays and surely those were fortified. The *Kamchatka* made several passes, each of them closer than the last.

"It's a dangerous game," Nam said.

Jodenny said, "It's not a game."

The *Kamchatka* started another sweep of the Roon ship's underbelly. Jodenny leaned forward, elbows on her knees, trying to make sense of the green scalelike attachments, the plates and protuberances and knobby features. She felt Myell's foot lash out against hers, and turned in alarm as he bolted upright.

"Stop them!" he shouted. No trace of the stutter remained. "Make them stop!"

A bright light flashed across the vidscreen. A thump vibrated through the *Kamchatka,* as if the whole ship had been slapped. The General Quarters alarm began to screech, tearing at Jodenny's ears alongside Myell's shouts.

"Stop them!" he kept shouting. The tendons in his neck bulged and he bared his teeth. He tried scrambling to the hatch but Ruiz's staff blocked him and started pulling him back. Jodenny tried to help, got an elbow in the face for her efforts, and was knocked off balance as the lifeboat unclamped.

"Emergency release!" someone yelled. "Strap in!"

The boat began to fall away from the *Kamchatka*. Myell was wrestled back to his seat and restrained. Jodenny hated to see Ruiz slap a sedative patch on his skin, but she didn't interfere. Myell slumped back, his eyes rolling up. The lifeboat continued to accelerate. Nam yanked Jodenny to her cushion and pulled down a safety strap just as alarms lit up across the bulkhead.

"Did they attack?" Jodenny demanded. "How's the *Kamchatka*?"

Nam pointed to a screen. "Repelled, but intact. Looks like only three or four lifeboats fell off."

"Can we go back?" Ruiz asked, his voice high with fear.

"No propulsion. We can't turn around," Jodenny said.

"Worse than that." Nam's expression was grim. "We're plummeting too fast. Whatever the Roon are using on Earth-based nav systems must be messing with our autopilot as well."

The officer in charge of the lifeboat, Chief Alvarez from the Data Department, wrestled with the helm controls. Interior alarms began to wail. A voice from the *Kamchatka* was issuing advice, but even Jodenny could see there was little that Alvarez could do. In his chair, Myell murmured a sedated complaint. She grabbed his hand, and for good measure grabbed one of Nam's as well.

"We're going to be fine," Nam told her. The vibrations of the lifeboat made his voice waver. "Understand?"

The tiny ship plummeted toward land.

CHAPTER TWENTY-SIX

Painkillers muddied Jodenny's thinking.

"Where are we?" she would ask, several times a day, and Myell couldn't always remember. Sometimes Nam would answer. Sometimes Dr. Ruiz would answer instead. Myell would listen carefully, then wander outside into the blistering, parched outback and forget everything they'd told him.

It bothered him that his mind seemed full of holes and crazy angles, but Ruiz told him he was getting better, and Nam would nod agreement before going back to the radio.

They were in Western Australia, Myell knew. They had been on a ship called the *Kamchatka*. Their lifeboat and several others had launched when the Roon did something to push the ship out of close proximity. The *Kamchatka* had suffered some damage but was still in orbit high overhead, on orders from Team Space. Nam talked to them every now and again on the radio. Myell listened, though it was hard for him to maintain focus on the way words worked, the way sentences flowed together and made sense.

He knew it hadn't always been that way. He remembered living on Fortune, marrying Jodenny, being stationed on the *Aral Sea,* joining Team Space. But he couldn't remember what it was like to have words flow out of his mouth like water in a river. Couldn't remember how to freely express what was going on in his head.

But the pictures . . . he could see pictures, day and night, pictures even when his eyes were closed, images of ruin and destruction that soaked into his flesh and sank to the bone. He couldn't shut them off completely no matter how hard he tried. Nam and Ruiz told him that the images weren't true, that the Roon weren't attacking.

"They will," Myell said.

Nam asked, "You're sure?"

Myell wasn't sure of anything anymore.

Sitting with Jodenny helped. When she held his hand, the burning cities and charred bodies behind his eyes faded into faint shapes that he could almost ignore. But she was groggy, in pain, fading, and fear made him afraid that just one more of his touches, one hot breath against her face, and she would be lost to him forever.

"Why don't they come for us?" he asked Nam.

"They are," Nam said. "But this place was the middle of nowhere even before the Debasement, and it's taking a long time to muster a land rescue. The Roon have grounded all airships, remember?"

Jodenny, the pregnant passenger, and two of the crew had been injured in the crash. The lifeboat carried plenty of water and food, but the hull was breached and of little protection against the heat of the day. The sunlight was indirect, diffused, victim of Earth's dirty atmosphere. It hadn't always been that way, because there was something Nam called the Debasement, which Myell understood to be a bad thing. Nam was in charge, but he was different from how Myell remembered him. Silent, mostly, his face drawn in deep lines.

"He's worried," Jodenny explained. "We're stuck out here and he holds himself responsible for all these people."

Karl raised his head from the nest in Jodenny's blankets. He too had been damaged in the crash, his fur singed and one paw bent. Often he curled up in Myell's lap, and Myell would pet him for hours.

Commander Nam sometimes talked about going for help. Ruiz told him he would die in the heat, or from snakes, or from any of the wild dingoes that circled the lifeboat at night. Because of the Debasement there were other things out there too, radiation-besotted, deformed, snarling. Nam scoffed at that notion, but on watch, at night, he was careful to keep the lifeboat's mazers close at hand.

On their third day in the desert Jodenny was groggier than usual, but she did open her eyes long enough to ask Myell how he felt.

"Hot," he said, which was the truth.

She gave him a crooked smile. "Memories all come back?"

He didn't think so.

"If I have to go . . ." Jodenny said, and swallowed hard. She touched his face with trembling fingers. "If I have to leave you, it's not because I want to, okay?"

"You can't leave," he said, stretching out beside her on the deck, scooting as close as he dared. "Can't."

She fingered his hair. "Sometimes we have to," she said, her eyes bright. "Sometimes we can't help it."

Myell whispered, "I won't let you."

That night, at sunset, two rescue teams arrived from Carnarvon. The crew cheered and even Jodenny mustered a smile. They crammed themselves into the flatbed vehicles and left all their gear behind. The flits turned west, toward the red sky, and in the excitement Karl was left behind with the wreck. By the time Myell remembered him, it was too late to turn back.

Jodenny was in a hospital in hell. The Carnarvon clinic hadn't been fully stocked or staffed before the Roon arrival and it certainly wasn't now. All forty beds were occupied by the ill or elderly, most struck down by dysentery or chronic illnesses. Other patients lay in cots in the hallways. The medical crew from the *Kamchatka*'s lifeboat were helping out the Aboriginal staff as best they could. If not for Dr. Ruiz, the only physicians would be a dentist and an unlicensed podiatrist. Post-Debasement Earth wasn't strict about medical staffing standards, especially with a nine-hundred-kilometer stretch to the nearest major city.

The hospital's air-conditioning didn't work, which made every room an oven. Ice was in short supply. The power generators were rationed, four hours off for every four hours on. Flies and roaches were a problem, as was overall sanitation. Nam had mustered up some volunteers to tackle the septic system, which was overtaxed and badly in need of new parts. Back on Fortune, it would take a few hours to get the parts made. On pre-Debasement Earth, it might take years.

"I'm afraid their bone knitter isn't working either," Ruiz said.

Jodenny squinted up at him from her lumpy, sweaty bed. Painkillers kept her broken hip numb, but could do nothing about other discomforts. "Can it be fixed?"

Ruiz squeezed the bridge of his nose. "No. We're trying to find another nearby, but the likeliest source is Perth. None of the flits around here could make it that far without running out of fuel. The Roon still aren't letting ships take off."

So she was to be laid up, crippled, for the foreseeable, horrendous future.

Myell came to Jodenny every day. His speech had gotten better since the crash but he looked haggard, weary, lost. Nam brought them both as much food and water as he could scavenge.

She said, "I'm glad you're here. I know you must be tempted to go off down to Perth, to do what you can about the Roon. Thank you for all your help."

He shrugged. "Least I could do."

Jodenny wasn't sure where Myell went when he wasn't with her, but sometimes he came to her with hair stiffened by sea salt, his face burned from wild solar rays.

"What are you doing out there?" she would ask.

He shook his head and kissed her cheek, which only made her worry more. The town wasn't safe. At night there were often gunshots, drunken singing, fistfights. The volunteer police force was vastly out-numbered by locals, stragglers, scavengers, and outback marauders looking for a place to lay up while the Roon ships roamed overhead. One tiny, thin strip of civilization, Jodenny thought, losing the battle against enemies outside and inside.

The clinic had no wallvids, but someone had a radio. According to news reports out of Perth, the Roon were still methodically scanning the whole of Earth. No more missiles had launched their way, no Team Space ships had tried another close approach, and no commu-nications had been established.

"But the *Kamchatka*'s still up there," Nam told her during his next visit. "I imagined that passenger petition has grown pretty long by now."

Jodenny asked, "Do you know where Terry is?"

"At the beach. I left him there a little while ago. One of the med techs is watching him."

"The beach?" Jodenny struggled to make sense of that. "Why?"

"He goes swimming. Throws himself into the waves and stays in the water for hours."

"He doesn't like the ocean. Never has."

"I know."

After that, Jodenny dreamed of sharks. Their fins sliced through the surf and their teeth bit into Myell's leg but it was her hip that flared into agony. She woke in the middle of the night, coated with sweat, biting into her lip. The med tech was late with the painkillers.

Jodenny turned her face into her pillow and wept.

She didn't see Myell again until that afternoon, and she begged him to stay with her. "Please," Jodenny said. "I don't want you going to the ocean."

"The water makes it easier," he said.

"Makes what easier?"

He waved his hand in the air. "Everything."

She persuaded him to stay the night on a cot that Nam found and set up near the window. Jodenny's roommate, an old woman with pneumonia who never received visitors, was in no position to object. The room smelled of urine and the night was like a furnace, the sky lit by fires from looting on Carnarvon's south side.

"Kay," he whispered in the orange-tinged darkness.

"Yes?" she asked.

"I wasn't always this way."

"Which way?"

"Broken."

"You're not broken." Jodenny peered at him as best she could. "We're just going through a rough patch."

He made a noise that might have been a laugh, then was silent.

Jodenny dozed fitfully. Dulled pain made her clench and unclench her fists. She was trying not to think of the *Kamchatka*, the Roon, the dying old woman in the next bed over. The smell of sickness wafted through the hospital, along with rot and bleach and blood and feces, and she wanted to scream, but didn't have the energy.

Sometime before dawn, she was woken from a restless sleep by Myell. He was standing beside her bed, his hair rumpled, his expression serene. She thought he might have been kissing her in his sleep.

"What's wrong?" she asked.

"I have to go," he said, almost a whisper. "I know what to do. How to stop them."

He sounded utterly confident. And that confidence scared her more than anything else could have done. She said, "Terry, no."

He kissed her, openmouthed, his lips warm and convincing, his hand cradling her head.

"Look at the ceiling," he said.

Jodenny tried to focus. All she saw were cracks in the plaster and a light bulb that didn't work even when the power was on. After a few more seconds of staring she thought she saw some kind of shape, an outline. An egret. She remembered swooping through the air with feathers in her nose and hands. The exhilaration of flight, and the bird's cry when it was attacked.

"It's a crocodile," Myell said.

"No, it's not," she said, and grabbed his hand. "There's nothing up there."

His gaze lifted. "I didn't tell you. I met crocodiles. Dozens of them. Free-not-chained. She kissed me in the ocean, and I couldn't stop her."

Myell's skin was warm, his eyes wide. Jodenny thought maybe he was sleepwalking, though he'd never done that before. They were so far gone from normal that anything was possible.

"Can we talk about it after breakfast?" she asked. "Can you wait that long?"

He bent very close to her. "Do you trust me?"

Jodenny trusted her *old* husband, her husband before Garanwa had done whatever he'd done, before brain damage and trauma and whatever else had gone wrong in his head. This man couldn't even tie his own shoes, but he liked to throw himself into the sea.

"Don't go," she begged.

Myell watched the ceiling. "Now it's a gecko," he said. "It's leaving. I have to follow it."

He kissed her again, brief and fleeting. Then he walked out of the room.

"Terry!" she shouted, trying to rise. "Come back! Get back here!"

Her frantic shouting eventually brought an overworked Aboriginal nurse, and the nurse finally found Nam.

"You have to stop him," Jodenny said.

"Stop him from what?" Nam asked, irritated.

"I don't know." Despite her broken hip, Jodenny started to pull herself up. She would throw herself to the floor and crawl across the outback if it meant stopping Myell from whatever craziness was going on in his head. "I have to go after him."

Nam pushed her back down. "Don't be stupid."

"He's out there, alone! He can't defend himself. He doesn't know what he's doing." Tears stung her eyes, and angrily she wiped them away. "He'll die, and you know it."

Nam grimaced. "If I leave you, you might die."

Which was true enough, though hard to admit. Nam had brought her food, had changed her stinking bedpan, was there when the med techs and Ruiz couldn't be.

Jodenny raised her head in challenge. "I'm not the one with the power to summon a token, maybe control the whole Wondjina network."

"You don't believe that."

"I don't, but you do."

Nam gazed past her to the dirty window.

"I'll go," he said. "I'll stop him. But not because of that."

The why didn't matter.

"Find him," she said.

CHAPTER TWENTY-SEVEN

Myell walked out of Carnarvon just before dawn, following the paths of the Dreamtime gods.

The town was not quite in ruins, because it hadn't been much to begin with. Back before the Debasement it had been a quaint outpost between the Indian Ocean and the Gascoyne River. But the long decades since had been rough. The trees and shrubs had mostly died off, and the tourists were long gone. The people who lived there had no place else to go and not much to hope for. The town was all they had.

And now Myell was leaving it. Leaving, probably never to return.

He had spent days by the sea, wading in the water, trying to talk to crocodiles. He had clutched Yambli's dilly bag so tightly that his knuckles ached, but the totems gave no answer. He had walked around Carnarvon until every street seemed familiar, every sad building like home. He had wandered through the clinic where Jodenny was, slipping through the rooms like a ghost. Nothing had made a difference, nothing had changed. He was still only half of who he had been. Maybe a third. An illiterate, impaired third, and he suspected that he was even worse than he believed.

Lying awake in Jodenny's room, the smells and sounds too strong for him to rest, he had peered into the darkness under her bed for hours. Watching shadows, waiting between heartbeats for mental acuity that would not return.

Then the crocodile came slithering across the ceiling. It peered at Myell with eyes darker than the blackness of the room. Its jaws opened, its teeth gnashed—

And Myell was back on Yambli's beach, the old crone sitting across the fire from him.

"What are you doing?" she asked.

He tipped his head back to a sky full of bright stars. The breeze off the ocean was cold and made his arms prickle.

"Waiting," he replied.

"Waiting for what?" Yambli poked the fire with her stick, sending sparks spiraling into the night.

"I don't know." Myell peered into her eyes but saw only his reflection. "There's no more time, is there? Everything's going to end."

Yambli poked him with the stick. He yelped.

"You've learned nothing," she said. "You are Jungali. There is no end, only a beginning."

A beeping noise brought him back to Jodenny's hospital room. A nurse paused in the doorway to hush a gib. Myell watched her come in and check on her patients. If she saw him lying awake on the cot, she said nothing.

When the nurse left, her feet disturbed the golden lines glowing on the floor.

Myell sat up slowly. Lines to follow. Garanwa's station, the ever-changing rooms, the songlines. He was in Old Australia, land of the

Wondjina, and he'd never thought to look for the songlines under his feet.

He closed his eyes and saw them weaving and unweaving beneath the hospital, beneath the town, all the lines, branching out like dried-up streams through the land, his to follow.

The hardest part had been saying goodbye to Jodenny.

The second hardest part was trying to persuade Nam not to join him.

He hadn't expected Nam to find him, never mind follow him, but when Myell reached a road that led east he heard footsteps behind. The sky was still gray with night. The drunks and rioters were sleeping, leaving the town quiet and still.

"Go back, Commander," Myell said, without breaking stride.

"The sea's the other way," Nam said.

"Not going there."

"Really? Going somewhere else?" Nam sounded out of breath. "Your wife was wondering. You left her without much explanation."

The gecko songline was pulling him now, strong like a magnet, always here, always waiting for him.

"What's at the end of this road you're traveling?" Nam asked.

"I don't know."

"You think maybe we could bring water, some food?"

Myell frowned. "You can't come. It's not your journey."

Nam pulled on the bandanna around his neck. He smelled like he hadn't showered in a while, and there was stubble on his chin. "Well, maybe, maybe not, but I promised Jodenny I'd come with you. She's a little worried."

The air smelled burnt, rotten, but there was a cleaner wind out there, singing over the countryside. Myell stopped and met Nam's gaze.

"I don't know what's there," he said, struggling again with words, their meanings, their shifting vagueness. "But it's not for you."

"So when we get there, I'll wait outside."

Myell said nothing.

Nam held his right hand up in a pledge. "You're not going alone, Terry."

Myell stared. Nam had never used his given name before.

"I'm coming with you," Nam said. "For more reasons than I can say. At the end of the world, it's rare that you get to pick your own exit."

Myell resumed walking. Nam followed.

The sun came up in the hazy east. The heat came up, as well. The road out of Carnarvon was littered for the first few kilometers with abandoned cars, rusty vehicles, old jeeps. The pickings were slim, no hope of water or food. Nam found a crushed bush hat and dropped it on Myell's head.

"Keep your brain from frying," Nam explained. "More than it has already, that is."

The debris gave way to acres of refuse that the townsfolk had hauled out in years past, before the effort became too much. Steel and glass, and plastic garbage bags, and small animals that scurried in between them, but the worst thing was the smell, and the flies that bit at their clothes.

"Great road you're traveling," Nam muttered, but didn't turn back.

Thirst made itself known, first a niggling tickle, then a strong itch, then the inside of him burning up, drying out. Myell had no canteen or water bottle. He had no way of knowing how far the road would take him, but he was walking with his ancestors now, and there was no turning back.

He was unsurprised that Nam grew increasingly restless, worried about their trek.

"Are we going to wait for rain? Manna from heaven?"

Myell didn't answer. He had nothing to go by other than the knowledge that this was the right path, that he was trusting the gods. He couldn't think ahead. But wasn't that foolishness? Was he so far demented that he couldn't tell instinct from psychosis?

"I don't know," he said, surrendering again to the song, to the intuition that this was the way it had to be, was always meant to be.

But it was hot, scorching hot, and he was parched inside and out. The day was cloudy, no rain. The landscape was quiet, just bugs and occasional scurrying animals in the brush, and the wind. He remembered that there were dingoes out here, and snakes, and other things eager to kill, but he told himself that he wasn't afraid. That everything had been planned for. Not by him, but by someone else.

Would have been nice, though, to see Jodenny one more time.

The horizon shimmered and shifted, skeletal trees stretched toward the sky, nothing but the crisscross to guide him, the ancient paths. A lonely land, baked dry, desolate enough to drive a man crazy.

"I'm not crazy," he said to Nam.

Nam was gone. There was no sign of him anywhere on the horizon.

That was crazy.

Myell paused, not sure if he should turn back. Had Nam fallen by the wayside? Had he said goodbye? For a moment Myell was sure that Nam had never been there, that he'd been walking this long road from Carnarvon with no companionship other than his own deranged mind.

In the end, he was alone.

He walked in the now, the moment, baked in the heat and misery, detached but feeling every jarring step in his bones.

"What did you expect, that this would be easy?" he heard Captain Kuvik ask.

Another hallucination. Kuvik was back in Supply School, sitting mired in regulations and invoices, running his command like a ship.

"There's more to being Jungali than just putting on the uniform," Senior Chief Talic added, his shadow keeping pace with Myell on the road.

Irritated, Myell asked, "What do you know about it?"

Talic replied, "You haven't gone through initiation. You haven't changed. Things that don't change end up dying. Isn't that what you said?"

"Leave him alone," Senior Chief Gooder said. His face creased with an encouraging smile. "Man's got a job to do."

Myell kept walking, listening to the chiefs bicker around him in voices like the wind.

Darkness finally came, bringing relief after the blistering sunlight. He slumped by the side of the asphalt, unable to trudge even one step farther. He had neither water nor food, only sunburn on his face and blisters on his feet.

He was lying on his back, no stars overhead because of the haze, when a loud, strange noise came from the highway. Some kind of machine powered by a combustion engine, misfiring, belching noise and chaos. It rolled on the ground instead of a cushion of air. Its headlights were weak but blinding anyway. Maybe it was a Roon scout, scouring the countryside . . .

The machine slowed to a stop. Its engine continued to grate and screech and make appalling noise. A man descended from the elevated cab. His outline blocked the light.

"Australia's pretty damn big," Nam said. "I thought we could use some help on your walkabout."

As it turned out, Nam's truck couldn't be turned off for fear that it might never turn on again.

"Engine's as old as dirt," Nam said from the front seat, which was a lopsided collection of springs and torn stuffing. The backseat wasn't much better. "Fuel's enough for a couple hundred kilometers, nothing more. Unless we find a gas station. What are the chances of that?"

Myell was stretched out with a wet cloth over his face. Every jolt of the truck sent shock waves through his aching body.

"There's some food in a box back there," Nam said. "Nothing too tasty, but it'll do."

Myell rummaged through the box halfheartedly and found something that he supposed was jerky. He bit it cautiously, and reached for the bottle of lukewarm water that Nam had tucked under his arm. Though he didn't remember asking Nam where he'd found the truck, Nam was telling him anyway.

"One of those roads we passed led to an old sheep station. The man there says it was his grandfather's place, way back. He's not much left for the world but he loves the military, said he would have joined up if it weren't for his wife and kids. It took some negotiating, but he was willing to lend me this truck, and the food and water, in return for an afternoon of swapping sea stories."

The truck was faster than traveling by foot, but louder and more grating. The engine was in constant danger of falling out from under the hood. The blowers spewed hot air that stank of grease. Myell managed to sleep a few minutes here, a few minutes there, though he was never completely unaware of the engine noise, of the stench. Part of him was still focused on the crisscross, the songline. When he could no longer see with his inner vision, he sat up and said, "Stop."

Nam slowed the vehicle to an obnoxiously loud idle. "What's wrong?"

"We've got to turn that way." Myell pointed off into the darkness.

Nam had some maps, badly wrinkled pieces of paper that he peered at in the dim light of flashlights. "I thought you didn't know where we were going."

"I don't. I just know that it's that way."

"Sure of that, are you?"

"More sure than anything."

"We'll be crossing overland. Rough going, even if we had the best ground vehicle on Earth."

Myell said, "We'll get as far as we can, and walk the rest if need be."

Nam gave him a sideways look. "You're talking much better."

Myell squinted at him. Words were indeed coming easier, he realized. His mind felt clearer, as if he were waking up from a long, muddy dream.

"Broken axle, here we come," Nam said, and steered the truck off the road.

The jostling got much worse. The truck didn't have a prayer of making it across any ravines or gullies, so Nam had to slow down and let the headlights pick out any potential hazards. Myell offered to spell him at the wheel, but Nam insisted that he was fine to drive.

Myell stayed with him in the front seat to make sure he didn't nod off. At oh-two-hundred a low, flat farmhouse appeared, and they got out of the truck to investigate.

Myell's legs were cramped from sitting for so long. He gingerly stretched them as they approached the farmhouse. No lights were on. No dogs barked. There was a barn, but its roof had collapsed. Nam knocked, and when no one answered he forced the door open.

The farmhouse was long since deserted, furniture covered with thick dust. It might have been a nice place, once. Musty curtains shrouded the windows. Photos of children hung in frames on the walls. The children were probably long gone now, maybe moved to the cities, maybe destroyed by the Roon.

Beyond the living room was a bedroom with striped wallpaper and a ceiling fan. Lying in the bed were two mummified corpses, their limbs entwined. Maybe they'd gone out together in a suicide pact. Maybe they'd taken poison. Or maybe they had been old and sick, and decided to die in their own fashion, their own choice.

He and Jodenny would never grow old together. He knew that as surely as he knew how to follow a songline, and the hard painful weight of that had lodged under his breastbone.

Nam had been investigating the kitchen, as if anything edible could be found after so long a time. Now he gazed past Myell at the dead bodies.

"We should get back to the truck," he said.

They left the dead to their rest and continued east.

The truck groaned and shuddered and went still five hours later. Myell said, "It's all right. We're almost there."

"Almost where?" Nam asked, propping open the engine compartment and scowling at the ruined machinery. "You don't know where we're going. You don't know how long until we get there. You don't know—"

Myell pointed past Nam's shoulder. "There."

Nam turned.

The sun was a low ball of fire above the horizon. Its rays slanted on an enormous hunk of ancient earth jutting upward. Myell's breath tightened in awe as he gazed on it. The rock was the largest he had ever seen, the largest maybe in the entire world, and they still had more than a hundred kilometers to cross before they reached it.

"Burringurrah," Myell said. "Garanwa's home. That's where we're going."

Though the need to keep going was like a deep, burning itch, Myell knew that neither he nor Nam could walk all day. They were both exhausted. The truck was like an oven but there were some old cloth tarpaulins folded up in the back, and they rigged those into a makeshift canopy. It wouldn't hold up under a strong rainstorm, but the chances of rain seemed slim.

They ate some more of the jerky and stretched out on the ground. Nam had found some more maps and even an old guidebook under the tarps. He thumbed through the pages with a frown on his face.

"It's a monocline," Nam said. "Largest in the entire world."

Myell tried hard not to think about Jodenny, so far behind them. Alone, in pain, no one to advocate for her.

"Three times as old as Uluru," Nam continued, the book close to his nose. "One point six billion years old."

She deserved more. She deserved a husband who would have put her needs first, not gone traipsing off across the outback on a quest to see a giant rock.

"She's fine," Nam said.

"Reading my mind?" Myell asked.

"You've got a lovesick-puppy look on your face," Nam said.

"She's all alone."

"She's a decorated military officer, broken hip or not. She knows how to take care of herself."

Myell turned his face away and hoped Nam was right.

Myell and Nam hadn't been gone for more than an hour when Dr. Ruiz came into Jodenny's room wheeling a bone knitter.

"Came in from Geraldton," Ruiz said. "Not the best unit, little rusty around the edges, but I think it will do the job."

Jodenny hoped he was joking about the rust, but she didn't dare ask.

The knitter might have been the most ancient model left in all of Australia, but it did its job well. By midafternoon Jodenny was able to walk with the aid of a cane. She discovered that the clinic was more crowded than she'd thought, more in desperate need, so their persistence in finding the knitter made her even more appreciative. Though she was tired, feeling brittle at the edges, she gave up her bed.

"You can't leave," Ruiz said. "You need a few days' bed rest or your hip could break apart under the strain."

"I have to find my husband," she said.

"Send out search teams. He can't have gone far."

She almost smiled. "You don't know him."

Carnarvon wasn't large enough for a Team Space outpost, but there was a civil defense troop stationed at the firehouse. Jodenny first had to convince them that she was indeed a Team Space lieutenant commander, but once they scanned her dog tags, the leading sergeant, a scared-looking young man named Hamilton, offered command of the unit to her.

"Our captain's been on a bender for weeks, can't be torn from his bottle," Hamilton explained. "The lieutenant went home to check on his family and didn't come back. That was three nights ago."

Jodenny said, "You'll have to carry on without them. I'm on a mission. I need a vehicle. Anything that moves."

Hamilton looked perplexed. "Nothing like that around here, ma'am."

"What about the flits that rescued us from the outback?"

"One's broken down, heard it's a goner. The other went up the coast to help out there. It won't be back until the end of the week or so. I'd try to reach it for you, but their radio's broken."

Jodenny put her cane aside and commandeered the radio. She tried using a nonemergency frequency to contact Team Space in Perth. But the operators she reached didn't know much, or didn't want to help. Some of them sounded drunk. At sunset she finally pushed off the headset. She brooded over a cup of coffee that Hamilton had rounded up for her. It tasted old and gritty, but she needed the caffeine.

"Maybe you should try the ham radio operators," Hamilton suggested. "There's still some old-timers around."

"Ham what?" Jodenny asked.

"Amateur radio operators. Got a language and world of their own. My daddy used to run his radio out of a little shack up near Meekatharra."

"I'll try anything," she said.

After several minutes of tinkering with the antiquated equipment, Hamilton was talking to a cheery-sounding man out of Kalbarri. That led to another radio contact out of Southern Cross and, much later, long after midnight, a chat with someone on the outskirts of Perth who promised he knew people in Team Space.

"I'll do my best, girl," he said cheerfully. "Don't hold your breath."

Jodenny rubbed her eyes in exhaustion. Hamilton said, "Best use that cot, Commander. Lie down before you fall down."

She obeyed, too tired and aching to argue. She slept until the brightness and heat of the day woke her. She was splashing her face with lukewarm water from a jug when Hamilton came running.

"There's a Lieutenant Sweeney calling," he said.

Jodenny hurried to the radio. "Mark?"

The connection wasn't good, but Sweeney's voice crackled through. "Ellen Spring?"

"The same," Jodenny said, a grin making her lips hurt. "How'd you get there?"

"Same as you. Damn lifeboat launched before we could stop it."

"I'm trying to get out of here. It's important. Chief Myell and Commander Nam need help."

Sweeney sounded frustrated. "I don't know what I can do. We're down here in Fremantle."

"You have to try," she said.

The transmission broke up. Jodenny sat back in the lumpy chair and cursed fate. She could not sit by for another day and do nothing. An old man with a straw hat went by on a bicycle. She imagined herself biking her way through the outback, pedaling until her hip fell apart. Already it was aching like a bad, bad tooth. Maybe she could find a DNGO, strap herself on its back, and make it carry her across the outback.

But even if she found some kind of transportation, she still had no idea which way Myell and Nam had gone.

"You said you've had sentries on the roads?" Jodenny asked Hamilton.

"Yes, ma'am. No one gets in or out without being seen."

"People want to get in or out?"

"We've had stragglers coming in, people afraid to be on their own." He scratched at an unhealthy-looking mole on his elbow. "Some other people here, they're leaving, taking their chances. Figure Perth might be safer if those lizards start landing and blasting away. Good luck to them, right?"

"Can you check with the sentries, see if any of them remember seeing one or two men leave on foot? Chief Myell, my husband, would be one of them. Commander Nam the other."

She described them both, adding that Myell might not be very articulate. Hamilton went off to check with his men. While he was gone, she studied a map of the surrounding region.

"Bill Gum didn't see them," Hamilton said when he got back. "But you could drive a herd of sheep past him and he might not notice. Tommy Reed said he was awake, but he was probably drunk or passed out. Hilly Dodd saw a fellow head out, followed by another. Could be your men. They were the only ones going north or so."

Jodenny traced the map with her finger. "What's this complex here?"

Hamilton peered at the spot. "Old NASA tracking station. Gotta neat history, that. They used it back when people were first landing on the moon."

"Does it still work?"

"Not a chance. Just a bunch of scrap metal. People like to shoot up the dishes with rifles and such." Hamilton leaned over the map. "Mostly that way you're going to find some abandoned sheep stations, some old tourist traps, a few sacred sites, but nothing worth pissing on these days. If you'll pardon my language, ma'am."

Jodenny didn't think Myell would head for any of those. "Sacred sites? Sacred Aboriginal sites?"

"Like that one." Hamilton gestured to a framed print on the wall.

"Uluru?" She had noticed the distinctive rock while Hamilton was gone—an enormous and imposing chunk of earth rising up from a flat plain, almost like a mountain with its top half sheared off.

"That's not Uluru," Hamilton said. "That's Mt. Augustus. The Wadjari locals call it Burringurrah. Not as pretty as Uluru. Not as famous. But bigger and older."

Jodenny stood up, snagged her cane, and crossed to the picture. "How far is it?"

"Oh, a right long distance. Three hundred kilometers or so."

"Could a person walk it?"

"Sure. Die of thirst or heat on the way, most likely."

It would be exactly like her husband to attempt an impossible walk under impossible circumstances.

Hamilton scratched at his mole again. "They say it's named after an Aboriginal boy from a long time ago. He was supposed to be getting initiated into his tribe, right? Manhood passage, stuff like that. But he ran away. Didn't want to do it."

Jodenny tried not to think about Myell and chief's initiation. "What happened to him?"

"Oh, they speared him. Right through the leg. Killed him with sticks and knives."

She immediately went in search of a vehicle. Surely somewhere in the town there was something she could rent, buy, or steal. One woman had a motorcycle with two dead wheels and no replacements. Someone else had a truck, but no gas. The town's petrol station had closed months earlier for want of fuel. She checked on the broken rescue flit, but the intake valves were hopelessly ruined.

"Can't they be replaced?" Jodenny asked.

"Sure enough," the mechanic told her. "Parts should be arriving from Sydney any week now."

Jodenny didn't appreciate his humor.

When sunset came she hobbled back to the fire station, watched Hamilton brief the oncoming sentries, and ate a cold dinner of bread and canned peas. Her hip ached more than she cared to admit, but all she could think of was Myell and Nam out there on their way to Burringurrah, lost and maybe dying.

She squinted at the horizon, at a growing yellow light, and rubbed her eyes against the hallucination. A whirlybird pulled into sight, ancient and battered but large enough for a pilot and some passengers. It was the ugliest, noisiest collection of flying equipment she had ever seen. Surely something like that couldn't fly for long without crashing into the ground or a tree or a mountain.

It landed behind the post office, and Jodenny was there when Mark Sweeney opened the back door for her.

"Where did you find this?" she yelled over the bird's noise.

"A museum!" he yelled back.

Hamilton, who'd come with Jodenny, said, "Better get on, Commander, before you get stormed."

Jodenny saw that a crowd was already forming—people who wanted out of Carnarvon and might do anything for a seat on the whirlybird. She climbed into the back, her hip twinging in protest.

"Carry on, Sergeant. Good luck."

"Yes, ma'am," he said, with a smart salute.

Sweeney tapped the pilot's shoulder. The whirlybird took off. Jodenny slid a commset over her head and Sweeney said, "This is Captain Cook."

"What?" Jodenny asked, sure that couldn't be right.

"Crook!" The pilot said, giving her a wave. "Peter Crook. Nice to meet you."

"Likewise," Jodenny said. "We're looking for two men on foot headed toward a place called Burringurrah. Do you know it?"

"Mt. Augustus?" Sweeney asked. "There've been unconfirmed reports of Roon scouts out that way. It's a big place, though. Eight or nine kilometers wide. Why are they headed there?"

"I'm not sure," she admitted. "You could drop me off near there, if you want. Get me in the region."

"Not a chance," Sweeney said. "You go, we all go. Crank it up, Captain Crook."

The whirlybird headed for Burringurrah.

CHAPTER TWENTY-NINE

The afternoon sun was high behind the western haze. Myell rubbed sleep from his eyes. He hadn't meant to nap the day away, but he'd stretched out and fallen into a deep, dreamless sleep. Nam was working diligently on the truck engine, trying to work a miracle with wire and tape and the tools he'd rustled up from the back.

"Try starting it," Nam suggested.

Myell climbed up into the cab. The driver's seat was more uncomfortable than Nam had let on. Myell eyed the unfamiliar controls. Though he'd watched Nam drive hundreds of kilometers, he hadn't paid much attention to how he'd done it.

"Turn the key and step on the pedal on the right!" Nam said. "Don't shift it out of Park or you'll run me over."

Myell did exactly as he was told. The engine made a rough gasping noise, belched, then settled into an irregular rhythm.

Nam slammed down the hood, threw their supplies into the back, and nudged Myell into the passenger seat. "There you go. Right as rain."

Burringurrah grew closer, its enormousness becoming more clear with every passing minute. The rock wasn't as symmetrical as Uluru, not as red tinged, but it was larger, maybe older. If Myell closed his eyes he could picture native Aboriginals worshiping in its shadows. Nam's books had mentioned caves and petroglyphs, and gorges full of ducks and swans, and lush flowers that grew during the wet season. Gum trees ringed the monocline's base, many dead from drought.

"This whole place used to be the floor of an ocean," Nam said. "Bet you didn't know that."

Myell admitted that he hadn't.

"I'll say one thing for you, Chief. Outer space, jungles, cliffs, islands, oceans, space stations, and ancient seabeds. You certainly get around."

They finally got as close as they could. Nam turned off the engine. The truck shuddered and went still in the dusk.

"You shouldn't have done that," Myell said. "You could have gone back."

"Fuel's out. Besides, I always figured this was a one-way trip."

Myell was glad for the company, though he told himself he shouldn't be.

"Up it?" Nam asked. "Around it?"

"Up," Myell said.

Nam adjusted the mazer and knife he kept on his belt. He reached for their flashlights. "I was afraid you'd say that."

Snakes slithered in the bushes as Myell led Nam on a steep switchback trail that was no wider than their feet. Darkness made the going all the more dangerous. The terrain dropped away quickly, ghostly gray under a dirty moon.

"How far do you think it is to the top?" Nam asked.

Myell tilted his head back. "Can't tell."

He soon fell into a plodding rhythm that kept him going upward. He didn't think he could have done the climb in the heat of the day, but night seemed to have cooled a bit. Nam, behind him, was having a little more trouble keeping up, but he waved off Myell's backward glances.

"Keep going," Nam said, breathing heavily. "Maybe at the top you'll finally let me know what this has been all about."

"You think I know?" Myell retorted, and that earned him a grunt.

One of their flashlights died after an hour, and the other was giving off only a weak yellow light. Myell feared they'd be left with no light at all. But the flashlight stayed on and the temperature kept dropping, and the slope grew steeper. He was sweating but had goosebumps. Couldn't wait until they reached the summit, but feared what they would find there.

Dead brush entangled his feet.

Jodenny, he thought, in grief, in memory.

"What is that?" Nam asked, his head turned to the west.

Myell tried to focus on a brightly moving light. "A birdie?"

Nam shifted on the trail. "No. I think—"

Rocks slid out from under his feet, and Nam fell.

Jodenny didn't know where Sweeney had dug up his whirlybird pilot, but she wished he'd done a little more searching. Captain Crook was clearly a man who liked flying. Liked it too much, maybe. He skimmed the ancient vehicle close to the ground, swooping and lifting and dropping for the fun of it. Music blasted through the commset, a screeching cacophony of some sort that she'd never heard before and hoped never to hear again. In the hot air of the outback night all she could do was hold on tight to her safety straps and peer at the dark landscape below.

"Do you have any spotlights?" she asked, shouting over the music.

"You're lucky we've got fuel!" Captain Crook responded cheerily.

Sweeney twisted around in his seat. "What the hell made them set out on foot?"

Jodenny said, "They didn't have any other way."

"Man could get his brains fried out here," Crook offered. "Straight line to hell. Your husband an Aboriginal, is he?"

"Not so much."

"What?" Crook asked.

"Turn the music down!" Jodenny ordered, and Sweeney reached for the dial.

Crook slapped his hand. "Nay on that, young man. I'll do all the touching around here."

But he did adjust the volume to a more manageable level. Jodenny asked, "How far is it to Burringurrah?"

"If we don't fall out of the sky first? Not so long," Crook said. "She's a good ship, you know. Found her myself in a junkyard and lovingly restored every last nut and screw and piston. Fast. No fancy computers for this darling, just a compass and my finger to tell which way the wind's blowing."

The whirlybird clattered eastward under cloudy skies. The engine noise and vibrations made Jodenny's teeth ache. She asked Sweeney, "Who else was in your lifeboat?"

"Some Engineering types, a few passengers. We splashed down off the coast and had to inflate the rafts. Got everyone off safely enough. Would have preferred to stay on the *Kamchatka*. The third lifeboat landed in Europe, I hear. I don't know what became of the fourth."

The ground rushing by below stayed dark no matter how hard Jodenny stared at it. She tried not to think of Myell and Nam down there, collapsed on the ground from heat or dehydration. Pawed over by dingoes or other wild animals. Nam was of Aboriginal descent but that didn't mean he had any outback skills. All she hoped was that he was using his military knowledge to keep Myell alive. That they weren't already dead.

They were hours out of Carnarvon when Crook said, "Good holy grief! Look at that."

Jodenny leaned forward between the pilot and copilot seats. Dead ahead, the plain of Burringurrah was an enormous silhouette. Smack-dab in the middle, hundreds of bright construction lights were pointed down into some kind of pit. She couldn't see what was in it. Several Roon scout ships were parked on the plateau, running lights shining like Christmas bulbs. Tiny Roon soldiers moved around the ships and pit, a deadly army.

"I didn't sign up for this, mate," Crook told Sweeney.

The whirlybird began to bank. Jodenny clutched Sweeney's arm and shouted, "You can't go back!"

Crook yelled, "I'm not putting myself in the devil's hands! I've got kids at home."

A blue-green light swamped the whirlybird. Jodenny fell back in surprise. The beam didn't hurt, but it silenced the engines and stilled the ship's vibrations. Crook swore and slapped his controls and said, "Fucking hell," but he obviously had no control as the plateau swung into view and grew larger in front of them.

"What's going on?" Sweeney asked.

"Tractor beam," Crook said. "They're pulling us in. Goddammit."

Jodenny peered out the window. A sense of inevitability, of predestination, calmed her thudding heart. "Prepare to meet the devil," she said, and sat back for the ride.

Nam cried out and fell a meter or so before being snagged on more rocks. Myell scrambled after him, desperate to keep him from plunging into the ravine below. He grabbed Nam by the arms and hauled him back up to the trail. Nam rolled in pain, and Myell asked, "Your leg?"

"Goddamn Achilles tendon," Nam gasped, in agony. "Snapped it before."

"Oh, Jesus," Myell said.

Nam was carrying the paltry medical kit that had been in the truck. Myell fumbled inside it, trying to find a patch full of painkiller, but the flashlight was unsteady in his free hand and Nam's distress was too loud, too close.

Finally he closed on the patch and slapped it onto the bare skin under Nam's trouser leg. It took a long moment before Nam's shudders stopped, though his eyes were still wide with shock.

"Should I splint it?" Myell asked. All his first aid lessons had fled. "Wrap it or something?"

"Don't bother," Nam said. "I'm not going anywhere."

Myell sat back on his heels.

Nam squeezed his eyes shut. "It's a dream come true. You've been trying to get me to turn back since we left Carnarvon."

"No," Myell said. "You're coming with me."

"Don't be an idiot! I'm not going anywhere."

Nam could indeed stay there, stranded on the side of the most ancient rock in the world, left to bake in the next day's heat. Slow death would follow, by thirst or hunger or wild animals. Or he could take another way out, and use the mazer he'd been carrying around since their rescue from the lifeboat.

"You have to," Myell said. "I don't know why. I don't know why *you*. But now that we're here, we've both got to get to the top, or it'll be all in vain."

Nam's expression narrowed. "You're lying."

Myell shook his head. "You've your own part to play in this, Commander. I can't change that."

Nam let his head roll back. "You and me, this trail, and I can't walk on my right leg. If that's your plan, it's shit."

"I know," Myell said.

And so they started upward together, up the ancient rock, Nam's right arm slung around Myell's neck. The going got rougher, slower, but Myell believed what he had said. Nam was just as important in this as he was. The end of a very long trip was in sight, and they were going to cross the finish line together.

Dead, perhaps, but no one would be left behind.

"Fucking crazy," Nam said, his voice a rasp.

Their water was gone, the canteens borrowed from the farmer empty.

"Stupid chief who doesn't know how to say no," Nam said later, as they struggled up the trail.

He didn't think they had any food, either.

"Stupid silly idiotic—" Nam said, the words like pebbles, drop drop drop, but Myell wasn't listening anymore, because they'd reached the top.

He stopped, gasping for air, sweating hard, Nam's weight almost impossible to carry anymore. The ground had leveled onto a rough plateau that stretched on for several kilometers. Myell wiped sweat out of his eyes. He played the flashlight over the ghostly landscape.

"There's nothing here but dirt," Nam rasped.

Myell rubbed his face. The tattoos abraded his palms. Maybe this whole one-way suicide trip had indeed been for nothing, and they would die atop the rock having achieved nothing but misery and suffering.

Then, in the blackness, something scuffled, something shifted, something breathed.

Artificial light switched on, blasting them from all directions. Myell shielded his burning eyes with his forearm. Nam did so too, and the miscoordination of their efforts made them stagger and fall and land on their asses. In the horrible illumination Myell saw upright reptilian shapes.

"Fucking shit," Nam said. "This is why you wanted me along?"

With watering, half-blinded eyes Myell stared at the rows and columns of Roon soldiers, a thousand lizards standing in rigid formation, their eyes black coals set in green faces, their body armor gleaming.

A Roon soldier grabbed Myell and lifted him upright so force-
fully that his right arm nearly wrenched free of its socket.
Other soldiers lifted Nam. Myell expected to live for only a few more
terror-filled seconds, and figured he might as well die fighting.

"Fuck you," he said, trying to pull free.

The Roon paid him no attention. Something clamped down on his
right hand, and he suddenly found himself unable to talk, move, do
almost anything but breathe. His head lolled painfully, his throat con-
stricted, his eyes froze wide-open. He began to panic, but then a curious calm washed through him like warm, clean-scented water. He
was lifted over one of the Roon's shoulders and carried through the

army like a sack of silent potatoes. Nam was carried off in the same fashion.

Myell's mind was clear, even if his body was helpless. The Roon smelled vile up close. Like a rotting corpse dug out of slimy mud. The soldier's armor cut into his stomach and chest and the steady jostling made him want to vomit. The Roon were utterly silent as Myell and Nam were carried through, and he had the uncomfortable feeling that they were going to be some kind of ritual sacrifice, that their deaths would be bloody and excruciating.

The army continued to part around them, lines dividing and falling away. Myell had no idea how far they were carried before the pace slowed. The lights on this part of the plateau were shining down into some kind of pit. He could see the silhouettes of equipment—large equipment capable of blasting through rock and dirt, of digging up something that had long been buried. Something hidden here, in soil that was almost two billion years old . . .

He had a strong, chilly premonition of what the Roon had found.

An order came, clicks and chitters in the Roon language. Myell was set down on the ground. The squeezing pressure on his hand was removed. He staggered upright. Nam, still hampered by his injury, grabbed for his hand and pulled himself up on one leg.

The Roon King stepped forward.

He was magnificent. More than three meters high, his head smooth where the others were ridged, a powerful jaw full of teeth, and two enormous wings rising from the white feather cloak over his shoulders.

Wings. Myell nearly lost his balance again, but somehow managed to stay on his feet.

The King loomed over them, still a few meters away, no recognizable expression on that alien face. Maybe he was a general, or a diplomat, or something other than a monarch, but it didn't matter. Myell's heart pounded like the drums of a military tattoo, so loud that surely every soldier in the Roon army could hear it, every soldier recognize the call.

He took his own step forward, though Nam tried to hold him back.

"Wait," Nam said.

"No," Myell replied. This was what they had made the journey for. This meeting, on Earth's exposed breastbone.

But once he was forward, once his relatively puny height was measured against the King's in the glare of light, Myell wasn't sure what he was supposed to do. Salute? Kneel? Kiss the King's claws, beg in supplication? Maybe he was there to surrender the planet formally. He had no authority, no invested power. He was utterly terrified.

But he was also Jungali.

He was the helmsman.

The King raised his left hand. Anna Gayle stepped forward. She was dressed in a gray feather cloak and dark robes. Her face was scrubbed clean, and her hair, red and lustrous, fell over her shoulders like a goddess's.

"Sergeant Myell," she said briskly. "Commander."

Nam spat in the dust. "Are you their prisoner, or their princess?"

Gayle smiled without humor. "Considering that you left me to die on Garanwa's station? Probably a little bit of both. But the Roon were smarter than us all along. They had transportation en route from the moment we landed there. Some kind of telepathy, I think. I'm not privy to it. I think it's safe to say they were looking for Garanwa all along. We helped them find him."

Myell closed his eyes briefly. An entire race of lizards, telepathically linked. Ships outfitted with interstellar propulsion faster than anything Team Space used. Weapons technology that humanity couldn't match or understand.

Nam said, in a strangled voice, "You're helping them."

She flicked her gaze to the King. Her voice was more monotone than usual, more flat. For a fleeting instant he wondered if she was drugged, or somehow under Roon influence. She said, "I'm just along for the ride, gentlemen. Doing my part to foster interspecies communication. Otherwise, the consequences are rather severe."

One of the soldiers pushed a man forward. The prisoner was dirty and emaciated, his hair and beard wildly tangled. The scraps of clothing on his legs and arms weren't enough to cover up dark bruises, ragged scrapes, and long gouge marks. The man landed on his hands and knees with a moan. He kept his head bowed to the King, but Myell recognized his profile.

"Commander," he murmured.

Not a flicker of acknowledgment from Sam Osherman other than the slight stiffening of his back, the tiny curl of a filthy foot.

"I said there were consequences," Gayle said mildly.

Machinery began to groan deep in the ground. Rocks tumbled and scraped and dislodged as an enormous Sphere was wrenched from the heart of the Burringurrah and slowly lifted into the air by gravity beams. Millions of years of dirt flaked from its brown encrusted surfaces. It was a dark, spherical moon larger than the *Kamchatka*. He couldn't look at it without flinching, couldn't breathe in the face of its power and might.

"What is it?" Nam asked.

"The First Egg," Myell said, the words scraping his throat. "First Egg of the Rainbow Serpent."

Chittering passed along the lines of soldiers. The Roon King held up his hand and they silenced. Wind whistled up over the edges of the plateau, stirring the King's cloak. Sam Osherman didn't look up, but his shoulders were shaking.

"This is all they want," Gayle said.

Myell rubbed his eyes with dirty fingers. "It's all there is."

Nam clutched him harder, still trying to stay upright on his one good leg. "What do you mean?"

"It controls every Sphere, every ouroboros," Myell said. "The Alcheringas. Not only the Little A and the Big One, but all there are in the universe—and there are so many more than we know about. It controls the planets the Nogomain built for us. It can control suns, and comets, and galaxies themselves."

The Roon King turned his face to the First Egg, his teeth sharp in the floodlights. Small Roon robots like DNGOs rose around the Egg, scanning it with lights. Searching for an entrance. The way in. But getting inside the Egg would accomplish nothing without a Nogomain to operate it. Without Jungali.

"How do you know?" Nam asked.

Abruptly Myell began to laugh.

Because it was pretty funny. Poor Garanwa, sick and dying, alone for so long, waiting for Myell. Who finally showed up, bringing Roon with him. Big mistake there. But the real mistake was Garanwa's thinking that Myell could handle the knowledge that had been transferred, that Myell's poor addled brain could be of any use whatsoever. No matter what useful pieces of trivia popped up now and then, they were simply jetsam floating on the surface of a poisoned sea. He wasn't Jungali. He couldn't control himself, or the rings, or the First Egg, or the fucking cosmos. He didn't *know* anything. He had failed every step along the way.

The Roon King turned back to him and made a clicking noise.

"I really don't know," Myell said, mirth bubbling down. "All this trouble, and I'm the last person who can help you."

The Roon columns parted, waves and ripples extending outward. Two humans were tugged forward, Jodenny and a man Myell tried to recognize—Sweeney, was it? From the *Kamchatka*. Jodenny, looking dirty and tired but otherwise well, tried to rush to him. She was held back.

"Terry!" she called out.

His sense of humor dried up immediately.

Gayle came to Myell. Her soft hand traced a path down his cheekbone and along his jaw. "As someone who recently lost a spouse to the ineptitude of Team Space, let me tell you. Give them what they want or they'll kill her."

He understood. Saw, in a flash like lightning, what had to be done. Kuvik had known. Yambli had known. The boy Burringurrah, fleeing the initiation rites of his tribe, had figured it out in the end. Transformation required sacrifice. Of one's self, and sometimes more.

"Fuck her!" Jodenny said. "Don't listen to her, Terry."

Gayle said, soft and insidious, "Or maybe they'll do to her what they did to Commander Osherman. Would you like me to describe it to you? Tell you what I've seen?"

Nam shoved Gayle away. The Roon soldiers closest by made a grab for Nam. Myell snatched the knife from Nam's belt and immediately drove it into the Roon King's side. The knife slid along the armor, found a weak spot, but didn't go far into tough leathery flesh. Instead, the Roon King struck at Myell with one of his clawed hands. Razors tore through Myell's cheek and jaw and neck and sent him flying through the air.

He landed hard on his side, agony thudding through him. Blood filled his mouth, hot salty blood, and more of it drenched his side, pouring from the deep gouges that he could feel, not see. He was barely aware of Jodenny's shouts, of Nam crawling toward him, of the Roon cheering on their King. Overhead, clouds rolled up against one another. A flash of lightning heralded the first rain in months.

Myell rolled weakly to his side, trying to spit up the blood, but he was choking on it, dying on it. In blurred vision he saw the First Egg light up with trails of gold and silver and blue, songlines crisscrossing its globe. How strange, how pretty. Like rivers of light, converging and diverging, cool and pretty and twisting upon one another in patterns established yet fluid, always fluid.

"Jesus," Nam was babbling, shaky hands trying to staunch Myell's bleeding wounds, but no fingers could plug the torn arteries in his throat, the vessels ripped irreparably.

Myell slumped, dizziness and weakness making it impossible for him to keep the weight of his head up. He couldn't breathe without a gurgle, couldn't drag air into his body. Part of him panicking, flailing, but the strength for that was fading, too, and he could barely keep his eyes gazing on the Roon King, who was staring at the beautiful First Egg and had no pity for dying humans.

Jodenny fell to his side. Myell tried to cup her cheek the way she had cupped his, that confused night in the *Kamchatka* infirmary. She had been so tender. Now his touch was rough with calluses, sticky with blood, and too tremulous to stay still for even a moment on her cheek.

"Where are you going?" she asked. "You can't leave without me."

Lightning zigzagged across the sky, along with first drops of stinging rain. The First Egg sang with light and then turned completely black.

Myell died with the image of Jodenny filling his vision.

CHAPTER THIRTY-ONE

Rain began to fall.

No gentle drops here. The water was hard and cold and hammering. The pelts bounced off the First Egg and filled the air with wild thumping, like a thousand men banging on drums. The Roon soldiers shifted uneasily, and the Roon King made a sharp, angry sound.

Jodenny was still kneeling at Myell's side. His eyes were open but glassy. His lips were blue in the harsh Roon light. She pushed on his bloody chest and blew air into his lungs but he had gone far beyond any place where she could help him.

Nam pulled her away. Jodenny tried to pull free, determined to provoke the Roon King into striking her as well, ending her life, but Nam said, "That's not what he wants!"

"I don't care!" she shouted back, into the cacophony of the First Egg's drums. Oblivion and void would be welcome—

But then she saw the plateau below Burringurrah fill with light, marvelous light, a sea of rainbow colors. The rainfall was making the ancient ocean bloom with neon reds, tender blues and greens, hot pink, silver whites, gold. Impossible, all of it. The colors reached up into the sky and became hot lightning bolts that pulsed, exploded, each bolt branching into a dozen more, each branch feeding back to the horizon.

None of the bolts touched ground but the charged electrical air made her hair lift, her skin itch. No thunder rolled down from the sky, or maybe the First Egg drowned it all out.

Jungali, said Myell's voice, somewhere in Jodenny's heart.

She spun to her husband but he was dead, horribly dead, his corpse being washed clean by rain.

The bolts slowed as if they were a vid image being stilled by an unseen hand. The dome of the sky became a pattern of hot-white tree branches, etched and sparkling in the blackness. The sea of light on the Burringurrah plain stilled and froze.

The Roon King, his head thrown back to the rain, his wings outstretched, turned into an unmoving statue. His soldiers also slowed to a stop, as surely as if they'd been turned to stone.

"Are they dead?" Nam asked.

Jodenny limped to the Roon King's side. She wanted to push him into the pit of the First Egg or maybe even cut off his head. Eat him, limb by limb. Gayle was nearby, also frozen. Her lips were parted in a word never to be completed. Jodenny could easily defile both of them. But Mark Sweeney, who had been standing by in silence, took her arm and said, "Commander," as if duty had any sway in this nightmare, as if rank could restore her to sanity.

Nam was struggling to stand, his right leg useless beneath him. Sweeney helped him up. A dirty, bedraggled man in rags was staring at Myell's corpse, no expression on his bruised face.

His bruised, *familiar* face. She had lain with that man in bed, had cupped his cheeks with her hands and tasted his lips.

"Sam?" she asked, and felt dizzy. "Sam, is that you?"

He didn't reply.

The First Egg drummed and glowed under the unforgiving rain.

"My God," Sweeney said, and Jodenny looked up.

Shards of the lightning branches broke off and began to tumble out of the sky. They fell silently and swiftly, and hit the ground at a precise spot beside the frozen Roon King. A dozen, then a dozen more, the shards coalescing, merging, until a white figure in Myell's shape and form appeared. He was taller than Myell, larger, not the same man, but some kind of creature born from the same body, as Garanwa had once been from a boy named Burringurrah.

The First Egg fell quiet. The rain eased into drizzle, and made a soft comforting sound as drops landed on the plateau.

"You're Jungali," Jodenny said.

He nodded. There was no smile on his face, but he looked kind, patient.

"You're the helmsman?" Nam asked, leaning heavily on Mark Sweeney.

"I am," he said, in a voice as sonorous as thunder. His gaze turned to the plain, to the rainbow sea still illuminated by the lightning branches above. He was watching something Jodenny couldn't see, or remembering something private and ancient.

"Will you help us?" she asked. "Kill them all?"

If there was anything left of Myell in him, she knew he would help. But this Jungali was a god, or something close to it.

"Not a god," he said. "Nogomain. We serve the Wondjina."

Jodenny took a deep breath. "Will the Wondjina help us?"

He turned his face to her. So familiar, yet so strange. His forehead was smaller, the eyes deeper, the mouth more lush.

"The Wondjina have always been helping. Who brings the lightning? Who births the crocodiles?"

She was too tired and grief-stricken for riddles. Jodenny turned away. The First Egg, quiet in the sky, caught her eye. It was no longer black. Its surface had changed to bright blue and green oceans, to brown land masses under wispy clouds, white polar regions covered with ice.

"You were given this world to learn in, to grow out of," Jungali said. "You conquered each other and ruined the land, battles that did not need to be fought."

"It's our nature to battle," Nam said.

"As is the Roon's," Jungali said. "These soldiers will no longer trouble you. But more will come from the stars. They're already on their way."

Up in the sky, the First Egg became a glassy vision of ocean and land. James Cook and his crew sailed the *Endeavour* into a tranquil bay. A tribe of Aboriginals stood on the shore, watching. Destruction rode the wind. Ruin. The lives of the indigenous people of Australia would never be the same. Their societies would be ripped apart by illness and war. Their children would be stolen off, their lands stripped from their control.

"Is that the fate of Earth?" Jodenny asked, bitterly.

Jungali gazed down on her. "Only if it must be."

The rain had stopped, though she wasn't sure when. She stared into the eyes of this creature that had come from Terry Myell but was not him. Would never be him again. She felt hollowed out inside, ready to die herself. Let the people of Earth take care of themselves. Maybe if she threw herself into the pit, or off the cliff's edge of Burringurrah—

"Your fate is elsewhere," Jungali said.

A crocodile ouroboros appeared, shimmering green with promise.

"No," Nam said. "We're not going anywhere."

Jungali touched Jodenny's cheek with fingers soft as clouds. "Your fate is out there. With them. Lead them. Show them the way," he said. So softly she might have imagined it, he added, "Take me."

Then the Nogomain was gone, vanished on the wind so thoroughly that she wasn't sure he'd ever been real.

Jodenny lifted Myell's corpse by the shoulders and dragged him into the ouroboros. She had done this before, on Garanwa's station. But now he was impossibly heavy, and rain and blood made it difficult to keep her grip.

"Help me," she said.

Hands reached in to help. Not Nam, not Sweeney, but Sam Osherman, whose arms looked stick-thin and fragile. He met her gaze for just one brief second before looking away. Together they dragged the body into the circle. Jodenny sat with him cradled in her lap, the ground cold beneath her legs. His head lolled. Blood glistened on his mangled throat and his eyes were closed forever.

"Warn them," she told Nam. "Warn Fortune, warn everyone."

Sam stepped into the ring. Above him, the lightning branches had almost faded.

Sweeney joined them. "I'm coming with you."

"No," she said dully. "Take care of Commander Nam. There's a whirlybird back there. And the pilot, somewhere."

Nam leaned against the statue of the Roon King for support. "I'll be fine," he said gruffly. "But where the hell are you going?"

Jodenny gazed one last time at the Australian outback, and the dark First Egg. "I don't know."

The crocodile ring flared with Myell, Jodenny, Sam, and Sweeney in it. Seconds before it took them away, before it swept her to a future unknown, Jodenny saw the great Rainbow Serpent curl down from the sky and snatch the First Egg in its mouth. It was a glorious snake, all color and light and power. It ate the Egg like candy, then bit its own tail and spiraled away into the sky. Later, she told herself she had merely dreamed it.

The bridge of the *Kamchatka* flashed into existence around them.

"Intruders!" someone yelled, and three security techs with mazers descended on Jodenny before she could even take a breath.

Sweeney ordered, "Stand down!"

"Commander Scott," Balandra said, her hands fisted with urgency. "What the hell is going on?"

Jodenny thought about answering, but she couldn't even begin to explain. Not about the corpse in her arms or the emptiness in her heart. Not about Sam, who was cowering in the sudden brightness and noise. Not about anything at all.

"Captain!" That was someone down at the Drive station. "We're moving. Autopilot has taken over."

Balandra moved down the bridge. Techs scurried out of her way. On the main vidscreen, Earth began falling away at an alarming rate.

"Engines engaged," another crewman reported. "Exterior sensors are going wild."

"We're headed for the Little A!" someone added.

"Too fast," one of the officers said. "Captain, there's no way our ship can be going this fast—"

Jodenny closed her eyes and held tight to Myell's corpse as the *Kamchatka* took flight and soared like a Great Egret. Air whistled by her ears, the winds uplifting and pushing and buffeting, the ground so wide and glorious below, the sky endless and full of promise. She felt as one with all the souls on the *Kamchatka*, passengers like Hullabaloo and Louise and the Fraser family, worried techs like Putty Romero and Hanne Tingley, Captain Balandra herself, Teddy Toledo and Leorah Farber, Sam and his awful pain—and she saw the threads that tied her to Team Space snapping and breaking in a painless but tangible way, like a quick yank, silk parting.

"Engines are stopped!" someone yelled, and there was chaos.

She blinked at the overvids, at a blue-green marble of a planet that was not Earth, nor one of the Seven Sisters, but a new world, virgin, unspoiled.

She kissed Myell's cold forehead and wept.

CHAPTER THIRTY-TWO

"Commander Nam, thank you," said the senator in charge of the Roon committee. Another day, another interminable government committee. Byron Nam wanted to scream, or throw something at the blank-faced men and women sitting on the podium.

"About the being that called itself Jungali—" he began.

"Commander," the senator interrupted. Bland tone. Mild, but firm. "Obviously you were hallucinating, in pain, and under extreme stress. That part of your account must be taken under study."

Bastards, all of them. Nam rose stiffly from the witness table, walked out of the room in his best uniform, and emerged into the bright sun of another day in Kimberley. Tom Gold was waiting at the curb, leaning against their silver-blue flit. He too was wearing his dress whites. His testimony had ended earlier that morning.

"They're all goddamn idiots," Nam said.

"I hear that." Gold opened the passenger door. "Give you a ride, sailor?"

Nam got inside. Gold turned off the autopilot and guided them through light traffic. The inside of the flit was tinted and privacy screened, and warm like a cocoon.

"They think they have all the time in the world," Nam groused. "That we'll see the next Roon ships long before they reach Earth, now that we know they'll be coming. That we can pull new weapons platforms out of our asses."

Gold said, "Sounds painful."

"We don't stand a chance."

"You don't believe that."

Nam stared out at the streets and pedestrians, at buildings and bridges. Civilians went about their merry business down Water Street, not far from Supply School. "Yes, I do."

"If you did, you and I would be hightailing it down the Big Alcheringa to hide," Gold said.

"I didn't say we shouldn't fight," Nam told him. "We should always fight."

Gold reached over and squeezed his hand. "There's the man I love."

Nam leaned his head back and closed his eyes. His Achilles tendon began throbbing for no good reason. It had been six months since he'd torn it on the trek up Burringurrah. The Team Space doctors told him that it seemed fully healed. To machines, perhaps. To gibs and medical DNGOs. But sometimes he limped so badly that he needed a cane, and there was talk of replacement surgery. He'd resisted so far.

"Are you thinking about her?" Gold asked.

"No," he said truthfully, but he would. At least once a day he would stop whatever he was doing and wonder where Jodenny Scott was. At

Burringurrah she had climbed into that crocodile ring with Mark Sweeney and Sam Osherman and her husband's corpse. No one had seen them since. Part of him wished he'd gone with her, and part of him was insanely glad to be back on Fortune with Gold and the chance to somehow stop the Roon, however wild and fantastically improbable that might be.

It didn't comfort him to think about the *Kamchatka,* which had disappeared from Earth's orbit immediately after Jodenny's disappearance from Burringurrah. Gone, completely. Not a shred of visual or scanner data to indicate what had happened to it or its crew and civilian passengers. The Roon ships had disappeared just as thoroughly from across Earth and up in orbit. The frozen Roon on the plain had likewise disappeared, and not even Myell's spilled blood remained in testimony.

All Nam could do about Jodenny was wonder what had happened to her. And grieve. Feel sorrow for Myell, who had died to become Jungali. Regret that he himself hadn't been Myell's biggest supporter, though he hoped in the end he'd done what he could.

"Hey," Gold said, tapping his knee. "We're home."

Nam opened his eyes. They had purchased a private home far from military housing. The neighborhood was good, not too crowded, not too old. Eucalyptus trees kept it fragrant. Gold pulled the flit into the garage, parked, and opened the kitchen door. Nam limped in after him. Sunlight spilled in through the oversize windows and the blue waters of the bay glittered past the edges of their backyard.

"It's your turn to make dinner," Gold said.

Nam flopped down on the sofa. "I'm not very hungry."

Gold gave him a stern look. "How can you single-handedly defeat the Roon if you don't keep up your strength?"

"That's not funny."

"I'm not joking," Gold replied. "Tell him, Karl."

Karl the Koala uncurled himself from a pillow by the patio doors and lumbered toward Nam. After Burringurrah, Nam had hired a couple of off-duty sergeants to trek through the outback and rescue the little bot from the wreck of the *Kamchatka*'s lifeboat. Karl's fur was still a little singed in places, and one of his eyes had a tiny crack in the lens, but he was otherwise in fine shape. Nam was hoping Jodenny might come back for the bot someday. He'd keep the koala safe until that happened.

"Rub belly," Karl insisted, and climbed up onto the sofa.

Nam obeyed. Gold opened the refrigerator, peered inside, and heaved a dramatic sigh.

"I'll take you to dinner," Nam said, surrendering.

"You hate eating out."

"For you, anything."

"Hmmm." Gold came to the sofa and sat beside him. "I can think of better things to do with the rest of our night."

Nam would recognize that lecherous look anywhere. Despite his gloomy mood, he felt the definite stirring of interest.

"Fine," he said. "We'll order in."

Karl retreated to a cushion in the corner, curled up in the sunlight, and smiled.

The cemetery was on a grassy, peaceful hill not far from the colony of Providence. Under the canopy of trees stood one lone headstone with no name on it. Jodenny couldn't explain why she didn't want Myell's name engraved into the rock. She suspected that Sweeney and the others thought she was in denial, that if there was no name she could pretend her husband wasn't dead, but that was ridiculous. Every single day she lived with the hollowed-out pain in her chest that reminded her he was gone.

And every day her womb grew bigger, her body swelling and curving as expected. Myell's last gift to her.

"I dreamed last night it was a boy," she said today, as trees swayed in the wind and grass tickled her bare feet. Though the day was sunny, rain was forecast for the afternoon. "I dreamed he could play the piano, just like you. But I don't remember you playing the piano. I never asked if you could play anything."

The leaves bowed and rustled above, and insects hummed in the grass.

"Maybe someone in the crew could make a piano," Jodenny murmured.

As if musical instruments were any kind of priority. Jodenny stretched out on the ground, letting the earth support her growing body. Junior, maybe waking from a nap, kicked her left ribs twice and then went still. Jodenny hadn't realized how much abuse from within pregnant women endured. Kicks and pokes and all sorts of twisting. If the kid wasn't destined to be a pianist, maybe he or she could be the colony's first gymnast.

Abuse and weight gain and fatigue, and daily fear that something would go wrong with the delivery. Jodenny was happy to endure all of it as long as this little piece of Myell continued to grow within her. Their only child. She told herself that it didn't matter but she wanted a boy, and planned to give him his father's name.

Another kick, harder than the last.

"Ouch," Jodenny complained.

Fat and lazy clouds rolled by in the sky until her view was blocked by Leorah Farber's concerned face.

"Are you sleeping?" Farber asked.

Jodenny frowned. "I don't think so."

"I've been calling your name."

She sat up slowly. "Is something wrong?"

"I wanted to tell you before you heard the gossip." Farber sat down beside her and pulled a blade of grass from the ground. She'd let her dark hair grow long in the months they'd been marooned, and the breeze blew it around her face. "Teddy and I are moving to the coast."

Jodenny hid her surprise. The Zhangs lived at the coast, along with a handful of other passengers who had rejected Captain Balandra's leadership.

"You're joining the dissidents?" Jodenny asked.

Farber twisted the grass into a knot. "Hoping for rescue doesn't make you a rebel. They need to believe Team Space is coming for us. I guess I need to believe it, too. For my daughter's sake."

Junior kicked again. Jodenny patted her left side, urging him to settle down.

"You could come," Farber said hopefully. "After the baby, if you're worried about that."

"I'm loyal to the captain," Jodenny said. "And someone has to keep an eye on Sam."

Farber grimaced. "He's crazy. And dangerous."

"He's been through more than any of us," Jodenny protested.

"More than you?"

"Much more than me," she insisted, even though no one knew what Osherman had endured at the hands of the Roon. He could not or would not speak. The *Kamchatka*'s medical equipment wasn't sophisticated enough to say for sure. Ensign Collins believed he was electively mute, but Jodenny didn't agree.

No one doubted that Osherman was still traumatized. He slept most nights in Jodenny's tiny house, curled up on a sofa from one of the ship's lounges. Often he had terrible nightmares that left him shaking and crying soundlessly. Sometimes he fled out the door into the darkness, and Jodenny let him go. The sentries reported that he spent a lot of time at the beach. He'd trimmed his beard and gained some weight, but he never smiled, never looked anyone in the eye, and kept a knife in his boot.

He scared people, Jodenny knew. But she didn't think he'd harm anyone but himself.

Farber tossed her blade of grass back to the ground. "You really don't think help is coming for us?"

"I think . . ." Jodenny started, and then paused. "I think no one knows the future. I have trouble getting through one day at a time. Help hasn't come today, how's that?"

"So far," Farber said.

"So far," Jodenny agreed.

The wind picked up, and clouds moved in front of the sun.

Abruptly Farber stood. "Come on. I'll buy you some lunch. A pack of emergency rations and the last known dregs of Ensign Sadiqi's coffee."

Jodenny glanced at Myell's unmarked tombstone.

"He's not there," Farber said gently. "It's just a body."

Just a body. *Take me,* Jungali had whispered, but for what? So she could bury the corpse of her beloved on this unknown world, far from where they'd hoped to make a home together. So his mortal remains could rot in the ground while she grew a baby and faced the rest of her life without him. Jodenny felt a surge of bitterness at the way things had turned out. But then Junior kicked again, and she told herself that anger was bad for the baby.

Still. If she ever met that Nogomain again, he was going to damn well answer some questions. She knuckled her eyes dry and lifted a hand.

"Help me up?" Jodenny asked, and Farber gave her a hand.

They walked downhill together, and made it to Providence before the sky opened up with rain, thunder, and lightning.

An hour before dawn, with Jodenny snoring softly in her room and Providence's moon heavy in the silver-black sky, Sam Osherman gave up on sleep and went for a walk.

He walked east, as he often did, toward the wooded peninsula that separated the bay from the wild blue ocean. The air was cool and clean. At the edge of sky and sea and land he sat on a jumble of rocks left exposed by the receding tide. If he watched the glinting sea closely enough he might see shark fins or a band of dolphins. Very rarely a crocodile might wander over from the marshes and peer at him with open jaws.

Nothing to see here, he wanted to say. Would have said, if the Roon hadn't stolen his voice.

He couldn't think of that. Couldn't touch those memories without their razor-sharp edges slicing new wounds into him. Instead he sat with his face turned to the east, thinking about the little life growing inside Jodenny, and the *Kamchatka* still in orbit with only a skeleton crew aboard. Most of the ship's cargo, equipment, and resources had already been stripped clean. There was no going back to Earth, Osherman suspected. And not much of an Earth to go back to, perhaps. Jodenny's child would never know the worlds left behind.

The sun began to burn its way up past the horizon. Osherman focused on the name Jungali, trying to summon the god that Myell had become. He'd tried it dozens of times already, maybe hundreds of times, with no success. His memories of the plateau were still shaky, still tenuous. A nightmare time of blood and pain and brilliant lights. But he was sure that somehow Jungali wasn't very far away, that Terry Myell's story was far from over.

And the Roon. The Roon were still out there, a prospect that made Osherman want to crawl into the deepest hole he could find and never emerge.

Out in the waves, a whale breached the sea's surface as if greeting the sunrise. It slammed back down again in a shower of spray, and its enormous tail gave a little wave.

Osherman slid off the rocks with renewed determination. For Jodenny and her baby, he would do his best to be sane today. He would not cower in fear, or claw at his own arms and legs, or give in to the impulse to burn himself clean. He wouldn't yield control to the wild voices in his skull. Wouldn't pay attention if the Roon King poked its slimy head out from behind a wall, if it blew its hot fetid breath into Osherman's own mouth. He would be *good,* he would be *strong,* and as he climbed the beach toward the settlement he hoped that maybe Jodenny would notice, and give him a smile or two for his efforts.

Just as he reached the edge of the woods, a dark blue ouroboros shimmered into existence on the sand. It was neither a snake nor a crocodile, but instead shaped like a man. A man bent in a circle, his feet in his mouth, his muscles smooth and untroubled, his face rapturous.

Standing in the ring was Terry Myell. A very surprised-looking Myell, but also one who was not dead or godlike in any way.

"Commander?" Myell asked, his voice distant. He raised a hand as if trying to reach past the ouroboros, but seemed constrained, trapped in some way. "Are you there?"

Osherman tried to answer, but his throat yielded nothing.

The ouroboros and Myell disappeared as quickly and easily as they had appeared.

Osherman touched the warm sand with his fingers. A different kind of hallucination, this, but one he could live with. Better than visions of the Roon King, better than night terrors in which he was a helpless, terrified prisoner wanting only to die.

He put his hands in his pockets and walked away.

In the trees above, a Great Egret peered down with beady eyes and then flew away, high into the sky, the land open and welcoming beneath her wings.

Far away, in a green sea cave, Free-not-chained nursed her half-human son and whispered, "My little Jungali. Your day will come."